Gregory Benford _____ the University of Cal___ ____, _____, a Woodrow Wilson Fellow and a fellow at Cambridge University, and an advisor to the US Department of Energy, NASA and the White House Council on Space Policy. Dr Benford is also one of the most honoured authors in science fiction. His many novels, including the classic *Timescape*, have won two Nebula Awards, the John W. Campbell Award and the United Nations Medal in Literature.

Also by Gregory Benford

FOUNDATION'S FEAR

COSM

By Gregory Benford and Arthur C. Clarke

AGAINST THE FALL OF NIGHT/
BEYOND THE FALL OF NIGHT

GREGORY BENFORD

THE MARTIAN RACE

An *Orbit* Book

First published in Great Britain by Orbit 2000
Reprinted 2000

A CIP catalogue record for this book
is available from the British Library.

ISBN 1 85723 999 7

Typeset by Palimpsest Book Production Limited
Polmont, Stirlingshire
Printed and bound in Great Britain by
Mackays of Chatham plc, Chatham, Kent

Orbit
A Division of
Little, Brown and Company (UK)
Brettenham House
Lancaster Place
London WC2E 7EN

To an idea and those who pursue it:
Mars in our time

PART I
IN THE HALL
OF THE MARTIAN
ENTREPRENEURS

It seemed . . . that if he or some other lord did not endeavor to gain that knowledge, no mariners or merchants would ever dare to attempt it, for it is clear that none of them ever trouble themselves to sail to a place where there is not a sure and certain hope of profit.

Prince Henry the Navigator,
assessing the motivations for sea exploration,
circa 1480

1

"WELCOME BACK TO MARS!"

She always opened these public broadcasts in the same way. Firm, friendly, positive.

"Viktor and I are here near the northern rim of Gusev Crater, doing some final surveying work."

Actually, we had to get out of the hab one last time. Take a last look around, have some time together before we're all crammed into that tiny Earth Return Vehicle, the size of a New York apartment.

"I expect most of you know the view pretty well by now."

I hope you're not already bored and out getting a sandwich.

"Still, those high ramparts to the east catching the afternoon sun, they're beautiful. A kilometer high, too."

Hope they don't recall that I covered nearly this same territory over a year ago. Completing a search grid isn't exciting, but maybe we shouldn't coddle the audience so much. And then, Axelrod's media types would just cut this part out anyway.

"The theme here is looking for unusual volcanic activity, whether fossil evidence or even current emissions. And biological clues, too—after all, I'm still hopeful. We have to keep a sharp eye out. Mars covers a lot of its secrets in dust! Nothing so far, but some of you may remember that over there—Viktor, pan across to the east, will you?—we located some lava tubes so big that we could walk into them. That was exciting! Marc later worked out from his radioactive dating equipment that the lava had flowed in them nearly a billion years ago."

Yeah, and not a sign of any activity since. I'll bet Axelrod's media managers cut this whole segment.

Not that I give a damn. I must've made over three hundred of these bright-eyed little talks by now. At least on this one there's something to look at. Going home, it'll be worse than those loooong six months getting here. Nothing to report but scientific details. No big cliff-hanger suspense about the landing, or about what we'd find, like on the way out. Maybe some about the dangers of aerobraking, but that's minor. I'll bet Las Vegas doesn't even give odds on us making it.

"So we'll just keep pushing. One more night out here, then back to base for the prelaunch trials. Should be exciting!"

This smile must be frozen on by now . . .

"So good-bye for now. Julia, from Mars to you."

She stuck out her tongue. "Auggghh! Doing this for two years and still I can never think of anything to say."

Viktor lowered the camera. "Spontaneous. Is better that way."

"God, if this wasn't in the contract—"

"Would not have made even a dozen, I know. You said maybe one thousand times now."

"Marc is so much better at this."

"Marc is not here. Want to make quick squirt for your parents?"

This brightened her. "Sure, roll 'em."

Julia struck a pose a little less heroic and shifted her feet. She was in her pressure suit, which bulked impressively but also, when Viktor went to a wide shot, showed its scrapes and blotchy color. It had started out a pretty royal blue, the best color choice of the four, but the UV and peroxides here had hammered it pretty hard. Now Viktor's yellow stood out better.

Viktor waved, and she said, "Hi, Mums and Dad. Here I am, back on survey. Had a good time on Kangaroo Island? Hard to keep the old eagle eyes peeled when I know we're headed back in just a few weeks. Man, am I getting worn down! Viktor's taking a break with me, the getaway special for the newlyweds."

Ooops, I'm blundering into that again . . . let's just change the subject.

"It's been kinda dicey with Marc and Raoul. Nothing basic, just prickly, irritable. They are, I mean. I'm the soul of warm sympathy, just like always."

She grinned, paused and looked around, wondering what they would appreciate about the landscape. Viktor panned with her gaze; he was really good at that by now.

"See that outcrop over there? I figure it was thrown

out by the meteor that made Thyra Crater. Signature splash effect, radially outward. So I was looking around, sniffing for signs of how much water there was here, maybe break open a few rocks and look at the mineralization. The usual, in other words. Nobody'll be able to say that at the tail end, I slowed up on the job!"

She sighed, feeling the old sensation of an emotional logjam: she could not switch from bright-eyed to real, not right away. She should have put some of the Thyra stuff in the public footage. Try again, then.

"I really miss you guys, as usual. Hope your viro treatments went easy, Dads. You looked great, last squirt I got. We had some trouble with the high-bandwidth signal, maybe lost your latest two days ago. Hope there's one waiting when I get back to base. I had a dream about taking a bath last night. Just that, nothing but the bath. Shows you what sensory delights I miss, huh? A long scrub in a big tub, the one we had in the old place, remember? Well, love to the rest of the family!"

Short, but she couldn't do any more without starting to go stilted on them. Maybe she had already. The first few months, she had replayed her squirts, both public and private, and edited them before the high-gain antenna sent them Earthside. Now she just let it go. History was history—over. If she scratched on camera, so be it.

"Was good," Viktor said, smartly shutting off the camera.

"Let's move."

She started toward the rover, its sulfurous yellow standing out violently against the pink sands and rocks. At midday Mars was a bit less red, because the light coming nearly straight down wasn't scattered as much by the perpetual fine dust that hung in the air.

In the distance a dust devil snaked lazily across the barren plain. They'd seen hundreds, nearly one a day. Kilometers high, they unceasingly threw the rusty fines of the surface into the thin atmosphere.

She had long ago given up yearning for green hills or ocean swells. Now Mars held for her a subtle but varied palette, its tans and rosy shades fraught with meaning. The mind adapted. Even so, iron oxides were a limited medium for nature's work. She kept the flatscreen in her personal room set permanently on a green Irish hill sloping down to a pounding sea. When she got back, she was going to find that exact spot and live there a while. Maybe forever. And hang on the wall a real-time flatscreen of Gusev Crater.

"What's that?"

Viktor peered out the big viewport and let the rover slow. "Cloud. Nearby."

The filmy white mist faded. "How far?" Her heart was pounding, her biologist senses instantly alert. A water cloud at this time of day meant an underground vent.

"Hard to tell. Could be on horizon, long way off."

"Or close. Damn, it's gone." She had caught it out of the corner of her eye and the haze had lasted only seconds.

"Was rising."

"Yeah, I thought so too."

They had skirted around some hummocky hills. To

save time Viktor was taking a fast route back to base, angling over a long sandy slope. The cloud had hung over the hills to the east, in an area they had not crisscrossed in detail because it was tricky terrain.

"Go in there, slow work."

One last try? "Let's go look anyway." Better late than never to find an outgassing vent.

An hour later she was ready to give up. Viktor was being good about it, carefully driving them across dry washes that had perhaps run with water or mud back before amphibians had first crawled up onto the beaches of Earth. They navigated around slumped pits that might have evaporated away ice deposits. Marc's seismology had probed this region, mapping ice layers several tens of meters below, plus some enticing tendrils that might be lava tubes. But eons of erosion and shifting dust had obscured most telltales.

"There!" he whispered.

A plume of yellow-white furled up from behind a low crest. "It's close!"

He floored the rover and its rumble echoed her quickening pulse. They had seen nothing like this through 500 days of patient crawling over the floor of Gusev Crater, a hundred fifty kilometers across. All along she'd harbored the hope that life would be hanging on underground, away from the cold and dry. With Marc she'd inspected the smaller Thyra Crater with microscopic attention, to no avail.

Over the rise, down a rocky slope toward a pit that didn't look any different from thousands she had seen before. Yet above this one a teardrop plume faded into the pink air, towering a hundred meters like a dirty exhalation of—what?

"Thermal vent, uh?" Viktor flashed her a quick grin.

"Hush. The gods of Mars will hear you and take it away."

He parked at the edge of the pit as she unclipped her gear from the wall mounts. The pit slope was fairly steep, and she got out all the climbing equipment. She had learned to keep it inside, where the fine dust could not get into the moving parts. Even the tough rope got worn away by the stuff where it rubbed.

Viktor sent Marc a quick radio message that they were going outside, and where they were. No need to get their hopes up with a description.

Out through the lock, consciously being systematic in moving the gear despite her excitement. Haste made accidents, and the lock was getting pesky, sticking around the seals.

Outside, she studied the whole area carefully, frowning. Steep, sandy descents were not her favorite. The fifteen-degree slope ran down about ten meters to a hole at the bottom about three meters across. It looked something like a giant ant lion pit. She guessed it was a volcanic blowout crater, rock walls obscured by the perpetually moving sands. "Looks like an old crater."

"See those rocks at rim?" Viktor pointed.

"Right, the yellow and white patches? Unusual discoloration."

"Condensate, could be."

"Hope so."

She had the irrational urge to sniff the air, guess

what the gas plume had been. They looped the cable and pulley rig onto the rover's back harness and winch. Going down the slope was a little tricky because the sandy dust had a funny layered feel, slipping away suddenly beneath her boots. A gritty skid. Viktor followed in her boot steps. They had secured the rope through their suit loops. She felt quite secure walking to the edge of the hole, but placed each step slowly to see if the rock rim would bear her weight. Months ago Marc had suffered a sudden fall when a shelf had given way, and he had limped for weeks. Looking down, she saw plenty of discoloration on the rocky throat that extended into blackness.

Viktor had knelt beside an outcrop. "Ice."

"What? Where?"

Pure water ice was improbable on the Martian surface. It would sublime away quickly. But the light orange film on the edges of the rocks near the hole glistened. "Vent," Viktor pronounced.

"Remember the gods," she said, absently.

"I go," he said, and without ceremony pulled his line tight.

"Hey, I'm the biologist. I want to take a sample of this film—"

"So take. I am captain, I go."

He started backing over the rim. There was enough room to let him descend by walking backward down the inside. She knelt and used a sterile wiper to collect the film, then secured it in a biosample baggy. She was nearly out of the baggies and here at last there was—

"Ow!"

She turned to see him wheeling sideways with a silky slowness she would never forget.

"Viktor!" With her cry she tried to stop his fall.

Barely below the lip, Viktor had caught his left boot during a power descent. When he tried to free the tip he managed to turn it, leveraging it with his whole weight. "Ah!"—his second yelp rang in Julia's suit comm when he hit the side of the hole on the rebound. His right arm smacked the wall vainly and a plume of red dust arced up and out of the hole.

"What happened?"

He tried to make the left foot bear weight. "Damn, hurts."

The dust began its lazy descent as she bent over Viktor's line. The top of his helmet was still in the light. "How bad?"

"Did not feel break."

"Hope it's just a sprain."

"I lost my hold with boot. Rock was slippery."

"It looks like ice on the rocks. Condensed out from the plume, I guess." She'd have to think about it later.

He hit the winch control and ascended to her level. She wrestled him clumsily over to the narrow edge of the hole and made him lay down. She unfastened the bottom of his insulated legging and ran her hands lightly over the ankle cuff of the pressure suit underneath. "Suit looks okay, no breaches. How's your self-med?"

The damned dust had settled on his faceplate and she couldn't see him, but knew he would be checking the readouts on the inside of the helmet. "Normal." His voice was thin and strained.

"Good. How do you feel?"

He shifted slightly, groaned. "Like yesterday's blini. Light-headed. Foot hurts like hell."

Keep him talking. Can't risk shock. She was no doctor, but her year of physician's assistant training snapped into high gear. She kept her tone light. "That's what you get for doing cartwheels."

"Unnnh. I can't move it."

She frowned, wondering how difficult it was going to be to get him back into the rover. Help was more than forty klicks away, and she was driving the only pressurized vehicle on the planet. Mission protocol limited the open rover to twenty-five klick trips, so the two of them had to manage it on their own. She thought of calling Marc on the emergency band, for moral support if nothing else. No, concentrate on Viktor. Plenty of time to analyze things in the rover. If she could get him there.

"Okay, enough laziness. Let's get you up."

"Aw . . . right." His slightly slurred voice worried her. They were all worn down, and shock could be setting in.

She slipped her left arm clumsily around his waist, feeling like a kid in a snowsuit. Suit-to-suit contact had a curiously remote feel about it, with no feedback from the skin. Still, she liked hugging him, even this way. They had slept together in a close embrace ever since the launch from Earth orbit.

"I've got some great stuff in the rover that'll make you feel like a new man."

"Want to feel like man I was."

"C'mon, get up."

"Why not pull me up on the line? I lie down—"

"Don't think I could."

"Pull with rover."

"Hey, I'm in charge."

"Aieee!"

With her help he heaved himself up onto his right leg, leaning heavily on her. Together they struggled for balance, threatened to go over the edge, then steadied. She had long ago stopped counting how many times the 0.38 g of Mars had helped them through crucial moments. It had proved the only useful aspect of the planet.

"Whew. Made it, lover." *Keep the patter going, don't alarm him.* "Ready? I'll walk, you hop as best you can."

Like a drunken three-legged race team, they managed to stagger slowly up the crater slope with the judicious assist of the winch. *You will work as a team,* the instructor at mission training had said constantly, but she hadn't anticipated this. Over her comm came deep, ragged gasps. Hopping through drifts of gritty dust, even in the low gravity, was exhausting Victor. Luckily the rover was just a dozen meters away.

Slow and steady got them there. He leaned against the rover as she struggled off first her harness, then his. She rolled him into the lock and set the cycle sequence. No time to brush off the dust, but she got off the coverall they used over suits to keep the dust at a minimum. She hooked it with her own to the clamps beside the lock. Skip the usual shower on entry, too. She climbed into the lock with him, sealed it. She hit the pump switch and oxygen whistled into the lock from half a dozen recessed ports.

With a wheeze, the cycler finished. She was jammed in and couldn't turn around to see him. She felt the rover's carriage shift. Good; he had rolled out of the lock and was lying on the floor.

The chime sounded; full pressure, 90 percent Earth normal. She turned off her suit oxygen, released the clamps on her helmet and as quickly as possible shucked her parka, leggings, and finally, her suit. She shivered as she stepped out into the chilly cabin: she had actually been sweating on Mars—a novel experience.

A prickly itch washed over her face and neck and already she regretted their dusty entry. The usual routine was to brush the suits down outside with a soft brush. Some genius from mission prep with a lot of camping experience had thoughtfully stowed it aboard, and it quickly became one of their prized possessions. The Martian surface was thick with fine, rusty dust heavily laden with irritating peroxides. Her skin had felt like it was being gently sandpapered all during the long months here—especially when she was tired, as now.

Fluffing her short black hair, she donned a red Boeing cap and went over to help Viktor. She upped the rover pressure to get him more oxygen, and together they gingerly peeled off his insulating layers and his suit. A look at his leg confirmed her guess: sprained ankle, swelling fast.

From there it was straight safety manual stuff: bind, medicate, worry.

"I love you, even zonked on painkillers," she murmured to his sleeping face when she had checked everything five times.

He had dropped off disturbingly fast. He kept up a front of invincibility, they all did somewhat or they wouldn't be here; it went with astronaut psychology. But he had the bone-deep fatigue that came from a hard mission relentlessly pursued. He didn't talk about it much, but the launch coming up was troubling him.

She was suddenly very tired. Emotional reaction, she diagnosed wryly. Still, better tend to it.

On Mars, you learn to pace yourself. Time for a cup of tea.

She looked around first for her tea cozy, carefully brought from Earth as part of her personal mass allowance. Nothing could've induced her to leave it behind—home was where the cosy was. She retrieved it from a corner of the cooking area. Originally light blue and cream colored, it was now permanently stained with maroon dust. When things got tough she sought the comfort of a proper cup of tea made in a teapot. There were precious few emergencies that couldn't wait until after a cuppa.

As the water heated she got on the emergency band and tried to reach the other two back at the hab. No answer. They were probably deep in the guts of the Return Vehicle, starting the final checks for the approaching test fire. She left a heads-up on the ship's message system, saying that they were coming back pronto, hurt. No way could she get any more done out here on her own. Anyway, Viktor came first, and any solo work was forbidden by their safety protocols.

With the robot arm on the front she unhooked the last solar-powered electromagnetic hailer from the outside rack and placed it in what she hoped was a good spot. It was always a judgment call. The winds were fickle, and the constantly shifting dunes had buried more than one.

She stared out of the forward viewport at the pale pink hills, trying to assess what this accident meant to the mission. Maybe just a mishap, no more. But Viktor still had plenty to do preparing for their return launch. No, this would screw up the schedule for sure. Her own work would get shoved aside.

And the vent—when would she get back? For about a microsecond she considered going down the hole herself. No, contrary to all mission procedures. Worse, stupid.

Face it, she thought—biology was not the imperative here anymore. She had made her big discovery. To the world, their expedition was already a big success—they'd found fossil life. But she wanted more than long-dead microbes.

And now they had one more accident to complicate things. *Plan all you want, Mars will hand you surprises.*

Like the accident that had gotten them all here.

2

"DAMN, STUCK AGAIN!"

She had been driving the Rover Boy, as they called it.

Rover was the telepresence explorer on Mars which had scouted the landing site. It was still operating after five years, thanks to the Mars Outpost program. There was a chem factory to feed Rover and backup electronics packages sitting in the Outpost base. Plus a microwave dish to keep in constant Earth contact through the three communication satellites above. She had trained with Rover from Johnson Space Center for years. Right now Julia was coaxing it across the tricky landscape, like a mother tending a toddling, balky child.

She was taking it around the edge of Thyra Crater, letting the autopilot on board negotiate the slope and rocks. There was no choice, given the time delay of over half an hour. Rover Boy was the most advanced model ever developed, but it had problems. Big, insurmountable ones.

"Where is it?" Viktor asked beside her.

"Stalled on a sand dune, looks like."

She thumbed through close-up processing commands, fingers drumming on the driver's console. Nearby hummed the station-keeping labors of the Jet Propulsion Lab.

At thirty-two, she had lost none of her impatience with life. What was more, she did not intend to. Piloting

Rover Boy with infuriating delays was more trying than she could ever let on, or else risk being scrubbed from the Mars mission. So her fingers danced uselessly, rather than slamming on the gas in Red Rover and trying to back out of the clogging sand fifty-three million miles away.

"Yah, the dune to the left, last time."

"Its onboards must've chosen to go that way."

"Looks maybe to turn wheels left, reverse out," Viktor said in what he probably thought was a helpful tone.

"It's a day's work getting out of a chuckhole," she said uselessly, sending the Reverse order and cutting the wheels to the right. Before they got free her watch would be over.

She glanced at her framed picture of the little Sojourner rover, one she had saved from her first brush with space excitement at age fourteen, way back in 1997. Sojourner had suffered from the same time delay problem—no way around the speed of light!—but its plucky nosing around had got Julia started on her Mars fixation. She brought it on her watches here, for luck. Today it didn't seem to be working.

Rover Boy was hugely bigger, better, but—"We're never going to get far from Thyra in slow-mo."

Viktor pointed to a smudge on the horizon. "Cloud?"

"Ummm." She thumbed up the last view in that direction, northwest. "Wasn't there last time."

"Unusual to have cloud at midday. Evaporate at dawn."

"Could be transmission error." It would take over an hour to get another look that way. She sent the order to swivel the TV cameras.

Julia sighed. She had still not come to terms with the simple fact that she and Viktor and the rest, fine folk all, were not in the six-person crew going to Mars in one year. Sure, they had known that half of the astronauts in training would form a backup crew. Sure, they might be in the second expedition. If there *was* a second. Unless the first crew found something damned interesting, that seemed improbable. NASA was already far over budget on this one.

Nothing to do but wait for the return signal, probably Rover barking back that it was still stuck. Viktor flicked the console view controls. "Let's catch news."

With a touch of pensive sadness she watched the TV feed from Cape Canaveral. There it stood, only moments from launch: the Big Boy Booster, as the media gang called it. She thought fleetingly of how everything on this mission was Rover Boy or Big Boy or some other closed-club name. How had that happened?

Atop its cigar-shaped bulk was the seemingly tiny Mars Transit Vehicle, ready to be flung into orbit for its first space trials. She thought of her friends in there, waiting to ride into the black sky and deploy the silvery cylinder, spin it up with the last stage booster as a counterweight, try out the 0.38 g for a month in gravity physiological trials—and felt another sour jolt of pure envy.

Into the last twenty seconds now. She reached out and clasped Viktor's hand. She could get away with that, tense moment and all—if anybody noticed. (Or had they noticed long ago, even before she and Viktor got together, and cut them both to the second team?)

"We have a burn," came the flat, factual incantation, used now for over half a century at the Cape.

The huge white booster, bigger than the Saturn V, lifted gracefully upward—and a spurt of virulent yellow leaped sideways from it. The explosion ripped apart the feeds just above the nozzles. Angry yellow climbed up the sides and, before she could gasp, engulfed the payload. Already the booster had begun to topple to the side.

It was the worst sort of accident.

Always feared, impossible to completely eliminate. A failed wall buffer at the high-pressure point. Fuel blockage. A pressure-driven chemical excursion.

The enormous, ripping convulsion destroyed the gantry, support structures—the whole launch area. The six crew tried to eject but the whole event was far too fast for even astronaut reflexes. They all died, mercifully fast. So did an electrician, standing half a mile away, struck by flying steel.

Julia went through the days of uproar in a glassy daze. Mourning for friends. Avoiding TV crews. Watching as the disaster undermined NASA's support in Congress. Letting the days creep by as the gray pall over her life slowly lifted.

Soon enough the strident voices from the House floor claimed an even larger victim than the booster. The entire Mars campaign was "halted for the duration," as one craggy-faced pol put it. The duration of what? Apparently, of the minimum-energy launch window that beckoned in 2016. After that, it would be 2018 before the next launch window. But once stopped, would the Mars program ever restart?

Slowly Julia sank into depression. She had been buoyed up for so long by the taste of opportunity. To have it snatched away so abruptly left a big hole in her life.

She had been riding on hope ever since, six years before, the United States had negotiated the Mars Accords. At the time it had seemed brilliant. The true trick of getting to Mars was how to do it without squandering anybody's entire Gross National Product. When President George Bush called in 1989 for a manned mission to Mars on the fiftieth anniversary of the 1969 Apollo landing, he got the estimated bill from NASA: $450 billion. The sticker shock killed Bush's initiatives in Congress. The price was high because everyone in NASA and their parasite companies tacked every conceivable extra onto the mission. An expanded space station. A moon base. Redundancy.

Multiple backup systems are the key to safety—but the more backups, the higher the cost. NASA's $450 billion program was an enormous government pork farm.

So a radical idea arose: the advanced nations could get this adventure on the cheap by simply offering a prize of $30 billion to the first manned expedition to return successfully from Mars.

European governments had long used this mechanism for risky explorations, going back to the Portuguese in the 1400s. In 1911, William Randolph Hearst offered a $50,000 prize to the first person to fly across America in less than thirty days. Human-powered flight got a boost from a $200,000 award claimed in 1978 by the

Gossamer Albatross. The method worked.

The advantages were many, and political: governments would put out not a dime until the job was done, and only reward success; only private investors would lose if their schemes failed. Politicians could be proud, prophetic patrons of exploration and, simultaneously, enemies of make-work bureaucratic programs. And if astronauts died, it was on somebody else's head, not an embarrassment to a whole government.

To win the Mars Prize, it would not be enough to fly a flags-and-footprints expedition. More like a treasure hunt, the Accords specified a series of scientific explorations—geologic mapping, seismic testing, studying atmospheric phenomena, taking core samples, looking for water and, of course, fossils or life. Samples returned from Mars would be immensely valuable: a full range of specimens weighing three hundred kilograms would be turned over to the Accords Board in exchange for the $30 billion. Anything over and above that was for the investors.

On the surface, the Mars Accords were international treaty obligations to open Mars for a global effort. Actually it was grudging support for NASA, whom everyone expected to eventually claim the prize. Julia and the other astronauts had been in training under this initiative.

But not now. Nobody else had taken up the challenge, and NASA had been slowly assembling an effort to fly at the minimum-energy planetary orbital window in 2016.

A week after the blowup, a day after the big state funeral, President Feinstein announced that the U.S. would "redirect its energies to near-Earth projects." Like building another wing on the space station, a notorious pork barrel beloved of Congress.

Mars seemed dead. All the astronauts were dejected, their years of training wasted. A few took sudden leaves. One went skydiving. Some started hanging out in bars, not part of the approved health regimen.

Julia tried to wear her Doris Day mask through the whole thing, but it kept slipping. She consoled Marc and Raoul, men who ditched good careers to train for Mars. Even then, she kept quiet about being romantically involved with Viktor. In the tight little world of astronaut politics, nobody knew what would happen next. Conceivably, just having kept it secret might knock them out of space station missions—the only game left.

Then a slim, beautifully dressed man walked in on the Mars astronaut team at Johnson Space Center.

He came with a trailing wedge of suited, alert men and women who formed a bow shock wave for him, enabling a dramatic entrance. He shook a few hands, traded short sallies, and worked the room almost like a politician. Julia knew she had seen him somewhere before. His gaze swept the NASA staff like a searching though affable spotlight. The whole room seemed to focus around him as people talking to the side stopped to watch.

His swift gaze found the dozen astronauts. He paused for effect, then asked, "Who still wants to go to Mars—on the cheap?"

John Axelrod. Ready smile, tanned good looks, darting blue eyes that gleamed with wary assessment. She had felt an uneasy fascination with him from the first moment.

His money originally came from Genesmart, a biotech firm he helped start, that brought to market Tourex, an antibacterial to combat Montezuma's revenge. It had become the indispensable traveling companion for tourists and business travelers worldwide. When he took Genesmart public, he was an overnight multibillionaire. But from his early years he had been the kind of man who would bet on whose bag came off the baggage claim carousel first. His interest in Mars ran back to childhood. He had been a washout in early astronaut training, but had kept a keen interest and had some insider, good ol' boy contacts at NASA.

He knew NASA's unmanned return ship, the ERV, had launched for Mars over a year ago. It had landed in Gusev Crater and refueled, using the Martian atmosphere, and was ready even now to fly a crew back to Earth. And he didn't want to see the Mars mission die.

"Plus," he had said to the astronauts, "there's money to be made."

In just a few wheeler-dealer days, Axelrod had put together a consortium of big corporations to win the $30 billion Mars Prize.

"But we estimated sixty billion dollars to go," one astronaut interrupted.

"That's with bureaucrats and paperwork." Axelrod grinned, white teeth against tanned skin. He looked to be in his forties, fit and bristling with peppery energy. "That, I'll cut."

He had a risky but inexpensive method for a red planet mission first suggested in the early 1990s. Instead of using NASA's costly orbiting return module, the

Consortium crew would return to Earth directly in the NASA return ship.

"But the ERV is government property!" an astronaut called.

"It's an abandoned ship. My lawyers will argue that the Law of the Sea applies here. With no crew, it belongs to whoever gets to it."

"That's not fair!"

"Life ain't."

"NASA will need it when they go."

"It'll be a junker by then."

Cutting the crew to four also allowed the Consortium to launch a smaller manned habitat vehicle. The crew of four would land near the ERV.

"That's dangerous, outside our design protocols."

"Mars is already dangerous, and outside your control. I'm gonna minimize costs."

"But with four people, there's not enough backup."

"I don't wanna back up. I want to go forward."

"If anybody gets sick—"

"There'll be a qualified doctor. But he—or she—will pull other duties, too. Everybody works, all the time."

"Four is still too few!"

"Hey, the fewer you send, the fewer we can lose."

This met only silence.

But . . . orbital mechanics were clear and cruel. The whole round trip would take two and a half years. Due to the shifting alignment of the planets, launch windows for trajectories needing minimum fuel are spaced about twenty-six months apart. The trip each way takes about six months, leaving about one and a half years on the surface.

When he finished, Axelrod stood back and hooked his thumbs in his belt and waited for more howls of protest. There was silence. His direct, no-BS manner had sobered the astronauts. NASA's big-bucks plan would have taken less than a year, round trip—expensive in fuel, but easy on the crew. The Consortium four would have to hold out on Mars, exploring and staying alive, for a grueling endurance test.

But it would be cheap. And they'd all get rich . . . if they got back. The salaries would range well into millions. Axelrod tossed off, "For the survivors, that is. And the widows."

"You can do all that for thirty billion bucks?" someone asked.

"Nope, twenty. Got to be a profit here, folks."

A long silence.

"Any volunteers?" Axelrod asked. The dozen astronauts all looked at one another. One stormed out, calling Axelrod a maniac. Three others expressed reservations and drifted out the door.

But eight were willing. Eager. Including Julia and Viktor, Raoul and Marc.

Over the next few weeks the eight candidates threw themselves into planning for Axelrod's risky Mars Direct concept, much as the original Mercury astronauts took a hands-on role in developing the first spacecraft. The ideas had been around for a while, pushed by the Mars Society. Axelrod just knew what to purloin. They had a joyous visit from Bob Zubrin, the Tom Paine of Mars who had pushed the earliest ideas about going on the cheap.

Graying but as hot-eyed as ever, Zubrin gave the staff meeting he attended an evangelical fervor.

Axelrod believed in the vigor of private capital, sure, but with the inexorable workings of planetary orbits bringing the launch window ever closer, he knew how to save time. He leased the Johnson Space Center facility for training astronauts—the cheapest, easiest, and quickest way to continue their conditioning.

Getting the private camel's nose under the NASA tent was not easy. But the Congressional timidity about going had a flip side: joy at a windfall of private money. The long-awaited crisis in Social Security, Medicare, and other overloaded social systems demanded fresh infusions of raw cash. Axelrod came to Congress with a delightful transfusion. Next year Congress would have to face painful cuts, but hell, that was next year.

Soon enough Axelrod was selling camera crews the right to film at JSC the intensive crew training. Grav-stress tests for aerobraking. The glitches in integrating and servicing the food, water, and waste systems. Not least, the medical nightmares coming up due to the six-month-long free-fall flight to Mars. The doctors were sure the crew would be too weak to function once they arrived, one major reason NASA had opted for a more expensive but shorter route. Never before had network anchors worried on the nightly news about zero-g effects, radiation levels, and the subtleties of orbital mechanics.

Even better, they debated a growing mystery. Axelrod's whole plan was based on buying, cheaply, the prototypes of hardware for NASA's doomed mission, then converting them into the actual flight modules. But certain key components were missing. No explanation, sorry.

The gone gear was particularly centered around the life-support systems. Julia suspected some of the more remote provinces of NASA were hoarding these for some other venture, in the wake of the agency's retreat from Mars. Who else would want to hold on to it?

This forced Axelrod to dig deeper into his own pockets to replace them. Grumbling, he did so. Julia got to see him grandly write a check for $2.3 billion. The cameras ate up the whole thing, of course.

Costs mounted. Estimates of future expenses soared even faster.

The whole world watched, and most betting was that Axelrod would fall flat on his underfinanced face well before liftoff.

One day Julia and Viktor were at a swimming pool with the married astronauts, Raoul and Katherine Molina. Twenty feet down, in full pressure suits, they were simulating zero gravity conditions that would occur in the six-month flight. Axelrod came charging in with his usual corps of assistants straggling after. He shouted out orders—after all, he paid the rent—and had them hauled out of the pool.

Dripping, irritated, weighed down by their heavy suits, the astronauts stood watching him. "Big announcement, guys. Had to tell you myself."

"Suit radios we have," Viktor said.

"This you don't wanna hear on those comms. Forget the pool work. You aren't going in zero *at all*."

Another money saver. He and his team had decided

on a Russian space habitat prototype that was designed to create artificial gravity in flight. The crew compartment module was connected by a cable to the last stage of the big booster rocket they launched with. By making these two modules revolve about each other, the habitat would feel an artificial, centrifugal "gravity."

"See," Axelrod said, "that cuts down on training and gear. Solves other problems, too—those medical worries, to start. Makes the plumbing work a whole lot easier, too."

So the Consortium mission was a go. But which four of the eight got to fly?

Julia had not been able to sleep the night before Axelrod's selection announcement. Neither had Viktor. She knew—she was next to him, tossing and fretting.

"You are more the favorite," Viktor said suddenly. "You must face going without me."

"Me, the favorite?"

"Better looking. Talk better, too."

She had never really considered the possibility that he wouldn't be with her on Mars. That only one of them would be chosen. She had never thought about their future, not in the terms he dryly outlined.

"Each have maybe fifty-fifty shot. Probability we both go, twenty-five percent."

"You're the best pilot."

"You are best biologist and general backup. But without knowing more, those are the odds."

She held him close. "I don't like to think of our lives together in terms of probabilities."

"Agree. Is too much like our daily work."

People weren't best considered, she felt, as racehorses. They just *were*.

Axelrod made his picks at a big press conference. Plenty of camera snouts, tons of tension. Feeding the eye-appetite of humanity. None of the astronauts wanted it that way, but Axelrod had licensed coverage of the event to a cable network on an exclusive.

"Got to raise capital, y'know. Send you folks to Mars with steaks and champagne."

And the team of four were, the married couple, Raoul and Katherine. The very telegenic pilot, Marc Bryant. And Julia.

But not Viktor.

The four chosen astronauts sat at a long table on the dais behind Axelrod. She looked at the others. Raoul and Marc beamed, Katherine was smiling her careful astronaut's smile that could mean anything. And Julia?

It was like a sudden lurch into zero g. Falling. *No Viktor.*

They were not just probabilities. She remembered thinking, *We're ourselves, not race horses.*

She sat beneath the glaring, searching lights and thought, *No Viktor. For two and a half years. By the time I get back, it will be over between us.*

3

THE CRACKLE OF THE RADIO STARTLED HER. "HOME TEAM here. Got your heads-up, Julia. How is he?" Marc's crisp efficiency came over clearly, but she could hear the clipped tenor anxiety, too.

"Stable." She quickly elaborated on Viktor's symptoms, glancing at his sleeping face. She'd had a year of physician's assistant training and was the official medical officer, but Marc had more field experience, and a med school degree. She felt relieved when he approved of her treatment. "Got to think what this means," he said laconically.

"We'll be there for supper. Extra rations, I'd say."

A small, very small joke. They had celebrated each major finding with a slightly excessive food allotment. Extra beer, too. She was in charge of brewing and they always had plenty on tap from the keg in the bio lab.

So far, they had not marked disasters this way. And they were having their share.

"My night to cook, too," Marc said, transparently trying to put a jovial lilt to it. "Take care, Jules. Watch the road."

Here came the heart-squeezing moment.

She turned the start-up switch and in the sliver of time before the methane-oxygen burn started in the rover engine, all the possible terrors arose.

If it failed, could she fix it? Raoul and Marc could come out in an unpressured rover and rescue them, sure, but that would chew up time . . . and be embarrassing. She wasn't much of a mechanic, but still, who likes to look helpless?

Then the mixture caught and the rover chugged into action. Settling in, she peered out at the endless obstacles with the unresting concentration that had gotten her on this mission in the first place. To spend five hundred seventy days on Mars you wanted people who found sticking to the tracks a challenge, not boring. One of the job specs for astronauts was an obsessive-compulsive profile.

She followed the autotracker map meticulously, down a narrow valley and across a flood plain, then over a boulder-strewn pass and down a narrow valley and across a flood plain, then over a pass . . .

Here, a drive back to base that proved uneventful was even pleasant. Mars was always ready to thunk a wheel into an unseen hole or pitch the rover down a slope of shifting gravel, so she kept exactly to the tracks they had made on the way out, a proven safe return. She had seen enough of this red-hued terrain to last a lifetime, anyway. Nothing out there for a biologist.

In the distance she caught sight of the formation she and Viktor had dubbed the Shiprock on the way out. It looked like a huge old sailing ship, red layers sculpted by eons of high winds. They'd talked about Ray Bradbury's sand ships, tried to imagine skimming over the undulating landscape. The motion of the rover always reminded her a little of being on the ocean. They were sailing over the Martian landscape on a voyage of discovery, a modern-day Columbus journey. But Columbus made three voyages to the New World without landing on the continent. He "discovered" America by finding islands in the Caribbean, nibbling on the edges of a continent. Still, he got a holiday named for him . . .

A sudden thought struck her: was that what they were doing— finding only the fringes of the Mars biology? Many people had speculated that the subterranean vents were the most likely places for life on this planet. The frontier for her lay hundreds of meters below, out of reach. She sighed resignedly. But it had been great fun, at first.

She slurped more tea, recalling the excitement of the first months. Some of it was pure fame rush, of course. Men on Mars! (Uh, and a woman, too.) They were household names now, the first Mars team, sure bets for all the history books. Hell, they might eventually eclipse Neil Armstrong.

She was first author on a truly historic paper, the first submitted to *Nature* from another world. Barth, Bryant, Molina, & Nelyubov's "Fossil Life on Mars" described their preliminary findings: it would rank with Watson and Crick's 1952 paper nailing the structure of DNA. That paper had opened up cell biology and led to the Biological Century.

What would their discovery lead to? There was already a fierce bidding war for her samples. Every major lab wanted to be the first to examine the fossils, maybe extract Martian DNA, if any, and determine the relationship between Martian and Terran life.

With her small scanning electron microscope she'd gotten decent enough pictures to confirm that these were indeed fossils, and not just wavy compression features in the rock. They looked strikingly like stromatolite fossils, tough layer cakes of bacteria. Some of the bacteria in living stromatolites on Earth were photosynthetic cyanobacteria, and thus green, but the Martian rocks gave no color clues.

She started on her favorite speculation: where did life start? Mars was smaller and so cooled first. Life could have arisen here while Earth was still a hot lava ball. Then it could have gone to Earth via the meteorite express.

Organized life-forms from Mars seeding Earth's primitive soup of basic organic molecules would have quickly dominated. *Martians invade, eat Earthly resources!* H. G. Wells with a twist. We may yet turn out to be Martians. Pretty heady stuff for the scientific community, and it would change our essential worldview. Full employment for philosophers, too, and even religious theorists.

The Martian meteorites with their enigmatic fossils had tantalized scientists for years. When first discovered, the big question had been whether the tiny shapes actually were fossils, because most people thought they knew that Mars was lifeless. *Now we know about that part, at least,* she thought.

But deep down she realized she'd wanted to find life, not fossils, and even more than that, L*I*F*E.

Marc was jazzed by the discovery of deeper deposits of fossils, separated by layers of sterile peroxide-laden sediments in the old ocean beds. That implied periodic episodes of a wetter and warmer climate.

But so far she had not found anything alive. Even the first volcanic vent they had explored had no life, only peroxide soil blown into it from the surface, like a dusty old mine shaft.

Before today, that is. And now they were about to leave, the subterranean reaches still unexplored. Damn!

After five hours Viktor was doing well, had regained his energy and good spirits. They even managed a clumsy but satisfying slap and tickle when she stopped the rover for lunch. In the cramped, fishbowl world of the hab, they'd learned to use the privacy of the rover to great advantage. Today she felt nervous and skittish, but Viktor was a persistent sort and she finally realized that this just might do both of them more good than anything in the medicine chest back in the habitat.

The route began to take them—or rather, her, since Viktor crashed again right after sex; this time she forgave him—through familiar territory. She had scoured the landscape within a few days of the hab. Coming down in the Gusev Crater, they got a full helping of Mars: chasms, flood runoff plains, wrinkled canyons, chaotic terrain once undermined by mud flows, dried beds of ancient rivers and lakes, even some mysterious big potholes that must have been minivolcanoes somehow hollowed out.

Her pursuit of surface fossil evidence of life had been systematic, remorseless—and mostly a waste.

Not a big surprise, really, in retrospect. Any hiker in the American west was tramping over lands where once tyrannosaurus and bison had wandered, but seldom did

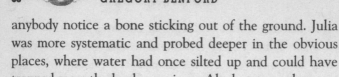

anybody notice a bone sticking out of the ground. Julia was more systematic and probed deeper in the obvious places, where water had once silted up and could have trapped recently dead organisms. Algal mats, perhaps, as with the first big life-forms on Earth. But she had no luck, even in a year and a half of snooping into myriad canyons and promising beds of truly ancient lakes. That didn't mean life wasn't somewhere on the planet. It had been warm and moist here for a billion years, enough for life to evolve, even if Mars had not supported surface life for perhaps three billion or more years.

She stamped her feet to help the circulation. Space heaters in the rover ran off the methane-oxy burn, but as always, the floor was cold. Mars never let you forget where you were.

She tried to envision how it must have been here, billions of years ago. This was her cliché daydream, trying to impose on the arid red wastes the romance of what they could have been, once upon a time.

Did life give way with a grudging struggle, trying every possible avenue before retreating underground or disappearing?

The planet did not die for want of heat or air, but of mass. With greater gravity it could have held on to the gases its volcanoes vented, prevented its water vapor from escaping into vacuum. Recycling of carbon didn't happen on Mars, the CO_2 was lost to carbonate rocks. The atmosphere thinned, the planet cooled . . .

Split from hydrogen by the sun's stinging ultraviolet, the energetic oxygen promptly mated with the waiting

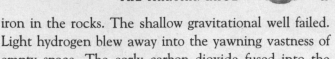

iron in the rocks. The shallow gravitational well failed. Light hydrogen blew away into the yawning vastness of empty space. The early carbon dioxide fused into the rocks, bound forever as carbonate. Had Mars been nearer the sun, the sunlight and warmth would simply have driven water away faster.

So those early life-forms must have fought a slow, agonizing retreat. There were eras when lakes and even shallow, muddy seas had hosted simple life—Marc's cores had uncovered plenty of ancient silted plains, now compressed into sedimentary rock. But no fossil forests, nothing with a backbone, nothing with shells or hard body parts. If higher forms had basked in the ancient warmth here, they had left no trace.

The squat hab came into view in the salmon sunset.

They had landed in the ancient flat bottom of Gusev Crater, whose distant ramparts reared over a kilometer into the rosy sky. A hundred fifty klicks across, Gusev was a geologist's playground.

One of astronomy's more arcane pleasures was eclectic naming. Gusev was a mini–United Nations. To the south lay the Ma'adim Vallis, "Martian Valley" in Arabic. Gusev himself had been a nineteenth-century Russian astronomer. Some French Planetary scientists working for the Americans had given the small crater near their base the Greek name Thyra.

She could see the slumped peaks of Thyra as she headed south. One of the major reasons to land here had been a tantalizing dark spot on Thyra's southern rim. Under telepresence guidance from Earth, Rover Boy had found promising signs that the spot was a salt flat left by a thermal vent. True enough, but when they arrived they found that the site had not given off anything for maybe half a billion years. A crushing disappointment, that first month. But if there had been venting, maybe there was still, nearby. She had lived with that ebbing hope for a year and a half.

Well, now she had her vent. And it had injured Viktor within a few minutes.

Looking like a giant's drum, seven meters high and eight meters across, the hab—their former command module—stood off the ground on sturdy metal struts. Sandbags on the roof cut their radiation exposure. Inside, the two stacked decks had the floor space of a smallish condo, their home for the last twenty months. A thousand carefully arranged square feet. Not for the claustrophobic, but they would certainly be nostalgic for it in the cramped quarters of the Return Vehicle they would shortly be boarding.

By now the hab was familiar to billions of Earth-bound TV viewers and Net surfers. Everyone on Earth had the opportunity to follow their adventures, which were beamed daily from Ground Control and carried on the evening news. Their webpage registered over a hundred million hits in the week following the landing. Mars had ceased to be space and had become a place.

Raoul and Marc climbed down out of the hab as she approached in the last slanting rays of a ruddy sunset, two chubby figures in dark parka suits. Only Raoul's slight limp from frostbitten toes distinguished them. The tracker system had alerted them. Thanks to the mission planners, they would not have to carry Viktor in. The rover mated directly to hab airlock.

But first, a little ceremony they had devised: salvaging water from the rover. Even with Viktor hurt, they followed procedure.

The methane-oxygen burn made carbon dioxide, which the engine vented, and pure water. She backed the rover to the conical return ship. The gaudy NASA emblem they had completely covered with a plated-on, red-on-white MARS CONSORTIUM in wrap-around letters a meter high. Axelrod had made a point of including that thumb-in-your-eye gesture in the payload.

Outside, Raoul and Marc hooked the water condensers to the input lines, so the chem factory inside could store it. They had full tanks of methane and oxygen for the liftoff, but water was always welcome, after the parching they had taken on the long flight here.

They waved to her. Their little rituals; the guys made the gesture as a way of saying "welcome home." In the bleak, rusty dusk, the cold of night biting already through to her, the symbolism was important. Mars was sharp, cold, and unrelenting, and they all felt it to the bone.

4

"VIKTOR, YOU SHOULD GET OUT, GO FOR A WALK."

"Thank you, no."

Julia walked around to where he sat on the couch, watching a news channel in Russian. The story seemed to be about the latest shuffling of governments. From her very limited Russian, Julia gathered that somebody had been president for the total span of three hours.

"You can't just veg out like this."

"Vegetables have right to be left alone. Plant liberation."

"I thought if we both go to Axelrod, explain how well we work together—"

"Work? Is what you call single entendre meaning?"

She got up and paced, not liking this edgy humor of his, but in an odd way respecting it. No astronaut was built to take failure. They all knew they could be cut from a list, and many had been.

But this list was the culmination of a lifetime, the A-grade ticket. Not just because everyone who returned would be wealthy—a rather new element in space careers, since NASA kept salaries at civil service levels for everybody. Because Mars was the sole destination that lifted the heart, that gave the inevitable risk a gravitas of immense historical and scientific heft.

And Viktor wasn't going.

He sat on the couch and watched the trivid and drank dark beer. He had quite a capacity, she had to give him that. He had arranged the five bottles before him in an exact pentagonal pattern.

"Look, *I'll* go to Axelrod."

"I do not wish you to go begging for me." He gave her a grave, owlish look.

"I don't think four people is enough for this, anyway. I could start there—"

"Four is the design spec."

"Look, all the thorough design studies at JSC showed—"

"That six was better. Of course is. But is not cheaper."

"We aren't even taking a doctor, for Chrissake, just me."

"You have year of emergency medical training."

"But it's not enough! What if I had to do heart surgery, or—"

"You are all excellent"—he paused to pronounce each part, *ex-cell-ent*—"condition. No heart attacks likely."

"Okay, okay, but we should have a backup pilot, right?"

"You say that because I am pilot-engineer."

"And if the pilot gets hurt? Not like a biologist breaking a leg, who cares? No pilot, nobody goes home."

"Marc is good pilot." He peered down the mouth of his beer, Anchor Steam Porter.

This non sequitur, she saw, was Viktor's way of saying that he was resigned to not going. "Hey, is this phlegmatic acceptance routine of yours just the Russian coming out?"

His head jerked up and he stared at her, mouth open. "What means phlegmatic?"

"Stolid."

"What means stolid?"

"What am I, a thesaurus? No, don't bother, a thesaurus is—"

"I know thesaurus."

"Passive, it means you sit on your ass and do nothing."

"Whole world is sitting on ass, watching glorious Twenty-first century on TV."

"Yeah, some truth to that." She sighed and collapsed onto the couch next to him. "And they'll be watching *us*."

"You. I watch, too."

"No, you're going. I dunno how, but I'm gonna get you there."

"You now say 'gonna.'"

"So?"

"Notice how everybody now talks something like that?"

"Oh. Like Axelrod."

"American Southern."

"We're taking on his mannerisms?"

"His ideas, too. Sounds to my ear, like."

"I hadn't noticed."

"I think is nothing wrong with. Is his money."

"And Microsoft's and Boeing's and Lockheed's and don't forget that fine old Russian Energiya, Inc."

"Very ancient joke." He suddenly turned and hugged

her in his bearlike grip. "Under capitalism, man exploits man. Under communism, is the reverse."

"Okay, I get your drift."

"So we rejected astronauts, we are angry but what can do?"

"I can—"

"No, me. I do for myself."

Except . . . she embraced him fervently and could not think of anything he could do. In him she felt the simmering, sour longing.

Three of the other astronauts had simply disappeared. Lee Chen, her instructor in exobiology, who had recently joined the astronaut program, Gerda Braun, a German engineer inherited from the European Space Agency, and Claudine Jesum, a French pilot. Where had they gone? Probably off to various ventures in the burgeoning low orbital business. But they had all left quietly, letting nobody know their plans. Astronauts were not usually very public in their passions, and even less so in their defeats.

Viktor had said he would remain behind to support the mission, serving in systems operations, trying out variant routines in the simulators as they flew to Mars and met unanticipated problems. Fair enough, she supposed, especially if he were positioning himself to fly in a later expedition—*if any*, she reminded herself.

But would their relationship survive this? She murmured into his shoulder and realized that Axelrod's decision had forced her to become something other than a standard, loyal team player.

The recognition surprised her. She did not want to

go to Mars without Viktor. Even if it meant staying home.

She hesitated at the double glass doors. On the other side was the plush outer office of Axelrod's huge suite at Genesmart. Here she was still safe, still one of the golden four astronauts picked to go to Mars. When she came out after their interview, what would she be? Just another failed candidate? How would she feel? She sighed inwardly. *This isn't going to get you anyplace, Jules, ol' gal. Let's get it over with.* She pushed through the door and slogged across what felt like miles of thick carpeting to her appointment.

Axelrod somehow managed not to be dwarfed by the massive desk. He came around it to greet her, moving in his usual kinetic style. To her mild surprise, he was the clean-desk variety of leader. The mahogany desktop held exactly two pieces of paper, one pen, and a pop-up computer flatscreen.

He clasped her proffered hand in both of his, then guided her to a seat in an alcove of the room, sort of a coffee table and chairs arrangement. The vastness amazed her; he had more room in his office than they would occupy on Mars. She wondered briefly if he had any idea what he was asking them to do.

An attendant who had been hovering in the background appeared with a rolling tray covered with an assortment of fruit drinks and mineral waters. She picked one and they made very small talk while she was being served. Then the tray disappeared and she knew she had to go for it.

"So, Julia, you're looking well. I can tell it's not your health that's bothering you. But something is." It was a question without being one.

"I wanted to talk to you about the crew selection."

"Something wrong?" He smiled, but his eyes were watchful. "I think I made a very fine selection."

"No, not wrong. Well, for me, yes. Raoul and Katherine are top-notch, and Marc is a fine pilot and geologist to boot. I guess I'm the problem."

"Don't tell me now you don't want to go."

"Oh, no, I do, all of my life I have, only . . . well, there's something you didn't know when you chose."

"Oh?" A little edge to the voice.

"Not that you could've known," she said hastily. "We were very careful, perhaps too careful." She smiled ruefully. "But NASA always discouraged socializing among the astronauts. Part of the Mr. Clean persona they favor. And it tends to weigh against you when mission crews are chosen."

"I see. But it happened anyway."

"Well, of course." A half shrug. "So you see, the problem is that Raoul and Katherine aren't the only couple."

"And Marc isn't your paramour?"

The old-fashioned term startled her. "No, or else there'd be no problem. And he's a fine choice . . ."

"But you'd prefer someone else?"

"Well, I can't ask you to yank him for that reason, so I came here to say that I've decided to pull out."

In rapid order Axelrod looked surprised, vexed, puzzled, contemplative, intrigued, then vexed again. How had so transparent a man risen so high in business?

Unless there lay his talent—to let his true self out to play, letting others see just who he was, and so solidifying their trust in him. If so, it struck her as an original method. Not calculated, but all the more effective for that.

Axelrod leaned back in his leather recliner and clasped both hands behind his neck, feet up on an ottoman, face now unreadable.

"Now you tell me."

"I couldn't go on without—"

"Rather than when it could actually have influenced my decision."

"I didn't know who you would pick. Or how I would feel, for that matter."

"But you do want to go."

"Oh, yes, but not alone. Not for two and a half years."

"And I'm supposed to send you to Mars? What if you get there and just don't feel like doing your job?"

"I wouldn't do that, I've trained—"

He laughed. "You'll have to do better than that when you face the press."

"Oh."

"Either tell 'em everything, or nothing. Me, I go the everything route."

"I noticed."

"More honest, seems to me."

"I'm trying to be honest. I just don't think I could stand being separated from Viktor that long, and leaving him behind."

"So it's Viktor you love. The Russian."

"Yes." Should she let "love" pass? She hadn't truly

owned up to that yet, even to Viktor.

"I understand." He gazed out the enormous broad window that was the entire wall of his office. "NASA liked him, top rated as a pilot, no problem there. How is he on TV?"

The question surprised her. She thought Viktor was very attractive, but not in the typical blond American mode of Marc. She smiled, allowed herself to say, "Well, I think he looks great, but I'm pretty biased . . ."

"Got presence?"

"Uh, I think so—"

"Do you think you can handle the right angle on this?"

She felt like a slow student summoned before the principal, not following remotely what was happening. She bought a moment by taking a sip of her drink. Axelrod gave her no help whatever, just leaned back in his chair and looked at the ceiling.

So far nothing in this conversation had gone the way she had anticipated. His silence was unnerving. Suddenly it occurred to her that when she left the mission, inevitably word would get out about why, and that would force her to reveal all of it to her parents. Her ex-astronaut mother would be all right, but her father did not like Viktor, the one time they met. So complication would not leave her life anytime soon . . .

"Surprise!" Axelrod sat straight up, face animated again. "I like the idea."

"What idea?"

"Of lovers going to Mars. Better ratings for the TV

coverage, for sure. First, a big wedding. Plenty of advertising spin-offs, if we play it right. 'What would *you* take on a Honeymoon to Mars?' Victoria's Secret could run up a whole line of low-gravity lingerie, I'll bet."

She wanted to laugh, but he was perfectly serious. And happy.

"You want Viktor, you got him. I stand by my crew."

Wedding? Marry Viktor? "I don't really know if we're ready for that yet."

Axelrod looked surprised. "I think it's got to play this way."

"Why?"

"The whole world is watching. I don't want people saying I'm running a program that flouts the marriage bond."

She looked at him, struggling to hide her incredulity. Hadn't he had three marriages already? Carefully she said, "I don't either. I just need a little time."

"Don't take too long."

"Well . . . it's all right with me, but I need to talk to Viktor."

"Sure, sure. But no marriage, no Viktor on this flight."

"Marc—"

"You wouldn't be sleepin' with him. Makes all the difference."

"Doing it on camera, that makes the difference here?"

"You bet." He smiled in a completely open way, no guile at all. Or was he really a quite accomplished actor, after all? She could not tell.

Then her astronaut training asserted itself. "Uh, won't the habitat have to be altered to take an extra crew mem—"

"No changes." Axelrod waved both hands in dismissal. "Too late for that, we're fabricating the hab right now."

"But—"

"I'll bump Marc. Tell you true, only big difference between him 'n' Viktor was, Marc's better looking and speaks well."

"Not . . . not piloting?"

"Viktor's a shade better, the simulations showed."

A wave of confused relief washed over her. Marc was a good friend. She had not seen this coming. "I never thought you would, honestly, I'm—"

"Don't have to. I'll do that. You think Mars, I'll think Earth." He winked. "Specialize. Now, then, let's pick the big date."

Viktor was tricky to deal with.

Not that he needed to be persuaded. Julia discovered to her surprise that he was happy with the idea of getting married. In his complicated Russian soul, what bothered him was her going to Axelrod in the first place. As pilot, he would be commander of the mission. He worried that he wouldn't be accepted as the clearly chosen leader.

But Raoul and Katherine didn't seem to mind the switch. Raoul had always had more in common with Viktor than with Marc. And as a couple they were preoccupied with some internal dialogue of their own.

Marc was furious. He blamed Julia, accusing her of plotting to remove him from the crew. Then he was gone.

Julia had the most trouble with her father. Harry referred to it as a "shotgun marriage" and wouldn't be cajoled into feeling better about it. In some ways, Australia wasn't really in the twenty-first century, she mused. He'd wanted Viktor to ask for her hand, not be told about her choice. And he resented Axelrod's forcing the decision. When he was offered a long-delayed consulting trip to Africa, he went, missing the wedding. Her mother, Robbie, would make the trip alone, in one of Axelrod's private jets.

Axelrod assigned each of the crew a media representative. They needed that. The impending wedding raised the issue of sex in space, and they became fodder for the tabloids.

They were now not just a team, but The Couples. Julia and Viktor, Raoul and Katherine. The press corps became an ever-hungry beast. Parents, friends, enemies, managers who had barely known them—all became suitable targets for microphone-in-face journalism.

NASA had created plenty of opportunities for the press to, well, press against the astronauts. Axelrod killed that attitude immediately. "Thing is," he explained to the four, "you are a commodity now. Don't want to oversell you."

Katherine said straightforwardly, "I'm not a commodity."

"Partners, then," Axelrod said smoothly. "Partners in the Consortium."

Raoul supported his wife's objection. "We have rights to our own stories, I believe."

"So you do." Axelrod nodded vigorously. He was sitting on his mahogany desk, and the four of them were alone with him, a rarity. He had ordered champagne brought in to celebrate the "consolidation," as he termed it, of the team.

Raoul said, "Then we should manage our own relationships with the media."

"You shall—when you can reap the benefits. Right now, you train."

Viktor said, "Good. No speaking to those fellows."

Axelrod smiled coolly. "Not entirely. But we'll orchestrate the press conferences. You keep your stories to yourselves, and our legal department will handle your separate contracts."

Viktor asked, "Contracts?"

"Your memoirs, interviews, so on." Axelrod beamed. "You are planning on coming back and telling your story, aren't you?"

They were officially media figures now. The world was steadily going Mars-mad and the four of them were at the center of it all.

First they were invited to all the big social events in Houston, thrown by people they didn't know. Later they received invitations from all over the country. Wannabe "megabillionaires"—a media misnomer—offered to send private jets to whisk them to posh mansions. Cost was no object. Your party was an instant success if one or more of the Marsnauts attended.

"Another big do," Julia said one morning, looking at the latest round of invitations. "This one's in New York. Wanna go?"

"To big doo-doo? I think not. Too much caviar is bad for astronaut training." He put a hand over his liver with a pained expression on his face.

It was a game they played. Julia would read Viktor the most outrageous of the invitations, and he would pretend to take them seriously.

It was their way of dealing with the craziness of it all. As astronauts, they had been faces in the crowd, lost among one hundred others. No one had recognized them in the street, wanted autographs, or invited them anywhere. Now suddenly they were hyperstars, megacelebs, their every move outside JSC stalked by crowds of paparazzi. Axelrod's security guards moved them between the training center and their secluded living compound.

Somehow she hadn't anticipated this roller-coaster life. At least the recent nasty talk in some of the down-market media had gone away, once their marriage was announced. Amazing, what a piece of legal paper could silence. Still, she felt that a lot of this had fallen upon her while she was busy doing something else. Like her job, for instance.

"I'd feel better about it if we weren't getting all this attention before we'd done anything."

"Yes. But maybe no time after."

A good way to put it, she thought sourly. *Maybe what we'll be remembered for will be our deaths.*

* * *

July 4, 2015. An Axelrod irony, "getting hitched" on Independence Day.

The wedding took place on Axelrod's private island off the coast of North Carolina, six weeks later.

"Just a simple garden wedding," he said to Julia and Viktor. "Leave all the arrangements to me. You concentrate on Mars."

And that was just fine with Julia. She didn't like weddings, had no interest in organizing one. She'd always thought vaguely that if she ever did marry, it would be in a judge's office with a couple of friends.

But here she was, in a long white dress, looking like someone from a bride's magazine. Her short brunette bob had been meticulously arranged; she was wearing a veil and had a bouquet of flowers in her hand. After months in training, she felt like a butterfly, emerged from the chrysalis of her astronaut coveralls. Axelrod had flown her in two days early, for a succession of mud baths, facials, hair and makeup consultations, and last-minute dress fittings. It would be more than three years before she had the opportunity to do anything remotely like it again, so she just smiled and went along with it all.

"Oh, my," Robbie said, dabbing her eyes. "You look gorgeous, Jules." She sniffed. "I do wish your father were here."

Julia felt his absence keenly. Harry was a devoted family man, and they had been close for years. The death of Julia's brother, Bill, had melded the three of them into a solid unit.

And yet he wouldn't come to her wedding. What was it he so disliked in Viktor?

In the absence of Harry, Axelrod would give the bride away. He was between wives at the time, so Julia's mother had flown in from Australia the week before to personalize the arrangements. But she hadn't been able to make a dent in the spectacle.

The media were divided into "invited" and "uninvited." Axelrod sent boats to the mainland for the former, the latter were reduced to buzzing the island in rented motorboats and helicopters.

Huge quantities of food and drink were ferried or helicoptered in. The JSC crowd and the media were serious partyers.

It was time. Her mother left. There was a knock on the door.

Julia hesitated one last moment before opening it to a beaming Axelrod in an ice cream suit. He was clearly relishing this.

"Ready, my dear?" He offered his arm and they walked through the cavernous mansion and out into the lush garden.

Her mother copied Julia with her letter:

TO: HBarth@mesh.com
FROM: RBarth@jsc.gov
July 5, 2015

Dear Harry,
You really missed a great party! The Axelrod island looks like all those old movies of the American South. It's not just a house, but a complex. Great

hunks of communication gear around. John must be able to reach anywhere on Earth he wants.

A huge white mansion with pillars, of course.

My suite was simply enormous. There was a fireplace in the bedroom, and the bathroom had a tub on a dais that Cleopatra would've loved. Hot and cold running help, too.

The "simple garden ceremony" was anything but, of course. Great drifts of food and drink, live music, tents, etc. Everyone danced and laughed until the wee hours. Half of JSC must've been there, and a lot of NASA brass from elsewhere. It looked like a convention for The Mars Society. And he'd invited a slew of reporters. They were pretty well behaved, had a special roped-off place to sit during the ceremony.

But the paparazzi were something else! There must've been a fleet of them buzzing the place with helicopters and speedboats! All for our Julia! But she was worth it. She looked really beautiful! And Viktor just couldn't take his eyes off her. He was just so pleased. I know how you feel about him, but I'm sure he does love her. He was very cordial to me, said he was honored to be joining Julia's family. His parents are gone, you know, and he's so far away from the rest of his family.

The actual ceremony was pretty simple. Raoul and Katherine were the attendants, and Axelrod stood in for you, of course. They'd decided on a civil ceremony, so John arranged for a judge—I think he was a North Carolina Supreme Court

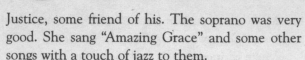

Justice, some friend of his. The soprano was very good. She sang "Amazing Grace" and some other songs with a touch of jazz to them.

The cake was incredible. It was Mars, of course, a huge red-icinged confection. Julia did her best to carve it—with a laser!

Julia's really not much of a public person. That was our Bill. So she had on her public face, and a bit of a grit-your-teeth smile at times. But overall I bet she enjoyed it. How can you not, when you're at the center of the universe like that?

Well, that's about it. I'm pooped. There'll be lots more pictures—I've only attached a few to this e-mail, so you can get an idea of what it was all about.

Hope your trip is working out like you hoped. Your last message about the poacher's camp sounded a bit gruesome. It's dreadful to think that the few remaining wildlife are being butchered—and for meat!

I hope it wasn't dangerous, riding along with the park rangers like that. We've heard so many dreadful stories over the years about game park incidents. Please be careful!

Oh, forgot one thing. The kids are honeymooning here for a few days. In fact Raoul and Katherine are staying on also. It's about the only place those four can get some privacy. I'm looking forward to a few days' peace myself. And it's a lovely place. I'll be flying back at the end of the week.

Miss you, you old curmudgeon! Take care of yourself!!

Much love, xxxx
Robbs

With Axelrod at her side, Julia launched herself into the wedding. In some ways this was the most terrifying part of the mission.

She hadn't yet gotten used to all the media attention—camera snouts, microphones, shouted questions. But it was impersonal. She was just an astronaut, an object caught in the crosshairs of the media. *This* was different. She knew a great many of the guests now staring wide-eyed and entranced (or so it seemed) at the spectacle. Despite her finery, she felt naked.

Axelrod leaned over, whispered in her ear, "Someone with a small nuclear weapon could take out the entire Mars faction."

It was just what she needed. The remark triggered her professional instincts. Axelrod was right. She caught sight of Bob Zubrin, Axelrod's Mars guru, and many of the longtime Mars researchers at NASA—Chris McKay, Carol Stoker, Nathalie Cabrol, Geoff Briggs, John Connolly, and others, some retired, all a bit grayer, but still enthusiastic.

Why are they all here? The dreamers . . .

And some schemers, too. They had come because of something none of them could quite put into words. Marriage, Mars . . .

And then she caught sight of Viktor. And all the rest dropped away. He was grinning in sheer delight. He stretched out his arm in an unplanned gesture of welcome. She took his hand and knew that this was the right thing to do.

Later, thinking about the ceremony, all she could remember clearly was the fond expression in his eyes. The right stuff.

5

JANUARY 11, 2018

DESPITE MARC'S BEST EFFORTS, DINNER WAS NOT A culinary success.

He was the foodie among them, forever trying out new variations of the limited range of kitchen stores. But they had long ago exhausted the narrow potential of the supplies for new tastes, and now everything they ate was too familiar to the tongue. No surprises.

Still, they did have luxuries. Marc's favorite duck in burgundy sauce from a trendy L.A. restaurant, authentic borscht from a San Francisco Russian bakery, blue corn enchiladas from New Mexico, kangaroo steaks, and holiday treats. The list was extensive. But frozen meals lacked that just-cooked, fresh taste.

Food and the mealtime experience were part of an elaborate emphasis on the crew's psychological well-being. There Axelrod had not cut back on the budget. No one on Earth really knew how tough it would be to live so long in a large tuna can surrounded by a hostile planet. So the psychologists intended the mealtimes to be extended breaks in the day. Chances to talk, relax, and eat good, nourishing grub. For Julia, plenty of comfort food—soups, meatloaf, chowder, oatmeal. They each had their own. "Evoke resonances of home," a psych guy had pontificated. As one wag put it, eating is the only enjoyable activity you can do three times a day, every day.

Months before launch each crew member had filled out an exhaustive dietary survey, and then had been interviewed by a dietician. Finally, a computer program called "Meal Creativity" took all the input and attempted to create a set of enticing menus that could be prepared in their galley. The menus rotated their individual choices and the whole pattern repeated monthly. Of course the meals were balanced nutritionally by the inexorable program, which tended to homogenize them. The mission eating experience was designed to be like repeatedly visiting a favorite restaurant. Sure, the menu was familiar, but familiar was reassuring. So the theory went.

They took turns in the tiny galley. On the outbound voyage Julia bowed to the public's expectation and dutifully did her time, but the others agreed that the results were definitely substandard, and she was relieved of cooking. Instead, she did extra cleanup.

That didn't bother Julia, a dedicated non-foodie,

who believed that eating was a somewhat irksome necessity. Food was fuel to power people through the day. Something to keep the "little gray cells" nourished, as her favorite detective said. But unlike Poirot's fastidiousness in cuisine, her palate was undemanding. She went through school with a minimally equipped kitchen. Dumping a box of macaroni and cheese into boiling water stretched her limits. Viktor joked that he sure as hell hadn't picked her for her kitchen skills. He had done most of the cooking for the two of them before the mission, and filled out her food survey. "Either that," he had said, "or risk eating junk food, or worse, Vegemite sandwiches, on Mars."

But there were limits to the technology. The microwaved frozen vegetables were especially resistant to creativity, but Marc kept trying. He and Julia worked in the greenhouse to grow fresh ones. He had asked for a wide range of spices as part of his personal picks. Some of his more infamous attempts had produced stomach-rumbling distress. Still, the food was much better than the freeze-dried horrors of NASA days.

"So what did you two do while we were gone?" Julia asked later over very slightly grainy pudding. The chocolate color disguised any visible traces of Martian dust, but the tongue found its sting.

Marc licked his spoon carefully. "Well, we were drilling into the giant gopher mounds again, ya know. Found something . . . interesting." He went back to his pudding.

Julia glanced over at Viktor. Something was up. You didn't live with people for two years without being able to read them.

Twenty years earlier, Earthbound scientists at NASA analyzing Viking photo data had discovered a field of dozens of regular, hundred-foot-tall hills just north of the small crater Thyra. They put forth a strong case that the hills were actually pingos, buried mounds of ice known from Earth's arctic. But so far, Marc's attempts to drill through what turned out to be layers of salt and rubble had been unfruitful.

"So what you found?" asked Viktor.

Marc stood up. With studied casualness he said, "C'mon, I'll show you. You can watch the robot vid. It's Raoul's turn to clean up anyway."

Aha. It's something big. She decided not to challenge him. *Just let him do it in his own way.* Anyway, she was enjoying the mystery.

She helped as Viktor got up clumsily and hobbled to the control room. The tape was already loaded and ready to go. Marc and Raoul must've planned this. Julia wondered, why the production?

They settled into chairs and Marc started. "Looking back over the robot's vid data, I found a hill where the morning fog seemed to have been a bit thicker or more persistent several times. Figured maybe the regolith covering was a little skimpier than on the others, ya know."

The base sported two open dune buggies the size of ancient VW bugs that the crew used for short sprints of less than fifty klicks round-trip. By taking both buggies, two people could haul the drilling gear. The buggies had been part of the Outpost Mars robot post established by NASA in 2010 to characterize the future landing site. The buggies had been telerobotically operated from

Earth, and later, from the hab at Zubrin Base. On arrival, Raoul and Viktor had added the seats to enable two people to ride in each buggy on manual mode. When not in active use, the buggies were sent out to robotically video areas of interest to the crew or to scientists on Earth.

Marc started the video. A large ruddy hill filled the screen.

Julia shivered, remembering the biting cold that morning she and Marc had first seen the fog over the mounds. Suit heaters cranked to the max, they had looked like colorful, quilted penguins. Their pictures now graced the cover of the Lands' End catalog, wearing the parkas and leggings now called Marswear©, of course. It was the latest rage in macho-type clothes, and the licensing fees helped pay for the mission.

On that trip they'd used the big rover. As they'd prepared to leave it, she'd grabbed her tea cozy and worn it like a knit ski cap. That was only the first time she'd used it as extra insulation.

Marc was talking. "You can see that it has an exposed side. So I decided to try drilling horizontally into that. Saved hauling the gear up on top."

He waved the remote and fast-forwarded the video, causing the two well-padded figures to waddle comically about as they positioned the gear and started drilling.

The video slowed to normal speed and the faint, tinny grind of the laboring drill came through. "Right about here we were in about thirty meters, going pretty slow through some resistant stuff, salts maybe, then all of a sudden the drill started to cut real fast. Right . . . there.

Raoul is monitoring the depth and he shouts to me that it's speeded up. I stopped it then so we wouldn't lose the tip. Now we're pulling it out, and you can see that the drill tip is smoking."

The camera came in for a close-up.

"Uh-oh," said Julia, automatically sympathetic.

"That's what it looked like, anyway, but it wasn't hot, wasn't even warm." He smiled, looking at Julia and Viktor slyly.

"So how could it be smok—oh, wait, it was water vapor!" shouted Julia. "You found water!"

Marc grinned. "Yep. The drill tip was really wet, and making cloud like mad." Mars was so cold and dry that water on the surface never passed through a liquid stage, but sublimed directly from frozen to vapor. The team had concentrated their efforts to drill for water in places where early morning fogs hinted at subsurface moisture.

On the screen the two suited figures were jumping about.

"So are pingos after all."

"Sure seems that way." Suddenly, Julia could see how pleased Marc was. She hadn't noticed much until now, so preoccupied was she with Viktor's accident and the vent.

"How far in did you go?" asked Viktor.

Marc turned off the video. "Just under ten meters. We went back in to confirm, of course. Got one hell of an ice core." He grinned again.

"What does Earth think?"

"I hope they're thinking: one more step towards a colony," said Julia.

"Well, they asked for all the particulars we could squirt 'em, that's for sure."

She was suddenly enthusiastic. "This is great news! Fresh water on our doorstep, practically." She had a sudden thought.

"It is fresh water, isn't it?"

"Yep. I used it in the soup."

"What? Native water? Did you run it through the mass spec first? It could be full of toxic metals."

He laughed. "Relax. Just kidding. I left the analysis for you to do. And a chunk of ice."

"Wow. It's like suddenly discovering you live next to a lake."

"More like frozen lake."

"A frozen bumpy lake."

"Typical Mars." This last from Raoul, who appeared from the galley with mugs of hot chocolate. "On Earth, you'd look for water in the low spots, stream channels. Here, it's backwards—water is in the hilly hummocks. An upside-down world."

His sardonic wit could sometimes cut through Julia's high moods, but not tonight. She was irrepressibly cheered by the discovery.

"A toast to the first lake on Mars," she said, "and to the discoverers."

They clicked mugs and drank.

"Can tell why Julia is so happy: she thinks we're going to build hot tub in the greenhouse."

"Now *that's* an idea. But first, what *does* Earth think?"

"Well, they'd prefer more cores to make sure all the

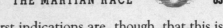

hills are pingos. First indications are, though, that this is probably good enough."

"Good enough for the government, as they say," said Raoul with uncharacteristic levity. Raoul was the top mechanic on the team, and ritually cynical about governments. He even disliked the fact that NASA had separately contracted with the Consortium to supply some geological data.

"Too bad we're not working for the government, eh?" shot back Marc.

Julia looked over at him, surprised. The brief exchange left much unsaid, but all understood the shorthand. Tensions were definitely building as the launch date approached. No one wanted to be the cause of a delayed return. The search for subsurface water had gone slowly, disappointing some of the mission backers, raising the specter that the team would be asked to stay longer to complete the mapping.

They didn't seem in a mood to discuss her going back to the vent. Time was pressing, and the next item was the engine test. She had better wait before bringing it up at all.

She knew through the years of working with these guys that timing was everything in prying up the lid of the male mind. She had learned that in the toughest of schools: NASA, and beyond.

After Katherine dropped out, there had been strong pressure to have an all-male crew. Many within NASA hadn't wanted a woman along at all. Adding one had inevitably made for tensions, but on the other hand, it also gave half the possible Earth audience somebody to identify with. And the Consortium could be subtle.

Even on Mars, the undeclared war between the sexes continued. As the sole woman on the mission, she had been the target of special psychological counseling during the final months before the launch. Her marriage to Viktor clarified what NASA delicately termed IRA, for Interpersonal Relationship Activities. Instead, they concentrated on how she could tell one of the "guys" that he was wrong without getting into a pissing contest. Someone was worried that she would bruise fragile male egos if she found fault with her crewmates.

She needed to be positive, supportive, but indirect, they said. No criticism of her crewmates. And they had her read old studies of the relationships between airline pilots and co-pilots. "Co-pilots on commercial aircraft use indirect hints to correct pilots who are making mistakes, even though these mistakes can be a matter of life and death," read one of the learned studies she'd been given. *Hollywood screenwriters got it wrong again*, had been her first reaction. All those airplane terror movies, and the cockpit scenes fraught with punchy dialogue, hadn't happened.

"Captains give more than twice as many commands as first officers, reinforcing the arrogance of rank. Airline accident reports, however, show that first officers often must correct captains' mistakes," she'd read.

She'd tried to imagine how this scenario would work on Mars. What if she had to tell someone he'd left the airlock open without seeming to be critical? No shouting, "Close the @#$%! airlock door or we'll all die!" Instead she was supposed to say, "May I borrow your scarf? There's a breeze somewhere." And then fall to the floor gasping for breath. What about something slightly more direct, like, "Oh, did you think it was getting a bit stuffy in here?"

She'd started to chuckle to herself. Okay, instead of "Your helmet isn't buckled down right," she could say, "What a novel way you've arranged your helmet. It's so much more *interesting* like that." Or, to Viktor, "I love you, but you're about to drive this rover off a cliff." By then she had been convulsed with laughter.

After that, she found excuses to stay away from the counseling sessions. The whole idea of having to assume a passive role was repugnant.

And ultimately, they just didn't get it: a few bruised egos would be survivable. Pussyfooting around stupid mistakes would not be. Mars never forgave.

6

AUGUST 2015

SHE HAD FELT TROUBLED, AFTER SHE HAD GOTTEN VIKTOR onto the crew.

She had gone into the meeting with Axelrod without a thought of pushing Marc off—she'd been prepared to resign. Her NASA experience should have warned her. Crew selection was the most Byzantine of all the rotations at NASA, fraught with personality and pull. Nothing was ever done for just one reason. In the Missions Operations Directorate there had been an intricate promenade of personalities and rank and "pull," traits that now seemed as distant and stylized as the mating dance of birds.

Still, at NASA, the art of picking crews took time and much influence-peddling, government style, and there was time to second-guess. Not here. Axelrod had done his calculations and acted with only a moment's thought. She lacked such decisiveness about people. Quite acutely she felt the soft inner squishiness of them, how easily damaged. With Viktor she shared a hesitant vagueness about emotional matters. This was the standard astronaut profile—strong on externals, weak on communication of internals, as current psych-talk had it. But that did not mean that she was unaware of people's feelings. Wounding Marc had been painful, even if she was not the primary decider.

There was precious little time to brood about it, though. After Marc left, they all swung into relentless mission training.

Using centrifugal gravity simplified many tricky engineering points. Plumbing and structural designs were far easier to make work with gravity to help. But there were plenty of new techniques to master. Despite this being a private venture, work got sliced into the same pigeonholes as at NASA: operations planning, robotics, computers, flight support, vehicle systems, operations managing, payload, habitats, EVA.

Axelrod had imported NASA veterans to run these, too. Soon the air was thick with acronyms, clipped sentences, and can-do mannerisms.

Then Axelrod called them into another astronauts-only meeting in his office, with thirty minutes notice. He sat on his desk again, carefully arranging the creases in his dark blue tailored suit before beginning.

"We're a team, right?"

Nods all around. Julia nodded enthusiastically. She liked these conditions. The NASA Astronaut Office had been a perpetual playground of primate rivalry. Pilots looked down on mission specialists. Veterans lifted eyebrows at the newbies. Military thought the civilians were soft. Doctorate holders felt themselves above all others; they were in it for the science, not the ride.

"I've got something to tell you that will *demand* that you pull together." Axelrod was savoring this, for some reason she could not detect. Then she saw: *he* was in the team, too. As close as he would ever get to being an astronaut. Luckily, he was more important than just another team element. He knew how to cut through layers of NASA fatty tissue.

The special demands of going to Mars with just four astronauts had disrupted the NASA style. Ideally astronauts were supposed to be interchangeable. That broke down somewhat under the space station's pressure for detailed specialists, and disintegrated under the work specs for Mars. Crews of four or six could not explore a whole world without a lot of special knowledge and techniques. So this team had few overlapping abilities.

"This is entirely top secret. Not even a hint to the press or anybody else, even inside the Consortium. Clear?"

They all nodded. Axelrod's assistants all left the room as if on signal.

"Remember that Mars flight gear I tried to buy? One-of-a-kind hardware? Well, NASA turned me down, then the ESA people. So I put some industrial espionage people onto tracing where it had disappeared to." He lifted eyebrows. "Guess."

Nobody did.

"I always like mysteries, just about the only kinda book I read. I go for the real detection stories, with clues you piece together. So let me give you an intercept my spy guys decoded. Engineering stuff." He arched eyebrows, apparently to warn them of approaching jargon. "It says, 'Configured in bi-modal, we can run after launch in 'idle mode' with thermal power output of one hundred kilowatts. Therms are removed and routed to a turbo-alternator-compressor Brayton power conversion unit using a helium-xenon working fluid. A finned radiator system (expendable on aeroassist braking) rejects waste heat. This also reduces decay heat propellant loss following propulsive burns.' Whew!"

Viktor said very quietly, "My Lord."

Axelrod took no notice. "So that clue led us to—"

"Someone is building a nuke," Viktor said.

Axelrod blinked, and for the first time in Julia's experience an uncertain smile flickered. "How'd you know?"

"That is describing how to use a nuclear thermal rocket to give electrical power," Viktor explained slowly.

"After boost phase, still have solid core propulsion system. There is plenty more energy left in the Uranium-235 plates. Run it at low level, circulate water or some other fluid, make all electricity ship needs."

The others nodded. To Julia it made sense. But Axelrod stared at Viktor, startled. "Damn it all, you're right. My spy guys took another three weeks to work that out."

"Do not know rockets."

"Well, they *said* they did. My staff thought so, too."

"Get new spies. I know couple Russians could do this job better."

"Y'know, I just might." Axelrod breathed in sharply and started with fresh momentum. "Maybe Viktor can guess who's behind that message."

Viktor frowned. He was not the kind of engineer who speculated, much less made guesses. "I smell some Russian work, but that makes no sense as only player."

"Right, kinda," Axelrod said. "They got some old Russian gear. A set of plates to lodge the U-235 in, plus a containment vessel."

"From old Soviet program? I heard the team at Semipalitinsk ran a nuclear thermal rocket in fixed mode for a thousand hours."

Axelrod nodded. "That checks. No environmental controls then, I guess."

Viktor snorted. "Was when people not scared of anything nuclear—bomb, rocket, or nuclear family, too."

Axelrod smiled uncertainly at this little joke. "My background report says that Soviet job worked just fine."

"Ran it underground, like nuclear test." Viktor tilted

his head, in his typical thoughtful pose. "No venting of exhaust gases to surface. Not much radiation count in the exhaust anyway."

Axelrod gazed around at his team, obviously liking his guessing game. "So who's doing it, guys?"

Nobody spoke. Julia knew that Axelrod thought in financial terms first, so she said, "Someone who thinks they can beat us to Mars and not spend thirty billion doing it. With all the new work a nuclear rocket requires, I don't think they can keep prices down."

Raoul said carefully, "There is enormous development work required. Nobody ever actually flew a nuke, y'know."

"Politically impossible to vent into atmosphere, these times," Viktor said.

Raoul nodded. "So they'll have to fly it to low orbit on a booster. Maybe a big Proton IV?"

Viktor nodded. "Is cheapest way up, sure."

Katherine said, "I don't know anything about the U.S. and Soviet programs, but I do know orbital mechanics. Surely they can't do all this development work and lift for Mars when we do? So they miss the window, and the energy price to catch us gets huge."

Axelrod slapped his palm on his desk. "Exactly. So they have to fly later, much later. We can't really guess what trajectory they'll choose. My spy guys haven't picked up anything about that."

"They could go for a smash-and-grab mission," Katherine said. "Miss our window and make the next one, twenty-six months later. Land, grab something, then fly home fast to beat us by a few days."

Axelrod obviously liked watching his team perform. "So what's stopping them?" he coaxed.

Katherine said, "It can't work. They wouldn't have time to gather all the samples, do the geology. Without a pretty detailed set that meets the Mars Accord standards, they won't win, even if they do get back first."

"You all agree? It seems impossible?" Axelrod swept the room with his concentrated gaze.

They all looked at each other and nodded. Julia wished they had time to hash this over, do some figuring on paper, but it sounded right to her. They could check it all later, of course, but Axelrod liked this seat-of-the-pants style. "So how can they win?"

"If we lose," Viktor said. "Fail. Blow up. Crash."

They had all thought of this, and only he had the courage to say it out loud, Julia realized.

Axelrod pressed them further. "So it's a big gamble for them, right? Nobody throws down maybe twenty, thirty billion on a toss of the dice like that. So there's gotta be a backup motive."

Julia was getting a bit tired of this teasing, but the man must have some point. How could he be so sure there wasn't somebody on this planet more foolhardy than Axelrod himself?

Raoul said suddenly, "If they lose, they still have the nuke."

A murmur of agreement as it dawned on them. Raoul said with zest, "A whole new kind of rocket. One that's two or three times more efficient than our boosters."

Axelrod beamed approvingly. "A ship they can sell to anybody who wants to do deep-space work. Plenty of money to be made in the next couple decades, opening up high orbits."

Viktor said, "Going to asteroids. Prospecting. Mining."

"Who has enough vision," Katherine observed thoughtfully, "to do that?"

"Too big for company?" Viktor asked. "Seems to me."

Raoul said, "Must be countries, sure—and they must be using Russia's old Soviet work. The U.S. wouldn't sell anything they have in storage from their old nuclear program, Nerva."

Viktor smiled dryly. "The mob at the top of Russia now, they will sell their grandmothers."

"Sell is the word," Katherine said. "They need the cash. But invest? I doubt it."

Raoul smiled. "What major players are left out of the Consortium? China. Europe. India. Probably not anybody from South America—they do not have the technology."

Axelrod laughed. "You all get A-plus. Right! Point is, I couldn't include the whole damned planet in the Consortium. So now some others are ganging up on us. We've got a European-Chinese collaboration on our tail. Call themselves the Airbus Group."

"It takes courage to leapfrog us," Katherine said. "A nuclear rocket. What are they using for shielding?"

Axelrod said, "It looks like they have liquid hydrogen as their initial fuel. After that, we don't know."

The room dissolved into cross talk as the crew speculated on the Airbus approach. Axelrod let it run for a few minutes, then waved for silence. He was a master at commanding a room, Julia noted, but could not see how he did it. Charisma was always in essence elusive but still apparent.

He grinned, a confident, tanned man with the budget of a small nation riding on his decisions. "My spy guys confirmed that Airbus bought some Soviet nuclear propulsion gear. Plus discarded U.S. government stuff done with contractors. Equipment we traced to an assembly building in South America, which turned out to be a blind. It's now in China."

"Makes sense," Viktor said. "They have big launch facilities. Buy Proton stages from Russian agency. Assemble there."

Axelrod folded his arms. "That's about all I know, except one more little mystery. Who will fly their mission?"

"Uh-oh . . ." Raoul said. Julia could see they had all thought of the same, obvious solution.

Axelrod grinned. "Right again. None other than your old crewmates—Marc and Claudine. Must say, I didn't think that when I rejected those two from this program, they'd turn up flying for a competitor."

"They'll need some others," Katherine said. "Probably Chinese, maybe Euros."

Axelrod agreed. Julia ground her teeth. "I would like to confront Marc. How can he betray his country by working for a foreign group, after all the years at NASA?"

She regretted it the moment she said it. *He's there because you got him bumped . . .*

"He's a private citizen and this is not a classified project—it's a public competition," Axelrod said, smiling grimly.

"We all know Marc fairly well," Raoul said. "He's like us. He dreamed of going to Mars all his life. And look, Julia, you didn't hesitate to have him dumped in favor of Viktor."

"I didn't! That was not my decision to make."

"It got made at your instigation," Katherine said mildly, not looking at Julia.

"I was going to quit—"

"So you say," Katherine shot back. "It sounded a little Machiavellian to me and—"

"I just didn't want to leave Viktor," Julia sputtered. "You have no right—"

"I'm only saying what a lot of people around here—"

Julia jumped to her feet. "Damn it, I had no idea—"

"Oh, come on—"

"Quiet!" Axelrod's booming voice cut through. "Sit."

Julia sat.

Viktor held up both hands, palms out, and said to all, "We do not run this show, remember."

Axelrod sat back, watching the strained faces slowly rotate toward him. "Right. I take responsibility. At the time I sure didn't think I was making things easier for a competitor, but that's how business works. There's always somebody coming in on your blind side."

Julia seethed inwardly at Katherine's remark. She felt guilty enough about her part in Marc's dismissal, but to be accused of having planned it . . . Still, her training told her to put the conversation back on a less emotional plane. "Marc is determined to get to Mars any way he can. They can't possibly carry out the trials we would have to just getting a nuclear rocket to a reliable state.

He and Claudine and whoever else—they're risking their lives, big time."

Raoul sat back, folded his arms. "We all know that the Chinese have been cutting corners on space for decades. This is new, cutting a corner nobody else has before."

Viktor's mouth twisted into sour agreement. "They are good. Skipped building space station, gained a lot of advantage. But nuclear!"

Axelrod's incisive gaze momentarily rested upon each astronaut in turn. "So you all think this is a credible threat?"

They all nodded.

"Dangerous," Katherine said, "but credible."

"Could work. A big advance, if it does," Raoul said.

"But we get to Mars first," Viktor said. "Tell Airbus, fine. We will leave a light on the porch for you."

They all laughed, but to Julia's ear there was a hollow ring to the sound.

7

AFTER DINNER IT WAS TIME FOR THEIR REGULAR VIDEO transmission. No groaning allowed.

They pulled Consortium logo shirts over their waffle-weave long johns and prepared to look presentable. In fact, they wore as little as possible when in the hab—loose clothing didn't aggravate the skin abrasions and frostbite spots they suffered in the suits. They kept the heat cranked up to compensate, but then nobody had to pay the electric bill, Marc pointed out. Competition was keen for creams and ointments for their dry skin rashes.

"My turn, I think," said Marc.

Julia smiled. "Janet on the other end tonight, then?"

Janet Conover was a former test pilot who had trained with them, and clearly had hoped to make the trip. Janet was a good mechanic, but Raoul was better. The Consortium had made a careful selection: individual talents balanced with strategic redundancy. The crew of four had to cover all the basics: mission technical, scientific, and medical. They fit together like an intricately cut jigsaw puzzle.

Tonight's broadcast was going to be somewhat sticky. They were going to have to describe Viktor's injury while reassuring their millions of regular viewers that they were okay and the mission was still on track. A considerable feat of bravado would be required. Maybe they would reassure themselves at the same time.

"Let's play up the water angle, not the ankle," Viktor said.

"Drama plays better than science," Julia said.

"So we must educate, yes?" Viktor jabbed his chin at Marc.

But Marc wasn't listening. The brief description of Viktor's accident had been squirted to Earth earlier, and he was downloading the reply. Due to the present time delay of six minutes each way, normal back and forth conversations were not possible, and communications were more like an exchange of verbal letters. At times the round-trip delay was only a matter of four minutes, sometimes it was forty. Mars's distance from Earth varies by more than two hundred million miles from closest to farthest approach in the course of each Earth year. Still, it was a big advance over earlier missions.

In the Sojourner era, it took twenty-four hours to execute a single command. NASA used solar panels on its robot vehicles, so when Sojourner was in Mars night, it was unresponsive. And part of the time Earth's giant antennae were on the wrong side of the planet to receive signals from Mars. The new comm satellites circling both planets ensured that they were always in contact with Earth, but there was still the delay time.

Early on, Earth and Mars teams agreed on a download at a specified time, to preserve the semblance of a conversation. At the short delay times Marc and Janet tended to handle the bulk of the communications. And there was a little spark in the transmissions.

They did a short, live video sequence at the same time each Mars day, after the crew's dinner. Because

Earth's day is twenty minutes shorter, they drifted in and out of synchrony with various listening stations on Earth. But they didn't worry about it. That was Axelrod's end of the business. The "Nightly Report from Mars" was great theater, but the Consortium also had a team of doctors scrutinize the footage.

The crew gathered around the screen to watch the latest video from Earth. It was Janet, all right, gesturing with a red Mars Bar. Mars, Inc., the candy manufacturer, had become a mission underwriter. Cautiously waiting until after the successful landing, they'd released a special commemorative wrapper—a red number featuring the four of them against a "Martian" backdrop. On Earth they had taken about twenty shots of the crew in their colored pressure suits—one each in blue, yellow, green, and purple—holding up a standard Mars Bar before scenic backdrops. They each got $5,000 per shot, and the Mars Bar people paid ten thousand dollars per pound to ship a box of the bars out for the follow-up ad campaign. It would have been irritating after a while, except that they came to relish the damned things, keeping one for exterior shots, where it quickly got peroxide-contaminated, and eating the rest as desserts. The cold sopped up calories and the zest of sugar was like a drug to Julia. She was quite sure she would never eat another, Earthside, even if she did get an endorsement contract out of the deal.

Julia had dubbed the red-wrapped candy the Ego Bar, unwilling to honor it with the name of a planet and an ancient god, and the team adopted the name. There had been some talk early on about producing another wrapper with Mars life pictured, but rocks with wavy lines weren't exciting enough, so the manufacturer had decided to just stick with the Ego Bar.

Somehow, the commercialism of it all still grated on her. But she had signed on with eyes open, all the same. She had known that market-minded execs ran the Consortium, but going in she had thought that meant something like, *If we do this, people will like it.* Soon enough she learned that even exploring Mars was seen by the execs as *If we do this, we'll maximize our global audience share and/or optimize near-term profitability.* Such were the thoughts and motivations on Earth.

Still, Mars the raw and unknown survived, unsullied. And deadly.

They all snorted when the expected question came in from Janet. She looked embarrassed, but what could she do? "And how are you feeling, with Airbus getting nearer and your own launch—"

Marc started before Janet was finished. "We'll wave to them as we head home."

It was what they always said.

Then they turned to the story of the pingos. Earth had already gotten the video footage, and in the intervening hours had reacted. Axelrod's press team had decided to play it up in a major way. Another great success for the mission: WATER on Mars! Janet duly asked the team a long list of standard questions: how much water had they found, what did finding water mean to the mission, etc. As co-discoverers, Marc and Raoul fielded the questions, leaving Julia free to think her own thoughts.

What *did* the water mean? She sat back and envisioned life on Mars with plentiful water, no longer a cold, dusty desert. Under a pressurized dome the greenhouse effect would raise the temperature to something livable. A colony could grow plants, have open pools of water, even fountains, if they wished. She smiled as she thought about strolling along tree-lined walkways from hab to hab without helmet and suit, then realized with a start that she would never do it. They were just a few weeks from launching to Earth.

A few *short* weeks, something inside of her said.

How odd. When they'd arrived it'd seemed as though they had such a long time ahead of them. Now, suddenly, they'd made a major discovery, but so late . . .

She suddenly remembered the sample she'd picked up outside the vent. She'd been so worried about Viktor she'd forgotten about it!

She mentally tuned back in to the broadcast, suddenly impatient to be off. Could she slip away? Janet wished Viktor a speedy recovery, and transmitted some medical advice from the ground team of doctors. The public part of the broadcast ended. Then Janet turned to technical details about the upcoming liftoff test. Viktor's accident was one more mishap to be overcome. Janet didn't fail to mention the obvious: the sprained ankle meant their captain would be less effective if anything went wrong with the engine test fire of the Return Vehicle. What should have been a routine test now loomed as a potential crisis.

There had already been plenty to worry about. The subject of the ERV had been a touchy one ever since they'd arrived.

Soon after touchdown they'd discovered that the Return Vehicle was damaged. A failure in the aerobraking maneuver apparently had made the Return Vehicle come in a shade too fast, crushing fuel pipes and valves around the engines. None of the diagnostics had detected this, since the lines were not pressurized. In some places where the damage went beyond mere repair, Raoul had been forced to refashion and build from scratch several of the more tricky parts. Working with the Earthside engineers, he had been steadily making repairs.

In this he drew upon not only his technical training, but his family's tradition of Mexican make-do. His father and uncle ran a prosperous garage in Tecate, just below the U.S. border. He'd grown up in greasy T-shirts with a wrench in his hand. Coming from a country with a chronic shortage of hard goods meant that "recycle and reuse" was not just a slogan but a necessity.

Viktor admired his work, and they understood each other at this basic level. The Russian space program, starting way back in the Soviet era, had always operated in the same way. Cosmonauts on Mir were expert at cannibalizing discarded electronic components to make repairs. Still, although Raoul was good at creative reuse and making novel pieces fit, he had never before had to work under this kind of pressure. Their return, and quite possibly their lives, depended on his repairs.

They ended the transmission on an edgy note. It was two months and counting to launch.

As soon as they signed off, Julia slipped away to her lab space, where she'd left the sample. She looked around at the usual clutter in her tiny lab. A mostly unused lab, she thought, since she'd not found anything living to study.

Ah, there it was. She held the sealed bag up to the light. The wiper material appeared to be damp, with a light orange smear in the center of the damp spot. What looked like drops of water had collected on the plastic of the bag over the damp patch. So there was water ice at the top of the vent! That was interesting by itself. It meant there was liquid water somewhere below the surface, and the cloud they'd seen was water vapor. Maybe all of them had found water today.

She slipped the bag under the dissecting microscope to have a quick look at the orange smear. It was probably just dust previously frozen into the ice, but she always checked anyway.

She looked through the eyepieces, expecting to see the familiar scatter of grainy dust and sand particles. Sure enough, they were there—but there was other stuff as well.

She rotated the nosepieces to get a closer view. Her heart caught in her throat. Trapped in the fine fibers of the wiper, it looked for all the world like cellular debris.

She sat back, her thoughts racing, reviewing in her mind how she had collected the sample and whether it could have been contaminated. The wiper had been clean, still sealed in its sterile wrapper, identical to all the others she had used unsuccessfully before this. And she had used the same technique as always. Except there was no second sample because of Viktor's accident. Could she have delayed sealing the bag? No. She remembered stowing it in her sample pack just before his first cry of pain.

She looked at the sample again. It had to be real. This *was* the stuff on the ice at the mouth of the vent. But what was it?

She changed nosepieces again, altering the size of the image, then fiddled with the light source to see it in different ways. It was actually quite difficult to make out, but after fifteen minutes she was satisfied. It seemed to be a very pale-colored, dried up scum coated with red dust.

Pale because it lived underground, that fit. But unmistakably organic. Life!

Her yells brought all three of her crewmates running, or in Viktor's case, hobbling.

They were a lot more reserved than she was.

"This is what you're excited about?" asked Raoul, after taking a look through the microscope. "It looks like nothing at all."

"Yes, but it's organic nothing."

"How do you know?"

"It can't be anything else."

Marc popped in. "What's up?"

"Julia's discovered organic nothing."

"Really? Let me see."

She'd learned from Raoul's reaction. "As a geologist, how would you interpret this?"

Marc settled onto the seat, scanned the sample, changed the magnification, altered the light source. Viktor arrived as he was studying it. "Hmm," said Marc. "There's water in here." He looked up. "Where'd you find this?"

"This is sample from vent?" asked Viktor.

Julia nodded. "Just outside. I swabbed one of the shiny frozen spots at the mouth of the vent as you started down. Here, sit down."

"Looks like sand particles and some dust in a wet patch," said Marc.

"What about the other stuff?" she asked.

"What other stuff?"

"There are bits of . . ." She was about to say "organic material," but said instead "flaky material."

"Wha'? Oh, yeah I saw that, what is it?"

"That's just the point, Marc, what is it? I think it's dried organic material, but what else could it be?" Julia was aware of her deflating excitement. What if Marc had a ready chemical explanation? And she'd been so sure.

"Some kinda weird—no, it seems to be a bit stringy . . ." He looked up. "I can't tell just by looking. You'll hafta try some chemical tests. Do you have any more?"

"Nope, that's it. There was more, only—"

"Science was interrupted to come to aid of fallen comrade." Viktor came to her rescue. "You think it's alive?"

"No. I think it's been freeze-dried, probably torn apart by UV and peroxide dust. But it was alive, and very recently. There was more of the stuff, probably blown out when the vent outgassed."

Raoul yawned. "When you scientists decide, come wake me up. I'm bushed. Lots to do, plenty of tests to run if we're gonna get out of here." He shuffled off.

Marc stood up. "Well, Jules, I just don't know what this stuff is. It could be organic, or some funny dried salt-like formation." He shrugged. "Find out what it's made of. Mars has fooled us before." He clapped Viktor on the back as he left. "Hope the ankle's not too bad, old man."

Julia watched him go, somewhat put off by his attitude. To Viktor she said, "They don't seem to care. What could be more important than finding life on Mars?"

"To go home, maybe? Organic scum is not exciting to lonely men." He reached up, put an arm around her waist. "I too long for home, but am not lonely, so is bearable."

As she hugged Viktor back she was already planning the next step in the campaign to return to the vent.

8

SEPTEMBER 2015

THE MEDIA WENT WILD WITH THE AIRBUS ANNOUNCEMENT.

By chance, that week there were no major wars, scandals, or tragedies to capture public attention. A covert program—prepared and sprung upon the world in one rather stiff press conference in Beijing—was far more

exciting than the Consortium's by-now wearying preparations. *A race for the Mars Prize!* the media sang.

At least the snout of the media pig rooted after Airbus for a while, leaving them in comparative peace. Time passed quickly for the astronauts as Axelrod's media machine purred busily day and night. Their cameras and constant, though ever-polite, questions got in the way of training. Antagonism rose in the Consortium crew. Countless times they complained, and Axelrod promised to tone it down.

Slowly it dawned on Julia that Axelrod loved it. Not just because a real race meant higher ratings, max coverage, and product endorsements, either. He had been a prominent figure before, but now he stood above all the many billionaires in a rich world, his cocky grin instantly known to anyone who glanced at a TV set. He kept this under control, but Julia remembered a comment from her father, early on: "Crowns work on the heads beneath them."

Axelrod was brilliant, but beneath the media blitz he was plainly growing more concerned. He had put up a lot of money and even with his vast holdings could not afford to lose the prize. Within weeks he had to sell trivid rights to make the monthly financial nut. The rather generous astronaut contracts began gnawing at him, because he could not touch the sums the four were already acquiring for interviews and book contracts.

The chancy air of racing fever could not disguise that, after all, this entire gaudy attraction could explode on the launch pad—gone in an instant, leaving behind only graveside tributes and a mountain of debt.

On a chilly evening she found herself sharing a limousine with Axelrod, coming back from a pointless backslapping banquet for Consortium bigwigs, and she pressed him on whether he could truly bring together all the elements before their launch date. "The money alone—"

He grinned. "Ah, my Julia, always worryin'. Any idea how much the Summer Olympics bring in?"

"Uh, a billion?"

"Last ones, five billion—and they last just three weeks!"

"But most of going to Mars is boring, just sitting in a tin can for half a year—"

"Sure, we don't sell that. We sell danger."

"The landing?"

"And the launches. Both of 'em, from here and there."

"Okay, that's a couple of tight moments—"

"There's tension building to that, y'know. Will they make it? What's the aerobraking look like, anyway? That kinda thing."

"You can't show much at landing—"

"Sure we can. I'm having a TV mounted just behind the aeroshell so we can see you guys skipping along the top of the air, landing—the works."

"And TV on the rovers?"

"Of course."

"How about in our suits?"

Her sarcasm was lost on Axelrod. He arched his eyebrows. "Too hard to fit 'em into the helmet, but we'll have great little portables. On live feed, right back to the hab, tight beamed to us here. Join the Mars Adventurers, you can ride along with the astronauts. Every time they turn a corner, you're seeing stuff nobody ever saw. Same time as the astronauts see it, too."

"I'm a little bothered by the whole feel of it."

"Might I remind you that Stanley of 'Dr. Livingstone, I presume' was a reporter. He paid for his fare to Africa and into the jungle with stories for a newspaper. One of the polar explorers, the one who got to the South Pole first, Shackleton—he wrote books, gave lectures, even showed the first movies of Antarctica. All to finance his exploration."

"Okay, that's history." She was wearing an evening dress, a sheath that showed too much of her bony clavicles. To argue with a man it helped to wear serious clothes, maybe working coveralls and boots. Here she felt at a disadvantage. "Now, these endorsements—"

"Got my sub-rights people on the job full tilt. We go for the outdoor gear makers, use their stuff on Mars. High-tech companies, they give us first-class stuff, we show you astronauts using their gizmos on Mars, and charge them for the privilege. Logos, brand names—plenty of room here."

"I don't like some of them. Athletic shoes? We can't wear those on Mars."

"In the habitat you can."

"Warm clothes—L.L. Bean, Lands' End, Archivo—those I can see."

"You should get a squint at the ski contract we're about to sign."

"Ski?" She laughed. "That's one product we certainly can't use."

"Look, the way we figure, some sponsors don't want in on something that could fail big-time. Fine, let 'em sell to the cotton-top market. But the young male market—they'll go for goods that look ballsy, just being associated with goin' to Mars."

"I have to give you this—you have audacity."

"Just market sense, is all. I'm gonna make you all rich and famous, you watch."

The crew began to feel rushed. They were coming down to the wire on training routines and nothing was converging right.

Viktor spent twelve-hour days in the simulator doing endless aerobraking trials. The avionics crews were having trouble getting the parachutes to deploy. The tests carried out at 80,000 feet kept finding that the chutes got snarled in the tumbling turbulence of Mach 3. Even the aeroshell, built by Martin Marietta to NASA specs, was showing dangerous signs of pitting and cracking as it slammed into the tenuous Martian carbon dioxide—all as simulated in wind tunnels, of course—at hypervelocities typical of their entry. All these problems had to be dealt with, and fast.

Axelrod had the astronauts running from one problem to the next, saying laconically, "I don't want you all to get stale, y'know." Then he would wink. At first Julia liked that gesture. After a dozen or so of them, they became supremely irritating.

Compared with the Consortium, the NASA style was infinite pains, infinitely prolonged. Katherine in particular was concerned that they were sacrificing safety to make the next launch window in just five months. As backup pilot she and Julia were training together, in simulators side by side with Viktor and Raoul. Julia had to keep track of shear and heating diagnostics while Katherine tracked their height, velocity, pitch and yaw, compensating for deviations from the flight path in a time-allowance window only two or three seconds wide. The work was usually difficult, often impossible, and always harrowing.

Axelrod was always around somehow, checking, cheerleading, and expecting more. One day Julia and Katherine crawled out of the sim pod at the end of a seemingly endless day, stiff and tired and reeking, and Axelrod had been there with some empty advice. He hung around the work areas a lot more than any NASA exec ever had, and Julia rather liked the effect. Everybody was more on their toes, and felt part of an effort that ran on zeal, not just money.

But today Axelrod's banter somehow seemed vacuous and Katherine whirled on him, spitting out, "You and your chatter! Running off to close more deals on rights while we bust ass here. We're putting our lives on the line and you talk profit, profit, profit."

Julia was shocked. Into the dead silence Axelrod smiled very slightly, as if he had been expecting this, and said mildly, "I put in three billion of my own. You lose your ass out there, I lose mine down here."

Katherine had calmed down then, but only for a while. Something was gnawing at her, Julia could feel it in the tremor of her voice and flickering of her eyelids. But Katherine would say nothing of it. The astronaut hardass carapace was not restricted to men. To get far at NASA the women had acquired it—including, Julia realized, herself. But she hoped she knew when to turn it off.

The psych boys were briefing them all in private about Extreme Crew Dynamics Challenges, as one of the lectures titled it, but here the whole idea of the tight-knit, teamwork crew fell apart: Katherine wouldn't talk. Julia's counselor believed that the two women were essential in defusing the tensions that inevitably would develop. But somehow the chemistry between the two was wrong. Julia didn't quite know why, not in a way she could describe, but she sensed it. Katherine dismissed the problem with a snort.

Pilots were often like that. Astronauts were superior pilots, and super-superstitious, far more so than ordinary air pilots ever were. Parts of the training grid had to follow just so, or it was bad luck. Never mind that they all counted on impersonal laws to get them through the harsh accelerations and intricate orbital maneuvers of deep space; they were still brooding primates afraid of nature's quixotic tricks, underneath it all.

Katherine, always super-rational in her manner, was no different. But she would not talk about anything personal, would not establish the links that would fend off trouble when they all lived in the same tin can.

So when Katherine took Julia aside for a stroll in the park near their simulation training building at Johnson Space Center, munching on an apple, Julia got her hopes up. No alarm bells went off, though Katherine's stiff-backed pace seemed odd.

"I wanted you to be the first to hear," Katherine said. "Even before Raoul."

"Well, I appreciate whatever—"

"This is big. Big."

"I sensed—"

"I'm pregnant."

"What!"

"It happens."

"But you—nobody—how could—"

"It happened."

"But medical won't like an abortion this close to—"

"No abortion."

"Huh?" Not brilliant, but Julia could not quite believe the conversation was taking place.

"Raoul and I are good Catholics."

"Abortion is out?"

"That's the way I feel."

"But my God, no astronaut gets pregnant accidentally."

"I did." Katherine's gaze was steady, almost blank, as if she were watching Julia's reaction under a microscope.

"So you're off the crew."

"I don't want to take the baby to Mars, no."

"My God."

"I told you first because I thought you'd be the most sympathetic."

"What are you going to do?" A useless question, of course.

"Raoul . . ."

Which turned out to be the real point. Raoul was torn.

Katherine told him that evening. The father was yet again the last to hear.

To her amazement, Julia heard all about his reaction the next morning.

Now that Katherine was not going, she opened up. Became a babbler. Told Julia how Raoul had been made speechless and round-eyed the night before, gone out, slammed the door. Had come back two hours later, confronted her. He had the same conclusion: "For an astronaut, there are no accidental pregnancies." Meaning that they all kept precise track of their bodies, the sometimes errant machines that carried them inside other machines into the black sky.

Julia had the bad luck to be alone with the two of them that morning. Raoul both wanted to talk and didn't, starting to edge up on the subject, then sliding away. Katherine was going to tell Axelrod and stand down from the mission. "But that'll scrap the whole flight," Raoul said at last.

"Possibly," Julia said carefully. "We could find a replacement pilot." Though she had no idea how.

"I will *not* consider an abortion," Katherine said.

They all stared miserably at the floor of their small coffee lounge. Between Katherine and Raoul hung the air of a played-out argument, nothing left to say.

"I've got to tell him." Katherine hauled herself to her feet.

"Let me think," Raoul pleaded.

"Got to," Katherine said forlornly, and left.

When he heard the news, Axelrod just gaped. Katherine described to Julia the man's stunned silence, his inability to muster any of that rogue charm. She had delivered the news and walked out, leaving him staring blankly at his magnificent view of the Johnson Space Center complex.

Raoul spent the day in his training exercises, not far from Julia. She understood him and wondered what she could do to help. Like them all, he wanted Mars, bad. More importantly to his crewmates, he was a master mechanic who had worked on Mars technology development constantly since his first missions to the space station. Without him their chances of survival were significantly worse.

Julia told Viktor, of course. "He must go," Viktor said. "Pilots are easier to replace than Raoul." He included himself.

Axelrod came and hauled Raoul away, brushing aside flight director Brad Fowler's objections to any interruption in the training schedule. For an hour Julia labored away at her tasks, knowing that up on the top floor Axelrod was attempting to persuade Raoul. Imaginary dialogues ran through her head while she toiled at integrating electronics and analog/manual systems, the legacy of the digital age. On Mars, brute force might well be more reliable than the latest snazzy chip from a hot manufacturer—but try to tell that to the whiz kids designing stuff these days.

Word had spread somehow among the crews and she could feel the unease in all the teams around her. The afternoon wore on. The PR people heard of it. She wondered who told them, then guessed that the savvy publicists had created a secret network of informants inside the Consortium, both to head off bad news and to ferret out the good. Nobody worked merely through channels, not in a seat-of-the-pants operation like this.

To Julia's amazement, Raoul came back to the training modules around six P.M., just as everybody was starting to show signs of wear. He had found Katherine and had it out. Unbidden, Julia and Viktor went to the coffee lounge and joined Raoul there. He wasted no words. "I will remain on the crew."

"My . . ." was all Julia could muster. "Axelrod—"

"It was not his arguments that made me stay. He even offered money, but no—it was the mission. I could not be who I am if I did not go."

Julia saw what he meant, something in the crinkled eyes and twisted mouth. Between him and Katherine things could not have worked. This way, though he would not see her for two and a half years, they would still have goals in common—the baby, and Mars. One goal each. Somehow this delicate equilibrium had been worked out during the long, bone-wearying day. She did not truly want to know how they had done this; some things were better left forever private. He would be gone before their child was born, and might never see it. But he could do nothing else.

For some reason, Katherine could not do otherwise either. Why had she precipitated this crisis? Some mysterious chemistry of motherhood, Mars, and . . . what? Julia had often wondered about this element in herself, the unlit cellars of her mind. Women astronauts usually had decided long ago not to have children. They had unbearably complicated careers. Katherine was mid-thirties, her clock ticking loudly. Had it simply swamped her other voices?

That evening Julia tried to talk to Katherine, more out of curiosity than any impulse to help the mission. But Katherine would not come forth. From that day on, she would not speak to the press or to the Consortium team. For all purposes, she simply vanished from their tracking scope, a fallen flyer.

A day later she ran into Raoul outside the simulator quad. He glanced at her, away, back. "Julia?"

"Hey, hi." She felt awkward and started to walk on.

"Uh, got a minute?"

"Yeah, sure."

"Come in here."

Into an alcove for suit-up prep. With all the work suites and suits, there was only room to stand. He turned and his eyes were big, brown pleas.

They were alone because the techs and support staff were off fixing some sudden glitch in the electronics, a colossal board malf nobody understood. Old boards, not the new top-of-the-line antimonide layers Axelrod was springing for, of course. They were going to Mars first class. Especially if it saved weight.

She waited and finally realized that he wasn't going to say anything. Couldn't. Maybe shouldn't.

"So, uh, how'd it go with her?" That was as much as she was going to give him. He had to come some of the distance himself, for Chrissake.

"I . . . we talked. You know, I know, *everybody* knows that . . . that she had to know."

"You said that."

"Yeah." A sigh of release, head lolling back.

"And she said . . . ?"

"She wouldn't really say, not right out."

"Uh huh." *God, other people's relationships.*

"But, I mean, we knew what we were saying."

More than I can say, but keep it coming, kid. "She admitted that she got pregnant knowingly? Even though it meant Mars was out?"

"Like I say, she never said it clear like that. But I got her meaning." He was opening now, his face less constricted, voice rushing on, tones more earnest yet less fevered. "Way I figure it, she was an astronaut all along, childhood dream and all that, like the rest of us. Only now she's done that. So it's a baby or Mars, and she wants the baby."

"Reasonable."

"You must've felt the same."

"Not actually. I like kids, but other people's are fine. Enough. I can return them afterward."

He laughed—a quick, light chuckle, and then the words came out fast again. "So she's getting rattled, too, I think."

"Rattled."

"I mean, this isn't NASA. Not today's NASA. It's like the NASA of the sixties, doing stuff for the first time, *every* time. People died then and everybody was sorry, sure, and they just kept going. Not like now. Somebody breaks a leg in the space station, there's people talking about it in Congress."

"You think she was scared."

He sighed, and to her surprise, lowered his head with a tired sadness. "Yeah, I think."

"Afraid of Mars, of the uncertainty." She was stalling. Plain old fear had not occurred to her.

"Maybe it got all scrambled up inside her. She's been an astronaut, a damn good one. Now she wants to be a mother. Doesn't need Mars." His head came up and he drew in a long breath. Something more coming. "And yeah, the way she was holding me at night all these months, the bad dreams and all—yeah, I think she was scared."

He was telling her as much as he was ever going to tell anyone. That Katherine had mixed motives—who didn't?—and one was the gut-squeezer nobody in the astronaut corps *ever* talked about.

"I . . . I see." Wow, real therapist stuff, here. "I've felt the same way. It is dangerous."

Raoul grabbed at this like a life preserver. "We all do, damn right. Only reasonable, I guess. Only with her, it got mingled in with the baby thing."

"No shame in that." She was trying to find a way to back away from this. She had no idea what to say to him.

"A woman like you, that's different. You aren't scared."

Now she really didn't know what to say. "I get by."

"Hey, they call you the Iron Girl, you know that?"

She had heard it, but only as a joke. Did any of the support crews really think that? *As others see us* . . . If only they knew.

She shook her head. "Undeserved."

"Well, coulda fooled me."

"I get scared about going this way, too." There, out with it. "It ain't NASA."

"Sure." Relief in his face, raised eyebrows. "Me, too."

"But it's the only way. For us, anyway. Give them a decade, Congress might get behind it again."

He nodded vigorously. "But not for us."

"And not for Katherine, not now."

His face suddenly filled with sadness. It softened and she wondered if he would cry. She saw the sacrifice he now glimpsed up ahead. Not only the danger, which had kept them all awake some nights or else they wouldn't be human. Piled on top of that was losing Katherine for years, not seeing his baby born, or maybe *ever*. She could not imagine what that was like for Raoul, a man who grew up in the shadow of the Latino community in SoCal.

"Katherine, she is strong." His face now firmed up after all that came through it in these moments. She saw a new Raoul, one who abruptly saw that he had a role to play, not a weepy soft one, but a solid part in a play he knew.

"Strong enough to get what she wants," she said helpfully.

"She will be strong while I am gone." He straightened, chin up, finding himself.

"Of course." And he was incredibly right. She got to be the tearful mother, he got to be the resolute father, the adventurous man, bringing home fame and fortune. And it would work.

"She's making the choice she wants." He nodded to himself.

"We all are. You, too." She managed a wobbly smile. He jerked a thumb up. "Mars or Bust."

Katherine's glacial silence was puzzling, vexing. But nobody spent time worrying. They all had a far larger problem: replacing her, pronto.

Axelrod held a meeting that night, most pointedly not including the astronauts. They found out about it only the next morning, in a staffwide meeting. Brad Fowler thought that he could not bring another pilot up to speed in time to meet the launch window. Katherine was geologist and backup pilot, but the entire skill-set she had carefully built for years was now integrated with the still-building mission technology. She had influenced avionics and control systems designs herself.

And now time was crushingly short: five months. Axelrod could not just pick some other astronaut left over from the NASA program and get him or her up to speed.

The all-staff meeting broke up in moody silence. Axelrod left the room without talking to anybody, the wind visibly gone from his customary billowing sails.

Julia was working on systems integration problems with a room full of engineers when the call came. They were about ready to break for lunch, so she grabbed a coffee, trotted to the main building and took the special VIP elevator to Axelrod's office. Viktor was there with Raoul and absolutely nobody else. Her pulse quickened. Axelrod liked dramatic announcements, and there was an urgent air in the room. Raoul and Viktor looked at her with relief, hoping to now get to business.

She refused a seat, took a sip of bitter coffee, and said

flatly, "What? Don't string it out like the nuke surprise."

"That's my Julia, always subtle," Axelrod said, utterly at ease. He even straightened his tie.

She felt her hopes rise. "I'm learning from you."

"I just spent half a billion bucks to keep you all from worrying. We've got to have a crew member we can work with now, right away. And he has to have the right mix of skills. Geologist and backup pilot."

A sudden suspicion dawned on Julia. "Marc?"

Axelrod looked startled, nodded vigorously. "He'll be here tonight. I've bought Marc back from Airbus."

"What!" Viktor said.

"Just how a baseball manager buys an outfielder," Axelrod said proudly. "The way I figured it was, they're a long time off from getting into the air. Hell, they don't have their main engines off the drawing board! These Chinese gentlemen—and a lot of Germans and French, too—they have time to train a replacement. We don't. So—money talks. Big surprise."

"In this case," Raoul said, "it must have shouted."

"Marc got half a billion?" Viktor's incredulous mouth stayed open.

"No, Airbus. I bought his contract. He wasn't too happy, so I gave him a li'l bonus." Quickly Axelrod held up both hands, palms up. "One I'm gonna give you three, of course. A clean million. Each."

"Good lord," Raoul said.

Julia felt the same. It wasn't the money, but the dizzying swirl of events. She could readily face danger, relentless drills, and high g's, but not the emotional wrenching of the last few days.

"You are the kind of capitalist we Russians do not know how to be," Viktor said with grudging respect.

"I'll take that as a compliment. I kinda thought you'd all like to have this settled right away." Axelrod grinned as if he had anticipated this; and he had. He snapped his fingers, and through a side door came three of his executives. Incongruously, they were carrying glasses. And champagne. "Figured we'd toast to the day, now that the Consortium crew is complete."

Julia accepted a glass—then, somehow, another. She did not quite hear the rest of Axelrod's rambling toast, her mind was so abuzz.

She was going to Mars with three guys.

No girl talk or consolation, as she had rather vaguely assumed. Not that Ice Queen Katherine had ever been forthcoming. Still . . .

There came a moment when Raoul had taken in a tad too much champagne and he leaned over to Viktor and said, "You two will be playing grab-ass all the way to Mars and back?" He murmured it mildly, only the words carrying his barbed meaning.

She brushed it aside, knowing abstractly that there would be a reckoning on this somewhere downstream. The celebrations soon widened as people came into the office and more champagne showed up.

Then one of Axelrod's minions was saying grandly, "We all feel the same here, and that's what helped us get through this crisis. Leadership, yes. But there's no *I* in the word *team*," he concluded with a flourish of champagne.

Julia had never liked these Consortium cheerleader types, with their solemn sayings. She especially didn't like them after a few glasses of what was actually a quite fine champagne. She wanted to applaud when Viktor stodgily replied, "There is in your word, *win*."

9

JANUARY 12, 2018

THE NEXT MORNING SHE SUITED UP AND TOOK THE SAMPLE out to the greenhouse. Under the protocols for handling possible Mars life, some of her equipment was set up outside of the hab. In a worst-case contamination scenario, they could abandon the greenhouse.

Attitudes about Mars life verged on schizophrenia. It was at once the most sought-after discovery and the most feared. Glory in the knowledge that we were not alone in the universe! Cringe in terror of the threat of alien life!

Using the portable glove box, she opened the sample bag. There was so little of the stuff, she decided to analyze it for Earth-like organic molecules by running it through the gas chromatograph. She didn't have enough to try multiple tests.

She was dying to try some quick and dirty chemical tests, assaying bits of the sample to see if the basic constituents of life—proteins, lipids, carbohydrates, nucleic acids—were the same here. Or at least close enough to respond to the same chemical tests.

But this way she'd find out if it was organic, and if it resembled Earth life in its components. It was a lot more work this way, and she'd have to wait to find out. *Oh well.*

She immersed the wiper in methanol. Starting the extraction was all she had time to do just then. The rest would have to wait.

Tick. Tick. Tick.

There was plenty of grunt labor to get ready for the liftoff test. Gear they had used on the repairs, supplies dumped months ago in a hurry, scrap parts—all had to be hauled away from the Return Vehicle. On the long glide back to Earth, every extra kilogram they carried made their fuel margin that slimmer, and it wasn't that fat to begin with.

Julia didn't mind the heavy labor. The low gravity helped but the laws of inertia still governed. Man-handling gear into the unpressured rovers to stow it for the next expedition—if there was one—at least gave her a chance to think; simple jobs didn't absorb all her concentration. She hefted a bulky package onto the top of a pile, puffed—and that was when all her frustrations surfaced and she decided to do some pushing of her own.

Through their usual heavy-carbo lunch she planned. Right after, she found Marc in the hab's geology lab, packing a core for transport.

"So what do we do now?" she asked. "Just you and me?"

Their last, long expedition in the rover was out, that much was clear. Safety protocols demanded two in the rover. Both mechanics, Raoul and Viktor, had to be working on the Return Vehicle. Marc was the backup pilot, so he would be needed to help Viktor, at least through the liftoff trial.

"You're going to tell me, right?" He grinned.

"I'm not going to sit around twiddling my thumbs for my last two months on Mars. Not when I think we've finally found Martian biology."

Marc said crisply, "You can't go out for a week by yourself, Julia."

"I know. Come with me, Marc. There's enough time left for a vent trip. Maybe even more than one."

The extensive Return Vehicle repairs had cut into all their schedules. For the weeklong rover trips, mission protocol decreed that one of the pair be a mechanic— Raoul or Viktor. When the two of them were tied up doing Return Vehicle repairs, Julia and Marc were restricted to day trips in the rover. Marc had filled his time setting off lots of small seismic blasts, and was surprised to discover extensive subterranean caverns several hundreds of meters down. So far they hadn't found a way into any of them, and Julia knew Marc was itching to get down there.

But Marc looked doubtful. "You did that already. I thought we agreed it was a bust. No life or fossils."

"Yes, but we picked a vent that was a blind alley. It didn't go down deep enough. The one Viktor and I found yesterday may be it. Finally."

Marc frowned, distracted by his chore. "You haven't proved it yet."

"I'm working on it. For now, consider the possibility that we stumbled on the entranceway to an underground ecology," she urged, caught up in her vision. "On Earth, anaerobes went underground or underwater to get away from the nasty poisonous oxygen atmosphere. They've thrived for billions of years in the most hostile places. Here on Mars, the anaerobes only had to fight the cold and drought. They must have followed the heat and gone underground."

Marc frowned. He had heard pieces of this argument before, his scowl said. He thought most life-on-Mars theorizing was just a way of avoiding the really interesting geology—sorry, areology—of this place. "Uh, where d'you want to look?"

"If my tests show the sample is organic, then of course the vent Viktor and I found yesterday."

Marc said, "We could maybe manage a few days in the rover, no more."

"Good enough. I'll start packing."

"Not so fast. We've all got to agree."

Squeezing in a half hour here and there, Julia ran her test. The results were relayed to her computer, in the paperless mode demanded by Mars. The problem of consumables like paper on long space missions was approached in a variety of ways.

Back in the days of Mir, the cosmonauts had been paper-deprived. They repeatedly requested something to write on, to no avail. It was simply too expensive, and there was no place to put the waste paper. In frustration the cosmonauts used cardboard from boxes, backs of food containers, and finally the walls of the station itself. The urge to express themselves, if only to write notes, turned out to be fundamental.

The psychologists studying spaceflight had duly noted this, so Julia was able to lounge in a comfortable flight couch after dinner with her personal electronic slate and call up the data squirted from the gas chromatograph in the greenhouse hours before.

For data, going paperless was simple: digital/electronic readouts instead of long scrolls of paper written on by ink-filled needles, covered with squiggly analog lines. Reams of paper were replaced by the newest digital storage techniques.

Julia enjoyed living without paper clutter and its attendant disorganization. Besides a few photos, the only piece of paper on her wall was a printout of the mission time line from just before liftoff. Featured prominently was the entry: 3/14/2018—Launch date!!

She fed the raw data into an initial converter program. As it scrolled across her screen, she felt a growing excitement, and some puzzlement.

She called across to Viktor, "It's alive!"

"What is alive?" He looked up from his reading. Books were tiny cartridges that fed into their personal slates. New ones came from Earth regularly.

"The sample from the vent, luv. It's clearly organic material." She couldn't help grinning.

"What does it mean, organic? Contains carbon?"

"Well, not just that. There are inorganic carbon-containing substances, like calcium carbonate. I mean, complex carbon-based molecules that are produced only by living organisms."

"Such as?"

"Oh, proteins, sugars, fats, that sort of thing."

"You found this in the sample?"

"Well, I found mostly degraded pieces of them. More amino acids—protein building blocks"—she said hastily, to his blank look—"than proteins. Nucleotides instead of DNA, that sort of thing. This stuff was freeze-dried and chewed up."

"Chewed? What could chew?" He was being maddeningly obtuse.

"It's just a figure of speech. Degraded is what I meant. And before you ask, I suspect a combination of the UV and the peroxides in the dust. Together they do a great job of sterilizing everything on the surface. I think I caught them in the act by that vent."

"You sure is not contaminated?"

"Well, more samples would be better, but that's all I've got, and I don't see how—"

"Is not very good argument."

She began to feel steamed. "But I can't go back to get more unless you all agree. And I suspect you won't agree unless I have more proof!"

"Is question of priorities right now. We must make sure ERV will get us back. That is first."

"What about afterwards?"

"Ask again then."

* * *

But she tried again at breakfast, laying out her results as they shoveled down the oatmeal. After communal hot cereal, they usually each nuked a precooked breakfast. *Mars Needs Calories!* It was a good time to set what they were doing that day.

Raoul shook his shaggy head. All the men were letting their hair grow out to the max, then would shear it down to stubble just before liftoff, including beards. The "Mars Bald" look, as Earthside media put it, went for Julia, too. In the cramped hab of the return vehicle, shedding hair would be just another irritant. If it got into their gear, especially the electronics, it could be dangerous.

He gestured at the injured Viktor. "Without him, we'll take longer to complete checkout. Marc, I know it's not your job, but I'll need both you and Julia to help. I want to eyeball every valve and servo in the undercarriage."

"Okay, I can see why you need all of us for that. But once it's done—"

"Until we've done the liftoff, planning is pointless," Viktor said in a voice that reminded them all that he was, sprained ankle or not, the commander. She had hoped he would reconsider overnight.

So far he had rarely needed to throw his weight around. Julia shot him a look and saw in his face the man who was the commander first and her lover second. Which was probably as it should be at this moment, she knew. Even if a part of her did not like such facts right now.

She said slowly, "I have a quick run we could do."

Viktor looked up from his recliner, "For jewels, I hope." He was not going to help her.

She grimaced, but went along with their laughter.

His jibe was completely in character. Viktor was deeply marked by the bad years in Russian space science following the collapse of the Communist economy. She recalled his saying, "In those dark years, the lucky ones were driving taxicabs, and building spaceships on the side. The others just starved." Not only research suffered. Some years there had been no money, period. Faced with no salaries, staff members in some science institutes found new ways to raise money, sometimes by selling off scientific gear, or museum collections. It was like her grandparents, who had grown up during the Great Depression; money was never far from mind. So Viktor made a fetish of following Consortium orders about possible valuable items: he scrounged every outcropping for "nuggets," "Mars jade," and anything halfway presentable. They all got a quarter of the profits, so nobody griped. Still, Viktor's weight allowance on the flight back was nearly all rocks—some, she thought, quite ugly.

"No, for science."

Viktor gave her a satirical scowl.

Raoul eyed her skeptically. "Your vent idea again."

"Yep. I want to go back."

"I've studied the whole area around it," Marc said. "My seismic profiles from last year show that it's honeycombed with subterranean caverns. Funny we never caught an outgassing before."

The Consortium wanted information on water and underground gases; they could use it on later expeditions, or sell the maps to anyone coming afterward. Marc had now processed some of the data; the rest he would work on during the trip home.

Raoul shook his head, scowling. "We've already got one injury. And we've looked in one vent earlier—it was no good, right?"

"It was just a small blowhole, not really useful—"

"Crawling down more holes isn't in the mission profile, not this late."

"True, but irrelevant," she said evenly. "There's new information. You know what I found. That *changes* the profile."

Raoul was the tough one, she saw. Viktor would support her eventually, if she could fit her plan into mission guidelines. Marc, as a geologist, had a bias toward anything that would give him more data and samples. He had been the most interested in her results, though dubious.

"It's too damned dangerous!" Raoul suddenly said. "Do you want to be the last soldier killed in the war?"

"Bad analogy," Julia said automatically.

"Well," Marc said mildly, "we could use our seismic sensors to feel if there are signs of a venting about to occur, and—"

"Nonsense," Raoul waved away this point. "Have you ever measured a venting?"

"Well, no, but it can't differ greatly from the usual signs on Earth—"

"We do not know enough to say that."

She had to admit that Raoul was right in principle; Mars had plenty of nasty tricks. It certainly had shown them enough already, from the pesky peroxides getting in everywhere—even her underwear—to the alarming way seals on the chem factory kept getting eaten away by mysterious agents, probably a collaboration between the peroxide dust and the extreme temperature cycles of day and night.

She said carefully, "But our remote sensing showed that venting events are pretty rare, a few times a year."

"Those were the big outgassings, no?"

"Well, yes. But even so, they are low density. It's not like a volcano on Earth."

"Low density, but could be hot?"

"Yes, I suppose—"

"Hot, and something that attacks seals on the suits. Our pressure suits do not provide good enough insulation. I believe we all agree on that."

This provoked rueful nods. The biggest day-to-day irritant was not the peroxides, but the sheer penetrating cold of Mars.

Raoul's style was to hedgehog on the technicals, then leap to a grand conclusion. She got ahead of him by not responding to the insulation problem at all, but going to her real point. "The vents must be *key* to the biology. We can't walk away now."

"That's the whole point. We should walk away— while we still can. We've been lucky so far, only minor injuries—frostbite, bruises, sprains, it could have been a lot worse. We have done enough on biology," Raoul said adamantly.

"Look—"

"No." He cut her off with a chop of his hand, the practical mechanic's hand with grime under the fingernails. "The ERV is our job now."

And they all had to agree. Getting back came first. In Raoul's set jaw she saw the end of her dreams.

* * *

Julia worked alone after that. The urge to be away from the others was like an itch.

After the last go-around she had nothing more to say to her crewmates. So when she finished her tasks she went straight back to the hab. She cycled through the air lock, suit-showered, shucked her helmet and outerwear, and moved to the flight deck. Hiking the room heat, she settled into the ergonomic chair and called up the latest e-mail from Robbie and Harry on the comm screen. Maybe it would distract her.

They had attached a New York ETimes article about the latest antics of the Protect Earth Party and a new group, the Mars First! activists. PEPA had terrorized NASA for years with their fears that a menace from space would be brought back on a Mars rock—or even a Moon rock.

In 1997, a National Research Council report on sample return from Mars concluded, "While the probability of returning a replicating biological entity in a sample from Mars is judged to be low and the risk of pathogenic or ecological effects is lower still, the risk is not zero." That was enough for PEPA. "Not zero" equated in their eyes to a certainty.

They—that is, the lawsuits—had made NASA agree to Chicken Little protocols to contain, sterilize, or abandon space samples from other planets. Robbie called PEPA the Andromeda Strain party.

After the launch accident, PEPA had looked for fresh meat. With their favorite target, NASA, out of the game, their entire pack of lamprey lawyers had descended on Axelrod. They started by charging that sending a manned mission to Mars violated the Outer Space Treaty of 1967.

"What the hell is that?" Axelrod had asked.

One of his assistants read it to him. He was being charged with planning a mission that was going to "produce harmful contamination of a celestial body," a treaty violation.

His reaction had been unprintable. His lawyers found a copy of the treaty. They discovered, of course, that it was a set of flimsy protocols with no teeth. And that it didn't cover future violations. Bottom line: PEPA couldn't stop him from launching or landing on Mars.

It had been a pleasure for Axelrod to grind their faces into this fact, in court.

But then, the article said, PEPA had been joined by the Mars First! activists—who, conversely, didn't want Earth to contaminate Mars. Both groups wanted the two planets to stay strictly apart, for opposite reasons.

"An unholy alliance of the absurd," Axelrod was quoted as saying in the article.

What, demanded MF-PEPA, was being done to ensure that indigenous life on Mars is protected from the ravages of Earth bacteria?

"Genocide, that's what it is," their spokeswoman exclaimed. "The so-called discovery of the New World all over again. European explorers brought diseases like measles, syphilis, and flu to the Indians, who died by the millions. Now we're doing it again, to a whole planet!"

They cited Ray Bradbury, whose fictional Martians died from earthly diseases. That it was fiction was a fine point they didn't appreciate.

And of course they sued Axelrod also.

Julia was amused by the article, but it also raised an interesting point. Did either planet threaten the other?

Traditional menace-from-space scenarios assumed an Earth-centric attitude. *Earth attacked! Outer space invaders!* The Andromeda strain, the Triffids, various evolved Martians, and lots of squishy aliens loomed.

And what was the fate of the fictional menaces from space? The Andromeda strain was done in by the pH of Earth's ocean after being rained out of the clouds. H. G. Wells's Martians succumbed to local microbes within a few days. The authors had reasonably assumed that a planet with a lively biosphere could put up a good fight.

But that was only fiction. Was there any real data to suggest that Earth could be at risk from an incoming Mars microbe?

First, it would have evolved in an oxygen-free, carbon-dioxide-rich atmosphere—anaerobic. Earth's oxygen-rich atmosphere would be the first challenge, vastly reducing where it could live. Oxygen is a potent poison even to many organisms on Earth.

Then, Mars has lain beneath a thin skin of carbon dioxide, thicker in the past but always carbon dioxide, for four billion years. Even so diminished, it still contains much more carbon dioxide than Earth's atmosphere. Even if Martian metabolism were not immediately

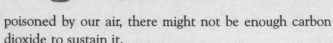

poisoned by our air, there might not be enough carbon dioxide to sustain it.

And finally, Mars has been delivering rocks to Earth for billions of years, without any resulting Mars plagues. So far, Earthly diseases have all been from Earth. And that's reasonable, because vastly different life-forms wouldn't pose a biological threat to Earth life anyway.

She remembered the Nauga, a stuffed monster toy invented by some ad agency to push a particular type of leatherlike vinyl cloth. The really interesting thing about vinyl was that it had been created in the lab by chemists, and it was a novel arrangement of atoms, a new molecule. After it was introduced, it was found to be inedible to all earthly life. There simply were no digestive enzymes that could attack the vinyl configuration of atoms.

To truly alien life, Earth was filled with Naugas.

She didn't think PEPA had anything to worry about.

But what about the Mars Firsters?

NASA had always tried to avoid cross-contamination. Spacecraft were assembled in a clean environment: an interplanetary condom.

Any microbes accidentally sent on the various landed robots should have succumbed to the aerobraking heat, then the cold, dry, and chemically hostile surface.

She remembered reading a short story about the first manned mission finding traces of microbial life on Mars, and then tracking it back to . . . a crashed Russian probe! A good story, and one NASA had tried hard to prevent from coming true.

But a manned mission was different. In their hab, they had brought a microcosm of Earth: four humans with all their tiny fellow travelers. Although we think we are individuals, we play host to colonies of bacteria, from our skin to the inner recesses of our gut. Not to mention the little creatures living between our eyelashes.

Four mobile Earth colonies and tons of food, frozen or dehydrated, carrying different microbes.

Even being careful, it was impossible to keep from liberating some organic material. Airborne dust blowing out of the hab included shed hair, skin flakes, human commensal bacteria, tiny mites that feed on human detritus, their waste pellets, and their bacteria. The built-in vacuum system in the hab kept up with most of the dirt, but there was no way to eliminate it all. The crew could not operate like a clean room for eighteen months.

And of course, when we arrived, we disposed of roughly a ton of frozen human waste, she thought. It's out there now, orbiting near Mars. Despite what Axelrod told the media, it's likely to come in for a landing sometime. When it enters the atmosphere, the plentiful microbes will most likely be incinerated crossing even Mars's thin atmosphere.

But what if they aren't?

Mars is covered with a reactive, peroxide-rich covering of busted-up crustal rock, sand, and dust that is essentially sterile.

Due to the wispy, ineffective atmosphere, sunlight rich in ultraviolet bathes the surface of the planet. Microbial life would be torn apart by vigorous chemical jaws. If Mars were lifeless, this was definitely the unwelcome mat to any bacterial life-form attempting a landing—apart from the cold and dryness. A hostile shore for life, indeed. But if Mars harbors life within, it was the first line of protection against tiny invaders. A rusty, defensive skin.

And what kind of life could exist on Mars? After four billion years of never having an oxygen atmosphere, it would definitely not be aerobic life. No, it would be anaerobic. But could we harm it?

We still think of Earth as the water planet, the blue planet, the planet of the oxygen breathers. "All life is ultimately dependent on the sun," children were taught. "Food chains begin with energy from the sun that is harvested by the green plants." But once again, it was our ignorance speaking.

Late in the twentieth century biologists found hydrothermal vents teeming with life deep on the ocean floor. The basis for the food chain was chemosynthetic bacteria, that had never seen the sun and couldn't use its light. Soon after came discoveries of life in boiling-hot springs, very acid water, coal mines, and even microbes living inside rocks. Life permeated Earth, didn't merely crawl its surface or swim in its seas.

All of the underground microbes were anaerobes, unable to exist within the reach of oxygen. That the biologists expected. But the biggest surprise was their DNA. Their genes were only 60 percent similar to all other life on the planet. They were the ancient bacteria, the archaea, persisting underground billions of years after the rise of the oxygen lovers. Did they retreat underground as the only refuge free from the deadly oxygen atmosphere? Is Earth's deep underground a refuge, or the cradle of life?

She paused to consider. There may be more life below ground than oxygen users on top. They have the whole interior of Earth, while we are confined to the thin biosphere on the surface. After all this time, billions of humans haven't touched the anaerobes on our own planet.

How could we few harm Martian life? *Hell, we haven't even found any.* Well, there was always the vent, but how was she going to get back there?

And she seethed with frustration again. She sent a private, coded e-mail to her parents.

Hi Mums, Dad,

Thanks for the ETimes article. Earth is as crazy as ever. (Except for dear old Oz, of course. Did I tell you I saw Australia last month, through the scope?)

So far you Earthlings haven't had much to worry about from Mars, but . . . Don't think I told you my great news.

Just before Viktor's accident, I managed to get a sample of organic stuff from the rocks around the lip of the vent. It was pretty dried-out and fragmented (it was frozen into some ice (!)). I've done a methanol extraction and run it through the GC and it's definitely organic.

Of course I've got a million questions, and I want to confirm if it could have been contamination, because it seems pretty similar to Earth life.

But the three mules won't delay the test even for a day!—and they won't really consider another EBA until afterwards.

I mean, I want to go home as much as anyone, but mygawd we may have finally found it!! So here I am sitting on potentially the greatest discovery of the whole trip, and what am I doing? Hauling boxes!

OK. Enough of that.

Hope you liked the last vid. Dad, hope you're doing well. Viktor is getting along okay with the bum ankle, but it's touchy getting a pressure bandage tight enough to give him some support without interfering with his venous return. Mars grav doesn't help at all with that end of it.

I keep wondering if he would've sprained it at all if we'd been under 1g all this time. Maybe we're more delicate than we think.

Lots of grunt work getting ready for that #$%$ liftoff test. I feel like an Aboriginal woman. The guys are so caught up in it that they've forgotten everything else. If it weren't such an old joke I'd say they really ARE from Mars.

Gotta go. My night to cook (that'll fix 'em!).

Much luv,

Julia

10

MARC ARRIVED, GRINNING MADLY FOR THE BATTERIES OF cameras, and fit right in.

Julia looked at him across the room. After the space of several months, she was impressed again by his gorgeous profile. He *looked* like an astronaut with the right stuff. Wide, guileless grin, perfect teeth, square jaw. Blue eyes, of course, and dark blond hair, slightly tousled. No wonder Axelrod's PR gang wanted him on the crew. He had the kind of looks that could kill at fifty feet. If they had fan clubs, she figured his would get the most mail, hands down.

And, of course, they did. But nobody let the crew see the numbers . . .

Raoul was compact and muscular, striking in a dark, Latin way—hell, all the astronauts were easy on the eyes. No coincidence. NASA didn't train people the public wouldn't want to watch. Katherine had been a knockout, and Viktor—well, she just couldn't judge. To her he looked simply wonderful. Objectively she knew he couldn't match Marc, but she was so much more *drawn* to him. He caught her eye and winked. She felt a stab of emotion. Despite her training, she flushed.

The new crew went out for beers and Mexican the first evening.

"Axelrod didn't need to offer the million-dollar bonus, either, tell you the truth," Marc revealed with a grin.

"Don't ever tell him that," Viktor said, smiling. Some part of him still liked the games and bargaining of what he called "late capitalism"—though what might replace it, he admittedly had no idea.

Raoul slurped his Dos Equis with relish. "Yeah, it would make him grind his teeth down faster."

"You would have come back on even terms?" Julia asked.

"Easy. I wasn't crazy about living in China, even at the top of the heap. Jammed, smelly, air so thick you could cut it."

"I hear you trained in Germany some, though," Viktor said.

"That was okay, but the leftover ESA gear they had was clunky. And the team Airbus had put together, it didn't jell."

"Chen?" Julia guessed.

"Him and me, we never got along real well."

Julia had a fond spot for Lee Chen, who had helped train her in practical exobiology. "He's old school discipline," she admitted.

"Autocrat prima donna, more like it."

"More German than Germans," Viktor snorted. He and Chen had not exactly hit it off, either, when they were all in the NASA Astronaut Office.

"Too true. I missed this Dos Equis, that's for sure."

Raoul joined him in a long pull. "We won't be getting any for a while, might as well enjoy the best."

"Ol' Chen-boy, he made it real clear. All his opera, and we're spear carriers."

"With Airbus supplying the Wagnerian music?" Julia asked lightly.

To her relief, between her and Marc there was no trace of the anger he had shown when he stormed out months before. He probably still blamed her for bumping him in favor of Viktor—rightly, of course, even though she had not planned it that way. Sometime it would come out and she would have to be ready. Viktor, too; Marc would see it as completely logical that they had hatched up the whole scheme. She realized that the two of them probably enjoyed a reputation for sly maneuver that was quite undeserved.

"Yeah, and the Germans hating living there so much, alcohol was one of the major food groups."

"Hard to keep sharp that way." Raoul's tongue was getting a little sloppy, probably from the effect he was criticizing.

"Yes. We heard there were plenty malfs," Viktor prodded.

"More than plenty, a surplus. From the first day, I had big doubts about the Chinese and Germans and French being able to put together a nuclear rocket in time. First time I saw their test-bed results, I was sure."

Julia dutifully drank some more of her light ale, aware that this was a male ritual she had better get the hang of, though knowing that some of the subtleties of barhopping would elude her. "They had all that old Russian data."

"Sure, and some from the old American Nerva project. Kept quiet about how they got that. But putting it all together with the avionics and control systems—not so easy."

"Data we have says are far more efficient rockets than LOX," Viktor observed.

"But still . . ." Marc leaned forward, almost whispering, "You wanna sit on top of that hot a pile?"

"If it got me to Mars and back pronto, sure," Raoul said.

"*If.* They're having trouble getting the fuel flow— liquid hydrogen when they boost from two hundred klicks up—to go through that cylindrical plutonium pile they're using. It gets too hot, then it gives them back pressure, heats up some more, and—whammo—the whole damned shebang can run away into—well, they dunno."

"I could fix it." Raoul looked bland, unconcerned.

"Welcome to, my friend," Marc toasted him.

Viktor said carefully, "They are on schedule?"

"No, that's the point," Marc said. "Fallin' behind every day now."

"Can they make the window?" Julia pressed.

"Don't see how."

They all beamed at their new crewmate.

Axelrod did too, the next day. He listened to all this technical detail with barely suppressed glee. "They won't be riding on our tail after all!" Handshakes all around.

But five minutes later his attention was elsewhere.

Now his PR people were worried about the publicity impact. Would people hate Raoul? He tried this out on Julia, "looking for the woman's angle"—as if there would be only one. "After all, he's leaving behind his wife, and child, to come. He won't see the baby until it's two years old."

"Maybe never," Julia said flatly, to see if Axelrod would react. Nothing. Well, maybe matters felt differently if your own rear was not going to be in an acceleration couch.

Axelrod was right, however. Some commentators took this up. *People* magazine did a big weepy feature on the issue. But by now the Consortium had made firm connections to a lot of media figures, those distant enough to look objective. They ran a counteroffensive, following a plausible line: Raoul was portrayed as a modern Odysseus going off on a voyage into the unknown to fulfill his destiny, no matter what it cost him personally. (Never mind that Odysseus had gone to war, won, then gotten sidetracked on the trip back in his involuntary odyssey, taking decades to hole up on various islands of the Aegean, several times with women not his wife.) This line seemed to work with the public.

Then the oddity of a lone woman going to Mars for two and a half years caught their imagination, deflecting attention from Raoul. The endless speculation—some quite ribald, and ignorantly assuming they would go to Mars in zero g—appalled Julia. She stopped reading the press entirely and never turned on the trivid anymore.

Still, there was relentless attention, and Axelrod had to let a tiny fraction of it focus on her. If all humanity was going to Mars along with the four, "We must know our companions," as one commentator put it. She was glad that she didn't have to get to know many on the immediate other side of the membrane, thank you, for she developed an instant dislike to most of the media mavens, who chose to wear their ignorance of Mars, space, and technology like a badge marking them as one with the Common Man.

Julia had to admit there was some point to the interviews, profiles, even in the lapel-hugging shows like *A Day in the Life Of*, and the like. There had been so many faceless astronauts among the hundred-plus needed to keep the space station aloft. From the old days the public knew John Glenn and Buzz Aldrin and Neil Armstrong and maybe Sally Ride, but from the station nobody remembered names, just grinning guys and gals riding rockets. Now there were only four to care about, and she was the singular figure.

She had the intelligence not to manufacture a public persona. Astronauts were by design sharp, crisp, automatically outgoing, shining with health, and always pressured. This she let carry her, staying inside her friendly but reserved carapace.

The worst of the public angle was the curveballs the media kept throwing her. In the middle of an absolutely innocuous talk with a worldwide morning magazine show, the kind-faced, motherly interviewer suddenly turned sharklike with, "And what do you say to those Asians who believe the Consortium is indulging in the worst sort of racism?"—apparently, by not having an Asian in the crew. Raoul, she was told, didn't really offset the Caucasian bias since he was an American citizen.

She countered by pointing out that Latinos were really mixtures of Caucasoids and Mongoloids, two of the three major racial groups. The interviewer shot back that the Consortium had no Negroid, the new "in" word for black.

Most embarrassing was the way she learned that Airbus was suing the Consortium over some tiny technicality. This took advantage of the legendary American habit of settling issues in court rather than by negotiation. A judge handed down a restraining order commanding Axelrod to stop development of the *Venture*—Axelrod's choice for the name—pending some obscure legal finding.

Julia had to field a probing, sneering interviewer who trotted out this news, hinting that the Consortium had stolen technology from both NASA and from the poor, media-neglected Airbus team.

He ignored the fact that, in classic Chinese form, Airbus was letting few media teams within miles of their facilities. Julia somehow managed to stutter and fake her way into a commercial break, then was missing when they came back on the air.

The order was dissolved within a week beneath the media glare. NASA gave a press conference to confirm that Axelrod was paying for everything the Consortium mission used. Airbus was thrown out of court.

Though Axelrod could not prove it, Airbus was still tying the Consortium in legal knots.

Suddenly the Securities and Exchange Commission was investigating Axelrod's finances.

A senator started complaining about technology transfer and safety. The Consortium vehicles were being launched on private rockets that were developed with NASA, right down to the solid launch assist boosters. Some vital U.S. secrets could leak—to whom, the senator did not say.

Since the primary international antagonist of the United States was the Chinese, who were half of Airbus, this made no real sense—but got lots of coverage anyway.

The tension between the two sides spilled out into the open, with tit-for-tat press conferences and incessant mike-in-the-face goading. The media had one great axiom: *You fight it, we write it.*

Axelrod proved too smart for them, though, by trotting his "Marsnauts" out when they were obviously tired, gaining sympathy. He even went along with the media term "NASAnauts" for the bland astronauts who were criticizing the Consortium. In all, Julia was grateful to be kept out of the fray, which just kept building.

Still, it had not escaped anyone that many Europeans and Chinese would like to take all that Mars Prize money away from the Consortium. And from the U.S., since the Americans put the most in the pot.

Nationalist rivalry got worse, like a grudge soccer match between whole continents.

Axelrod didn't find everything he needed on NASA's shelves. The Consortium had to fabricate important components. That proved comparatively easy, though expensive. Axelrod grumbled and paid. Mating the fresh cut-metal parts with the conventional wisdom of decades proved harder.

The NASA designs were pricey, the engineering incomplete, and what hardware that did exist needed modification. The habitat had to be cut down, reengineered, and simplified—after all, they were no longer running under the ludicrous zero-g orthodoxy, which complicated everything from the kitchen to the toilets. Flying with 0.38 g made life simpler, but many standing NASA methods developed for the space station now had to be scrapped. Connectors, electronics, systems integration—all had to be done with a fresh vision, to meet a stepped-up deadline.

It was legendary in aerospace that gear got built faster in the dry, lonely techno-outposts where there was nothing else for the engineers to do: China Lake, Rockman, Palmdale, White Sands, other forlorn dust-bowls. So Axelrod's teams had bought space and people in all those places, and the metal and composites grew apace in splendid dry isolation.

Crews for the space station were normally selected ten to twelve months before launch. Fine, so long as the equipment was ready. Here it wasn't. More headaches.

The Consortium had to squash together development and training, a feat unheard of since the Apollo days.

Single-system training came first, weeks of working with instructors who were building the payload and landing systems while they trained the astronauts. It was a field day for overachievers.

The confusions would have been comic if lives had not been on the line.

Mission simulations came next, bringing all four crew together in the habitat-cockpit mock-up. Here they practiced everything that could go wrong and the few things that could go right—endlessly.

For starters, nobody had ever built a combo habitat and cockpit. The two functions had diametrically opposed demands. Habitats should be comfy and convey largeness; cockpits should be rugged and tight. They had to fly the bulky hab and land it on Mars, but return would be in the ERV, already in place.

The habitat-lander was a big aluminum and steel tuna can with a central cylinder that served to reach the air lock at its base. The top level was living quarters, the bottom held their Mars exploration equipment and the cockpit. There were no side windows, nothing looking straight ahead, where the craft would slam into the Martian atmosphere at speeds of several kilometers per second. Viktor would have to fly using TV screens alone. Fair enough; aerobraking required senses of flow speeds, spiking temperatures, and pressures, not eyeballing.

Four months before nominal launch date, joint integrated simulations began in earnest. To this grueling party everybody got invited: operation control, flight director, habitat monitors, techs—eighty-six people in all.

In a way, a whole-systems exercise was a game. The crew wanted to make no errors, while the flight director tried to make them die in dozens of different ways.

Their flight director, the ever-smiling Brad Fowler, had left NASA three years before for private consulting and many more bucks. Axelrod had topped whatever he was getting and then some, by all accounts. Brad was happy to be back running a real program of exploration, though he tried hard not to show that too much.

"Must admit," Viktor said, "systems personnel are best money can buy."

Julia countered, "Best, period. Half these guys quit NASA to come here."

The others were from private corporations that were essentially NASA feeder outfits. It was an open secret that NASA's stand-down from Mars had sent the whole organization into a tailspin from which morale might never recover. If not Mars, what *was* the point of having a space agency? That had simplified Axelrod's problems immensely. People would sign on just to have a hand in getting to Mars, even for jobs that were below their capability ratings.

So here they all were, one happy gang all wanting to go to Mars, and a dozen times a day dying in the simulators. Brad Fowler smiled at them every day, obeying a standard NASA commandment: *Thou shalt smile, but not grin.* Confidence, not arrogance. His teeth shone like a white flag against skin as weathered as beef jerky, from decades in the Houston heat. He gave them the same opening mantra, "Morning, all. The tougher we are on you here, the easier it'll be on Mars."

Each time Julia thought to herself, *Yeah, right, you sadist.* Even though she knew what he said was true.

The rules of the simulation game were, no *Challenger*-level disasters. Nothing beyond their control, when the only response possible was to say your prayers. Sure, those events could happen, but there was no point in simulating them.

Instead, they got what Julia thought of as *instant obstacles.*

Failure of a subsection of the electronics board. Fuel pump shutdown. Cryo malf. Leak in the vector-keeping system lines. Big-time pressure drop.

Miss the first sign and that wedged you against the

clock, trying to restart a procedure while fluids spurted out into space or pumps locked up nice and tight. One of these—or all three—come at you while the habitat is scooping deep on its first gulp of the Martian upper atmosphere.

In a typical "exercise," Viktor was trying to fly an avionics structure that more nearly resembled a refrigerator than an airplane. Raoul was performing mechanical CPR on the fuel feeds that had just redlined. Julia and Marc were running backup, taking over problems that the others had discarded as nonessential.

That didn't mean they couldn't kill you, only that they wouldn't do so *right now.*

Like, say, a pesky waffle in their aerodynamic trim. Sure, there was plenty of theoretical backup on this, books full of Navier-Stokes three-dimensional flow-field solutions for their aeroshell shape. They also inherited thick studies of how the reacting flows of appropriate CO_2 chemistry worked out with the preliminary thermal protection system (TPS, in NASAspeak). No problem there.

But when Viktor handed off the problem to Julia as he struggled with the Mach window, she couldn't find the right operating regime for their vector-control jets. Viktor had to take it over and fly the bird by hand, not even looking at the overshoot trajectory plots that an anxious ship computer kept flashing up on his right-hand screen.

No matter that they had bought from NASA a "robust 3-D Conceptual Fluid Dynamic code capable of radiating, turbulent, and dusty flow simulations." Viktor had fifty-eight tons at his back and no wings to lift them out of trouble. He had to skate on the filmy upper blanket of CO_2 by feel more than by numbers.

So when the vector problem grew to fatal levels, he snatched it back from her and tried to correct the sliding yaw the whole craft was developing. The simulation was *good*. It yanked them around, buffeted them like a bad roller coaster, meanwhile yowling in their ears like a drumroll from hell. Not a great aid to abstract thinking.

Running out of luck got to be a habit. Engines went out at just the worst moment, when they were pulling maximum g's. Headwinds maxed up to kill their lifting speed. Boards went dead, running lights and all, just before a critical command had to pass through them.

Nothing in nature said that only one thing had to go wrong at once, after all.

Brad reminded them of that far more often than he needed to. Maybe there *was* a bit of the smiling sadist in him.

Maybe NASA had selected him for that. Or Axelrod had.

Every time they failed to recover from a malf, they looked at each other, knowing that the feed camera was showing their dismay to the whole goddamn team outside. Everybody was thinking the same thing: if this were Mars, they'd be dead. Little chunks of red stuff spattered across the already red planet.

They needed their coffee breaks.

A few months of this and maybe the magic point would come. NASA termed it "crystallization"—when a crew thought as one, knowing when and how to do the right things at just the right times. So that they didn't get in one other's way, blundering through the complex, interacting systems commanded from the tight little cockpit.

Crystallize too early and a crew got cocky, bored. Too late and they couldn't fly at all, because they weren't seasoned.

Hitting the right point as the launch window started to open was why Brad Fowler's job was more like an artist's than an engineer's.

Or a psychotherapist's.

Viktor had started his career during the slow revival of the Russian space program, post-Mir. His father had worked on keeping Mir aloft, laboring in the mission control center that was a brooding mausoleum hulking beside a pothole avenue. Though his father had been a flight controller, to make ends meet he had to drive a taxi in his off hours.

After Mir, Russian cosmonauts had lawyers and contracts and agents, in a parody of neocapitalism. They got bonuses for doing EVAs and running orbital experiments. Viktor was already used to doing telecasts from orbit endorsing snack foods and sweaters. Russian institutions had a long habit of covering over embarrassing lapses and outright failures, so the Consortium's up-front attitude—if it doesn't work, let's hear pronto, then fix it—had been delightful.

At night he lay in bed with Julia and could talk about things like this, things that to another, ordinary woman would have been petrifyingly dull. But to Julia it was the world she lived in, his experience in it different and strange and movingly sad. What she thought of it did not matter. What did was that she heard and felt through his halting, awkward English the pain of a life lived in tougher places, harder times.

Hearing it helped him. And her.

But all the wonderful, warm communication only served to offset the complexity and strain of their working days, which now stretched to fill all but sleep. And sometimes it invaded sleep itself. She would awaken to find Viktor pacing, moody and unable to speak. Sometimes she felt that way herself, for reasons she could not name.

But they helped each other through those times and emerged in the morning whole and sometimes even rested. Able to smile for the cameras that sometimes got through security and dogged their footsteps as they fetched the morning Houston *Times*.

The tragedy of Mir and the International Space Station alike was that they did not confront the deep problem of living in space.

Instead, they camped in space. They used disposables, taking in food and air and dumping their waste, never closing the loop.

Only when it became embarrassingly obvious that the ISS had nothing much to do did NASA's attention turn to the obvious next goal: systems for true exploration, Mars. Recycling water and air, separation of solid waste, air chemistry—these had gotten worked out in orbit with painful slowness.

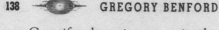

Centrifugal gravity was a simpler matter. In 2008 the method got a simple trial in orbit, standing off the ISS a few kilometers for safety, keeping astronauts—NASA-nauts—in fractional g for a year.

They performed so well that the zero-g faction in the JSC Life Science Directorate had tried to suppress further work, fearing for their jobs. All they had learned from four decades of endless study of zero g was that it was a bad idea. But after the fractional-g trials the cat was out of the zero-g bag. There were at least some 0.38 g orbital studies to support Axelrod's leap to the simple configuration they would fly to Mars and back.

After all, this wasn't even what the media called rocket science—an interesting cliché misnomer, for rockets are engineering miracles, not scientific ones—tricky but not exactly challenging the limits of knowledge. It was Newtonian mechanics, and as long as the cable deployed all right between the upper stage of the booster and the habitat, all that remained to do was give each a burst from the hydrazine thrusters and spin the habitat about the dead weight of the empty upper stage shell at a few revolutions per minute.

Maybe the best fresh aspect of the Consortium was the absence of paperwork. In Julia's experience, every flight up to the space station produced more paperwork mass than the payload weight. Axelrod cut all that.

"No point in a bunch of Cover Your Ass memos if we fail," he said happily. "Point isn't the paper we generate, but the paper we lose—thirty billion dollar bills."

Then, as far as Julia was concerned, petty geopolitical

and personnel matters lost their importance. Harry, her father, collapsed in a golf game.

He was diagnosed with one of the newly emerging killer viral diseases, the zoonosis class that migrated from animals to humans, fresh out of the African cauldron. They traced it back to the hunter's camp in west Africa he and the park rangers had found—Harry's spite trip. The animals the poachers were butchering harbored a viral disease ready to make the leap to humans. Harry's prognosis, in the long term, was grim— five years at best. Short term? Nobody knew. He could be dead in a month, if myriad details of blood chem went wrong on him. For starters, he was embarking on an intensive drug regime.

She got the news from her mother, Robbie. Julia had been lucky to have a mother who had dreamed of space and had married a biologist. Not just a loving, loyal husband, but one whose mind wandered to other planets. In those ancient days, the 1970s, the manned space program was solely short shuttle trips. Harry had enthusiastically supported Robbie's astronaut training, postponed his academic future so they could live near JSC, and worked for the exobiology group at NASA.

Her concession to the family was to return to Australia for the birth of Bill, then Julia. Toward the end of her leave for Julia, her mind full of the upcoming resumption of her career, she turned the wrong way into the path of a pickup truck. In the accident, the top of her femur was pushed through her shattered hip joint. Five months in hospital and then a long rehab.

After that she walked with a limp. The folks at

NASA were sorry, and offered her a desk job, but her career in space was finished. She was repelled by the idea of becoming a bureaucrat, and with Harry, decided to stay in Australia. Harry snagged a position at the University of Adelaide and they settled into the academic life.

Julia had caught the space bug early on from her mother. An old videotape of the "Martian Chronicles" was her favorite movie. When grown-ups asked what she wanted to do when she grew up, she always said primly, "I'm going to swim in the canals of Mars." That earned her little amused murmurs and a pat on the head. By the time she learned that there were no canals, it had become her mantra.

When she was fourteen, Harry and Robbie's old NASA connections got them invited to the celebrations surrounding the July 1997 Mars Pathfinder probe arrival: *Back to the Red Planet!*

Live video feed from Mars was piped into a makeshift auditorium, looming enormously real on a huge screen. Around her she had felt the press of excited bodies. A group enthusiasm filled the room, actually a screened-off portion of the giant exhibition hall. There in the buzzing dark she was mesmerized. Later on, they went upstairs to a small room where she spent twenty minutes driving a radio-controlled rover toy around a patch of sand and rocks. Tacky, really, just plastic. But it was enough. After that, she read everything about the mission, put up posters of the Sojourner rock garden on her wall.

And her parents had gone not just for her, but for themselves.

Julia considered dropping out of the team to be with her father. She went through a hard night, thinking about it. She had not been able to rush to his bedside because there were some aerobraking trials on for tomorrow and she had to be there. And through the long night she was fully aware of the damage she would cause to the Consortium plans. None of it helped her sleep.

But when she talked to her parents on visiphone, Harry wouldn't hear of it. "Mars has always been your dream, sweetie!" he had exclaimed, frowning at her with Old Testament fury. "Mine, too."

"And mine," her mother said wistfully.

So during a long, intermittently awkward call, they reached a negotiated cease-fire. Harry would take his experimental drug treatment. They would all stay linked closely throughout the two-and-a-half-year flight. And, Harry added, "I'll be the first to kiss you when you come prancing down the gangplank. I'll push that Katherine out of the way, I swear I will." Harry had decided opinions about the whole Raoul-baby-Katherine business. "I damn well promise."

February 2016.

Time ticked on.

Launch readiness review. Nobody wanted to hear anything but the crisp, can-do NASA style. But this was seat-of-your-pants private sector, and in the eyes of everybody, especially leathery old hands like Brad Fowler, there were too many open items, too much unrehearsed.

NASA flights were like grand operas, the score and cast selected long before, the outcome ordained. This was more like a musical comedy they improvised as the band was warming up.

The solid rocket motors were time-honored technology, and still just a tad tricky. Maybe more than a tad. Stacking the whole assembly, booster and solids, had an uncomfortable resemblance to building a house of cards. Axelrod had paid the better part of a billion bucks to get full use of the Cape's facilities, right up to and including the Vehicle Assembly Building.

The crew flew into Runway 33, right next to the soaring square profile of the biggest building in the world. They marched out in their Consortium uniforms— Axelrod had insisted on the red-blue spandex suits—and stood there staring up at the VAB. They milled around like insects beneath the building's bulk until the press corps arrived, halting at the Axelrod-commanded respectful distance.

In the shimmering Cape heat the reporters and their big sun-shaded cameras looked a lot like old 1950s movie Martians, and Julia treated them pretty much that way— as objects of loathing. She had enjoyed enough exposure, thank you. The best thing about Mars, right then, was not the exploration and frontier and unknown and all that, but the fact that there would be nobody else there.

All four lined up behind a single microphone and spoke a few platitudes for what a PR type called "footage effect"—just enough to get a flash-recognition on the news, not enough to actually make a story out of it.

And what story could there be? Astronauts on their way uphill to the Big Empty. Luckily the reporters and VIP guests alike had to keep the twenty feet distance commanded by the quarantine rules, to avoid the crew picking up a head cold. Not a good way to go into a launch. No viruses to Mars either, couldn't have that.

Once they were into the hab and belted in by the ground crew to the adjustable acceleration couches, the checkoffs went smoothly and then the waiting began.

Julia had been through this already, they all had, and so she knew that the worst moment was before they lit the Roman candle under her. It was right *now*, when there was only waiting and too much thinking with not a damn thing to do. Astronauts were people built to be busy, not at their best when stuck immobile. When the prickly fears could come inching up the spine.

Tick, tick, tick.

Her whole life did not flash before her, but pieces of it flapped by like anxious seagulls as her attention darted around the cockpit. Voices buzzed in her headphones and she tried not to think of sitting on top of two million kilograms of supercold hydrogen and oxygen, two basic molecules yearning to kiss each other and explode in their elemental passion, to fling them at the empty eggshell blue sky.

They were all alone out here in the rippling tropical heat, all their relatives and friends and public standing a respectful five kilometers away because if anything went wrong . . .

Liftoff.

There was nothing about *lift* in it. Instead, there was huge noise and rattling and shaking and then a hard hammering and a pressing weight. The hab was being shaken profoundly, as if by an angry giant that could jar and jiggle in all directions at once.

She had done it before, but every time there was the same momentary terror, far too late. *Why am I here?*

They spent a day in near Earth orbit, checking out systems before casting off into the deep.

Microgravity bothered the brain. The perception of primordial primate unease busied the mind with the business of trying to offset shifting fluids in the skull. Senses kept screaming to the mind that *we're falling!*—all the time. Fretting about survival led to dumb astronauts. Julia found, just as on space station flights, that her reflexes were doughy, her thoughts muddy.

Plus, half those in zero g got sick. No matter if they had been there before, as all four had. This time it was Julia's turn. She had always felt a bit superior to her NASAnaut companions on space station flights, as they grew woozy.

She felt odd, then ill, then a lurching, hideous nausea. The "queasy cruds" struck arbitrarily, with an impartiality she found insulting. She was an old space hand! On her way to more important destinations than crummy old orbit! Her stomach was betraying her.

The medicos still couldn't prevent it or predict it. This proved to be of little comfort. But there were little pills that got it under control within a day. You turned green, threw up, weren't much good for anything, and then you got okay. Yippee ti yi yay, space cowboys!

Or cowgirls. As fluctuations would have it, the men were fine.

Hurried preparations went on all around her in the cockpit/hab while she lolled in her g-couch, following Viktor's orders and not thinking about the food he offered and looking out the port at the big creamy world she was about to leave. The return ship was full of fuel, waiting for them on Mars.

Planets perform a grand gavotte, forcing humans to dance to the same grave rhythms. Viktor checked and rechecked their ship. The most fuel-stingy method of reaching Mars, or any other world, started by slipping away from Earth's nearly circular orbit on a long, slow tangent. Their boost would start them on this glide, an ellipse that paralleled Earth's orbit at one end and that of Mars at the other. Sliding like a bead along this smooth course, they would swoop near Mars at a velocity very nearly that of the planets.

But getting there meant hitting the window. Leave a month late and the fuel cost ran up enormously. Leave half a year late and no rocket imaginable could get you around the long loop in time; you would chase Mars all around its orbit—watching the blue-green world dwindle away, as every second, that oasis of air and water fell behind another 33 kilometers. Even moving that fast, a thousand times the speed of the Apollo missions to the moon, it would take six months to ride the 400 million kilometers.

Axelrod did a 'cast with them, saying confidently, "We're going to Mars!" to big background applause. She tried not to throw up, for several reasons.

All systems were *go*. So they went.

11

THEY HAD ALL BEEN SHAKEN UP BY THE AEROBRAKING ON arrival. Sure, the simulations had been tough—harder vibrations than at liftoff, gut-wrenching swerves as they hit high-altitude turbulence that nobody had predicted (and what if they had?).

Coming in, they had to lose several kilometers per second of speed. Doing that by rocket braking would have imposed a considerable fuel cost. So they used friction, just like ordinary brakes. Slamming into even the tenuous CO_2 atmosphere meant heating their aeroshell to the same temperature range that the Shuttle tiles had to endure.

The hard-hammering jolts came in all three axes at once. *Like a dog shaking a rag doll,* she thought as her stomach lurched. She tried to pay attention, through the shattering noise—a wall of sound that threatened at each new shrill note, as if the whole hab were starting to come apart. And through that came the incredibly calm drone of Viktor's voice, somehow close and personal in her headset.

"Coming up on max delta, heading at four four three seven, coming close to margin on that. In the envelope, adjusting for pitch, altitude four eight seven."

He was talking to Marc but it had a hugely comforting effect on her. She knew that he was documenting every step in real time, so that if something failed, at least there might be some record of what went wrong. One of the pre-positioned orbiting comm satellites for the Mars Outpost program was receiving whatever signal could escape the plasma discharge glow that made them look like a fresh orange comet high up in the Martian day.

She held on through it all, praying to Viktor, not God, to bring them through the long agonizing minutes while they skated around a quarter of the planet. Wind friction howled and the rugged shell in their nose turned bright red, shedding its nose tiles like a spaceship with skin disease. Then—*whang! whoomp!*—they blew the aeroshell and the heavy hand of deceleration lifted a bit.

The hab rotated abruptly, pulled by the deploying parachutes into a wrenching one-eighty. Noises trickled away. A sudden silence.

They were swaying beneath their chute canopy and suddenly she was cheering, they all were. Falling, still, but slower—

Their rocket flared with a roar, working with the chutes. Viktor was calling out numbers, getting smaller—their altitude, seventeen, fourteen . . . in kilometers. They had crossed hundreds of millions of kilometers and now just eight klicks . . . five . . .

She had held her breath. Amateurish, but to hell with that.

Liftoff had been rough, sure, but they had not had to hit a patch of sky a few klicks across. Just anywhere in orbit would do; correct for it later.

This time Viktor had to put them smack next to the Earth Return Vehicle, the ERV. Sure, close enough to reach with a dune buggy would be okay, though inconvenient for the next year and a half.

Viktor had liked Raoul's going outside to dump their dung—saved a ton of mass that didn't have to be gingerly lowered onto Mars with their precious fuel. He used the extra fuel now, bringing them in at less than one hundred klicks/hour to a near hover a few kilometers up. He used the radar altimeter, the Outpost Mars location finder beacon. And not to forget the external camera that was feeding the view to Earthside, making Axelrod millions per moment.

"Easy, heading one eight three, drifting north . . . I see the site. ERV. Looks like home! . . . Coming up . . . got parking spot all picked out . . ."

A roaring. "Plenty dust . . . touch . . . Engines off!"

After the eerie first hour, the magic of Mars lifted enough to make Raoul walk over to the ERV. First priority was his checkout. It was a pleasant stroll, crossing ruddy rock-strewn land they had seen a thousand times through the dune buggy TV eyes. Julia ambled off to the left, kicked a rock to see it tumble away in the delicious low g. Then she heard Raoul groan in her suit comm.

By the time she got to the ERV, Raoul had crawled up under it. She saw what he had—a dark stain on the sand, maybe as big as two hands across. Small. But enough.

The ERV had had no human to guide it. Given that, its performance was miraculous. It had touched down within 2.3 kilometers of the exact center of its ellipse. A tribute to NASA's skill.

But Raoul quickly found that it had come in off-level. No problem, but a strut had jammed against a boulder. At its descent speed, the jar and wrench had crushed fuel pipes and valves around the thruster.

"How come none of the diagnostics detected this?" Marc demanded.

Raoul had just crawled out from under the cowling, while the others stood waiting nervously, looking at the twisted strut.

"Those lines were not pressurized," Raoul said.

Viktor said nothing, just ducked and went under to look for himself.

When he emerged he was frowning. "A yaw failure in aerobraking maneuver, probably. Ship came in too fast. Only a shade too fast would do it."

Marc swore.

"How bad is it?" Julia asked.

"Not too bad, I think," said Raoul. But he grimaced, which told the true story. "And I am without a real machine shop," a phrase they all would get very tired of hearing. "I will have to improvise."

After the shock of it the men said little. She understood—why stress the obvious? Fix it, or die.

Julia sat at the comm, savoring her last mug of tea. Soon enough she and Marc would have to suit up and go outside the hab for the liftoff test. Raoul and Viktor had just left. She'd felt a thump as the outer door of the air lock closed after them.

They generally worked in pairs. Backup systems were the order of the day, always. Redundancy was the key to survival.

On Mars, the threats were redundant also. If the cold didn't get you, the atmosphere would. If both of them failed, the dryness was always waiting. Not to mention the damned toxic dust.

The buddy system had a proud tradition on Earth, from scuba diving to NASA, she mused. On the flatscreen she watched as two colorful suits, one yellow and one purple, walked outside across the landscape, one skipping lightly, one walking carefully, toward the ERV.

Although they had trained in the Devon Island arctic base, there it was only the cold you had to defend against. A wrap of wool across the face had protected Shackleton, Amundsen, Peary and the other crazy pole seekers of a century ago. And their technology had been barely sufficient to shield them against even the one peril. Plenty of frozen bodies at both ends of the Earth. With the new fabrics—warm, lightweight, basically self-regulating to release excess moisture—you really only had to be careful for your nose and lungs.

Not until Everest were the twin threats of cold and airlessness combined. The lethal zone, they called the upper reaches of the mountain, where even the best prepared ventured at extreme risk, losing brain cells to anoxia and becoming weaker by the day. *This whole planet is a lethal zone.*

Sitting here in the hab, a mug of tea in her hand, in comfortable sweats, it seemed safe enough. But they never forgot that outside Mars waited, implacably hostile. Not a bad place, just not one tailored for humans.

Sometimes, in her dreams, she imagined there was something, an unseen terror, lurking just outside her door. If she stepped out unprepared, she would be lost. Rationally, she knew it was just anxiety over having to be constantly prepared that gave her the dreams—but the afterimage remained.

Living on Mars was really more like living in the wet ocean, ironically, than at dry and cold Devon Island. That joint NASA/Mars Society facility had been built just about the turn of the millennium to prepare for a manned mission to Mars. There they were drilled into the habit of always suiting up by the numbers before going outside, going through an internal checklist of necessary gear. This amused the permanently Earthbound staff, some of whom had become quite cold-tolerant, and dashed between buildings in indoor wear.

But Julia had never become accustomed to that first great shock of cold air when she went outside. Ironically, on Mars, so much colder than the arctic, they never felt it. You'd have to be suicidal, or crazy, to step outside without a pressure suit and helmet. Best estimates were that you could survive less than thirty seconds.

So, on cold, dry Mars, like divers they checked and rechecked air tanks and connectors, heaters and sensors—their own and those of the ever-present buddy.

And they watched each other's backs. Always. And so they had survived a year and a half.

The liftoff test came after two days of hard labor.

They had been burning methane with oxygen in the rovers for over 500 days. But that was with carbon dioxide to keep the reaction heat down, acting like an inert buffer much as nitrogen did in the air of Earth. The ERV boosters would burn at a far higher temperature. The many engineering tests said the system would withstand that, but those were all done in comfortable labs on Earth. The test ERV had not been sitting on cold, dusty Mars for four years. And did not involve a system that had ruptured on landing. Or one that Raoul had labored month after month to fix. His extensive labors had hampered the exploration, casting a shadow over their long months here.

They'd debated doing just an engine test, maybe even a partial pressurization.

"Maybe we should just warm it up this time," said Marc.

"You mean do the test in steps?" Raoul looked worn and tired from the accumulated tension.

"So why do test at all?" Viktor's voice had an edge that they all knew by now meant he was keeping his feelings under control. "It works, it doesn't work. We should find out as soon as possible."

"It might be safer," said Marc.

"Partial test is only useful if it *doesn't* work." Viktor's finger jabbed the air, though careful not to point at anyone. He needed to express himself but had learned to not irk others at the same time.

Marc said, "If you lift off and come down wrong, maybe the wind blows you some—"

"Weather is calm. And I know how to fly straight up."

Marc nodded. Julia said carefully, "The logic seems compelling."

"Yeah, if we test-fire it too many times we risk other problems," said Raoul. "Can't beat the devil."

The men looked at each other. Somehow this had turned into a minor challenge-response between the three, leaving her out of it. At times like this, when the technical expertise was wholly outside her realm, they treated her like Mrs. Viktor.

"We go for it?" Viktor insisted.

The others nodded.

A warning call from Raoul made her crouch down.

They had decided to limit this test at ten percent of max liftoff, enough to see if anything blew a pipe. Just in case, it would have only Raoul and Viktor aboard. Viktor could run the subsystems fine from his couch. Julia also suspected he and Raoul didn't want any distractions.

She and Marc took shelter a few hundred meters away, ready to help if something horrible happened. The stubby Return Vehicle stood with its chem systems detached and gear dragged away, looking a bit naked against pink soil as thoroughly trod as Central Park in Manhattan, but with more litter.

She and Marc had nothing to do but pace to discharge all their adrenaline. The damned cold came through her boots as always and she stamped them to keep the circulation going. Even the best of insulation and boot heaters couldn't keep the chill from penetrating through the soles. It was early morning, so they would have a full day of sunlight to make repairs. If necessary.

She seldom came out this early into the biting hard cold left over from the night. Quickly enough they had learned the pains of even standing in shadow, much less of Martian night—skin stuck to boot tabs, frostbite straight through the insulation. Raoul's limp resulted from severely frostbitten toes after hours of making repairs in the shadow of the Return Vehicle.

He had said he hadn't noticed the chill. That meant he got involved tinkering and shut off those alarms in his mind. They were all focused, semiobsessive types, big on getting details right, or else they would never have been chosen to come.

She closed her eyes, trying to relax. They were about to land on Mars for the second and last time, after a trip of only a few meters or so, think of it that way.

Such odd ways of taking each moment, relieving it of its obvious heart-thudding qualities, had sustained her through the launch from Earth and their aerobraking. Months of tedious mission protocols and psychological seminars had given her many oblique skills.

"Ready," she heard Raoul through the suit comm. "Starting the pumps."

Viktor responded with pressure readings, flow rates. She saw a thin fog form beneath the rocket nozzle, like the vapors that sometimes leaked from the soil as the sun first struck it.

More cross talk between the pilots. Their close camaraderie had been so intensive the past few days that she and Marc felt like invisible nonentities, mere "field science" witnesses to the unblinking concentration of the "mission techs," as the terminology went. Then Raoul said, almost in a whisper, "Let's lift."

A fog blossomed at the Return Vehicle base. No gantry here, nothing to restrain it: the conical ship teetered a bit, then rose.

"Nice throttling!" Marc called.

"Wheeeee!" Julia cheered.

The ship rose twenty meters, hung—then started falling. A big plume rushed out the side of the ship.

Crump! came to her through the thin atmosphere.

A panel blew away, tumbling. The ship fell, caught itself, fell another few meters—and smacked down.

"All off!" Raoul called.

"Pressures down," Viktor answered, voice as mild as ever.

"My God, what—?"

Then she started running. Not that there was anything she could do, really.

PART II
A MARTIAN ODYSSEY

12

AT LEAST THE DAMAGE WAS CLEAR. BRUTALLY. THE PANEL had peeled off about a meter above the reaction chamber. Inside they could see a mass of popped valves, ruptured pumps, and tangled lines.

"Damn, I built those to take three times the demand load," Raoul said.

"Something surged," Viktor said. "Readout shows that."

"Still, the system should have held," Raoul insisted, face dark. "The seals must've leaked."

"Overpressure was probably from double line we made," Viktor said mildly.

"Ummm." Raoul bit his lip. Julia could see his pale face through his helmet viewer and wondered if he felt defeated. He was looking intently at the ruined assembly. "There seems to be a stain *inside* . . . dust! There's dust inside the line!" He turned to Viktor, "It's the seals all right, and having two lines made it just that much worse—twice as many seals." Then he nodded briskly. "That's it, all right. We should check with the desk guys, see if anything else showed up during their test fire, but I'll bet that's it."

"Double line was their idea."

"Right. We'll go back to the original design."

Somehow this buoyed them. It had to, she reflected. Either they got the system working or they wouldn't dare lift. The Airbus crew would have to rescue them—a huge *maybe*—getting the glory and the $30 billion.

"Should I contact Ground Control now, or wait until we get back to the hab?" Marc asked.

"They control nothing," Raoul said. "We're in control."

"Is damned right," Viktor said, laughing in a dry way.

"Okay." Julia grinned uncertainly and Marc followed suit.

"I suppose we should wait, talk to Earthside before we pull anything out and start refitting," Raoul said.

Viktor's voice crackled in the suit radio, his accent more noticeable, "Nyet, nyet, no waiting. You go ahead. Can't sit here and wait for Airbus to take us home."

As they were cleaning up and preparing lunch, a chime announced that a priority vid had arrived. Julia knew it was from Axelrod, as usual catching them together at a mealtime. By consensus looks they agreed to wait until later to review it. Axelrod's messages were usually harangues—as Marc put it, "The latest bee up his ass." And today was going to be epic because he had seen the failure, heard their reports.

They ate slowly.

Axelrod was livid. "NASA's repair blew out? What kinda shit instructions did they send you?" He was pacing around his office, vid feed clipped to his collar. "That's why they call them whiz boys, ya know. They can't find their whizzes without instructions. Detailed instructions." He paused for breath. "First they sold us a defective ship, then they fuck up the repairs. Someone's on the take to Airbus, I promise you."

Viktor had been the first to notice that the monologues had slowly changed in tone, from the friendly go-get-'em team chats to daily rants.

Axelrod was being worn down by constant media pressure, amidst the capital drain that the mission was costing him. In addition, relations between him and NASA, always edgy, had deteriorated. He no longer trusted their communications team.

The problems dated to the very first days of Consortium mission planning, when Axelrod announced his plans to use the ERV to get his crew home. NASA had resisted, and the whole project teetered.

"Who's gonna stop me?" Axelrod had said. "You want to send guards to Mars to keep the team out?"

After two months of hassling, they had reached a settlement—the Consortium could buy the ERV for $1 billion. Up front. But elements in NASA never forgot Axelrod's original presumption.

When Raoul discovered the damage to the ERV, Axelrod was furious. He lashed out at NASA in the press, described the ERV as "a derelict piece of government surplus equipment," and demanded his money back. This proved unwise.

Having already spent the money—after all, it was the government, and that is government's job—NASA refused. Instead it offered to help model the repairs with a duplicate ERV sitting in a hangar at Johnson Space Center.

Axelrod became increasingly hostile, threatening to file suit to recover all costs for the mission unless the ERV could be repaired.

NASA, in turn, hinted that smooth communication with the Mars crew could be a casualty of any open breach of contract. If he filed suit, they said with solemn sincerity, the government lawyers would almost certainly not allow them to deal with Axelrod anymore. Even worse things could happen . . .

In fact, he had hinted darkly to his crew, NASA was already not transmitting his vids to them reliably.

On screen, Axelrod continued to pace. "If we lose because their piece of shit equipment won't work—listen, Raoul, I want you, first thing, to—*arrrrrrp*."

The screen went blank.

"That won't help his state of mind," said Julia mildly. She was relieved not to have to listen to him any longer. "He's so paranoid about NASA." She sent back a "Did not receive message" reply.

Raoul shrugged. "Just another comm satellite glitch."

"Does seem to happen more with boss's vids," said Viktor.

"Well, he *is* on the horn more than anyone else. So it would happen more to his vids."

Julia knew what all four of them were thinking. That

if he had followed the original mission plan, the one they had all signed on to, they wouldn't be in this fix.

The original Mars Direct plan included a second ERV. This spacecraft would be launched about a month after the crew, on a slower trajectory. On arrival, it would land about 1,000 kilometers from the first mission, refuel itself, deploy its robot probes to recon the area, and await the second manned hab. Or, it could be used as a backup in case of trouble with the first ERV, and land at the first base.

But there was no second ERV at Mars Base. Or even an awkward 1,000 klicks away.

The nearest ERV was at a distance of 40 million miles, safely stowed in a NASA warehouse at Cape Canaveral.

Viktor had been handling the comm that evening, about a month into their outward journey, when Axelrod's squirt came through.

At a delay of about a minute and a half, it was more like verbal e-mail with both parties on-line than a conversation. This the psych team had not anticipated—these almost-conversations, surrealistic, displaced.

So they worked it out by themselves. Only one of them responded to Axelrod at a time, although the others felt free to suggest things to say.

"Hi up there, crew! How's the weather? Oh, yeah, that's right—no windows."

After this ritual joke, Axelrod was brisk, efficient, upbeat—sending along hails and tributes from various countries and luminaries. Somehow these fixtures of his messages never ebbed. Julia suspected the psych advisors of massaging them.

They let him run down. "Hey, we can read the calendar, even a minute behind time," Raoul said to the camera on their callback. "We're waiting to hear about the backup ERV launch. It's today, right?"

Somehow the delay seemed to stretch unbearably. They had all picked up something in Axelrod's breezy manner. When he came on again his face was sober, studied, wary. "I been meaning to tell you, but things get in the way. Mostly, money. Or lack of it. Right, the lack of money is the real root of evil." A sigh. Eyes veered away, then back. "I couldn't get it off the ground. Couldn't get the funding. I mean, I *tried*. Thing is, I'm down to nickels and dimes here. No reserves, running off income from the ads and promotions and all. I was never as rich as people said, y'know. Plenty of my holdings, they were mortgaged one way or another . . ."

He paused, took a sip of what looked like water. Julia wondered if it could be gin. She had seen him drink it that way before. Champagne for public, gin off to the side.

He freshened. "See, NASA kept pilin' on more costs, and it was always up front, too, no cost deferment. I tried everythin', bonds, floatin' a dummy corporation for future proceeds, the whole damn game. It just wasn't there. I couldn't get the capital together. My backers wanted out, even. So to cut costs and hold it together here on the ground for you guys up there . . . well, we missed the launch window."

Very slowly, as Axelrod went on with his rambling

confession, Raoul said, "Son . . . of . . . a . . . bitch."

It came out like an angry prayer.

They took a week to work off their anger. Plenty of gym time.

NASA had organized itself for decades around the implicit assumption that astronaut safety was not just the first rule, it was the only rule. But they weren't NASAnauts anymore.

They all spent more time in the exercise circle. Marc ran for hours on the treadmill, so much that Raoul complained that he was going to wear out the bearings. Since the treadmill would turn into a conveyor belt for off-loading at the landing site, this was not an idle complaint. Julia used the stationary bicycle, but worked out a lot of her feelings in push-ups, isotonics, and chin-ups. They all liked to exercise alone—time spent away from the others was getting steadily more precious—and though none of them was a very verbal type, they had to talk it out, too.

The second ERV was backup. It was to have come screaming in after they had settled in on the ground, providing perhaps a more distant base camp for far forays. The extra ERV wasn't necessary, in the day-to-day sense. Without it, nothing in their mission profile altered.

But the reassurance of having another way to get off the planet—that would be gone, for the whole 1.5 years they spent on the ground.

Not that they could do anything, of course.

But talk they did. They had to arrive at a consensus statement about the "unfortunate shortfall" the Consortium had suffered, how they "fully understood the difficult choices that the corporation had to make," and that they "would shoulder these new burdens with a sense of confidence in the long-term outcome of the mission."

It took a week more before they could all say such things to the camera.

There was help, though. Before leaving they had each sat for hours of "template setting" for a hotshot new software. Facial Management could cover for you if you were agitated, naked, fresh from the shower, or just hungover. The media managers reassured the crew that their slips and errors would be smoothed over and made better by the software. All their errors would be morphed and toned long before it went into the lucrative media mix that was paying many of the Consortium's daily expenses.

And they could review the results, if they wished, before release. They all did at first. Few did after a few months. It was eerie, watching yourself say things more confidently, with tones that carried the right accents and emphasis, complete with expressive and seemingly sincere lip movements, lifts of eyebrows, and utterly believable looks of complete candor.

"Old joke about what prostitute says to customer," Viktor observed. "Sincerity, it costs extra."

It got them through the roughest patch.

But they never forgot.

She brought up the unthinkable as a way of edging her way around to her own agenda.

What the hell, they were all exhausted from laboring on the repairs, and it had been three days since she had last mentioned the vent. Long days. And then a grand failure. Time to think the unthinkable again and do some planning.

As they were finishing lunch, Julia turned to face her three crewmates. "Okay, suppose we can't get this thing fixed. Then what?"

Raoul's face darkened, but he said nothing.

"Have to hitch ride home," said Viktor.

"But when are they getting here?"

The Airbus mission had been well cloaked, Chinese style. Publicly, Airbus said only that their crew had launched more than a year after the Consortium, and would arrive at Mars "soon." Some sketchy bio stuff about the crew of three, nothing more. A few "under wraps" leaks, but those proved to be planted.

The Germans at Airbus let their Chinese partners play the inscrutable card. Secrecy only heightened suspense.

Axelrod's moles had confirmed that it was indeed a nuclear rocket, put up on a Chinese three-stager, into a two-hundred-kilometer-high orbit. There, systems checkout took eight days—which meant they either had some minor trouble or were being very, very careful; maybe both.

Then a trial burn, which the Chinese government denied had "a significant nuclear component," double-speak for *We don't give a damn what all those European and American protesters think.* NASA and the National Security Agency both analyzed the burn optical signatures, and sure enough, it was hydrogen exhaust warmed by a medium-hot nuclear pile, design unknown.

Axelrod had sent them close-up shots of the craft, imaged from the Keck telescope complex. "It is big, sleek," Viktor had observed. "With specific impulse two and a half, maybe three times ours, they can use that much less fuel. Hydrogen—fine for getting speed up, best choice. But they are not bringing liquid hydrogen to surface of Mars?"

The Consortium intelligence operation thought the fuel for the return part of the mission could not be hydrogen, though. "Keeping hydrogen at very low temperatures, landing it, then using it to return—no," Viktor said decisively. "One heat leak and they scrub the mission. No, they have some other plan for later."

But what? Nobody knew. A day later, Airbus had laconically announced a decision for *Go*. Their big boosting burn into interplanetary space was a long, hot, silvery plume scratched across the night sky.

It had been eight months since the Airbus launch. Because of the configuration of the two planets, the trajectory guys at Johnson assumed that they were doing a Venus flyby mission. In effect a planetary handoff, the nuke would slingshot around Venus halfway through the trip, picking up extra delta vee. The physics resembled bouncing a tennis ball off a moving freight train, so that the ball came off with the train's velocity added to what it had.

That was the only way to get to Mars, launching when they did.

"Venus flyby takes ten months," said Viktor. "So they get here two months from now. Our launch window. They get here in time to see us leave."

If we leave, Julia thought but did not say.

* * *

But Axelrod had sprung a surprise, right after the Airbus launch.

"Been keeping this secret, didn't want the negative publicity," he admitted on his next priority vid. "I laid a side bet for you guys. Cost me plenty, let me tell you, and I don't just mean money. I had to tip my hat and bow for this one."

Raoul whispered, "Which means he had to pay more than he bargained for."

"You knew about this?" Julia shot Raoul a glance.

He shrugged. "Axelrod said to keep quiet."

"I went to our fellow explorers, those German Airbus management types. Followed Raoul's estimate of what he might need, if his on-site repairs don't quite work out. Dickered. Finally got Airbus to fly his box."

Cheers and shouts from all four of them. Julia glanced at Raoul again. *Keeping secrets.*

"I got the weight of all that gear down, way down. Had to. Engineers here said it's the best they can send. Parts, tools. Airbus will get it to you somehow."

"Tell them just look for only humans on Mars, we be here," Viktor said happily.

"They're under no guarantee to land at your site. They may go somewhere else, they won't say." Axelrod shrugged modestly. "Thought you guys would want to know. I hope it kind of makes up for not flying the second ERV."

It didn't for Julia, not entirely. But she had to appreciate the way he brought it off. His last flourish was impressive: "And I had to lay out a cool one hundred million dollars for them to fly it to you. Biggest freight bill in history, got to be. At least I'll get in the record books for that."

They had popped one of Viktor's last bottles of champagne over this message. "Welcome to the captain's table," he had said grandly. "Part of special mass allowance."

The voluptuous curve and weight of the bottle was wasteful to Julia's eyes, and wonderful. After nine months on Mars, they had needed a celebration. He had even produced caviar, eyes gleaming—the best pale sturgeon, in a delicate little box.

Help was on the way. And so was the competition.

"I was speaking to Katherine," said Raoul slowly, visibly trying to wrench his thoughts away from the engine failure. "They can cut the time by using more fuel. Leave Earth faster, and power decelerate at Mars." He toyed with his coffee mug.

"I, too, worked out most available orbits," Viktor said. "They come in with big velocities, eight kilometers per second. Have to lose that energy with a long aerobrake, I think."

"So they could be here anytime?" asked Marc.

Raoul shrugged. "Basically."

"We don't even know where they're going to land," said Julia. "They have to land near here or we can't reach them."

"It's a big planet," Marc said.

"Up to boss to arrange passage with Airbus."

"Okay. Even if they get here soon, they have to refuel—"

"With what?" asked Marc. He looked at Raoul and Viktor. "What can they use? What are they using now?"

"Hydrogen, probably," said Viktor. "Is lightest—most bang for mass." Raoul nodded. "What they use to go home, that is anybody's guess."

"What else could they do?" Marc demanded.

"What we did—or the ERV, I mean," Raoul said. "Bring hydrogen. Run a chem plant to pull in CO_2, make methane and oxygen and water. Even with a big nuclear reactor to run a bigger plant, that's several months' work."

Marc pressed, "You're sure?"

Raoul nodded. "We'll beat them home, I'd say."

"There are too many unknowns about Airbus," said Julia, "and I don't understand how they affect *our* mission." *I never expected this would become a technical discussion about nuclear rocketry. Time to edge us back to the vent trip. Guess I was being a little too sneaky about my intentions.* She looked pointedly at Marc. "I'm trying to go someplace else with this discussion."

"Well," said Marc, "even if they get here tomorrow, they still have to fulfill the prize conditions if they hope to win. We've collected the geological data, taken the core samples, done the meteorology, and surveyed the hell outta this corner of Mars. If they hope to win, they'll hafta do the same. That'll take time."

"It's useless to ask how *much*. It took us almost a year and a half."

"But we squirted all the data back to Earth. They know where to find everything." Marc's upper lip wrinkled with exasperation. "No dry holes for Airbus!"

Julia said mildly, trying to keep them talking despite their fatigue, "How can they use that?"

"They can't reach water very easily," Marc said. "I mean, they had to launch with some kind of plan, and I hadn't found any ice back then, when they were figuring out their mission profile."

"With lot of power, people can adapt," Viktor said, toying with his cup.

"Yeah, that nuke can do a lot of work," Raoul said.

"So there are plenty of maybes," Julia said forcefully. "But the orbital mechanics, they can't change."

"Even nuclear obeys Newton," Viktor said with a grin.

"If they miss the launch window in two months," she said, "how long are they here for? Another two years?"

"Got to be," Viktor said. "They freeze through winter, like us."

"We had cold, but at least it was clear. They'll get the southern summer first, with its dust storms," Marc said. "Nasty time to get much exploring done."

"Remember, they had no choice," Julia said. "They launched late into a screwball trajectory. Going in as far as Venus, they've come through about twice the heating we had. Probably took a lot of fuel loss from boil-off, right?"

Raoul nodded. "But they have that extra push from the nuke. They could carry more of everything—"

"Speaking of that, what's our supply situation?" She asked it although everybody knew the answer. She was afraid to let the conversation get out of the channels she wanted.

"The ERV has seven months times six people," Marc said automatically, since he was in charge of provisions. NASA had provisioned it to return a full crew of six to Earth. "We've got maybe six weeks' worth here for each, not counting greenhouse food."

"I am surprised that we have not eaten it all," Viktor said with an artificial lightness.

A clear signal to her. She saw that he, too, had caught the sense of gathering tension in the room, apparent in tone but not so far in words. Their advisors had trained "the couple," as they termed it, in "counter-conversational" tactics, useful to defuse conflicts.

Julia nodded, letting a silence grow for a moment, hoping that would help. Indeed, Viktor was right. They had devoured so much after the landing, as they adjusted to the heavy labor and constant cold, that early estimates showed them running out weeks early. So they had tapered off, watched their cold exposure—the real culprit, it turned out, not the muscle work—and got their eating rate down. Mars imposed harsh demands on the body, burning between five and six thousand calories a day. "I asked because we may have to be here until the very end of the launch window."

"Why?" Raoul demanded suddenly.

"I mean, if the repairs take longer than we think—"

"They won't." He chopped the air with his hand. "I know the problems, we can make good progress."

"I'm sure—"

"Right, Viktor?"

"I believe *our* fix, it is correct. Not the double line."

A *white lie*, Julia thought. Viktor was plenty worried about the repairs.

Marc gave Viktor a skeptical scowl. "You're sure?"

"No one can be sure until we have another test," Julia said in what she thought was her best perfectly reasonable voice.

"I am sure," Raoul said.

"You were sure before the test, too," Marc said evenly.

"What does that mean?" Raoul shot back.

Julia tried to head them off with, "Look, I don't believe—"

"Repairs, that's your whole reason for being here," Marc said, again with his deceptively easygoing manner.

"Rocks, that's your reason," Raoul said. "Which is harder?"

Marc said, "I'm just saying—"

"Maybe say less, would be better," Viktor put in.

"Harder isn't it," Marc said. "Getting the job done, that's it."

Raoul said, "I explained out there, pretty clear I thought. We been sitting here in this sand, these 'fines' you geologists call them. Not just grit, but *peroxide* grit. Smaller than anything on Earth. Microsand! It gets into those systems, eats away, works on them for years while every day and night the temperature goes up and down, maybe a hundred and fifty degrees in a few hours. No way anybody could simulate or duplicate that on Earth. So no way to plan for it. No way. That ERV, it's been here three years. We're lucky any of it works."

Raoul stopped abruptly, breathing hard, the moment teetering on a precarious point.

"Absolutely," Julia said. "No way any engineer could know what that would do. Even the Outpost experience, that was with simpler systems, easier couplings, lesser pressures—right?"

It was a calculated risk, taking one side. Marc could run up his aggravation curve, go over the top. And she needed his support for more exploration.

But Raoul had to come ahead on this one, she sensed. If he lost heart, or even slowed his relentless labors, they were all in even more trouble.

She thought again of her strategy in initiating this discussion. Get everything out into the open, agree on tasks, relieve some of the tension. And get the okay to go exploring.

She looked at Raoul and said carefully, "Well, I'm relieved you and Viktor think the ERV can be repaired, but we have a supply problem if we miss the launch window. I think Axelrod *or* NASA—and I'm not going to get in the middle of that one—should get that second ERV on its way, loaded with two and a half years of supplies."

Raoul looked very unhappy, but did not object.

"Either that, or confirm that Airbus can take us back at the launch window," she finished.

Marc said, "Yeah, why haven't we heard from them? We know the crew, why the bloody radio silence?" He was still angry, but had found a new target.

"Not very likely they can help," said Viktor. "Even with a nuke, mass is mass. Seven people plus food is no doubt more than they can carry."

"You're sure?" Julia sat up, startled.

"From its dimensions, from simple scaling laws—

yes." Viktor looked at each of them in turn. "Do not expect miracles."

"Damn," said Raoul. "I'd been hoping . . ."

"Who wants to go limping home with them anyway?" Marc grimaced. "Christ, after all this time, we've worked our asses off doing those inane manufacturing tests, collecting all those samples—and all for nothing."

Before the conversation veered again into confrontation, she leaped in with her trump card.

"Raoul, I have no reason to doubt your assessment of the dust problem. You and Viktor can't be expected to fix the unfixable. If all the seals are exhausted, or the metal is fatigued, it's a major miscalculation on NASA's part. It's a *planning* failure, not a mechanical glitch. The ERV you're trying to fix should've been only the backup, to give us reserve fuel and an oxygen supply. Our return ship should've launched just after we did, not two years before. Earth needs to send us a fresh vehicle."

Raoul looked at her with surprise.

Through Viktor, Julia had sensed Raoul's growing frustration with the repairs. Every time he looked at a new system, he found the same creeping disintegration. He was attempting a Sisyphean repair, and the weight of the boulder threatened to crush him. But he wouldn't give up. Couldn't. Latin pride plus astronaut training equaled superman image.

Viktor had the last word. "Raoul and me, we want to test again—with our single line—and soon. If there are still problems, we go ahead with Julia's idea."

Nods all around. Nobody spoke. Their fragile peace worked best with silence.

He was the commander and had taken the decision. A big hill had been crested. She'd caught them off-guard with her assessment, and it had worked.

But Julia was still unsatisfied. She gritted her teeth.

Damn. I couldn't quite get there. It'll have to be after the next test. But maybe this was more useful. After all, it's 40 million miles to the nearest grocery store.

13

JANUARY 14, 2018

EARTHSIDE MEDIA REACTION WAS INTENSE. THEY ALL FELT it, even behind the thick screen the Consortium kept between them and the rampaging media.

She got a long e-mail from Robbie and Harry, plus all the other relatives. Once you were famous, she had learned, every distant cousin was on the doorstep. They remembered poignant moments from childhood, fraught with portent for the future Mars voyager—all on interview shows or in op-ed pieces, and so what if Julia herself couldn't remember those episodes?

Okay, she had to admit to herself, she had gotten

cynical. Years of exposure to the Mesh's worse problem—having an essentially infinite number of pen pals—had sharpened her sense of the absurdity of it all. Here she was in very real danger, and she was expected to take time to answer letters about it.

The others felt the same, but each handled it in a different way.

Viktor had long since stopped sending anything but bland visuals to anyone but his mother. Raoul sent long e-mails to Katherine and a very few others. Marc, though, wrote general letters that got reposted to a huge list of "intimates." Julia did the same, trying to make them less stiff than they needed. The Consortium had contractual rights to see these group letters, scooping off any reasonably good writing for "on Mars" journalism pieces under their bylines, polished up by staff and licensed out by Axelrod. Showbiz.

Even in this crisis, the system worked. Habit, mostly, and they all had found during the long flight here that they needed the time away from each other, to speak to another audience than the same three mugs they confronted each breakfast.

They had met only one other real crisis, and it had been the same then, though compressed.

Three days after their boost out of low earth orbit, well beyond the moon, they had done the spin-up for centrifugal gravity. Carefully Viktor blew the bolts that freed for deployment the cable-gravity system.

This was the scheme the Magnum booster had been going into orbit to test. The postmortem showed that a pump failure lay at the bottom of the spectacular blowup that had killed the original Mars crew.

So no one had actually done the entire run-through, from launch to spin-up. There had been trials at the space station, but no trial could simulate every dynamical aspect. And astronauts were trained to be professional skeptics about any piece of new gear.

They all huddled around the cockpit as Viktor checked systems and then blew away the unneeded outer manifold. Their external camera showed a clear separation. The cable came snaking out, then, as the upper stage of their Magnum eased away.

"Clean snake," Viktor had said in a precise, controlled voice that could not hide his joy.

The cable had to take the full eighty-five tons of the habitat plus the upper stage, all subject to 0.38 Earth g, the Mars normal. Viktor let it unfurl fully, two hundred meters like a slick fishing line dwindling away. He fired the hydrazine thrusters. Plumes blossomed from both the long tube of the empty upper stage and the habitat. They accelerated smoothly, upper stage becoming their counterweight.

"Some of the manifold bolts don't fire correctly," Viktor noted, eyeing the video. "See?" Small motes tumbled in the darkness along the cable, winking on and off in the sunlight.

Raoul said, "Right. That seems minor. They came off the separation cowling, I guess."

"Should stay with cowling," Viktor said.

"Good riddance."

They were all in their acceleration couches by then, feeling the return of partial gravity. Julia had felt 0.38 g in the centrifugal spinner of the space station, but as she got up and walked around this felt subtly different. The other system had used a short, ten-meter rotation arm, and when she had walked then her inner ear sent out faint alarms. None here.

Raoul was running the video camera for Earthside, plus the in-cabin fixed one, as Viktor pulled a champagne bottle from the refrigerator. Viktor's eyes popped in mock surprise. "Drink on board?!" for the home audience. They all laughed and beamed and watched Viktor pour an enormously expensive long pale golden stream into Julia's glass, falling in slow-mo in the new gravity—

Thunk.

"What is?" Viktor's brow wrinkled.

They sprang to the external video. Tumbling away into the blackness was a sharp piece of ragged painted metal and a bolt attached to it.

"Damn!" Viktor said. "Cowling fractured."

Raoul studied the dwindling shape. "Must be those bolts didn't come free easy, stressed the frame, tore it."

"So we spin up, we run into it." Viktor wrenched his mouth around, as he always did when a piece of inanimate matter did not behave.

Marc glanced at the cockpit board. "We got a light on the internals."

They all turned as one. Julia was still cradling the glass she had not drunk from.

"Water pressure," Marc said. Plumbing was one of his subsystems, though Raoul had responsibility for the overall ship systems, plus their integration.

"We're losing it," Raoul said. He punched in a

question and the systems inventory showed them digits declining. "That's a pressure drop."

They looked at each other, each reaching the same conclusion as Viktor: "Cowling punch a hole in outer habitat jacket."

The hab was a cylinder with water-filled walls that functioned also as a radiation shield. Once they landed, the water would also provide thermal protection against Mars's bitter cold. Ingenious, but the designers had not anticipated the danger of collisions to the precious water supply.

"It's that thin?" Marc asked. "Just a piece of metal—"

"Moving a few meters per second, yes, could," Viktor said. "Did."

Raoul had done a quick calculation. "Dropping, but not fast. This is a tiny leak, maybe as big as a thumb."

"We can't live with that," Marc said.

"Got to go EVA." Viktor scowled at Raoul. "We."

It would have taken a month to lose their water through the hole, which was halfway up the habitat outer skin. Which meant that they would die perhaps four months before reaching Mars.

Raoul went outside first. They had to use the surface suits not really equipped for this kind of repair—the downside of going lean and mean. It was worse than a zero-g excursion—the only kind any of them had ever performed—because they could not de-spin the habitat. The hydrazine was gone. Their mission profile provided for losing their angular momentum as they approached Mars by simply blowing the cable, setting the upper stage and cable into a long orbit into the solar system. There was no propellant to adjust their centrifugal gravity up or down after they had reached the 0.38 level.

Raoul had to go out the main lock with Viktor. They rigged a line around the lock lever and stepped out into the 0.38 g pull. Julia had watched it all on the video, her heart thumping. This was an utterly untried exercise, something nobody had ever done, not even in the station trials.

They worked their way around to the handholds thoughtfully set in the habitat skin. Progress was slow. Raoul gave a yell when he saw the thin plume of water foaming into a white fountain from the jacket.

Julia could barely see him on the forward vid screen, around the curve of the habitat. Nobody had thought of this problem, of course, and nobody had thought of how crazily the stars veered when you were wheeling around in a big circle every minute. The sun's glare swept like a spotlight across the hab's skin, followed by a thirty-second night. The swift change in the light levels alone was disorienting. Add to that the pinwheeling stars . . . It was hard enough watching it from inside.

Raoul got to the spot while Viktor played the line out. "Some of the debris from the manifold bolts is stuck in here. I'm pulling it out."

She could see more water billow out, turning to vapor, making it hard to work. He worked for ten minutes on the job and then said over comm, "I can't make a patch hold against the pressure. These weren't made for positive pressure at all, y'know."

"Got to be can block it," Viktor insisted.

"You come up here and try."

This was not a jibe, but a legitimate request. EVA operations were legendary in zero g. Done in a suit not optimum for the task, clinging to a wall in 0.38 g's—as they all agreed, it was an astro-nightmare. Viktor tried and failed, too.

They were running out of suit time. The Earth link was full of nonadvice, the sort of hand-wringing that was Mission Control's first reaction to the unexpected.

"I don't think we've got anything aboard that can take positive pressure in a vacuum for long," Marc said.

A long silence. Julia could hear Viktor's labored breathing over her suit comm.

Julia said slowly, "I can think of a trick. Let me look into it, guys. Hold on."

"Is what we are doing."

"I've got to check some things."

"Make it fast," Raoul sent, voice filled with knotted frustration.

She found a circular sealant layer in the maintenance kit. The hardest part of the operation proved to be climbing up to the hatch opening, near the habitat ceiling. There she opened the emergency access to the water system. The entire habitat was sheltered by a layer of water a hand's length deep. Water's hydrogens give, ounce for ounce, the best shielding against the solar wind and cosmic rays that lance through the inner solar system. Not that their water blocked all of the speeding particles. But since water is also the great essential in the life-cycling system, Axelrod had sprung for an ample supply. Every kilogram of the stuff had cost more than a normal astronaut's annual salary to launch to Mars, and every minute one of those kilograms was fizzing off into the vacuum outside.

She felt tight apprehension as she dropped the brilliant blue patch into their water supply. It sank.

"We can live with the taste," she said airily. It came out brittle and high-pitched.

Her idea was that the suction of the leak would draw the patch to the inner part of the puncture. Long moments ticked by. The digits on the internal monitor showed steady loss. Raoul and Viktor clung to the hull, watching their vital supply vent into pearly fog, then nothing. Julia waited with them.

"Hey! Is stopped."

The fog thinned.

"Here, slap this on again," Raoul said.

With Raoul's external patch, the blockage from inside held.

She learned later that the entire drama had taken nearly two hours. It seemed like longer in memory. Nobody had noticed that the video cameras were following their motions, overridden by Earthside and slaved to Mission Control. The entire planet had anxiously watched Raoul and Viktor, or at least the portion of their helmets visible over the curve of the hull. And they had seen her scale the wall and drop the patch in. In an ordinary vid show this would have been boring stuff. In real time, it was high drama, living history.

Julia was upset at the vid coverage, at first. It was too much to ask that they star in a home movie that might have ended in their deaths.

Never mind that their losses meant that it was going

to be a dry voyage. To keep adequate shielding water in the walls meant using less in the life cycle. Short showers, very careful cooking and cleaning. Finish all drinks. No wastage. Like living in a desert.

But their quick, efficient teamwork had enthralled the globe. It was the first time they'd confronted a real crisis together, not a training simulation.

Raoul emerged as an instant media hero, mostly because he was in camera range more of the time than the others.

When it was over they all slept most of the first week, not wholly from fatigue, but from the need to escape the sense of a closing vise around their lives. Recovery was slow. Each spent time talking to their personal counselors.

Axelrod loved it. "The worst trips make the best stories," he said, and meant it.

Stories—they realized that they were now immersed in what was, for everyone on Earth, an ongoing serial story. And in the long dull days following, they relaxed in the tiny social room of the circular hab and began to invent their own versions. They began writing their memoirs. There would be four solid best-sellers out of this, no problem, already under contract with fat advances paid.

Amateur writers all, they started out with titles which they tried out on each other.

"I think I'll call mine *Mars or Bust*," said Marc.

That got a laugh from Raoul. "More like *Mars and Busted*, don't you think?"

"I know—*Mars ~~or~~ and Busted*." They howled with

laughter, delayed release from earlier terrors.

"Together on Mars," suggested Viktor, grinning at Julia.

Axelrod had a surer sense of drama. Faster than the crew, he had long ago realized that folly was acceptable to the public if it was *his* money at stake. If the taxpayers were paying, they demanded certainty, safety—and then got bored if it was dull, dull, dull. Apollo 11 had been a perfect technical masterpiece. *Apollo 13* the movie grossed hundreds of millions.

Some thought all this undignified. NASA had trained many to think that only emotionally repressed pilots spouting acronyms were The Real Stuff. Largely without planning, the Mars crew had become media icons, each standing for some faction of the metapopulation. Raoul was the Minority, Marc the Good Guy, Viktor the Lovable Foreigner.

Of course Julia had to play Stalwart Heroine, Feminist Pioneer. Of course; only she couldn't remember her lines.

Long before the famous water crisis, they had gotten used to being celebs: the Bright Stuff. By the time they launched there were Mesh betting parlors on chances for a booster blowup just like the last one. (Not great odds, either: 23 percent for failure, Viktor reported.)

The analogy that seemed to frame it all was Antarctica. Scott, Amundsen, and Shackleton had made their classic races across frozen wastes, high drama in a place distant, hostile and worthless. Mars was a comparable canvas for the twenty-first century.

For Shackleton, self-promotion had been essential all the way. He had paid all his expenses with media tie-ins, one way or another: auctioning off news and picture rights before he left, taking special postage stamps along to be franked at the south pole. After he made it, his bestseller had nine translations. He spruced up his expedition ship into a museum and charged admission. With a lecture tour and a phonograph record, a first film of the Antarctic and countless newspaper interviews, he made his way into history—and prosperity. Even when he could not reach the pole, he returned to Europe with a sound bite: *Death lay ahead and food behind, so I had to return.*

By the time they actually reached Mars, the world had gotten used to this modern manifestation of the same phenomenon.

Name That Peak! Again, Shackleton had done it first, sticking the names of his patrons on spots in the Antarctic. Beardmore Glacier, its name bought for $34,000—big bucks, in those days. How about selling rights to name the Valles Marinaris, a 2,800-mile-long trench? Axelrod asked the question and there were plenty of takers lined up. In principle the lucky "donor" could then title the chasm for anything, but it seemed unlikely that the sort of hard driver who became a media tycoon or retailing genius would go for anything except his own place on the Martian map—price suitably adjusted to the size of the geographical object, of course.

The International Astronomical Union stiffly disputed him in court, since they had rights to name astronomical objects. But Axelrod claimed "explorers' rights," his lawyers basing their opinions on early eighteenth-century legal precedent. The case got bogged down in several courts. Axelrod kept selling anyway. He even published a map showing prominent craters, plains, and mounts with their proud new names. Olympus Mons became Gates Mountain.

Once on Mars, the beat went on.

Live from Mars, It's Saturday Night!—she and Viktor had made millions by exchanging scripted lines before the camera, all to be duly synchronized with straight lines from Earthside pop stars. It was fun, in a way. There certainly wasn't much to do on a Saturday night on the real Mars, a dead blackness a hundred degrees Centigrade below zero outside.

So in a way, the media frenzy that leaked through to them, as they labored on ERV repairs and rested in silence, had a familiar old-shoe flavor.

To Julia, it was a lifeline. They all needed one.

14

JANUARY 15, 2018

As it turned out, Axelrod anticipated Julia's scenario. After the ERV engine test failure, his NASA-naut detractors were quick to point out that *their* mission profile wouldn't have left the crew without a backup.

"Your mission never left the ground," was his widely reported response. This was a heavily edited version of his real retort, according to Janet, in a private correspondence to Marc. She had been in the comm center with Axelrod when the exchange took place.

In public, Axelrod defended his mission plan as conservative and downplayed the danger. Nevertheless, he told the crew, he was "feeling out" Airbus about "a possible cooperative strategy."

For the first time in months, Julia saw glimpses of the old Axelrod in the vids he recorded. The rambling, overly familiar discourses to the crew were replaced by controlled, almost formal squirts. Delivered in measured tones and intended to be reassuring and supportive, these almost certainly had been heavily massaged by the psych advisors. And probably face-filtered for warm and fuzzy expressions, too.

Despite the crew's dislike of having to rely on Airbus, even Raoul had to grudgingly admit that it was "good to know the bastard is working on getting us back."

Axelrod's actions seemed to Julia to be a glimmer at the end of the tunnel. Maybe candle-sized, and flickering in a high wind. For most of the day she thought about the negotiations taking place on Earth for their return, while she played gofer for Raoul and Viktor. She decided to try again.

After dinner she turned to Marc. "Okay, suppose we can get off at the launch window. With our ERV or with Airbus. What do you think we could do now with the highest impact?"

Marc looked surprised. Nobody answered for a very long time. In their weary faces she read a vast reluctance to face this issue. She realized with a start that the three men were already finished with the exploration part of the trip. They were completely focused on packing up and going home.

But she was not.

Finally Marc said slowly, "Geology, maybe."

Viktor laughed sourly. "Scratch scientist, find fanatic."

Marc bristled. "This vent thing is making me rethink—"

"Geology, we have plenty," Viktor rumbled on. "A cold, dry desert with red rocks and ancient water erosion. Not much better than the Viking pictures."

Raoul said reasonably, "Julia, this is an old argument. Of course the Viking landing spots were purposely picked to be flat and boring and dry. Not the best places to look for life, but the safest to land. Now we know Viking could never, anywhere on Mars, have found microbes that retreated below ground when the seas and lakes dried up."

"Over a billion years ago, I estimate," Marc put in. "Maybe two."

"We don't know that those fossils are the whole story," she said. "Stromatolites on Earth were the beginning, not the end, of evolution."

Viktor called, "Ah, your new version of the old Sagan argument. While Viking was licking dust into the biology experiments, an undetected Martian giraffe walked by on the other side of the lander."

Julia bristled but did not show it. Sometimes she wondered if Viktor had to occasionally show that he was not an automatic ally just because he was her husband. "You know I'm not really expecting Earth-type animals, but I'm keeping an open mind about other possibilities."

Marc blinked. "You really think we'll find something alive in that vent?"

"I certainly think we should look. We're probably never going to be here again, any of us." She looked around at them. "Right?"

This they had never discussed. In some ways the surface mission was the safest part of the expedition. Their coming launch was risky, and the aerobraking into Earth's atmosphere would be more tricky than their rattling deceleration in the comparatively soft Martian atmosphere. Still, the sheer wearing-down of laboring in the harsh, cold dryness of Mars had sobered them all somewhat. When they returned home—or if—they would be wealthy, famous. Would they do this again?

"I might come back," Marc said.

"I, too," Raoul said, though without the conviction he had before.

"I am honest enough to say that I will not." Viktor grinned at them. "I will have a wealthy wife, remember."

They all laughed, maybe more than the joke deserved. Warm chuckles, after a filling meal, served to remind them that they were a team, closer than any contracts could bring them. This was a highly public, commercial enterprise, of course, but none of it would work without a high degree of cooperation and intuitive synchronization.

Julia looked at the others, their clothes emblazoned with the logos of mission sponsors, all quite soiled. Through the Consortium's endless marketing they had endorsed a staggering array of products. But this grand adventure was not itself a product. They were destined to be a team forever, no matter what happened in the future.

Marc said, "The metals, that's why I'm here. They'll be more important than fossil life, in the long run."

"Not so," said Viktor. "Asteroid belt is where we will go for metals. Mars is where we build base to mine the asteroids. Going to be much cheaper to boost from here than anyplace else."

Raoul emerged from the pint-sized galley toting his coffee. It was in a large mug, incongruously solid ceramic, in sharp contrast to the rest of their lightweight plastic dishes. Katherine had hand painted it with flowers for him early in their courtship, and he had toted it with him as part of his personal mass allowance. Only he ever used it, of course. He sipped and scowled. "So we've just wasted our time looking for metals on Mars? Suits me. If we jettisoned all of the damned ore samples there'd even be room to breathe on the return."

Julia said, "We shouldn't be limited by what we think we know. Or what we think we're going to find. A biologist named Lovelock pointed out, well before the Viking landings, that there was probably no life because the atmosphere was in chemical equilibrium with the surface. Spectroscopy from Earth showed plainly that there was nothing in it but boring CO_2 and nitrogen."

"Good argument, you have to admit," Marc said.

"But it assumed life would use the atmosphere as its buffering chemical medium. Unlikely, because it's so thin . . . so, what about life that has long abandoned the atmosphere?"

"How could it do that?" Marc looked puzzled.

"Life may be holding on deep underground. Using emissions of, say, hydrogen sulfide, as an energy source. That's just a guess, of course, but we'll never know if we don't look. And we can't do that except through the vents."

"Good theory, but until we get the ERV fixed, there's no use talking about what else we could be doing." Raoul had his set look, jaw solid and eyes narrowed, announcing his position.

They had been through all of this before, of course. In the course of two years you get to know each other's views pretty damn well.

Life at Zubrin Base—their unofficial name, in honor of the hot-eyed founder of the Mars Society—settled into a dull routine of ERV repair, machine shop work, and normal maintenance. Through the long hours Julia dreamed of the vent, heard the clock ticking in her head, and seethed inwardly.

After a frustrating morning of hanging around doing trivial gofer tasks for the repair effort, she headed for the greenhouse. The task of trying to grow food on Mars was hers. A colony would need to produce much of its own calories to avoid the kinds of supply problems faced by Napoleon's army in Russia.

One of the best-kept secrets of the space station age

was that the astronauts had not been living in a closed system. Far from being self-sufficient, Mir, Skylab, and the International Space Station had been just end points of Earth's delivery system. Oxygen, food, and water were ferried up, depleted tanks were returned to Earth, and garbage was just dumped, to eventually burn up on reentry into the atmosphere.

It fell to private, Earth-based experiments to start work on the problems of recycling within closed systems. The Biosphere II project in the Arizona desert had become a legendary cautionary tale by the time Julia joined the NASA astronaut corps. That two-year experiment in the 1990s had hardly been a success—everyone lost weight, medical emergencies led two people to be evacuated, and there was a mysterious loss of oxygen from the system.

Finally, fresh air had to be pumped inside to save lives. The culprit turned out to be the slow chemical curing of the tons of concrete in the buildings, binding oxygen within the walls of the structure. It was a complete surprise to the mission designers.

Closed life-support systems were still not practicable. Even on Mars, the crew used the local atmosphere to chemically fabricate their oxygen and water. That's what the ERV's chemical plant had been doing all this time, using hydrogen brought from Earth to produce methane and oxygen. When burned as Rover fuel, it produced waste carbon dioxide and precious water. What had been in most short supply was hydrogen. But since Marc's discovery of the frozen pingos, future missions could use indigenous Mars hydrogen from water.

Food was still an unsolved problem. Julia was working on a series of trials proposed by NASA and contracted with Axelrod, following on years of research by earnest nutritionists.

They had long ago established that in the long term, the colonists' diet would be vegetarian. It made sense to eat plant protein directly, rather than lose 90 percent of its energy by passing it through an animal first. So early on, the Consortium crew had set up an inflated plastic greenhouse next to the hab. They covered it with recycled parachute material, scavenged from their landing, for extra UV protection for the plastic.

In an inspired move, Raoul had hooked up the air-exhaust vent from the hab to the intake of the greenhouse. Warm air enriched with CO_2 for photosynthesis, but with enough oxygen for plant respiration, flowed into the greenhouse, displacing the arid CO_2 of Mars. The heat helped to keep the plants from freezing overnight.

After about two months, Julia's plants were growing strongly, and her tests showed that the oxygen content in the greenhouse was more than adequate for humans to breathe.

The hab's air system provided clean, moisturized air at ⅓ Earth sea level pressure, like living on a mountaintop at 23,000 feet but with plenty of oxygen. So they didn't feel altitude effects, and had lots of energy, but the air tasted flat.

When Raoul opened up the return path for the air, they clustered around the duct in the hab and waited. That first whiff of greenhouse air proved to be a great morale boost for the crew, their first non-canned air in over eight months. Greenhouse air was processed through plants, and it carried with it the fresh smell of Earth.

Never much of a gardener at home, Julia came to prize her time in the greenhouse. Inside she could work without helmet or gloves. With just a skin suit on, she could shuck her Marswear insulated outer garments.

What she enjoyed best was looking through the rows of plants, through the clear side walls to the dusty red landscape beyond. She could imagine then that Mars was a hospitable planet, and that humans would someday come here to stay.

She'd shared these feelings in a brief missive to the Mars Society, and had been inundated with e-mail from would-be colonists. The idea of growing food on Mars was immensely symbolic as well as practical.

About three dozen types of plants seemed suitable for colonists' diets and the hydroponics system, including cultural superfoods like wheat, rice, and potatoes, various beans, and popular vegetables like broccoli and tomatoes. They'd grown some of these in the hab during the flight to Mars, in a prototype tank system called the Garden Machine.

Once on the surface, Julia established large hydroponic trays, then moved on to tests using Martian soil.

When she'd first heard of the project, she'd been skeptical. But in the large folder of research reports there had been just enough biology to interest her. No one really knew, for example, what the combination of low gravity and low sunlight would do to the plants. Earth-based agronomists had done their best to gene-engineer them for the light levels, about 43 percent of Earth's, but the gravity effect was a virtual unknown. As with centrifugal gravity, the tests simply hadn't been done.

So Julia's work was cutting-edge research in its own right. As she'd planted her first seeds, she felt a kinship with ancient hunter-gatherers, taking the first tentative steps toward agriculture by poking seeds into the still-mysterious ground. Their experiments had culminated by populating an entire world. Maybe hers would do the same.

Not as exciting as deciphering Mars life, but it was still satisfying. And they could eat the results.

There was something very calming about being surrounded by green leaves and vines, nodding gently in the endless updraft of the air from the hab. The floor level was distinctly cooler, as she and Viktor had experienced, even though it was set on an insulated pad and Raoul had managed some inductive coil heaters. They had taken advantage of the absence of Raoul and Marc, off on a rover trip, to make love amidst the plants. It had been an exciting, though chilly, experience. It'd always been a big turn-on for her to look over the shoulder of a lover into the foliage of a tree. Viktor joked that it showed she was a real primitive.

They all went to the greenhouse when they were tired of the endless sunset hues of Mars. Or when they longed to see something alive that wouldn't talk. So she wasn't too surprised when Marc slipped in the quick way they'd engineered, to retain the air.

She smiled to acknowledge him, then turned back to her plants, prepared to ignore him. Privacy was precious, and they'd adopted the Japanese habit of not intruding on one another's space.

But Marc wanted to talk. He popped his helmet and parka, and came right over.

"Got some results you might be interested in."

"Oh, what's that?"

"Did the isotopic dating on the pingo ice core, thought you'd want to know." He looked expectantly at her.

"Well, of course I want to know. What'd you find?"

He grinned slyly. "It's not what I expected."

"Too old to date?"

"Nope."

She stopped working, turned to look at him. He was drawing this out on purpose. That was Marc's style when he had something important to say. He let you know by making a little drama out of it. Like the discovery of the pingo water.

"Do I have to guess or are you going to tell me?"

"Before I do that, do you remember the scenario I described for Gusev in particular, and Mars in general?"

"Sure. Basically, you said the planet's engine had died, in fact some time ago. The fossils we found were old, belonging to a long-ago wet and warmer time. The fact that they were in two different levels separated by sediments and volcanic layers meant that there had been another warmer, wetter time. Gusev held a lake at least twice, and that's why we found the fossils inside the crater."

"Okay, given that scenario, how old would you expect the ice to be?"

"Pretty old, maybe a billion years or so."

"Not a bad guess."

"Is that what you got?"

"Nope."

She was beginning to feel exasperated. "Well, then it isn't a good guess."

"No, no, it's a good guess. It's just that my scenario was wrong."

"How?"

"Suppose I told you the ice was young—very young, in fact, for Mars."

"How young, or do I have to guess again?"

"Say, ten million years old."

"But that's—"

"Way young, right." He rushed on. "Not only that, the ice seems to be all about the same age, within the limits of dating error. So it all came up at once."

"Wow. So what's the bottom line?"

"The planet's not quite dead. There's probably volcanic activity still going on in that big cone, Apollinaris Patera, about two hundred klicks north of here."

"Wait a minute, that means—"

He grinned. "Yep, your vent could be nice and warm down below, probably always has been. A comfy place for life."

They were both grinning, like two schoolkids with a common dream.

They didn't wait for dinner to call up the satellite downloads. As usual there were routine situation analyses—"sit-als"—done Earthside, from the raw data their hab systems shipped out automatically. The satellite web above kept Mission Control in constant touch, which could be a pain. Now that they were in trouble, it was a comfort.

Marc insisted on going through the sit-als first, but there were no red flags. When every breath you take is brought to you by a complex set of overlapping functions, chemical and hydraulic and electrical, you pay attention to early warning signs.

Then Marc palmed the console to General Messages and there was Axelrod, as they had hoped. Gray trousers pressed to razor-sharp, blue yachting jacket, yellow shirt, matching gray tie; a color treat. Julia tried to read his mood and failed. Probably pointless, given the face filters.

"Hope you-all had a good day. Ever'body here's awaiting your update on the repairs. I know it's slow work, but you're the best. I've got every confidence in you."

"Quick compliments," Raoul said, "always a bad sign."

"I've been negotiating hot and heavy with Airbus, just like I said I would. Offered them a lot, I got to say. If their nuke is so powerful, you'd figure they could take some of you back, right?" He blinked. "Not that I'm thinkin' you'll need it, of course. This is just for backup. Only . . ."

Unusually, his eyes drifted off camera. "Uh-oh," Marc said.

Axelrod's eyes swept back and Julia could tell he was suppressing very real anger, eyebrows pressing toward each other. "They turned me down flat. Just not interested, they said. No deal possible, this Chinese guy says to me, smooth as a swindle."

Axelrod had enough sense to sigh, look down at the floor, give them time to absorb this. Julia could feel the rising rage around her, laced with suddenly tightened mouths, downcast eyes.

"They launched hoping we couldn't fix the ERV," Marc said. "Damn! They must be celebrating now."

"A calculated risk," Raoul agreed. "Betting against me."

"Against us," Viktor insisted. "We are a team."

"Vultures," said Julia. She could feel her mind racing, searching for an angle, a new plan, a way out.

Axelrod gazed at them forlornly. "Wouldn't even *discuss* options. Like talking to a man who holds all the cards. They just smiled and 'expressed concern'"—here his eyebrows rose, then crashed down again—"and said they did not want to deal with us at all. *At all.*"

"They just brushed us aside?" Julia asked incredulously. *All our hopes, our plans, our hard work here . . . what will it all add up to if we can't get home?* She felt a thin tendril of despair.

Viktor scowled. "Me, if I were Airbus, I would worry about us later. After I am on the ground."

"Why do you say that?" asked Julia.

"They must be approaching fast," Viktor said crisply. "They will be worrying about aerobraking. Their trajectory, if they land soon, maybe two weeks from now, it brings them in with higher delta vee than we had. Maybe seven, eight kilometers per second. That is a lot of energy to burn up."

"It's only possible if they're a smaller ship than ours," said Raoul.

"They can't have much room on board, then," Julia said, groaning inwardly.

"No, this isn't coming from the Airbus crew," Marc said. "The goddamned suits are calling these shots."

"Do they wear suits in China?" Julia asked. "More like uniforms."

"Meaning this is essentially decision of government?" Viktor said calmly, plainly trying to keep the discussion focused and professional.

"Airbus is a collaboration of businesses that might as well be state bureaucracies," Julia said. "Who knows how they think?"

"Or if," Raoul added.

"Look at it positively," Julia said, though she certainly wasn't feeling that way. "Maybe they are just counting on Raoul's fixes working, once we get that repair kit they're delivering."

Marc said sourly, "Yeah, the hundred-million-dollar kit."

"Somehow I don't think that's it," Raoul said somberly.

Axelrod had continued speaking through their discussion. The words ". . . your fuel?" came clearly across as Raoul stopped speaking.

"Hey," Julia said. "What's he saying? Are we recording this?"

"Sure thing," said Marc, sitting down again. "In fact, this *is* a recording. The squirt came in while we were doing sit-als."

"Back it up. Let's hear what he said about fuel."

"Keying search on words 'at all,' okay."

A brief pause. Axelrod again stared at them from the screen, eyebrows lowered. "At all," he said. He shook his head in disbelief. "I'd even put the fuel in the ERV on the table to get the discussion going." His voice lowered. Quietly he said, "Bottom line is, they don't think they need us to win. Now, my info is that their nuke is too small to be carrying fuel for the round-trip. Maybe you have some ideas about what they could use, besides our methane/oxy? I'd love to hear them." He suddenly looked squarely into the vid pickup. "I have no idea what they're planning, but just to make sure, have you thought about protecting your fuel?"

A shocked silence descended on the crew.

Axelrod looked apologetic as he continued. "Now, my lawyers tell me the Law of the Sea defines a derelict as an unmanned vessel, so as long as someone is aboard the ERV it can't be salvaged by someone else."

"What's he talking about?" Julia yelled. "Airbus is going to *steal* our fuel? Oh, God, the man's mad."

"Maybe not," said Viktor amiably. "Why pay when can just take?"

"That's a ridiculous idea," said Julia. "What kind of mind would dream up something like that? This isn't 'Terry and the Pirates,' this is real life. We know the Airbus crew. They're like us. Astronauts! Civilized people! They don't act like that."

"Do, and did," said Viktor. "Mutinies aboard ships not uncommon in 'civilized' British Navy."

"I take his point," said Raoul. "Thirty billion dollars

is a lot of money. People have killed for a lot less."

Julia looked around. "Marc? Do you agree, too? Am I the only one who thinks this is crazy?"

Marc shrugged. "I dunno. It seems far-fetched, but there's no harm being prepared. Maybe one of us *should* sleep in the ERV."

He looked at Viktor.

Viktor shrugged. "We wait until Airbus arrives, or until we get better information about situation."

"My repair shop's already there. I can go," said Raoul.

"Good. Is settled." Viktor stood up. "I go cook dinner."

That's all it takes, thought Julia sourly. *They're blithely preparing for an invasion from Earth! From planetary mission to action film in the space of a few minutes.*

She felt her anger welling up. Out there, just a few tens of meters below the ground, was Mars's greatest secret, and she would never get there at this rate. Not while her crewmates played their ridiculous little boys' games.

She stomped her way back to her cabin.

15

THE NEXT DAY SHE GOFERED AGAIN, BUT THERE WASN'T much business.

Raoul spent most of his time in his ERV workshop, carefully fashioning collars around the plumbing he had repaired. A lot of the wrecked metal he had to melt, recast, and rework on a lathe or hot-press foundry. These tools were little miracles of lightweight design, hauled from Earth at his insistence.

His judgment had paid off in spades. Without these beautifully engineered instruments they would have been doomed from their first day here, unable even to begin repairing the damage the ERV had suffered on its landing. But now Raoul complained, when he was tired and down at the end of every day, about how little he had brought. Every evening he found a new variant on "If I'd just brought a . . ."

So Julia gave him—and Viktor, who with his bum ankle labored as well as he could at detail work in the ERV shop—all the help she could. But a machinist she wasn't. After a few mistakes Raoul discouraged them from even coming into the ERV bay where he worked.

Getting in and out of anything—ERV, habitat, the pressured rover—was so laborious, they kept the "lock-pass-throughs" (a NASA term) to a minimum. And with every one they brought red dust fines into the ERV, even with the two-shower system designed to wash them away.

So by midmorning she was out of work. She was getting away with a nonprotocol method, running errands for Raoul and Viktor in a skinsuit instead of the bulky, full-pressure lobster shell she should have used. The skinsuits were highly elastic jobs that sealed the wearer up at high enough pressure to work, without using the pressure joints and elaborate infrastructure of the big suits. Of course, even with a battery pack and electrical wiring to heat it, the skinsuit demanded an outer layer of arctic-style jacket and leggings. She felt like the Pillsbury dough boy, but better off than she would in the full pressure, tin can suit.

And nobody had ever mastered the cycle in a lobster suit, either. She pedaled the tricycle around on her errands, the movements far easier in her skinsuit, and relished the almost nostalgic feel of it.

Biking on Mars! Even with three balloon tires to keep her gliding over the sand, it *felt* like a bike ride. Cruising along summer avenues, or cross-country, had been a childhood pleasure. She could not help but cast her mind a mere half year ahead, when she would be biking down to the shimmering beach with her parents, a warm wind sending her hair streaming, Viktor laughing beside her . . .

Maybe, she reminded herself sternly.

After two years, the crew functioned smoothly together, anticipating one another's needs wordlessly. The efficiency of true teamwork bore fruit: now they were ahead of schedule for the next engine test.

Still, she could not let go of her own itchy ideas. The night before, she had lain beside Viktor in the cool darkness and let her thoughts run. Or rather, spin pointlessly, with no traction to guide them.

She needed a good, solid talk, but sensed that Viktor was too distracted to really hear her. Time to have a session with Erika, her Earthside counselor. She was trying to think of a way to work it in when Marc came inside with another task.

As biologist, she managed the hab's life support. The air scrubbers needed adjustment and filter changes. It was her turn to do the housekeeping, too. They fought a steady battle to keep dust down. Their suit shower plus self-shower converted the virulent peroxides on the dust surface to oxygen, a useful gain, and left her with watery soil for the greenhouse. They used a toilet that neatly separated solid and liquid waste, and the urine got recycled.

The one trick the bioengineers had not managed was converting the solids to anything useful or even nonsickening. Let the next expedition "realize existing in situ resources," as the NASA manuals had put it, by composting.

The biological protocols demanded that they bury their waste here. Now their third capsule of wonderful waste was ready. "Let's do it now," Marc said. "One less item on the list for the final checkout."

It took two hours for her and Marc to get the awkward plastic liner out of the hab underskirting and onto the hauling deck of the dune buggy. Amazing, how large half a year of four people's shit was! A big, brown mass inside a mercifully opaque plastic sack, compacted and frozen solid. They had to do this—in full pressure suits, of course. Marc had already dug the pit for it a few klicks away, using Rover Boy's backhoe. The peroxide dust would probably eat through the plastic within a few years, but then it would also neutralize the biological elements of the mess. Here was the bizarre surface chemistry's sole advantage—it made the risk of contamination tiny. No isolation lab on Earth was remotely as hostile to organic chemistry.

Mars taught hard lessons. How much Mother Earth did for humans without their noticing, for one. Recycling air, water, and food was an intricate dance of chemistry and physics, still poorly understood. She had to tinker with their systems constantly. Let the CO_2 rise and they could all be dead before anyone noticed anything wrong. Watch the moisture content of the hab's air or they would all get "suit throat"—drying out of the throat until voices rasped.

Humans were walking litterbugs. The four of them shed human dander, duly vacuumed up and used in the greenhouse for valuable proteins and microorganisms. Early on, she had set out a sample—"a dish of dander," she had called it in a published Letter to *Nature*—and Mars had killed every single cell within an hour. This surface was the most virulent clean room in the solar system.

Finally she could distract herself no longer from her inner conflict. She told the others she needed a break and went into the hab. "Good, rest," Viktor sent on comm.

First, she showered twice and had a tiny glass of cognac—a minor breach of rules—to put the dung job behind her.

As soon as she had water on for tea, she turned on

some piano pieces by Chopin. They all had divergent musical tastes. Viktor liked awful, moody Tchaikovsky and Mahler, Raoul some skippy South American steel-drum bands, Marc syrupy string gloop. Seldom could they agree on music over the hab speakers for long. Instead, they listened to their headphones. Safety dictated that they not play music while in their suits, because sound was a useful warning.

Chopin's brilliant, fast runs were soothing as she sat herself before the vid camera, needing a talk session. The real-time link was open, as it should have been, so she unloaded all her pent-up pressures on her counselor Earthside—Erika the Eager, Julia's private name for her. Julia had gone for days without sending anything to Erika, and now, alone in the hab, she found all sorts of largely unsorted emotions gushing out.

"Erika, you asked me last time why I was unsatisfied with the mission, and I stalled. Okay, here's the truth. Home!—sure, I want to get going. Sometimes, the call of it is an ache in my heart. My Mums and Dad, and the—what's that old saying?—the cool green hills of Earth . . ."

The trouble with delayed therapy was that her monologues lacked shape. With eight minutes' time delay, real ping-pong discussions had proved impossible.

Still, they helped. She went on.

"Leaving Mars . . . Y'know, behind me I can feel the yearning of millions, of a whole civilization reaching out. I want to bring them something really *big*."

As she talked it out, she understood better. Why *had* the issue of life here come to loom so large in the contemporary mind? It dominated all discussions and drove the whole prize-money system. Viktor and Raoul thought economic payoffs would be the key to the future of Mars, but they were engineers, bottom-line men, remorselessly practical. Just the sort you wanted along when a rocket had to work, but unreliable foreseers, particularly in their prophets-of-profits phase.

Certainly profit had motivated Axelrod to mount this whole huge project. But there was more to it than that.

She suspected that the biologists themselves were to blame. Two centuries before, they had started tinkering with the ideas of Adam Smith and life-of-the-party Thomas Malthus, drawing the analogy between markets and nature red in tooth and claw. The dread specter of Mechanism had entered into Life, and would never be banished, not after Darwin and Wallace's triumphal march across the theological thinking of millennia. God died in the minds of the intellectuals, and grew a rather sickly pallor even among the mildly educated.

All good science, to be sure. But to Julia, the biologists had left humanity without angels or spirits or any important Other to talk to. Somehow our intimate connection to the animals, especially the whales and chimps and porpoises, did not fill the bill. Humanity needed something bigger.

"So the way I see it is, behind our being here is a restless, unspoken craving. It's the scientific class, people like me, reaching out—through the space program, through the radio listeners of the Search for Extraterrestrial Intelligence—for evidence that we intellects aren't alone. *That's* why our discovery of fossil microbes satisfied nobody, not even me."

She poured into words her sense of the tragic desolation outside. Mars had fought an epic struggle over billions of years, against the blunt forces of cold and desiccation, betrayed by inexorable laws of gravitation, chemistry, and thermodynamics. Had life climbed up against all the odds, done more than hold on?

"To me, evolution of even bacteria in such a hellish, dry cold is a miracle. But I can't leave it at that!"

She went on about trying to persuade the others, the varying positions of each, then remembered that this wasn't a strategy session. And Erika would not enter into any quarterbacking, anyway. Each counselor kept professional confidentiality and stayed out of crew disputes.

"So, well, just wish me luck. And don't try to talk me out of it!"

The trouble with therapy at long distance was that she would have loved a response *right now*. She paused, feeling awkward. "I just have to face up to the others, I guess."

She could get an answer that evening, after Erika had a chance to think and frame something suitable; the counselors were on instant demand by the Consortium.

But as she punched off with her usual wry salutations, Julia realized that she did not really need a reply. Once the pressures were out, she felt much better.

The vent beckoned. And there was such a short time left.

16

SHE TOOK A CALCULATED RISK THAT EVENING, BRINGING up their first day here.

They were all tired and edgy. Mars had worn the corners off them. As she watched the weary figures riding a dune buggy back from the ERV in the stretched shadows of twilight, the memory came back sharp and clear.

Partly it was the contrast. After landing they had left the Mars Landing-Habitat Module—soon to be just "the hab"—all four together, stepping off the landing pads together on cue, so there was no single First On Mars. That was planned; even Axelrod liked the gesture.

Before them lay a sandy vista streaked with radial blast marks from their landing exhaust. A few kilometers away reared the hilly walls of Thyra Crater, craggy and darker red, the minor welt a mere punctuation mark compared with Gusev Crater. A hundred fifty kilometers across, its ramparts reared all around them a kilometer high, catching the slanting rays of early morning like a vast shining wall.

Her first thought had been, *It's even more beautiful than I had hoped.*

The others felt something similar, she felt, but they carefully said nothing. This portion they had debated endlessly. As the hab cameras and their own handhelds watched, each of them made a gesture. None knew what the others planned. A large fraction of the human race would discover their decisions at the same time—or rather, after the time delay for transmission.

Each had done something quite characteristic.

Viktor had planted the Consortium flag. "But for the whole world. Remember that Mars belongs to no one country. It is for all of us."

Marc had been undecided about what to do. In the end, his geologist's curiosity led him to turn over a rock. "This is igneous, but plainly shows signs of water erosion. Already something exciting!"

Julia looked under Marc's rock for signs of life. Nothing, of course, but she had felt a thrill to actually get a sample into her gloved hands.

Raoul had bent down, scratched a straight line in a rock ledge nearby.

"What, you're drawing a line?" Julia asked, laughing. "Us on one side, Airbus—if they ever get here—gets the other half of the planet?"

Raoul smiled. "Nope, it's a one. One day. And we have five hundred and seventy to go."

So that evening, when she reminisced, she hoped it would make them think about all that had happened to them here. She even recalled their celebration of Katherine's baby two months after Raoul became their hero by sealing the water leak. Anything to bind them together, she figured.

When she received Erika's return message, and played it on her slate, she was pleased to see the counselor give the same sort of advice. "Plant thoughts about what they're really there for," Erika had said in her warm, soothing tones. "Let your shared past do the work for you. Don't harangue."

This was further than Julia could remember Erika going. Did the tight little circle of counselors and psych types have an agenda, too? No matter; if they were allies, all the better.

She cooked that evening, a luscious beef stroganoff done in rich creamy style with a lot of freeze-dried mushrooms. It was damned good, and they had the last bottle of red wine with it. Moods lightened. Raoul fell asleep at the table.

Seven weeks to go before the absolute optimum minimum-energy orbit for Earth.

Message from Earthside: No communications from Airbus, no update on their position. The German side of the operation did send a note that their team had the capability of sending down the "repair kit" Axelrod had paid so dearly for. It could come in on a small aeroshell and parachute to within approximately twenty-five kilometers of their site. "If the Mission Commander so decides," the German message concluded.

"Hundred million and they do not deliver to door," Viktor grumbled as he made coffee.

Raoul was silent and distracted, staring into space as he ate. Over breakfast Julia signaled to Marc, took a deep breath and made her pitch. The last few days' work had pushed them hard. More than that, it had nudged them across an unseen boundary in their feelings. For them, Mars was a onetime experience. Once they left it would be all over.

But she had to try. She crept up on the subject, reasonably indirectly—or so she thought.

Raoul's head jerked up. "This is going to be about that vent trip again? I thought we laid that to rest. You didn't find anything the first time."

"Absence of evidence is not evidence of absence," she shot back.

Raoul frowned. "Besides, there isn't time. We've still got the test to do."

"We're ahead of your schedule," said Julia.

Viktor cut in quickly. "Under normal circumstances, would be true." He gestured at his ankle cast. "With this, I am clumsy. It takes longer to do everything." He peered at Julia. "I need your help."

They all knew that a public admission of weakness cost him a lot, and it touched her. He had said as much when they lay in each other's arms. But she was determined not to be swayed. She refused to meet his eyes. *Damn. Why did women always have to choose? He never would've asked that of a man.*

Impassioned, she used her Columbus argument—how could they go home when there was the chance they had only nibbled at the edges of discovery? Columbus never set foot on the continent that bore his name.

Nods, but her little speech moved nobody.

Marc gave her a quick glance and she saw that he was going to come to her rescue. After days of grunt work, the scientist in him yearned for this last chance as much as she did. The dung job had somehow united them, without their ever discussing it.

He gave them all his easy smile. Again she had the

flash recognition that he could quite easily have become an actor of the Tom Cruise type. He was naturally mellow, the sort of man everyone liked immediately.

"We can do it in two days," Marc said amiably. "We'll work here tomorrow morning, fine. Get a lot of gear set up in the ERV. Then we drive Red Rover to the site and set up the pulleys by nightfall. Next day we'll explore the vent and come back. Minimum time lost. Plenty of room left before the liftoff test." He looked at Viktor and Raoul. "Bottom line is, we feel we have to do this."

Technically, the two scientists could amend mission plans if they felt it was warranted. Viktor could overrule that. But he shook his head, opened his mouth—

—and a priority message popped up on the board, softly buzzing. When they called it up, there was Axelrod.

"Hi, my guys! I got to come at you right away on this one. No news from Airbus, no, but I been thinking about that vent you found. It could be a big thing, and I don't like the idea of walking away from it."

Julia frowned. When they had reported on Viktor's ankle and the vent, Axelrod had barely spent a sentence on anything but the injury. Now he was all concern, shaking his head with folded arms, the camera shooting him from below as he leaned back on his mahogany desk under soft indirect lighting.

"If you can find time in your schedule—and only if— I'd sure appreciate it if you could give that place another look-see. Maybe Julia and Marc, if they can be spared?" A winning grin. "Thing is, we're all of us back here proud of all you've accomplished, but if there's something in that vent that bears on life on Mars—life still, well, alive—we'd sure like to know it. That would enhance the value of this expedition for all humankind. Think on it, will you?"

He gave them a salute as his image faded.

Silence. One by one, the men turned to look at her.

Julia said, "You think I went to him."

"And you didn't?" Raoul's scowl was frankly disbelieving.

"No. Not a word."

"You were in here a long time yesterday, all alone," Marc said.

"I called Erika. That's all."

"You're sure?" Raoul's scowl did not go away.

"Damned right I'm sure!"

Viktor had kept his face blank the whole time. His eyes bore into her. "Then this is serious for two reasons," he said gently.

"Axelrod's giving us orders, that's pretty serious," Marc said. "*We* are in charge of scheduling on the ground."

"Is true," Viktor said, "and if was just that, I would not be getting, as you say, my shorts in a knot. We could maybe spare you two for a day. But big point is that the counselors are not reliable now."

They all nodded. A cardinal point for the last two years had been their private transmissions. Nothing was more personal than their counselor chats. There they could pour out their feelings, whine and complain, vent anger, lapse into depression or self-pity or anything they liked, and it would not get back to anybody on Earth. Or Mars. A release.

"Damn bastard," Marc said.

"Yeah," Raoul said sullenly. "How long has he been piping into everything we send? Even"—he sat upright—"my talks with Katherine." His jaw clenched.

Viktor's face was composed, giving nothing away, but she could tell it was a struggle for him; his fingers had knotted into tight bunches, their tips white. "Why does he give this away now?"

"Maybe he just slipped up, didn't realize we'd figure it out," Marc said.

"Or maybe he doesn't care whether we know, not now," Raoul said bitterly. "Now that we've got to bust ass just to get home. So what if he piles on the work? So what—"

"I think is his error, you are right," Viktor moved into Raoul's building tide of anger. "He thinks maybe we are too tired to figure him out? And he smells a big story here, maybe the biggest—and has already sold to TV or somebody."

Julia said, "I don't think he's quite that bad. It could be that Axelrod simply wants to get one more triumph out of this expedition. He's sure we'll come home, and he wants us to have the most glory, the most discoveries, we can."

Marc looked at her with genuine curiosity. "You're ready to put that positive a spin on it? It was your conversation with Erika he tapped into."

She shrugged ruefully. "Don't I know it. Who is the leak? We'll never really know, not until we get back and get these clowns alone to ask."

Viktor said softly, "Did Erika give any sign later? That she had . . ."

"No, none I could read."

"So we can't know," Raoul said. "Either Axelrod eavesdropped or Erika ratted."

Marc said, "How long it's been going on, we dunno that either."

"So we put it aside," Viktor said decisively. When he was being captain his sentences rose at the last word, cutting off debate. It worked well, and Julia had always wondered if he was even conscious of it. Better not to ask; it might kill the effect for him.

"We just forget?" Raoul asked.

"Until we get Earthside, yes," Viktor said. "And in meantime we consider what Axelrod says at face value."

Julia said, "We might as well."

A long silence—while they searched out their feelings, Julia guessed. And how did *she* feel, anyway? Betrayed by Erika—if she was to blame. By Axelrod, maybe. But without proof of either, there was no point in belaboring the issue. Like so many things, it had to go on the shelf, marked DO NOT OPEN UNTIL ON EARTH.

She had developed a whole category of such matters. It helped to know that she was not accepting defeat, just putting off a battle.

Raoul looked pensive. "Well . . . okay. A while ago, I was going to say that I do want to go over the thruster assembly again. Some pressure releases might need adjustment after that misfired burn." He hurried on, "But I can do it alone."

Julia understood that Raoul wished to take responsibility for the repairs, needed to have time alone with his handiwork. He would be just as happy not to have two itchy scientists underfoot. Then he could take as much time as he liked, obsess over every detail.

A long moment passed. They skirted the edge of a rift.

Finally Viktor nodded agreement. He had followed Julia's arguments carefully, hoping to be convinced. Now he snapped back into mission commander mode. "Da. All right. Two days only."

Julia's heart soared. She flashed him a brilliant smile, leaned over, and ignoring mission discipline, gave him a big kiss. Spending one final night in a hellishly cold rover would be the price, but well worth it. They all beamed at her and she saw that the many currents between them had suddenly, unaccountably, met and merged.

Worn down they might all be, yet there was a bond between them now that none could express.

She restrained herself from kissing every one of them.

17

THEY SET OUT THE NEXT DAY AFTER LUNCH. THE panorama of Gusev crater opened before them as they moved north across the rumpled, pitted floor that told, to a practiced eye, a story running back over billions of years. She watched closely the shifting scenery in its lurid pinks and rusty splashes, knowing she was seeing it for the last time. Somehow, each vista seemed fresh.

The Mars Outpost program, starting in 2009, had left at the site several long-lived robotic scientific experiments, the Rover Boy, and a small chem plant that sucked carbon dioxide from the atmosphere to make methane and oxygen. Above the outpost orbited three communication satellites, supplying constant contact with Earth. With several more satellites left over for navigation and surveillance of the area, Earth had known just about as much about the Gusev Crater region as it could without putting people on the ground. Maps galore. But all that technology had missed the most important facet: the wonder of it.

Nearly four billion years before, a huge asteroid had splashed into the crust here, opening a deep crater that nothing had been able to fill. To the south, as the highlands drained of water, a deep channel called the Ma'adim Vallis had cut through the kilometer-high crater wall, flooding it. A cooling lake had stood here for many tens of thousands of years—so Marc said, after careful study of his corings. It might have lapped at the highest cliffs. White-water rapids rushed from the highlands, sending great sheets foaming down in roaring waterfalls. Then the big volcano to the north had erupted, spewing lava and gas and water into the crater. Several nearby impacts had sent more liquid gushing from the warmed crust. Several times the crater's lake had frozen over, only to melt when an asteroid smash or the fitful climate of Mars allowed.

All this history was written on the ramparts that towered over them as they marched north in Red Rover. Marc had traced it all out.

"Y'know, my work here has been damned interesting," he said as he carefully edged them over a sloping sand dune and down the face. "I can't shake the feeling that it's been mostly a waste, though—except for the pingos."

"Come on!" Julia said, not taking her eyes off the moving scenery.

"No, that's the way I feel. Take that long trek we went on, through the subsidence morphology terrain and on up the Ma'adim Vallis. I got to show that a helluva lot of water ran through there once. Measured, bored, traced out the meanders—the works. Even found some benches to prove that there were earlier floor levels, which got undercut. So there was a big river running through that valley, a thousand klicks long and a klick deep. Where did it go?"

"It's somewhere under our feet, you told me," Julia said helpfully, letting him run.

"Only place it could be, yeah." Marc gazed morosely out at the ruddy cusp dunes and car-sized rocks. "I spent over a year trying to get some Mars ice, and only here at the last do I get lucky. Some geologist I am."

She reached over and clenched his hand. He had been more closed up lately and this was more direct than he usually could be. "You worked your tail off."

"Remember when I climbed up that wall in the Ma'adim? Thought I saw a real tributary mouth up there. Busted that tail of mine climbing four hundred meters, pinning myself to that rickety rock the whole way. I got to tell you, I was scared. Didn't want to say so, but I was."

"I could tell."

"It was that obvious?"

"People say all sorts of things when they're exhausted."

"I was, when I got back, wasn't I? Damn fool stunt, but we didn't have enough gear to do it in a two-team rig." His eyes never left their course but she could tell his inner recollection was more vivid than the rumpled plain before them. "So I violate protocols—"

"*We* violated them. I was holding your drop line."

"—risk my stubborn neck, and it turns out it was no feeding stream at all. Just a wale. No smaller channels in the upland surface to feed the ol' Ma'adim. No runoff, so no rainfall. Only needed one!—to prove there had been rain. Couldn't find it."

"There had to be rain."

"Prove raindrops fell, four billion years later? The academics will want more than rock cores and arm-waving."

"You've got the ice cores."

"Which prove there were lakes. Sedimentary layering for sure. But the water could have oozed out of the ground.

Fluid erosion features, that's all I've found. No little creeks, no feeder drainage networks carving up the plains."

"The water is hiding underground. It's staying away from the sun, which would break it down. Smart water."

He laughed, dispelling his own mood suddenly. "Smart water, dumb geologist."

"It wasn't dumb to build that enhancement on the drill."

"Raoul's idea, mostly."

"But you made it work."

"It was simple, once I thought to try it. I took too long."

"Drilling into the pingos from the side? It wasn't obvious to me."

"If they'd sent a wildcatter with common sense—"

"And your first five tries failed. A wildcatter would've walked before that."

"I was lucky to find it in six."

"Okay, so not all those pingo hills have water under them, at least not so shallow."

"It was just good luck, last-minute luck."

"Your 'luck' was mostly sweat and intuition."

They reached the first of the pingo hills in midafternoon, running exactly in the tracks of Marc and Raoul's last expedition. Protocol: avoid new dangers. A new route would hold unknowns, perhaps deadfalls or a rock slide just waiting for a passing vibration to start it downhill.

Marc kept up a lazy discussion of the vent, and she answered, but her mind was elsewhere. She had devoted her life to space, but in the end it was this hostile yet beautiful land that she loved.

Until now, all active astronauts had been exclusively near-Earth-orbit guys, never out of sight of the looming custard clouds below. The deep range of the blackness between the worlds felt utterly different from near-Earth space, where the great ice cream planet hung over you like an ever-changing artwork of milky white swirls and hard blues and misty greens, encased in the precariously thin eggshell film of pale air.

Just going to Mars had changed that forever. On the long voyage they had hung between the eternity of diamond-shard stars as though frozen in their embrace, unmoving but for the hab's gravity-giving cartwheel. No reassuring Earth hovering nearby. Longer and longer pauses within radio conversations, until those became impossible.

Awaiting them was a real place—ruddy mystery, not just a slice of vacuum. Living here was different in a way she could not name. Not like a space station, though there were locks and gear and procedures in common. Not like the moon, though it had dust and dryness. She had never been there, but she knew that Mars resembled the moon, with bad weather and more danger. But more, it had a deep history it concealed artfully.

She wrestled with this, tried to talk about it with Marc, and could not find the words. Traditionally astronauts were minimal talkers. Here they still slung around the space cadet lingo now and then, but as the mission wore on they found English more useful. TWAs—three-word acronyms—faded, especially after you forgot what they stood for. But personal stuff was as hard as ever. Finally she descended to cheerleading. "Look, we give

this vent a good shot, then we can go home with more than we had any right to expect."

"I still want to find out if it ever rained here."

"And I want to find out if those fossil microbes in your cores were the last Martians, or the first."

"Lots of luck. Me, I've got my eyes on other prizes."

It was quite like him to leave a leading question open like that. "Such as?"

"My agent, Carlos Avila? I got good news from him. A contract for a co-lead in a big new syndicated space epic."

"Wow. Movie?"

"No, vid."

"Think you can pretend to be a big-time space guy?"

Marc gave her a smile that might as well have a canary feather sticking out of it. "I start a month after we get back."

"You've got the looks for it."

"Hey, Carlos said we all do, for stuff like that. It turns out that actors are usually short, compact people. Something with the way our features photograph."

"I'm not short."

"Not *short* short. Compact."

"We're strong, sturdy."

"So was Arnold Schwarzenegger. He was also shorter than you."

"Really?" She laughed. All four of them were light. Astronauts generally were, to fit into tight spaces and consume fewer expendables. So far they had not suffered for it here; the 0.38 gravity helped.

She mulled over the idea. "So we should all go Hollywood?"

"What's left, after Mars?"

Somehow the question stuck with her. *What's left?*

An odd sensation, looking down the slope of her life from this pinnacle. It was hard for her to think that this was truly *it*, the last big thing she would ever do. Going back would be six months of boredom followed by endless Earthside ticker-tape parades and fawning fans. Pleasant enough, maybe, but astronauts were not attention-hounds. They wanted to *do*, not just *be*. Acting in fake spectacle vids and making speeches to the Rotarians . . .

She shook her head. *Stay in the present. Mars isn't over . . . yet.*

When at last they rolled up to the vent she insisted on going out. That meant suiting up and Marc didn't want to. Getting into a lobster suit was a chore and he was comfortable where he was. "Let's do the setup in the morning."

"Nope, I want to eyeball the site. And I want to spend all the time tomorrow underground."

So they violated protocol. He watched her on the external camera while she checked the vent in the waning sunset light. Carefully she followed the boot prints she and Viktor had left, partly filled in by dust already.

"No change that I can see," she sent over comm. "No signs of another outgassing here, either."

Disappointing, but then, ice would have sublimed away here within a few days. Her heart pounded just to see the place again, even if it was a rather unimpressive little hole in the fading light.

She carefully walked back up the incline, remembering hauling Viktor this way. Their boot prints were wind-
blurred.

She unhitched the two winch assemblies and freed
the climbing harnesses from their mounts. Cables were
still neatly coiled, the yokes ready. Neatness counts, especially on Mars. The cables were incredibly strong and
light, the best carbon fiber. Thin wires threaded through
the carbon also carried their suit comm transmissions
back to Red Rover, for relay back to base if they needed it.
Carefully she checked the connections and sent a hailing
signal to the ship, whose onboard answered automatically.

"All set!" Job done.

Now for a reward. The first month here she had
often gone out to witness the splendid ruby wonder of
sunset. Dawn was even better, with ice clouds that
quickly vanished, but much colder. Already a hard chill
came stealing up from her boots.

What she had truly come out to see was rising as the
glorious crimson sunset began to fade. A ruby radiance
suffused the horizon, and above it rose a lustrous blue-
white dot. Earthrise.

A resplendent smudge, brimming brighter than
Venus. She peered closely and could make out the small
white point to one side. The only primary-and-moon
visible to the naked eye in the solar system.

Until now, that tiny little interval had been the full
extent of the human reach. On the bigger creamy-blue
dot, a million years of hominid drama had been acted
out, blood and dreams playing on a stage a few miles
thick, under a blanket of forgiving air.

Then those brawling hominids had reached out. Half a century of sweat and ingenuity and courage had taken the species to the other dot, its alabaster, beckoning brilliance.

Now she could stand here and see the twin worlds of her birthplace for their true nature, a small neighborhood wonderland gliding through a hard darkness. One world was an airless desert, the other a moist promise.

The ground she stood upon had also held promise, once. Water had swirled here, Marc said, a kilometer deep. Volcanoes had belched and fumed into that ancient lake bed. Cooked by heat and violence, organic chemistry had worked its slow magic. Life arose and briefly bloomed.

What had it come to? Anything?

18

JANUARY 19, 2018

SHE WOKE TO THE BITING TANG OF BLACK COLOMBIAN perking in the pot, the scent mingling with a buttery aroma of pancakes, the sizzle of bacon in its lake of fat, all lacing in their steamy collaboration to make a perfect moist morning—

And then she snapped awake, really awake—on the hard rover bunk, hugging herself in her thermoelectric blanket. Once all her waking dreams had been about sex; now they were about food. She wasn't getting enough of either, especially not since Viktor's ankle.

The sprain would heal by the time they were on the long glide Earthward; their rations would not improve until they were back eating steak. She pushed the thought of meat out of her mind and sat up. First feelers of ruddy dawn laced a wisp of carbon dioxide cirrus high up; good. Today she got to burrow, at last.

"Hey Marc! I'll start the coffee."

No dallying over breakfast, though the hard cold that came through the rover walls made her shiver. She peered out the viewport as she munched a quick-heat breakfast bar. They would run on in-suit rations today, no returning to the Spartan comforts of the rover.

By the early pink glow the cable rigs still looked secure, anchored to the rover's twin winches, which revved up nicely with a thin electrical whine. Marc didn't trust the soil here to hold, based on some nasty close calls. So first they arranged cross-struts of monofilament cabling, to take lateral shear as they went down the steep incline. She helped drive into the loose soil a Y-brace that would keep their lines from scraping on the rim.

Care taken now would pay off in speed down below. They each had a separate winch and driver, rugged and light. Metal cable was much too heavy to fly to Mars, and not necessary under the lighter gravity. So far the peroxide dust did not seem to have affected the tough fibers. So far.

The first part was easy, just backing over. She always felt a bit funny, stepping backwards down a steep drop. They had practiced in Nevada deserts, but here the utterly unknown was at her back, where she couldn't see it. A ruddy sunup was just breaking in pink streamers across the distant hills. Shadows the color of dried blood stretched across the hummocked land.

At the rim the rock was smooth, and this time, dry. There was no trace of the ice and intriguing organic scum she had harvested with Viktor only a week earlier. Any vapor from the vent had evaporated away. The Martian atmosphere was an infinite sponge.

The vent snaked around and steepened as the pale light of late dawn from above lost out to the gloom. The rock walls were smooth and eight meters wide.

"Big hole," she said, "once you get inside."

"Promising," Marc allowed. "Gotta be cautious about geology we don't understand yet."

They reeled themselves down, letting the winches do the work. Quickly they reached a wide platform and the passage broadened further. Every ten meters down they checked to be sure the cable was not getting fouled. They were both clipped to it and had to time their movements to keep from getting snarls.

Cautiously they edged along the ledge, headlamps stabbing into the darkness. She was trying to peer ahead but her eyes were cloudy for some reason. She checked her faceplate but there was no condensate on it; the little suit circulators took care of that, even in the cold of full Martian night. Still, the glow from Marc's suit dimmed.

"Marc, having trouble seeing you. Your lamp die?"

"Thought I was getting fogged. Here—" He clambered over on the steep slope of the ledge and shone his handbeam into her face. "No wonder. There're drops of something all over your faceplate and helmet. Looks like water drops!"

"Water . . . ?"

"We're in a fog!" He was shouting.

She saw it then, a slow, rising mist in the darkness. "Vapor on Mars?"

"A water-ice blend, I'd say. Condenses out pretty fast, see?" White crusts coated nearby rocks.

"Not pure water."

"No, probably hydrogen sulfide and stuff, too."

She wanted to snap her fingers, but of course her gloves stopped her. "Yes! It could be a fog desert in here."

"A what?"

"Ever been out in a serious fog? There's not much water falling, but you get soaked anyway. There are deserts where it doesn't rain for years, like the Namib and the coast of Baja California. Plants and animals living there have to trap the fog to get water."

She thought quickly, trying to use what she knew to think about this place. In fact, frogs and toads in any desert exploited a temperature differential to get water out of the air even without a fog. When they came up out of their burrows at night they were cooler than the surrounding air. Water in the air condensed on their skin, which was especially thin and permeable.

Julia peered at the thin mist. "Are you getting a readout of the temperature? What's it been doing since we started down?"

He fumbled at his waist pack for the thermal probe, switched it to readout mode. "Minus fourteen, not bad." He thumbed for the memory and nodded. "It's been climbing some, jumped a few minutes ago. Hmm. It's warmer since the fog moved in."

They reached the end of the ledge, which fell away into impenetrable black. "Come on, follow the evidence," she said, playing out cable through her clasps. Here the low gravity was a big help. She could support her weight easily with one hand on the cable grabber, while she guided down the rock wall with the other.

"Evidence of what?" Marc called, grunting as he started down after her.

"A better neighborhood than we've been living in."

"Sure is wetter. Look at the walls."

In her headlamp the brown-red rock had a sheen. "Ice! Enough water to stick! Last week some of this stuff was all the way up to the entrance."

"I can see fingers of fog going by me. Who woulda thought?"

She let herself down slowly, watching the rock walls, and that was why she saw the subtle turn in color. The rock was browner here, and when she reached out to touch it there was something more, a thin coat. "Mat! There's a mat here."

"Algae?"

"Could be."

"Hot damn!"

She let herself down further so that he could reach

that level. The brown scum got thicker before her eyes. "I bet it comes from below."

She contained her excitement as she got a good shot of the scum with the recorder and then took a sample in her collector rack. Warmer fog containing inorganic nutrients would settle as drops on these cooler mats. Just like the toads emerging from their burrows in the desert?

Analogies were useful, but data ruled, she reminded herself. Stick to observing. Every moment here will get rehashed a millionfold by every biologist on Earth . . . and the one on Mars, too.

Marc hung above her, turning in a slow gyre to survey the whole vent. "Can't make out the other side real well, but it looks brown, too."

"The vent narrows below." She reeled herself down.

"How does it survive here? What's the nutrient source?"

"The slow-motion upwelling, like the undersea hydrothermal vents on Earth."

Marc followed her down. "Those black smokers?"

She had never done undersea work, but everyone was aware of the sulfur-based life at the hydrothermal vents. Meter-long tube worms and ghostly crabs. They harvested from the bacteria that existed on chemical energy in the warm volcanic upwelling. The vent communities on Earth were not large, a matter of meters wide before the inexorable cold and dark of the ocean bottom made life impossible.

She wondered how far away the source was from here. Kilometers?

Down. Slow, careful, watch your feet.

In the next fifty meters the scum thickened but did not seem to change. The brown filmy growth glistened beneath her headlamp as she studied it.

Poked it. Wondered at it.

"Marsmat," she christened it. "Like the algal mats on Earth, a couple of billion years ago."

Marc said wryly, puffing, "We spent months and only found fossils, up there in the dead lake beds. The real thing was hiding from us down here."

Ten meters more. Reeling out the impossibly thin black cable, the life cord.

The walls got closer and the mist cloaked them now in a lazy cloud. "You were right," Marc said as they rested on a meter-wide shelf. They were halfway through their oxygen cycle time. "Mars made it to the pond scum stage, and it's still here."

"Not electrifying for anybody but a biologist, but better than just fossils. This is more than just algal scum. It implies a community of organisms, several different kinds of microbes aggregated in, okay, slime—a biofilm."

She peered down. "You said the heat gradient is milder here than on Earth, right?"

"Sure. Colder planet anyway, and lesser pressure gradient because of the lower gravity. On Earth, one klick deep in a mine it's already fifty-six degrees C. So?"

"So microbes could survive farther down than the couple of klicks they manage on Earth. They're stopped by high heat."

"Maybe."

"Let's go see."

"Now? You want to go down there now?"

"When else?"

"We're at oxy turnaround point."

"There's lots in the rover."

"How far down do you want to go?"

"As far as possible. There may be no tomorrow. Look, we're here now, let's just *do* it."

He looked up at his readouts. "Let's start back while we're deciding."

"You go get the tanks. I'll stay here."

"Split up?"

"Just for a while."

"Mission protocol—"

"Screw protocol. This is important."

"So's getting back alive."

"I'm not going to die here. I'll go down maybe fifty meters, tops. Got to take samples from different spots."

"Viktor said—"

"Just go get the tanks."

He looked unhappy. "You're not going far, are you?"

"No."

"Okay then. I'll lower them down to the first ledge if you'll come back that far to pick them up. Then I'll come down too."

"Okay, sounds fine. Let's move."

He turned around and started hauling himself up the steep wall. "Thirty minutes, then, at the first ledge."

"Yeah, fine."

"Julia . . ."

"See you in thirty minutes," she said brightly, already moving away.

Into utter darkness. Marc's helmet light receded

quickly. The slope below was easy and she inched down along a narrow shelf. Paying out the cable took her attention. Methodical, careful, that's the ticket. Especially if you're risking your neck deep in a gloomy hole on an alien world.

Despite the risks, she felt a curious lightness of spirit—she was free. Free on Mars. Maybe for the last time. Free to explore what was undoubtedly the greatest puzzle of her scientific life. She couldn't be cautious now.

Her brother Bill flashed into her mind. Marc reminded her of him, but was much more wary. Bill had taken life at a furious pace, cramming each day full, exuding boundless energy. They went on exploring trips together as children, later as nascent biologists. He was unstoppable: up and out early, roaming well after dark. There was never enough time in the day for everything he wanted to see. "Slow down, there's always tomorrow," people would tell him.

But his internal clock had served him well, in a way. He was cut down at age twenty-two when his motorcycle slid into a truck one rainy night when sensible people were home, warm and dry. Looking around the church at his funeral, Julia felt he'd lived more than most of the middle-aged mourners. Bill would've approved of her right now, she was sure.

A flicker from her handbeam brought her back. She looked down, shook it. The beam brightened again. Damn, not now.

"Marc! Bring some batteries, too. My handbeam's getting feeble."

A long pause. Had he heard? She relied upon the

signal going up the thin wire in her monofilament cable, then getting rebroadcast from the rover to him. A useful backup for times like this, when they were out of line of sight. But did the connection still hold, after 500 days exposed to the brutal weathering here?

"Yeah, copy. Had to get up that last long climb."

"Easy does it."

The harness and yoke under her arms was making it impossible to move around. She wrestled it off and held it in one hand while she worked her way around a protrusion. It felt good not to be tied up. She was getting the knack of moving down here. Slow, steady, letting her eyes pick out telling details.

The mat was thicker here, as she'd guessed it would be closer to the elusive source.

She landed on a wide ledge and moved briskly across it, mindful of time passing. The floor was slippery with Marsmat but rough enough so she could find footing. *Sorry*, she said silently to the mat, *but I've got to step on you.*

Her handbeam flickered again, died. She shook it, leaned forward to look at it with the headlamp, then felt a sudden hard blow to her forehead.

The lamp went out.

She fell backwards. It was like a dream, plenty of time but nothing to grab.

Slow-motion, into the Martian darkness.

19

SHE BECAME AWARE OF A FAINT TINNY CONVERSATION interspersed with crackles.

Ghost voices . . . sounded like . . . she concentrated . . . Viktor . . . and Marc.

Of course! It was her suit comm. *How dopey of her not to recognize them right away!* Now what were they saying? Something about Airbus and a landing. More crackles. She was too far underground to hear clearly. She gave up. *Marc would tell her later.*

She lay there, waiting for the surprise to go away, automatically checking her suit readouts. All normal, no damage. She'd dropped the handbeam in the fall. *Must've run into an overhang.* Utter pitch dark.

Where was her damned handbeam? There was a faint glow to her left. *That must be it.*

She started to get up, noticed a feeble luminescence ahead of her. Confused, she sat back down. *Take this carefully.*

All around her, the walls were developing a pale ivory radiance.

She closed her eyes, opened them again. The glow was still there.

No, not the walls—the Marsmat. Tapestries of dim gray luminosity.

She reviewed what bits she remembered about organisms that give off light. This she hadn't boned up on. Fireflies did it with an enzyme, right. Luciferase, an energy-requiring reaction she had done in a test tube a few thousand years ago in molecular bio lab. Glow-worms—really fly larvae, she recalled—hung in long strands in New Zealand caves. She remembered a trip to the rain forest of Australia: some tropical fungi glow in the dark. Hmm. Will-o'-the-wisps in old graveyards, fox fire on old wooden sailing ships . . . could there be fungi here?

Damned unlikely. She couldn't even get mushrooms to grow in the greenhouse. Wrong model. She shook her head. Waves breaking at night into glowing blue foam during red tides in California. Those are phosphorescent diatoms. What else? Thermal vent environments . . .

Deep-sea fish carried luminescent bacteria around as glowing lures. *That's it.* The lab folks had fun moving the light-producing gene around to other bacteria. Okay. So microbes could produce light, but why here? Why would underground life evolve luminescence?

Bing bing bing—the warning chime startled her out of her reverie. She flicked her eyes up. The oxygen readout was blinking yellow.

Thirty minutes' reserve left. Time to go back.

As she got up she brushed against her handbeam. She picked it up but left it off. Navigating by the light of the walls was like hiking by moonlight.

Gingerly she made her way up to the harness and yoke. It had been dumb to take them off, of course. But sometimes even stupidity paid off. She might have missed the luminescence if she hadn't fallen, her handbeam knocked off.

Pulling herself up gave her time to think, letting the winch do the work. She could feel her excitement burn in muscles that seemed more supple than usual. Warmer here, for sure. She turned her suit heater down. Life hung out in the tropics.

Before she reached the tanks, she heard Marc's impatient voice. "Julia, where are you?"

"On my way. Pretty close." She rounded a jut in the vent walls, into the glare of his lights. The walls faded into black.

"Where were you? You're way late, damn it. The tanks were here on time—hey, where's your headlamp?"

"Ran into an overhang. Smashed it. Marc—"

"Handbeam too? What'd you do—grope your way back? Why didn't you call?" He was clearly angry, voice tight and controlled.

"I found, I found—"

"Julia, calm down, you're—"

"Turn off all your lamps."

"What?"

"Turn 'em off. I want you to see something."

"First we switch your tank."

She sighed. It was just like Marc to fuss over details. Looking down at the sidewalk for pennies and missing the rainbow.

When she finally got the lights off he could see it too. There was a long moment of utter shock. He seemed to know it was better to say nothing.

Then she heard something wrong. The faint hissing surprised her. Mission training reasserted itself.

"What's that? Sounds like a tank leaking."

Automatically she checked her connections. All tight. "Marc? Check your tank."

"I'm fine. What's the matter?"

"I hear something, like a leak."

"I don't hear anything . . ."

"Be quiet. Listen."

She closed her eyes to fix the direction of the sound. It came from near the wall. She shone her handbeam on the empty tank, bent down low, and heard a thin scream. Oxygen was bleeding out onto the Marsmat.

"Damn. Valve isn't secured." She reached down to turn it off. Stopped. "What . . . ?"

The Marsmat near the tank was discolored. A blotchy, tan stain.

"Damn! We've damaged it." She knelt down to take a closer look, carefully avoiding putting her hand on the wall.

"What happened?" Marc took one long step over, understood at a glance. "My vent gas?"

"Uh-huh. Looks like it."

"What a reaction. Damn! And fast!"

"Oxygen's pure poison to these life-forms. It's like dumping acid on moss. Instantaneous death."

He looked around wonderingly. "We're leaking poison at them all the time in these suits."

She nodded. Stupid not to see it immediately, really. Like scuba gear, their suits vented exhaled gases at the back of the neck, mostly oxygen, a bit of nitrogen, and some carbon dioxide. A simple, reliable system, and the oxygen was easily replaceable from the Return Vehicle's chem factory.

Marc shook his head, sobered. "Typical humans, polluting wherever we go."

"If the stuff is this sensitive, we'll have to be really careful from now on." Julia straightened up carefully and backed away from the lesion.

They stood for a long moment in inky blackness, letting their retinas shed the afterimage of the lamps. Finally Marc asked, "Where's the light coming from?"

"Marsmat glows. Phosphoresces, is more correct."

"How can it do that?"

"Don't know. The more interesting question is why."

A long pause in the darkness that seemed to press in on all sides.

Marc said, "Did you hear? Airbus is incoming, within hours."

"No, too much static. I could barely recognize your voices. What'd Viktor say?"

"They got a message relayed from the satellite. Airbus will be in tonight. We're to be back by then."

"Damn. I'd hoped . . ." She sighed. "What did you tell him?"

"Not much. I didn't want him to know you were down here alone, so I was pretty brief."

"Good move."

"How's Airbus going to deliver Raoul's repair kit?"

"They don't say. Maybe drop it to us?"

"What's their landing site?"

"Viktor says they just don't answer that. Or other questions, either."

"So okay, big mystery, standard Airbus bullshit. That doesn't have any effect on us here."

"I guess not. Good to know Raoul'll get his kit, though."

"Yeah. Let's think in the here and now, though."

She knew now that time and oxygen would set the limits. They had this day and now were to return to the base. Solid orders. Team loyalty.

"Plenty of oxy up there," Marc said later as they rested and ate lunch—a squeeze-tube affair she hated, precisely described in one of her intervideos as eating a whole tube of beef-flavored toothpaste.

"So we trade tanks for time."

"Viktor's gonna get miffed if we don't check in at the regular time."

"Let him." She wished they had rigged a relay antenna at the vent mouth. But that would have taken time, too.

Tick, tick, tick.

"I don't want us to haul out of here dead tired, either."

"We'll be out by nightfall."

"We won't be so quick going back up."

Field experience had belied all the optimistic theories about working power in low gravity. Mars was tiring. Whether this came from the unrelenting cold or the odd, pounding sunlight (even after the UV was screened out by faceplates) or the simple fact that human reflexes were not geared for 0.38 g, or some more subtle facet, nobody knew. It meant that they could not count on a quick ascent at the end of a trying day.

"You want geological samples, I want biological. Mine weigh next to nothing, yours a lot. I'll trade you some of my personal weight allowance for time down here."

He raised his eyebrows, his eyes through his smeared faceplate giving her a long, shrewd study. "How much?"

"A kilogram per hour."

"Ummm. Not bad. Okay, a deal."

"Good." She shook hands solemnly, glove to glove. A fully binding guy contract, she thought somewhat giddily.

"Viktor's counting on using some of your allowance to drag back more nuggets and 'jewels,' y'know."

"It's my allowance."

"Hey, just a friendly remark. Not trying to get between you two."

"Thanks for the thought, but I'll deal with Viktor. Ready to go? We're eating into my hard-bought hours."

They returned to the ledge where Julia had her accident, two hundred meters further in. On the other side of the fortuitous overhang they found a pool covered with slime on a ledge. It was crusty, black and brown, and gave reluctantly when she poked it with a finger.

"Defense against the desiccation," she guessed.

Marc swept his handbeam around. The mat hung here like drapes from the rough walls. "Open water on Mars. Wow."

"Not really open. The mat flows down, see, and covers this pool. Keeps it from drying out. Saving its resources maybe?"

She scooped out some of the filmy pool water and put it under her hand microscope.

Marc said, "It's just algae, right?"

She did not answer. In the view were small creatures, plain as day.

"My God. There's something swimming around in here. Marc, look at this and tell me I'm not crazy."

He looked through the scope and blinked. "Martian shrimp?"

She sighed. "Trust you to think of something edible. In a pond this small on Earth there might be fairy shrimp, but these are pretty small. And I don't even know if these are animals."

She hurried to get some digitals of the stuff. She scooped some up in a sample vial and tucked it into her pack. Her mind was whirling in elation. She studied the tiny swimming things with breathless awe.

So fine and strange—and why the hell did she have to peer at them through a smudged helmet?

They had knobby structures at one end: heads? Maybe, and each with a smaller, light-colored speck. What?

Could Mars life have taken the leap to animals, bridging a huge evolutionary chasm? On the other hand, these could be just mobile algal colonies, like *Volvox* and other pond life on Earth. Whatever they were, she knew they were way beyond microbes. She bent down over the pool again, shone her handbeam at an angle.

The swarm of creatures was much thicker at the edges of the Marsmat—feeding? Or something else?

She couldn't quite dredge the murky idea from her subconscious. The arrangement with the mat was odd, handy for the "shrimp." What was the relationship there? Some kind of symbiosis? And how did the swimming forms get to the pool?

She and Marc climbed down from the ledge, playing out cable. As they descended the mist thickened and the walls got slick and they had to take more care. The cable was getting harder to manage, too. She could not stop her mind from spinning with ideas.

On Earth, hydrothermal vent organisms photosynthesized kilometers deep in the ocean, using the dim reddish glow from hot magma. The glow became their energy source. Could some Martian organisms use the mat glow? Wait a minute—

"Marc, did you notice anything peculiar about the shrimp?"

He paused before answering. "Well, I don't know what they should look like. They looked sorta like the shrimp I feed my fish at home."

"Did you notice their eyes?"

"Uh . . ."

"The knobby ends, those had lighter specks, remember?"

"Yeah, what about them?"

"So you saw them too."

"Why, what's the matter—Oh."

"Right!"

"I see, they shouldn't have eyes."

"Good for you. I'll make a biologist out of you yet. On Earth, cave-dwelling organisms have lost their eyes. Natural selection forces an organism to justify the cost of producing a complicated structure. You lose 'em if you don't use 'em."

"So if they have eyes—"

"On Earth, we'd say they were recent arrivals from a

lighted place, hadn't had time to become blind."

"But that's impossible. The lighted parts of Mars have been cold and dry for billions of years. Where would they have come from?"

"I agree. So my next choice is that it's not dark enough here to lose the eyes."

"That glow is pretty dim."

"To us, maybe. We're creatures from a light-saturated world. Our eyes aren't used to these skimpy intensities. Closest parallel on Earth to these light levels are the hydrothermal vents. There are light-sensitive animals down there, even microbes able to photosynthesize."

"Maybe they're not even eyes."

"They're light-sensitive. The critters clustered under the beam from my scope."

"Wow."

"I need more information, but at the very least it suggests that the glow is permanent. Or at least frequent enough to give some advantage to being able to see. And that means there should be something that can use the glow as an energy source. Maybe the mat is symbiotic—a cooperation between glowing organisms and photo-synthesizers?"

"Yeah . . . That suggests the glow is primary. What's it for?"

"Don't know, just guessing here."

"Curiouser and curiouser, as Alice said."

"I didn't know boys read *Alice in Wonderland*."

"It seems to fit what we're doing."

"Down the rabbit hole we go, then."

She gazed down and saw at the very limit of the weak

lamplight bigger things. Much bigger. Gray sheets, angular spires, corkscrew formations of pale white that stuck out into the upwelling gases and captured the richness. One spindly, fleshy growth looked like the fingers of a drowned corpse, drifting lazily in the currents . . .

She shook her head to clear it. *Stay steady, here.*

Below the level of the pool ledge twisty side channels worked off at odd angles. These ran more nearly horizontal, and they explored them hurriedly, clumping along until the ceiling got too low. No time to waste crawling back into dead ends, she figured. They headed back to the main channel and then found a broad passage that angled down. It was slick and they had to watch their footing.

The mats here were like curtains, hanging out into the steady stream of vapor from the main shaft of the vent. Some seemed hinged to spread before the billowing vapor gale. She was busy taking samples and had only moments to study the strange, slow sway of these thin membranes, flapping like slow-motion flags.

"Must be maximizing their surface area exposed to the nutrient fog," she guessed.

"Eerie," Marc said. "And look how wide they get."

"There's sure as hell a lot of biomass here."

"Wonder if any of it's edible."

"Hungry, huh?" They both laughed, a bit tensely.

At turns in the channel the mats were the size of a man. She took a lot of shots with her microcam, hoping they would come out reasonably well in their lamp beams. Gray and translucent, under direct handbeam she could see her hand through one.

These forms owed their origin to the warm, moist eras of the Martian antiquity.

The mats—and what else?—lived in such labyrinths as this, all around the globe? They could harvest the moisture billowing from heat below, and perhaps melt the permafrost nearby. At the edges of Earth's glaciers lived plants that actually melted ice with their own slow chemistry.

The thermal vents and their side caverns could be extensive. With an exposed surface area as big as Earth's, there was plenty of room for evolution to experiment.

Marc whispered, "Nothing like this pale ivory cavern on Earth. For sure."

Ruled as it was by boisterous, efficient aerobic life. Anaerobes had long ago retreated to inhospitable niches like hot springs and coal mines. In that infertile ground they survived, but remained as microbes, spawning no new forms. On Mars, oxygen-loving forms never evolved. The atmosphere escaped too soon.

Julia gently caressed a mat as it lazily floated on the vapor breeze. Plants, flourishing in the near vacuum. She could never have envisioned these . . .

She dropped down a few more meters, blinking. How much was she seeing and how much was just illusion?— the product of poor seeing conditions, a smudged helmet view, her strained eyes—

"Hey. Time."

She felt her fatigue as a slow, gathering ache in her legs and arms. Experience made her think very carefully, being sure she was wringing everything from these minutes that she could. "How far down are we?"

Marc had been keeping track of the markings on the cable. "Just about one klick."

"What's the temperature?"

"Nearly ten. Almost toasty. No wonder I'm not feeling the cold."

"This vent could go down kilometers before it gets steam-hot. And we've just reached the cavern level."

"Julia . . ."

"I know. We can't go farther."

"It'll be a long, tough climb out. Soon be dusk up there."

Be getting deathly cold on the surface, and fast, yes.

She was on a small ledge, about five meters below Marc. A strange longing filled her.

"I know. I'm not pushing for more, don't worry. Biologists need oxygen, too."

Automatically she started to cut a small sample out of the closest mat, a thick hanging curtain suspended just within reach. It was surprisingly tough, like thick kelp. She found she was puffing with the exertion. Her suit exhaled with a slight hiss. Suddenly the mat whipped around, pinning her against the rock wall. She was in the dark, as if someone had closed a thick curtain in front of her.

Marc responded to her yell. "Jules, where are you? I can't see you."

"Here!"

"You're behind that mat?"

"Yeah." *Breathe deeply, speak clearly.* "Must be some kind of reflex reaction. I was trying to take a sample, and this hanging mat slammed against me."

Training reasserted itself. Marc answered in calm astronautspeak. "What is your position? All I can see is the cable."

"I'm standing on a small ledge, being held against the wall by a lot of mat stuff. Can't see anything."

"Still got your scalpel?"

"Negative. Must've dropped it. It wasn't much good anyway. This stuff is tough."

"You say it moved. Did it fall on you?"

"Negative. It swung around." She had a quick thought. "It must be suspended from above. Can you see how?"

There was a short pause. "It's hanging from what must be a hinged branch just below me. The branch protrudes from a thick trunklike structure close to the wall."

She struggled ineffectually. "Try to make it move away again. I'm pretty stuck. And I don't want to risk burning out my winch motor."

"What do you suggest?"

"Kick it!"

She could hear his breathing over the suit radio. Reassuring, somehow. He was only a meter away, but she couldn't see a damn thing but the blotchy pattern on the mat.

"*Unh! Unh!* Anything happen?"

"Negative. What'd you do?"

"Thunked it with my boot a couple times. Didn't seem to have any effect."

"Well, something I was doing caused it to move."

"How do plants move, anyway? No muscles, no nervous system."

"Don't know that this is a plant. Still, even plants on Earth can move. Lots of 'em track the sun, and some can instantly collapse their leaves in response to a stimulus."

"Oh yeah, I remember that, uh, sensitive plant from botany class."

"But there's a downside. They have to grow the leaves open again, and it can take days."

"Cheery thought." There was a short pause. "Say, there's another one of those brown spots forming on your mat. It must be your suit exhaust."

The thought struck both of them at the same time.

"Hey, what about—"

"Yeah, I'll try a short blast from my intake."

"Marc? Just tease it with the oxygen. We want it to twitch, not collapse."

"Right."

The seconds ticked slowly by. Then she heard, "Okay, I'm in position now. Ready to start. One-second jet coming up."

The mat pressing against her shuddered.

"It just twitched."

"I barely grazed it. I'll try a couple more short blasts—"

There was a sudden feeling of lightness. The mat heaved violently away from her. Her helmet was hopelessly smeared.

"Climb, Julia! Quick!" Marc shouted.

"I can't see. Visor's smeared." She grabbed the lines to be sure they were unsnarled. A quick command to the winch cranked her up. "Tell me where I'm going."

"Go! You're coming up alongside it. Good! Just keep

coming up. Okay, you're level with the hinge. If you clear it you're home free— Yes! you're clear!"

She struggled on another couple of seconds, then stopped, sweat pouring off her face, suit fans humming. "Wow, hot on Mars. Surely a first." She felt curiously exhilarated and exhausted at the same time.

"We've got a one-klick climb ahead of us."

"I know. I'm okay. Just gotta clear my visor. I want to vid that hinge, then we can go. What incredible stuff we've found!"

She went into automatic drive on the way back. Run the winch, negotiate around the ledges and rocks, run it some more. Steady does it.

They stopped for new tanks at the ledge, took another food break, then finished the climb. They didn't say much. Astronaut training; talk breaks concentration, which you need all the more as you tire.

But she could feel her mind working in the background, processing and sorting all the new information. When she sat down to write her report, it would all be there.

It was dusk when they reached the surface. She climbed up into a ruddy sky darkening in the east.

The residual moisture on their suits froze to rime and fell from their suits as a dusting of snow. The flakes fumed away within seconds.

Marc dismantled and stowed their climbing rig as she carefully settled her precious samples, sealed safely away from their oxygen atmosphere. She was already planning how to culture them in the greenhouse.

Then they were off, Marc carefully following their tracks back to the hab.

They'd squirted the briefest of "we're back" messages before making final preparations for leaving. Now, a mug of hot tea in hand, she started to put in a call to base.

The radio crackled to life. "Company is coming," said Viktor.

"Where?"

"They are being, what you call it?—coy."

The next hour they were silent, letting Red Rover's sway massage them. Marc heated up a thick beefy soup and they wolfed it down. In the dark she moved the rover more carefully, following the microwave reflector telltales they had dropped on the way out. The pilot program kept her on track pretty well, so all she had to do as they approached the pingo hills was keep an eye out for really large rocks. The rover's ranging radar did a fair job at that, too, but they had had enough near scrapes during night drives to made her cautious.

She was peering out the forward port—calling it a "windshield" was too much of a compliment to Red Rover's speed—and so was the first to see it.

A hard, hot fire moving in the sky.

Marc had seen it too. "Airbus," he grunted.

A boom slammed into the rover, startling her. "Shock wave?"

"Reentry profile, lessee—that puts them maybe twenty klicks up," Marc said.

"Through their aerobraking, for sure. Pretty low, wouldn't you say?"

"Yeah. Bright as hell!"

"Nukes run hotter."

"We're seeing the exhaust plume. It's squashed, see, pushed back by ram pressure."

"Look, I can see its light reflecting on the ship."

A shiny silver needle atop a ball of orange fire.

"It's close!" Marc stood up in excitement.

"Going to land at our base?" She thumbed on her mike, preparing to tell Viktor.

"No, look, it's—we can see it clearly! It's coming *here*."

"That's crazy!"

But true. The fireball came steadily down, slowing, prowling across the cold night sky sprinkled with unwinking stars. The plume's brilliance made the stars fade as it got closer. They craned to look up as the blaring light arced toward them.

"It's coming down wrong!" she shouted.

"They must be off-target. Shooting for the hab, but fifteen klicks north."

"We copy," came Viktor's voice.

"It's coming down in the pingos," she spoke into the mike.

"Wait, it's stopped." Marc pressed his face against the port. "Hovering there."

Sand and pebbles rattled on the rover. A steady roar was getting louder—the sound of the rocket exhaust.

Julia realized that they were still moving, on autodrive. She turned to face directly toward the hard, fierce flame that hung on the horizon, then stopped the rover. The plume came lower, kissed the soil.

"It's maybe a klick away from us," Julia called to

Viktor. "You figure it somehow locked on our carrier wave, mistook it for the hab?"

"Dumb mistake, if so," Viktor said.

"It's hovering," Marc called. "Maybe they're confused."

A big rock tumbled into view of their headlights. Hammering grit rained on them. Abruptly a loud *smack* rang out and she saw the glass before her face starred with thin white lines.

"Turn around!" Marc said. "It's blowing a lot of crap around."

She steered them sideways, enough to still see through the small side window and not expose the forward port. "Viktor, it's still just hanging there."

"No," Marc said, "it's drifting to the south."

"Looking for a landing spot?" Viktor called.

Pebbles sang against the roof. "Nobody would take this long to land," Julia said.

"Look, fog!" Marc pointed.

"Clouds under the plume," Julia reported to Viktor.

"Sure is not dust?" Viktor asked.

"No, it's white!" Marc shouted.

Julia remembered the fog in the vent. "Water!"

"They are using water rocket?" Viktor said. "Axelrod's agents, they say the fuel is something else—"

"There wasn't any fog before, not on the way down," Julia said. "This is new."

Big billows of creamy clouds boiled out from beneath the gemlike flame. They reflected the brilliant light upward and she could see the shiny ship holding steady, several hundred meters off the ground, coasting slowly away to the south.

The ship slowed, hovering over the crown of a hill.

"The pingos!" Julia cried. "It's blowing all the dirt and rocks off them, burning through, exposing the ice buried in them."

Pebbles clattered against the rover skin, then eased away. Suddenly more fog burst from beneath the plume.

The roaring exhaust got louder. The ship coasted away again.

"It's opening up several of them," Marc said wonderingly.

They watched, dumbfounded. Again, after a moment's intense blowtorching of a pingo, white clouds jetted up.

"It's moving again," Julia reported. "No, wait—coming farther down. Dropping."

The radiance spread out at the base of the ship. "Landing! It's setting down."

The roar muted, abruptly fell silent.

Her ears rang. Even in the thin atmosphere, huge sounds could carry.

"They're here. Landed," Marc whispered.

For a moment no one spoke. Julia blinked in vain to get the afterimages from her eyes.

Viktor said, "Solves a minor technical question. What fuel will they use to go back? Water."

She was dumbfounded. "What?"

"They took the trouble to save labor. No need to drill, like us. Blow off top of pingo." Viktor chuckled in appreciation.

"My God," Marc said. "They're going to fly home on Martian melt-ice."

Viktor said, "Is very intelligent. I will have to compliment their captain. If they let us come aboard."

PART III
OUTPOST MARS

20

SHE SPLURGED ON WATER. BEFORE BREAKFAST SHE TOOK A long warm shower, even longer than last night's. Not exactly champagne, but a festive gesture.

The day down the vent in a cramped suit reeking faintly of old sweat—despite the new self-cleaning liners—had left her with aching muscles. Not so much from all the grunt work, but a suit never let you get the best leverage. The designers had never fixed the basic problem that most of the suit's weight hung on the shoulders. She had built hers up into hard slabs of muscle, these last 500 days, but they always wailed. Untended to, they got other muscle groups to join in the concert.

Long experience had taught her to pay attention to her lower back pangs. She had one big goal: to study the vent samples she had waiting outside in the greenhouse. Worrying hurts could throw off her pace and judgment.

She dialed for steamy-hot water plus blue-ion gouts

to stimulate her. When she reluctantly quit, she stepped out into one of her thick towels (a personal mass expense) and onto one of the few sensual details worked into the otherwise Spartan bathroom. The bath mat was cleaning up when she came out, but did not mind being stepped on. It crawled with cilia-like fibers, sopping up droplets, tissue shreds, and emitted a little oxygen to boot. It was actually a hybrid creature: fibers in the top of the mat had embedded algae, much like a polar bear's fur coat. The algae were gene-engineered to photosynthesize maximally from the special full-spectrum lights in the hab. This produced more oxygen than the bottom fibers used in their cleanup work.

They called it Roger the Rug, and let it creep around the whole hab, cleaning corners and nooks. Roger was the most advanced biotech they had, deceptively simple.

She needed the pampering. Trouble started at breakfast.

"We will all go to greet our friends and losers of the race," Viktor said.

"I want to stay here," Julia said. "I've got plenty to do—"

"Axelrod's orders. We look like happy people welcoming fellow brave explorers."

Raoul said, "'Showing them around the planet,' was the way he put it."

"When did this come in?"

"While you were oversleeping," Raoul said.

"Like me," Marc said. "That descent really took it out of us."

"Let me see Axelrod's song and dance," Julia said, quickly finishing her oatmeal.

Last night they had sent a quick report to the Consortium, with a few shots from her videos of the Marsmat. Axelrod had sent a bunch of "guidelines" for handling Airbus, but Julia had ignored all that talk in favor of putting her samples in order. Then she had crashed. That billions of people were at a fever pitch over the "race" mattered not at all to her.

She and Marc watched Axelrod's message on the big screen. "I can't believe our luck," he began, "finding life and getting the repair kit, all in one day."

"They were correlated," Marc remarked wryly. "We just barely squeezed in the vent descent before Airbus got here."

"Yes," Julia said, as Axelrod went on with superlatives, "but the PR people won't present it that way."

Axelrod said, "As big a discovery as this is, Julia and Marc, you've got to realize it raises problems. I'm keeping it quiet for now, see? Announcement in a day or three. We've got to be *really sure* to observe the—what's that name?—oh yeah, Planetary Protection Protocols. No Mars life in the hab or the ERV. No exposure of you crew. Samples stay outside, always. No glove box work in the hab. My people tell me this is a *minimum* that we *have* to follow, or there'll be hell to pay."

"The real trick will be to keep any of it alive," Julia said to the others with growing annoyance. She yearned to get outside and see if any of the samples had survived the night under the conditions she had rigged in the greenhouse.

"Now, I know you'll both want to get right on those samples, study the hell out of 'em." Axelrod smiled warmly. "But there's this other big deal, Airbus. I want the best coverage. Those Chinese, they seem to be calling the shots from back here, and they're as media-stupid as ever. No good camera shots from them, except for some pretty night-landing stuff. They just sent out a footprints-and-flags video, been on all the media. A copy of how you guys handled it. That guy Chen and the engineer, Gerda, they stepped off together. That woman, Claudine, she was a half step behind—dunno why."

"Who cares?" exploded Julia. "Damn it, how trivial can you get? We discover the first alien life in the universe, and he's worrying about who steps off the blooming nuke first!"

"Let's see what else is bothering boss, okay? Then we can discuss," said Viktor. This was a clear warning to Julia.

She glared at him but said nothing.

"He's worried," Marc whispered. "Look how he runs on."

"Maybe he's afraid they'll hold the repair kit for ransom?" Raoul asked.

"—so our footage will be *much* better. You guys welcoming them, showing them the territory. Smiles, all smiles. Give 'em a ride in the dune buggy—be sure to take it along."

"He thinks the technical problems are solved," Marc said.

"Yes," Viktor said. "Raoul plus kit, game is over."

Axelrod beamed. "Can you believe it? Ol' Airbus is

giving away their video feed! Anybody wants, can run it. Not only are they losing the race, they're losing all the media money."

Marc said, "He's going to want us to outperform them on camera."

"No thanks," Julia said. "I don't want to—"

"So Julia," Axelrod said earnestly, projecting warmth and concern. "I know how you feel about your big discovery. I'm sure you understand, though, that you and Marc have got to be in the welcome. Can't have just half our guys show up! People will wonder why. We don't want questions, not while you're finding out just what we've got there, scientifically."

"Grumble grumble," Julia said. "Maybe it makes sense, but—"

"He's got a point," Marc said.

Axelrod beamed. "With all the excitement, plus Raoul putting the finishing touches on the ERV, that's plenty of cover for you to get something done—just as soon as you wave hello."

She grimaced. "Logic okay, but I don't have to like it."

While the others got the dune buggy checked out—anything standing exposed on the surface needed a going-over after a few days, they had learned—she ducked into the greenhouse. The vent samples were in the glove box, looking the same as last night. The box stood against one filmy wall so that it could operate at Martian ambient pressure, venting directly out. Though its atmosphere was filtered, the positive pressure from the greenhouse would pull any leak outward. She wanted to start some simple experiments, but already the others were waving at her.

The hour-long trip to the pingos she spent planning her research strategy. Riding on the dune buggy was much more fun than using Red Rover, because your view was wide, even in the lobster suit. As they approached she studied the fog rising from the several pingo hills Airbus had scoured out. The pearly mist poured up like slow-motion smoke. The rocket exhaust had blown deep holes in the pingo hills, now open fuming pits. Milky crusts spattered the nearby rock flanks. Debris from the blast wave stretched away in long, dark fingers of freshly exposed gravel.

"They'll have to dig into that," Viktor sent over comm. "Mine ice and then warm it up in a kettle."

Raoul said, "No, something more efficient. Run a pipe through the ice, melt it where it is, pump it out."

"Whatever they do," Viktor said, "will take a lot of time to make so much fuel."

Raoul chuckled. "Axelrod. This morning he asked if Airbus would separate the water into liquid oxygen and hydrogen, maybe? Still thinking like it was a chem rocket."

They all got a laugh out of that, but Julia knew it was pure nerves driving the mirth. Instead of fretting over meeting Airbus, though, they fell into technical talk.

A big virtue of nuclear rocketry was that ordinary water was a perfectly fine "fuel" because it simply served as mass to shove out the nozzle. The true fuel was the uranium or plutonium in the reactor core—a compact cylinder no bigger than a Volkswagen. Water pumped into it exploded into steam and jetted out the back.

The Magnum booster that had sent them here was also a steam rocket, its energy gotten when liquid hydrogen combined with liquid oxygen. Nuclear rockets just skipped all the trouble of handling ultracold fluids. They could fly anywhere in the solar system where ice could be found, then fly home on local "fuel."

She let them rattle on, aware that something was working in the back of her mind. With the first glimpse of the ship in the distance, she felt her perspective change suddenly. This was not just two crews of astronauts meeting on assignment. She, Viktor, Marc and Raoul were about to welcome their first visitors from Earth to their home on Mars.

The Airbus ship gleamed on the Martian sands like a shiny tower. It *looked* like a futuristic spaceship, Julia had to admit. Compact, slender, and much more impressive than their clunky, utilitarian hab and ERV. They halted the dune buggy and she took several panoramic video shots, on direct feed for the waiting Earthside millions.

"We prepare to welcome the crew of the *Valkyrie* to Mars," she said for the sound track.

Raoul checked the radiation count as they ground across the dunes to the blasted landing site. "Their pile has cooled off to very low levels," he announced. "No higher than ambient now."

She was glad they'd had the night to let the nuke subside. Nobody was very clear about the Airbus operating mode, and some high-efficiency piles could leave a lot of short half-life isotopes to fry the surroundings. Not here, luckily.

The slender ship had its pile riding just over the nozzles, with the fuel tanks stacked above to shield the two passenger levels. They parked at the foot of a large elevator, craning their necks to see the ablation shield that capped the elegant spire.

All this slick engineering had ridden into medium-high Earth orbit atop a Proton booster stack bought from the Russians. Then they had fired up the nuke and boosted. They kept the upper Proton stage for centrifugal gravity, copying the Consortium. Airbus had kept quiet on technical details of the Venus flyby, but that had not been a demanding maneuver, just coast through a looping orbit, picking up delta-vee from the planet. Unmanned spacecraft had been using the same trick since the 1960s.

There were tracks of a rover and boot prints all around the ship, but by radio Viktor knew they were all inside. The Consortium four rode up in the elevator. The cycle-through at the air lock was complicated. They had to shuck their lobster suits after their antiperoxide shower. Nobody mentioned a second shower, though it was standard after you had worked on Mars for a while. A few hours in the suit made you as rank as a plow horse. They formed up and went through the big air lock together.

And here came the big moment: Julia traded turns with Marc videoing the handshakes, greetings and exchanges in Chinese, Russian, French, German, and English. Once performed for the domestic audience, as usual, the only useful shared tongue was broken English.

She was shocked by Lee Chen's lean, lined face. He

had grayed a lot since she had last seen him, in Texas during mission training. His hairline had receded, and he seemed slightly stooped. She wondered if the trip had been difficult. "You're looking great!" she lied.

"You, too," he lied back.

Two years into the mission, and she knew it would take her a week in a makeover salon to look presentable. "We've got plenty to discuss," she said. "The only two biologists within fifty million miles."

"I have memorized your papers in *Nature*, of course."

His polite, professional formality, despite their knowing each other half a dozen years, now made her uneasy. *But the BIG discovery, I can't tell you . . .*

"You'll be able to do plenty of backup work around here . . ." *What an understatement!* How to get the conversation away from this?

Marc turned to Claudine. "Ah, good to see you again."

She was French, and on this mission, pilot and medic. Julia and the Consortium crew had known all the Airbus crew from NASA training, but not always well.

Alongside Claudine, Julia always felt like a rough-cut Colonial. The Frenchwoman was remarkably self-possessed, her long ash-blond hair controlled, today in a bun. Her gestures were graceful, and she moved with economy. To Julia she had always represented old-world manners. She was astronaut-short but with a slender build. Like all the astronauts, she was good-looking and photogenic, with regular features.

She nodded. Marc pressed, "You're staying here? Not just stopping to drop off the mail?"

Laughs, a little nervous. "We plan to stay here," Chen answered. "Your site intrigues us."

He's the designated talker, thought Julia. She shot a quick glance at Marc, who was keeping his face carefully blank.

Chen was pouring a ritual sweet drink—plum wine.

"To the first social event on Mars," Julia said.

They all toasted the moment. She videoed it.

What do we talk about next? Are we companions in space or competitors? And how do they feel about Marc? Residual bitterness?

"So, what d'you think of the scenery?" asked Marc. "A bit skimpy on landscaping, but then we've been busy."

Claudine smiled, "It's like all the videos you 'ave sent back. You are quite ze celebritees now, you know."

Julia searched for undertones, but the French woman had been impeccably correct, gave away nothing. Julia remembered now that while Claudine's mouth smiled easily, her wide-set hazel eyes often did not.

Julia smiled ruefully, gestured with her minicam. "Welcome to Mars TV, the series. Condition of our employment, I'm afraid." She felt, somehow, like a bull in a china shop.

Chen said, "We hope to profit from your many explorations."

Soon enough the seven formed groups. Captains Chen and Viktor conversed as they moved through the narrow passageways, with Julia coming behind.

Raoul and Gerda Braun, their engineer, traded lore. Julia remembered her as a determined-looking woman with a somewhat chunky build. Today her round face was all smiles. Her light brown hair was braided and on the top of her head, and the effect was oddly Tyrolean. She seemed solicitous, worried by the myriad repairs Raoul had been called upon to perform.

Julia remembered that Marc and Claudine had done their heavy-duty training together in Germany and China; they paired off quickly, she showing him ship details. With more time to plan, Airbus had some niceties, like built-ins. Claudine seemed unusually focused on Marc, though, her expression more animated.

Mars has a lot of past, and so do we.

Finally, Raoul could restrain himself no longer. "Say, about that mail . . ."

Laughs again. The repair kit was a foam-steel box that Raoul cracked immediately after Chen ceremoniously presented it. His eyes flew over the parts. He nodded, smiled. "Just the ticket."

"Ticket home, I hope," Viktor said.

Chen insisted on giving them a "tour" of the ship, if that was the right term for seven people crowding around each other in the narrow passageways, low ceilings and general cramped air of the living quarters and small bays. Their staging area had held the rover they had already deployed, workbenches, cabinet stores, a machine shop that Raoul instantly inspected with gleaming eyes. He asked for one or two tools and Gerda gracefully offered them up.

"I would be happy to assist, if need be," she said in a flawless English accent.

Raoul looked at her intently. Julia remembered that her crewmates had not seen another woman for two years, and Gerda was somewhat similar in appearance to Katherine. She was quick and intense, and gestured a lot with her hands. Her dark brown eyes were set a bit too close to her prominent nose, but the overall effect was handsome. "I would certainly appreciate that. Let me get you on your back when I do." His face froze. "I, I mean, let me get *back to you* when I do. Need some help. I mean."

Julia had never before felt an entire room of people hold their breath. Smiles all round, but nobody said anything.

"Ah, and over here . . ." Chen led them away to another wonder of the Airbus design.

Julia started breathing again.

On the trip back they all got a huge laugh out of it, of course.

They were quite merry, and Raoul took his ribbing well.

Airbus had treated them to a sumptuous lunch—a chicken dish frozen from a fancy Beijing restaurant, Chinese beer, a sticky German pastry dessert. "Not really better than our grub," Marc said, "but, thank God, *different.*"

"They sure outclassed us on the dress code," Raoul said.

I noticed you appreciating the women, for sure, Julia thought.

"They have pressed work suits especially for landing," Viktor said dismissively. "Show business. Let them work here a month, they look like us."

"Threadbare, stained, beat up," Raoul agreed. "I sure would hate to spend the next two years in that chicken coop they've got."

"And already they have been for over half a year," Viktor said.

"Everything does seem small," Raoul said. "The whole ship does, in fact. I'd like to crawl up under that cowling, see how the nuke is pinned in—"

"Crawl under ERV's skirts, if that's on your mind," Viktor said, earning another round of guffaws.

"I wonder where they've got their supplies stowed," Raoul persisted.

"It did not look to me like there is enough carrying capacity for years of the supplies," Viktor said.

"Another layer of storage, I'd guess," Marc said. "Between the fuel tanks and that equipment bay. Use the food for shielding from the nuke, that's the way I'd want it."

Raoul nodded. "They had more time to design and build. Their engineers probably thought of a few more twists."

"Those bedrooms of theirs are *tiny*," Julia said.

"Maybe they all sleep together," Marc deadpanned.

Viktor grinned. "Sell that story to the tabloids, make another million."

"Hey, don't think I couldn't," Marc said. "You should see what some of the big shows are hinting at. Two women, one guy, going to Mars for years. My uncle sent me a squirt on that—therapists talking, giving it some intellectual covering fire, while the host makes cheap jokes and they show 'suggestive' videos."

"Better than three guys, one woman, for years?" Julia asked mildly.

"Lots better," Marc said. "Plays to male fantasies and all."

She shot back, "How about female fantasies?"

"No market," Viktor said. They all laughed, a little ruefully.

21

JANUARY 20, 2018

IT WAS MIDAFTERNOON WHEN THEY REACHED ZUBRIN Base. By unspoken consent, Marc parked the dune buggy by the ERV. Raoul and Viktor manhandled the repair kit off the buggy, grunting. Mass weighed less on Mars, but its inertia was the same. They disappeared quickly into Raoul's fix-it shop.

"Look at them go." Julia smiled at their retreating backs. "Kids with new toys."

Marc snorted. "And I suppose you're not eager to get at those bio samples?"

"Not at all, but I'll race you to the greenhouse anyway."

In their lobster suits this was a joke. Over the months they had learned how to walk without looking like overstuffed teddy bears, but the suits were cumbersome.

As they approached the hab, she was struck by how clunky it looked compared to Airbus's sleek nuke. The shape of a giant tuna can, its lines were not improved by the rows of sandbags they'd stacked on the top for radiation protection. Still, it had the familiarity of home, and they'd lived in it fairly comfortably for almost two years.

A thought struck her. "Hey, Marc, what're they gonna do for rad protection in that nuke? They can't do what we did, that's for sure."

"Maybe they have some fancy shielding under the skin of their craft."

"No one talked about it when you were on their project?"

"Uh-uh. We didn't even know if the thing could fly at that point. But it's a good question."

By the time they emerged from the hab in skinsuits and insulated Marswear parka and pants, it was about 4 P.M., and across their rosy pink work yard the shadows were lengthening, blue streaks across a red landscape.

They walked the thirty meters around the hab and alongside the length of the inflated walls to the greenhouse air lock, moving in the slow-motion skipping dubbed "Mars gait" by Earthside media. Julia regretted the lateness of the hour. Still, it was late spring and the sun would be up for several more hours.

She entered the greenhouse eagerly, shucking her outerwear and helmet. She was elated to finally have some biology to work on. Early in the mission, she had repeated the robot Viking biology experiments, hoping to find something different. She spiked samples of the Martian dirt—"regolith" to Marc—with water and nutrients, sealed them in small pressure vessels, and incubated them. She then checked for any gases produced by the metabolism of life-forms in the soil.

This time life is looking for life directly, no robots in the way.

To avoid the embarrassing possibility of introducing her own microflora into the experiment, she had initially worked with the samples only outside, under the cold red-stained sky. But in her pressure suit and insulating outerwear she was clumsy, and each step went slowly. They all had special two-layer gloves that allowed them to peel back the heavy insulation down to a thin, flexible inner glove. But her hands got quickly cold and stiff and it wasn't like working bare-handed.

In response to her complaints, Viktor had fashioned the greenhouse glove box. The elevated greenhouse temperatures kept the water from freezing and speeded up the results enormously.

Sure enough, as in the Viking experiments, there was an immediate response of dry surface peroxides to the water. A spike of oxygen. When that had run its course, she bled off the gases and resealed the pressure vessels. Nothing further happened. Viking and all the other probes had found only chemistry after all, no evidence of life.

She'd tried this experiment with samples plucked from Marc's cores, and anyplace that looked promising. And she'd never found anything different.

Finally, she'd streaked a plate with a dirty spoon after dinner one night, and cultured some vigorous Earth bacteria. These she ran through the same experiment, with fresh Martian dirt. After the initial spike of oxygen from the chemistry, she'd gotten nothing more.

The peroxides had savaged the microbes, ripping apart cell walls. It was quite clear why the robot landers had found no signs of organic chemistry. For Earth life, Mars was like living in a chemical blowtorch.

But this time it was different. Waiting for her were living samples.

She went straight to the glove box. *Time for a good look at this critter.*

On Earth, she'd had many discussions with other biologists about how best to proceed with an unknown sample. All agreed: before slicing, dicing, or extracting, spend some time observing. Get all the clues possible from the living organism.

She plopped the sample from the underground pool under the dissecting scope. That would give her a good overview of the sample, live and in 3-D. She'd collected some of the water with the swimming forms—Marc's "shrimp"—and a piece of the closest mat.

Under the scope they didn't look much like shrimp. They were small, pale red, motile forms, moving through the water with beating, whiplike projections. Under good magnification, they looked even less like shrimp, and more like motile colonies. They seemed to be made of several distinct types of cells held together by a flexible matrix. At one end was a knobby protuberance—she didn't want to call it a head—with a lighter spot.

When she first turned on the light, they were moving very sluggishly, and there were just a few. Again, they clustered under the spot of light in the dish. After a few minutes, they became more energetic. More started to appear.

But from where? She scanned over the rapidly thickening group. Moving the spot of light sent them into frenzied movement until they had relocated the light.

She caught the edge of the mat in her field of view. That was the source. They were swarming from—*under? inside?*—the mat.

She increased the magnification, focused on a thinner patch. *There.* She watched, fascinated, as a round, pale red blob embedded in the slimy matrix of the mat began to move under the light, popped out, and swam off. She moved the focus to another one and triggered the built-in vid.

"Hey, Marc," she called, "come look at this! Your shrimp are popping out of the mat."

Marc had been working on one of the long trays they used for growing crops. He'd come to relish gardening during the long months of the mission, often volunteering to help Julia in the greenhouse. She could imagine him pottering away in a garden in his later years.

As he approached she got up and gave him her seat. She straightened up, feeling chilled and stiff. The greenhouse was warm enough for just the skinsuit when she was moving around, tending the plants. She set the floor heater to a higher setting. Working in outerwear would be too cumbersome here. She rubbed her thighs for warmth. Even her boot heaters couldn't fight off the chill seeping from the floor. Darn this cold planet!

Marc watched a while in silence.

"Wow. What are they doing?"

"I'm not sure. Something I did triggered it, though. The light, maybe."

"I mean, what's the use of swimming to a wall-hugging life-form?"

"Good question. Same goes for photoreceptors—they're of minimal use underground."

"So . . ." He frowned. "The shrimp evolved on the surface of the planet?"

"Sure seems that way. During Mars' warm, wet past. These are fossil features."

"Man, that was a long time ago." He looked up, frowning. "On Earth, cave creatures are blind. How come these primitive eyes lasted hundreds of millions of years underground?"

"There must be positive natural selection for a swimming, 'seeing' form, or else mutations would destroy the genes coding for these features." She paused, thinking furiously. "So either they need eyes to get around in the mat glow, or there have been several warm, wet periods, maybe lots of them . . . or the mutation rate is drastically lower here."

"Hmm. Well, that could be, y'know. Underground, there are no cosmic rays, and Mars has fewer radioactive elements than Earth anyway."

She raised her eyebrows. "Oh?"

"Yeah, there're more heavy elements the closer a planet is to the sun. Also, the heavier elements on Mars are concentrated in its core. No tectonic recycling up to the surface as on Earth."

"I never thought about that. Cosmic rays and radioactive decay account for a lot of the background mutation rate on Earth, so on Mars—"

"It's probably a lot lower," he finished.

"Damn. Too many choices. Wish I could talk to Chen about this. I just hate this secrecy."

He stood up. "Yeah, there're lots of things I'd like to ask Airbus too."

"Such as?"

"Such as if they want to use this facility, for example. I'm harvesting beans today, but I could also be planting some for them. I mean, they'd be no good to us, 'cause they don't mature for two months or more, when we're long gone."

"Unless—" She stopped.

"Unless we're stuck here?"

"It crossed my mind."

"Well, uncross it. We've got to get off this rusty ball of slag," he growled.

She was surprised at his vehemence. Time to deftly change the subject.

"I'm still thinking about how small their ship is. It's definitely ERV-sized."

"Smaller. NASA intended the ERV for a crew of six. That nuke is sized for four, max."

"Exactly. How are they going to live in something that size and actually *do* something? I mean, you can survive in something the size of a New York studio during transit, because there's nothing to do, really."

He shrugged. "Maybe they plan to use the hab after we're gone."

"Hmm. I never thought of that. Wouldn't they have to ask the Consortium? And tell us? So we can leave it up and running for them? And they're not very close—for moving in, that is."

"They can just reposition. The nuke is much better for that sort of maneuvering, I'll bet. "

"I was thinking along a different track. Suppose they're not here for very long."

"A flags-and-footprint expedition? That won't win them anything. But we're just guessing again. We don't know. It's like dealing with Brer Fox and the tar baby."

"I agree, *we* don't know much at all. That bothers me. But what gets me is we're sitting on the biggest news to hit Earth in centuries. And I can't tell anyone! To hell with private ventures and prizes if this is what it means."

She was surprised at how agitated she was. Maybe it was contagious. *Time for another session with Erika.*

"Well, I don't know what to say. We just gotta ride with it for a while, I guess." He stretched. "Back to my beans. Have fun with your shrimp."

She plunged happily back into her work. Outside, the wind whistled softly around the plastic walls. It was another reason she enjoyed the greenhouse—the sighing winds. Sounds didn't carry well here, and the hab was so insulated it was virtually cut off from any outdoor noise.

She was keenly aware that these were probably the only samples she was going to get, and there were many tests to run. As well, biologists all over Earth would want samples. She decided to try to grow some more. *After all, we've grown Earthly crops here . . .*

After some thought, she settled on a variant of the standard greenhouse mist chamber. On Earth these were used to induce cuttings to grow roots. Here she hoped it would encourage the mat to grow. *If it likes light, heat, and water, that's what I'll provide.*

She set it up next to the outside wall of the greenhouse for light. She prepared a shallow tray with some neutralized Martian soil for substrate. She guessed that the peroxides would be bad news for even the indigenous life. Rigging a sprinkler system came next, then concocting a watery brew of inorganic elements to sprinkle it with. *Dunno what it uses for energy—there are Earth organisms that like sulfur, even one that uses manganese. So I'll give it a metal cocktail and it can pick what it likes.* She made it airtight—duct tape to the rescue!—and provided a Martian air supply by splicing it into the glove box duct.

"Okay, I'm off." Marc's words broke into her musings. Julia realized she'd been completely lost in her work. "Is it time already? What's for dinner?"

"Greenhouse surprise." He held up a bag of vegetables. "I feel goulashy tonight."

"Mmmm. I've got to finish up here, then I'll be along. I want to try culturing the mat, see if I can keep it healthy. It'd be a pity to have to bring back only preserved samples."

"Shouldn't be too difficult. Keep it in a cold, dark, airless closet."

"Yeah," she said absently. "I wish I knew for sure

what triggers the swimming forms to pop out of the mat. But then I don't know why there are motile forms at all."

"Yeah, where would they go?"

"They swim, so that implies water. Lakes, rivers, oceans. Do you think there's open water farther down in the vent?"

He shrugged. "Could be. It's warm enough for sure."

"Doesn't help me much. I took several samples going down, and there are actually more swimming forms in the mat that's high up in the vent."

"Up high? Why would that be?"

"Well, I've got a crazy idea. I fooled around with the conditions in their sample dishes. Add water, and a few of them pop out. Warm it up, and more come out. But when you add light, they come *pouring* out. Water, heat, light . . . all together what do they suggest?"

"Ah . . . good times topside?"

"Yes. Your warm and wet episodes. Maybe the motile forms are the seeds, or the explorers. Bits of mat get blown out of the vent during outgassings. When conditions improve on the surface, the bits of mat land in a puddle, or a lake. The motile forms pop out and swim away to colonize it."

"Ingenious. I like it," said Marc, catching her enthusiasm.

"My problem is timing. What's your best guess about how often it could've happened?"

"A warm and wet time? My cores in Ma'adim Vallis covered a couple billion years of Mars history. From crater wall evidence there were at least two big, long-lasting lakes in Gusev crater. And I found several other layers with fossil microbes, as you recall. So, averaging something that I probably shouldn't, maybe every four hundred million years there's a major warming period. It's preceded by heavy volcanism. That provides the CO_2 to warm up the planet for a while."

"Four hundred million years is a long time to wait for a swim."

"Well, in between times, there are those upwellings of crustal water triggered by gosh knows what. Volcanoes, maybe. That gives them more chances."

"That sounds better."

"Yeah, and outgassings with bits of mat probably happen on a time scale of months, or at most years. So if there were a flood event, the mat could take advantage of it."

"Marc, you're a genius. Spiffy geology—sorry, areology—on demand."

He left humming. A happy geologist.

Outside, the sun was setting, and she knew the temperature was starting its steep plunge to subzero range. The thin atmosphere didn't have enough mass to buffer temperature changes. From one minute to the next it could change by twenty degrees Centigrade.

The dune buggy cruised slowly by, churning sand. She waved at Viktor enthusiastically through the murky sides of the greenhouse. They all knew to go back to the hab at sundown, another safety procedure to minimize risk.

After her shower she met Viktor in their bedroom. She unwrapped from her waffle-weave robe and sprawled, relishing nudity. The robe was cozy and allowed Raoul and Marc no tantalizing glimpses; no point in making it any harder on them.

Early on, she and Viktor had arranged their two cabins so that one was a bedroom and the other an office. They met there before dinner to unwind together on the nights when neither of them was cooking.

Innumerable nosy media pieces had dwelled on the tensions between a crew, half married and half not, complete with speculations on what two horny, healthy guys would feel like after two years in a cramped hab with a rutting couple just beyond the flimsy bunk partition. What tensions would emerge?

So far the answer was, nothing much. Raoul and Marc undoubtedly indulged in gaudy fantasy lives and masturbated often (she had glimpsed a porno video on Raoul's slate reader), but in the public areas of the hab they were at ease, all business.

There was no room for modesty in the hab, four people in a small condo for two years. They had unconsciously adopted the Japanese ways of creating privacy without walls. They didn't stare at each other, and didn't intrude on another's private space unless by mutual agreement.

Nobody had thought much about what the hab would be like if the newlyweds—well, it had been well over two years now, most of that time in space—got into a serious spat. Maybe on the half-year flight home they would find out. She would worry about that then; for right now—

Viktor was already in the cabin when she arrived, fairly humming. She kissed him warmly. "I had a wonderful time in the lab. How was your day?"

"My afternoon, you mean. You forgot we had lunch together? At newest bistro on Mars? Airbus Café?"

"I forgeet noothing, you old Rooussian bear." She liked to think that her accent was maybe lousy, but funny. At least he had never complained.

She looked around the room fondly. Add a TV set, a couch, and some beer, and they could be in one of those Hong Kong stacked microapartments. It was amazing how good it felt to be working again.

Viktor must've sensed her mood right away. "Okay. Tell me about Marsmat. What is it?"

"I sectioned a few pieces and looked at them with every microscope I have. It's a complex biofilm, all right, with layers of different types of organisms—anaerobic one-celled organisms, I guess."

"Has had billions of years to work."

"Subsurface life on Earth isn't as advanced as this, though."

"Conditions different."

"Ummm, yeah. Here the valiant anaerobes didn't have to fight a poisonous atmosphere of nasty oxygen."

"How advanced is this Marsmat? Or should call Marshroom?" His eyes twinkled.

"Leave terminology to the pros, please. The mat seems to be more advanced than a standard Earth biofilm, but maybe it only looks that way because it's bigger. There's a system of channels for transporting fluids, so even the interior cells get nutrients delivered and waste taken away. Like a communal circulatory system."

"Where is pump?"

"There doesn't have to be one."

"How does water move around?"

"Well, I think it moves vertically, not around."

"How do you get water to top of mat without pump? You said there was hundreds of meters of it."

"If the water column is unbroken, evaporation from the top pulls the water up. It's just like a tree. Evaporation from the leaves sucks the water up from the roots."

"So mat is flat tree?"

She looked at him with raised eyebrows. "That's not a bad way to look at it. The channels have some kind of stiffening in them. They remind me of xylem tubes—" She stopped at his slightly strained look.

"Am engineer."

"Okay. Botany lesson. A tree has a lot of narrow tubes—the xylem—that transport water up to the top—darn near four hundred feet for the tallest redwoods. The xylem tubes are dead, so the water isn't pumped up, it's *pulled* up—passively. Biology taking advantage of physics. It would work the same way here, only because of the .38 g's, a tree on Mars could be much taller."

"How tall is mat?"

"Don't know. We were down close to one klick and the structures were getting bigger. There was mat material way up in the vent, within a few tens of meters of the top. So, it extended several hundred meters at least."

"Is pretty tall, even on Mars."

"Well, I'm just working with ballpark estimates here. Plus I don't know for sure how the water transport works.

For example, there were cablelike structures running vertically and horizontally—looked like a circulatory system. Maybe they were full of water tubes. And—"

From the kitchen came the sound of the dinner bell. She stopped, suddenly out of gas. "Gosh I'm hungry."

Viktor laughed. "Pavlov was right. Ring dinner bell, get hungry."

She savored the air. "Mmmm, we're having goulash. Marc spent hours picking veggies. Let's go."

She never got around to asking him about his day in the ERV.

22

MEALS AFTER A DAY OF OUTSIDE WORK WERE SERIOUS matters. Marc had concocted a delicious beef dish loaded with greenhouse produce, a variant of his now-famous Mars Goulash. His original recipe had been an instant success, on both planets. Millions of people ate it regularly, and demanded more. The crew's subsequent book, *Recipes from Mars*, was the hottest-selling cookbook ever, part of the Mars fever that gripped Earth since their mission began. Never mind that most of the recipes were from their mothers, reworked by the NASA nutritionists.

The first ten minutes were mostly sincere compliments uttered through mouthfuls of it.

"Say," she said to perk up matters, "I'm figuring out how to announce the vent discovery."

Marc said, "Let ol' Axy's people handle it."

"Not done right, you get more woo-woo stories," Viktor said.

"You mean worse than that one about you?" Raoul grinned. "RUSSIAN STARTS DIAMOND MINES."

Julia said, "Remember that first month? ASTRONAUTS VISIT FACE ON MARS."

Marc added, "Followed by ANCIENT EGYPTIAN TEMPLE FOUND!"

Raoul shook his head in disbelief. "After you and Julia turned up those fossil cells, it was DINOSAUR BONES IN MARS ROCKS."

Viktor said, "Of course right away followed by COVER-UP OF ANCIENT DINOSAURS FROM MARS."

Marc said, "Those were the real woo-woo press, though. Media crap. But the *Tokyo Times* had that big feature SAND SKIING ON MARTIAN SLOPES, with pictures. All from a shot of me falling down! Just digitally add skis and go with it."

"Remember the *Frankfurter Zeitung* piece METEOR ATTACK! when we had a tiny hole?" Raoul said.

"The news shows played the sound of it for days," Julia recalled. "And then somebody changed that little whistle into a pop song background and paid Axelrod royalties."

Viktor nodded. "No money made from MARS QUAKES one, though. Maybe because no quake."

Raoul said, "The truth never stops them. You guys forgotten FIRST BABY DUE ON MARS?"

Julia laughed. "That came right before ABORTION RIFT SPLITS MARS COUPLE."

Viktor added, "Then was DIVORCE ON MARS? CONSORTIUM NOT TALKING."

Marc said, "Hey, they didn't let any of us off easy. LOVE TRIANGLES RUMORED AT GUSEV, that was in some Chinese paper."

Raoul grimaced. "It never ends. This last week, my media summary had CONSORTIUM TO AIRBUS: 'WE'LL SHOOT YOU DOWN' and NUKE ROCKET STERILIZES AIRBUS CREW. And that was after my gofer program supposedly edited out the real crap."

"How can a program know nonsense?" Julia asked. "Or the public? When Marc found ice, some supposedly respectable show features BURIED ANCIENT CANALS DISCOVERED. Science gets treated like candy."

Raoul said, "Axelrod told me once that journalism is the first draft of history. I hope not for us."

Viktor said soberly, "Our world has not enough to excite it. So it makes up things."

Julia nodded intently. "They have the usual wars and scandals, celebs and accidents. But what's to *do*? Shave a fraction of a second off the hundred-meter race, if you devote your younger life to it. Be the hundredth person to climb a certain high peak—never mind Everest, the crown is a trash heap now. Most of the people in our own countries are just sitting at home and

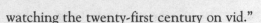

watching the twenty-first century on vid."

"Not us," Marc said quietly.

"Thank goodness!" Julia said. "Maybe being here so long makes me see it better, but geez, how *trivial* most lives are."

"Not here," Raoul said. "Here, it's desperate."

"And now we are desperate to leave it," Viktor said.

They ate in silence for a while, Julia still thinking. Marc switched the music to Mozart, their signal for dessert—strawberry shortcake, her favorite. When she could tear her mind away from her stomach, she looked over at Raoul. She could tell by his drawn, solemn face that it had been a long day and he was distracted. Precisely because it was all-important, nobody had mentioned his repairs.

As they finished up, Raoul announced, "We should all listen to Earthside's latest."

"Spare me," Viktor said. "You look, I lie down."

"No, I replayed some of this, it's important."

They settled in before the big screen. She and Marc had filed the obligatory story of the first social call on Mars, with all their footage. The first item in the priority vid was a squeezed, edited, and enhanced version. Raoul wanted to speed through it but the others wanted to see how they came off—not bad, of course, with emphasis on beaming faces rather than the fuming pingos.

Then came an anxious Axelrod. His yachting jacket was a bit rumpled and he looked worried.

"Your coverage was aces on the Airbus meeting. Got to let you know, though, that all of us here want to get your impressions of what they're planning to do. Any chance they'll finish their recon in a few months? I mean, and get all that ice melted and into their tanks? Raoul, Viktor, the engineers here need your assessment of their capability."

"How can?" Viktor talked back uselessly to the screen. "We see no gear, no hoses or mining equipment."

"Tell him to ask his spy guys for that," Marc joined in.

"—and keep track of how they're setting up. I mean, are they uncorking one of those inflatable habitats we heard about?" Axelrod flashed on the screen photos of trials done with blowup habs, one deployed in orbit.

"Never get me in one of those," Raoul said. "No radiation shielding." He had been strict about sandbagging the hab roof on the first full day after their landing. He had even strung more over the lip, to get more coverage. Viktor had remarked to Julia that after all, Raoul was hoping to have more children.

"—and their supplies. Point is, my guys, we're wondering down here if Airbus would maybe do an end run around you. Take off maybe a month or two after you do, but catch up on the return. With enough water, the engineers tell me, they could."

"Impossible," Raoul said. "They might have the tank volume, but mining that ice, no. It's a big job."

"—so we're depending on you to fill us in on everything you see. Go over there, sniff around. Invite them to the hab, big dinner and all. Maybe give them the rest of your booze, see if that loosens some tongues. I'd say, get them off by themselves for that, so they're not under Chen's watchful eye alla time." Axelrod smiled shrewdly. "See, we're putting out the story that we welcome these latecomers and all. But I smell a rat."

"He's off-base," Raoul said.

"True," Viktor said. "They cannot do all the Accords want, plus make their water reaction mass. Not in few months."

But Axelrod wasn't nearly through. On the screen popped the "pork chop" plots that showed the orbitally ordained launch windows. A big broad spot at the center was the minimum-energy zone. The window was broad, but its edges steep. Just above the spot was a high ridge-line when the energy costs became huge.

A glance told the story: Leave Mars between late January and late March, the dates laid out at the bottom. For these there were orbits for which the energy required to reach Earth was at the absolute minimum. On the left-hand axis were the arrival times on Earth.

"Now, I know you got all this in mind, Viktor, but just lemme see if I'm right here—"

Deciding on a trajectory was in principle simple. Pick a launch date, draw a straight line up into the minimum-energy spot. Depending on exactly which long ellipse Viktor chose, there were different arrival dates at Earth. Draw a horizontal line across the contours to the left-hand axis, tell your loved ones when to expect you in their sky.

"—if I'm readin' this right, you guys could launch right now and hit damn near the minimum. The contour at January 22, in a couple days, is just a bit higher than the absolute minimum. I read it to be eight kilometers per second of velocity needed. That's versus waiting for the bargain rate on March 14, uh, 6.1 kilometers per second. Now, I know that's not a minor difference. My guys tell me so we're talking maybe seventy-five percent more fuel needed. Not a small order."

"Energy goes as the velocity squared. You bet is not small," Viktor said.

"Impossible," Raoul said flatly.

Axelrod came from a business culture where much could be bought with smiling self-assurance, Julia realized. He was emphatically not a scientist. Deep down, she suspected, he believed that nature could be cajoled into behaving differently if you just found the right approach. He looked grave, then earnest, then respectful—the same sort of lightning-quick repertory she had seen from him in their first solo meeting. She did not doubt that he genuinely felt all those things, either. She had watched him carefully for years now, under the unique need to fathom his true meaning when she could not immediately interrogate him.

Finally, he beamed with renewed confidence. "But somewhere between now and March 14, there's a place where you guys can launch. I dunno where. I leave that to you." He leaned toward the camera, arms crossed. "But as soon as you can get off, do. Beat Airbus back, if they're planning to try a smash-and-grab operation. Hell, you get home quicker, anyway!"

Raoul froze Axelrod's confident smile. "So he has learned some orbital mechanics."

"Not very well," Viktor said. "Those total flight lengths, the diagonals—they show even Axelrod that if we leave earlier, we take more time."

Marc chuckled. "Maybe he thought we wouldn't notice?"

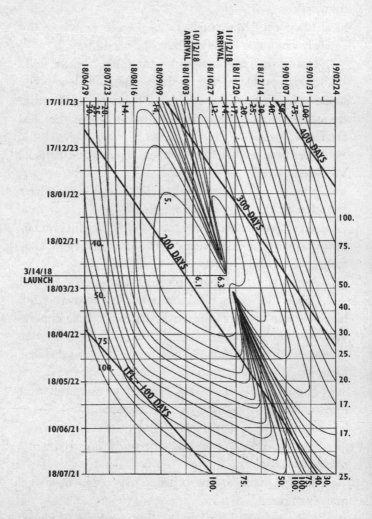

"No, I doubt that," Julia said. "He's not a detail thinker."

"You got it," Marc said.

"He's hiding a lot of anxiety," Julia said.

"Has thirty billion dollars on the table," Viktor said.

"So he probably figures the earlier you leave, the sooner you get there," Raoul said. "He didn't notice that the earlier launch dates are all further above the '200 DAYS' diagonal."

"We leave earlier, take longer, arrive little earlier," Viktor pondered.

"How's our incoming velocity?" Raoul said. "Can't read that from these pork chop plots."

"Will have to check," Viktor said. "All would bring us in with small speed. Between them all, is maybe one kilometer per second difference."

"Any trouble with our aeroshell?" Raoul pressed him.

Viktor shook his head thoughtfully. "No, is rated high. We can burn off the delta vee easily. Like coming back from moon almost."

"Okay then," Raoul said decisively. "We can do what he wants."

"Not so fast," Viktor said. "Matter of margin here. I like to have extra fuel, maybe twenty percent."

Raoul said, "That's a lot—"

"For ship standing on Mars for years, not so much," Viktor shot back.

Raoul glanced at the others. "We could drop our mass load some."

"Not much," Marc said. "It's just food, water, mostly."

"Personal effects, it's maybe enough to make a one percent difference," Raoul said.

"If drop all, could be," Viktor said.

Julia could tell Viktor was sitting back, letting the talk run to see what would come out. Even she could not read him all the time. Maybe that was the signature of a good captain. "I've got very little disposable."

"The most we have, masswise, is Marc's samples," Raoul said, not looking at Marc.

"Hey, the Mars Accords *require* those," Marc said.

"Not all of them," Raoul said.

"Damn near." Marc stood up. "I'm not compromising—"

"No point to argue," Viktor said smoothly. "I set safety margin. Marc, I need the total mass you're carrying back anyway."

Marc bridled. "You're not thinking—"

"Right, am not thinking. Just counting. Let me see total mass from everybody."

"You're going to shave the margin that close?" Julia asked wonderingly.

"I think about it."

"Next we'll be discussing Raoul's big old coffee mug," she said in an attempt at lightness.

It failed badly. Raoul's face clouded.

Julia said, "Just kidding. What bothers me about this talk is that I've got plenty to do on the vent life. I need a month, easily, to—"

"Plenty of time to do that on the trip home," Raoul said.

"I can't, not and keep to the bio protocols. I'd have

to work in the little onboard glove box, and there's not nearly enough room in there to carry out my experiments on—"

"Science isn't the issue here," Raoul said. "Let 'em do that Earthside, then."

"The samples will die! I don't know if they'll even survive tonight—"

"If they don't, that settles the issue, then," Raoul said.

She made herself take a deep breath. "It does not. I might want to go back down there, do more—"

"No more trips," Viktor said. "Raoul is right, science over."

"It's too early to say that! I—"

"It is too late," Viktor said calmly, turning to her. "Game now is get back fast."

"If we leave the big questions unanswered—"

"Airbus can answer," Viktor said. "They have time."

"But, but—" She could not see a way around him. "Look, let's hear the rest of Axelrod's message."

This was pretty transparent, but then, they did not know that she had specifically sent Axelrod a quick question about when to announce her discovery, tacked onto the Airbus reception footage.

Sure enough, Axelrod quickly moved to answer. After a little cheerleading, he said, "Oh yes, Julia. I'm not going to go anywhere with the life story. Sure, it's huge, but I've got lawyers on my tail here. The Planetary Protocol people, they'll go ballistic when we announce. I want to do that *after* you guys have lifted off. No stopping you then—and I think that's what's at stake here. Somebody—hell, maybe the Feds—will slap an injunction on me, try to stop you coming back at all. I mean it. You got no idea what this circus is like, back here."

"Oh no," she said weakly.

"—and Raoul, I want your verdict on the repairs, right away. Before you knock off for today. I know you're tired, all of you, been working hard. But we gotta know back here, make plans." He paused, beamed again. "Plans for your victory celebration, soon as we know the launch date."

They sat in silence as the screen went gray with static.

Julia fumed. "Damn him. This is the biggest story—"

"He knows the situation there," Raoul said.

"He is boss," Viktor said.

"Well, he doesn't control everything," she said. "I can blow the story any time."

Raoul's eyes bulged. "What!"

"Tell my parents, just let it slip. They'll know what I mean."

"You wouldn't," Raoul said.

"I would." She put more confidence into her tone than she felt. "Axelrod can't suppress news this big! We'll have a devil of a time explaining why we stalled."

"He is boss," Viktor said simply.

"If he told you to dump your gemstones, would you do it?" she said sharply.

Viktor looked affronted. "Is my personal mass."

"I'd say we may have to put all our cards on the table," she said in what she hoped was a calm manner.

"Hey," Marc said, "let's cool this off a little."

"I'm tired," Raoul agreed. "Got to call Earthside and report, too."

She tried to think of a way to smooth matters over. Better not let everybody sleep on unresolved issues. "How is it going?"

"Pretty well." Raoul smiled. "I'm replacing all the seals I can."

"Can?" Marc pressed.

"I'd like to replace every one. They've been standing in that damned peroxide dust for years. Impossible to tell if they have micropore damage, not without putting every square millimeter under a microscope. The temperature swings stress the material, crack it, peroxides get in, eat away—a nightmare."

For Raoul this was a long speech, especially lately. Julia said, "They only have to work once."

"Right, one clean shot. That's all I'm asking for." Raoul smiled wanly.

Viktor said, "As soon as I say we can lift, we go. Okay?"

There wasn't any real doubt. He was captain. But Julia seethed.

23

THEY SPENT ANOTHER DAY IN HARD, EARNEST LABOR. Raoul and Viktor were refitting every possible seal, testing every valve, examining electrical interfaces, endlessly checking, checking, checking.

There was plenty of gofer work for Julia and Marc. He, however, was more than willing to take some of her chores. That freed some of the day for Julia's greenhouse experiments. Just why Marc was so willing she did not question, though she suspected that his anxiety over the ERV exceeded his interest in the vent mat. Maybe he was trying to help everyone, bridging the growing gap in their interests with his work.

She forgot all that as soon as she stepped inside the greenhouse.

The mat samples were indeed growing. In the mist chamber the pieces had expanded and merged, nearly covering the available floor space. Where they touched they blended seamlessly: this was a surprise that hinted at their complexity. Individual bacterial cultures would maintain a perimeter, whereas cultured tissue from higher plants and animals would be expected to blend together. In a few places there was a hint of more complex structures.

She had enough material to start some more sophisticated biochemical tests. She gingerly cut off a piece of the mat, bracing for some kind of reaction. But nothing happened.

She froze, then thin-sectioned tiny pieces of mat for biochemical staining and microscopic examination. Under the microscope the colors showed that the basic constituents of life—proteins, lipids, carbohydrates, nucleic acids—were the same here, or at least close enough to respond to the same simple chemical tests.

"All right!"

This was already a big step. Although the biologists had been betting that Mars life would be carbon-based, no one had known for sure what she would find. Some had speculated it could be silicon-based—even some kind of self-assembling mineral life. But so far matters were a lot less strange.

Doing all the tests carefully took a lot of time, and she was more than ready to quit when she saw the dune buggy with the guys trundle slowly by.

The next day was equal parts tedium and excitement: careful, slow work rewarded by glimpses of the fast-growing and ever more complex biofilm. On her stretch breaks she stared through the plastic walls of the mist chamber and thought, *I'm looking at aliens.*

The words brought no fear, just wonder.

She was ready for the next step, to find out how close it was genetically to Earth life.

She used standard lab techniques and extracted what seemed to be DNA from the microbes. So how similar was it to Earthly DNA?

DNA spells out the amino acids, which then construct the cellular proteins—both the structural brickwork and the busy enzymes that do the cell's business. If Martian DNA spelled in the same language as on

Earth, it would mean unequivocally a common origin for life.

Time for biotech on a stick.

She prepared to run some comparative tests using the DNA of terran microbes she'd brought along. Basically, you unzip the double-stranded DNA helix by heating, then mix the soup of single strands with single strands of a different DNA. When the mixture is cooled down again, strands that are similar enough pair up.

Ten years earlier she'd have had to run through a series of tricky lab protocols. She'd done it often enough in grad school, but it would've been difficult under greenhouse conditions.

Luckily, development of elegant new chip-based technology and new theory had allowed her to bring to Mars a library of what was hoped to be representative genes from Earth organisms. These were mostly from microbes, and heavily biased toward primitive anaerobes, the archaebacteria.

Craig Venter, an Axelrod-type biotech entrepreneur, had sequenced some of Earth's smallest microbes and found that they shared about 300 genes in common. He argued that this was the minimum genome necessary for life. This notion was somewhat controversial, but had enough promise that Julia's gene library included Venter's selection.

The new technology was kin to simple home-use pregnancy and glucose test sticks. Unique sequences from microbial genes were attached to tiny glass chips in a rectangular array. Each was tagged with a fluorescent dye.

If the Marsmat DNA recognized a similar sequence by pairing with it, the dye would fluoresce. Picked up by a small charge-coupled detector, the results were displayed on Julia's electronic slate. The similar sequence "hits" would light up in the array, like a bingo card. The number of hits was the number of genes the Marsmat had in common with Earthly microbes.

That afternoon, her first test—using Venter's 300 "essential" genes—came up with seventy-nine hits.

Seventy-nine . . . what did that mean?

It was an equivocal answer. It was enough pairing to indicate that life on both planets used the same four-letter alphabet and probably the same language.

She longed to talk to Chen, or her old friend Joe Miller in Texas, or her dad. To work alone on a discovery of this magnitude was crazy. She could miss something important—*would* certainly miss something.

The automatic lights came on, startling her. It was dusk, and she'd have to hurry to beat the plummeting temperatures back to the hab.

The rest would have to wait.

As she suited up, she felt like Dr. Frankenstein working away in splendid isolation in his drafty old castle. But even he had Igor to talk to.

As she came out of her shower at the end of the day, Viktor was out in the public area, talking to the big screen. She paused. The screen view was of ruddy hills catching the first slanting beams of sunset. In the fore-ground stood Lee Chen in a brilliant sky blue hard suit.

"—found some interesting outcroppings on the

eastern slope. We went where you didn't—your tracks are still here. Our aim is to gather a wider range of samples, building upon what you have learned already."
Chen walked slowly to the left, opening up the view, and the camera panned after him. Julia could see the shadow of their rover.

"They are using our relay satellite," Viktor whispered to her.

"Some kind of deal with Axelrod?"

"Or NASA. I am not sure of rights."

"—and with Gerda I am preparing to take cores in areas similar to those of Marc and Julia. My goal here is to verify independently and yet in different terrain the stratigraphic density and dating data you acquired."

"Good idea," Julia said, leaning into their camera's field of view. "We've been wondering why we couldn't hail you."

Chen nodded. "A relay problem. I hope it is solved now."

"You have been out, all three, for three days?" she asked.

"Yes, testing our equipment. Our comm bands are not yours. Connection through satellite is best, we find."

"Cold enough for you?" Viktor asked mildly.

"We are adjusting. Temperature varies so much. Shadows are chilly always. At least, with the atmosphere so thin, it cannot chill us so quickly as the ground. My feet are always cold. What did you do to avoid this?"

"Put heating pads in the rover," Viktor said. "And come inside now. Do not go out for view of night sky."

"Very good advice. We violated it last night and Claudine may have frozen a toe."

"*Hoog!*" Viktor winced. "I the same, first week."

"But I am calling for more than a check-in," Chen said. "We will be back at the ship tomorrow. Please come for lunch with us."

"Thank you. We will come." Viktor glanced over his shoulder.

"I realize not all may be able to visit. Preparations for your launch—"

"I at least, and Julia," Viktor said, "What can we bring?"

"We have plenty of food, do not worry."

A few more pleasantries and Chen signed off. Julia said, "What was that about?"

"Maybe they are lonely."

"Or want to find out how our ERV work is going?"

Viktor grinned. "Billions of dollars being gambled on our ERV, Earthside, I hear on news."

"You mean, besides Axelrod?"

"Betting. I wish I could do myself."

She caught a mischievous twitch of his mouth. "You tried, didn't you?"

"Wanted to transfer my bank funds to my mother, she make bet. Some kind of rule stopped it, they say."

"Axelrod?"

"I suspect. Does not want heroic crew gambling."

"Good for publicity, if we bet on ourselves."

"But surprising? That it is not. He cannot sell for news value."

She kissed him quickly, as she heard Marc come clumping into the air lock with Raoul. "Once we get back, you'll lose that veneer of cynicism."

"Is genetic to Russians." He left to prepare dinner.

"I'll be in soon to help, ol' bear," she called after him.

For the first time in days she checked in for her personal mail. A long one from Mums and Dad came first. Her parents were sitting on the living-room couch, smiling but strangely stiff. As she watched their routine greetings she felt guilty about threatening to leak her big vent-life news through them. Using your family as a pipeline was tawdry, even if it might be necessary. She hoped that matters would never come to that.

Amid such musings she sat bolt upright. Her father was saying in his matter-of-fact way, "—turns out it's pretty serious."

She thumbed back. What had she missed, daydreaming?

"We wanted you to be the first to hear, in case it got out into the damned media and worked around to you. The other shoe's dropped on this darned virus, and it turns out it's pretty serious. Unfortunately, it's affected my liver, caused a cancer. In that way it's similar to hepatitis IV, only it moves much faster. Dunno what you know about liver cancer, but according to the docs, you don't get a discrete tumor. Instead, it just infiltrates throughout the liver tissue, so it's difficult to treat. The standard menu of treatments is not very appetizing: chemo, radiation, liver transplant. I'm not doing anything right away until we look around some more." He took a deep breath, as though exhausted. "Sorry to drop this on you, with all the stuff you're dealing with right now, but Robbie and I felt you should hear it without embellishments." He smiled wanly and sat back into the cushions.

She halted the vid, checked quickly for the date it was sent: two days ago! *Oh, Lord.* Remorse washed over her. *I've been so wrapped up in everything here, they must think I don't care.*

She blinked, feeling an almost physical ache at the prospect of her parents facing this alone. Bill was gone, and she was millions of miles away. Would she be back in time?

Without waiting to see the rest of the message, which she expected would be full of "interesting" news items, she squirted a short greeting and good wishes, with the promise of a longer message soon. She felt an intense desire to tell them about the Marsmat, to give them something else to think about. *Gotta check with Axelrod about a secure feed, then I'll tell them.*

She was aware of an inner turmoil. She sat back, consciously cleared her mind, and relaxed. On the vid-screen, the colors outside were darkening rapidly. She thumbed the controls to the back camera, so she could see the sunset. She'd always liked watching the sunset on Earth, even parking her car to get out and gawk if a particularly good one was in progress. Here on Mars she tried to watch as often as she could, with Viktor if possible. It was one of the quiet moments they shared. Raoul and Marc didn't seem to care much.

Tonight's sunset was fairly typical—yellow sun in a blue-gray sky. Earth's glorious sunsets were red, but on Mars the daily red gave way often to blue skies at dusk. She stared at it until the screen was black, then reluctantly turned it off. If the engine test went well, she wouldn't be seeing many more.

She felt a yearning both to stay and to get back to Earth. It was going to be hard to leave, knowing it was forever. She could hear Viktor rattling dishes next door in the galley. Despite the physical hardship and the constraints, she'd been happy here.

Well, luckily, I don't get to decide.

She went into the kitchen and shredded the cabbage viciously.

"We're piling up the social obligations here," Julia said as they approached the Airbus ship's elevator. Its name, *Valkyrie*, sprawled in big letters across the shiny white crown in an electric blue.

"I am thinking we not get to repay," Viktor said, "until on Earth."

"Leaving that soon?" Marc asked, huffing audibly into his suit mike.

"I estimate we could make our safety margin within three weeks," Viktor said.

"I agree with the calculations," Raoul said. "Cutting it a little close for comfort, launching that early, but—"

"Wow! Headed for home." Marc beamed as they closed the elevator door and started up.

"We not discuss this at lunch," Viktor said, looking at each of them in turn.

"No launch at lunch, check," Marc said happily.

"We are here to find out what we can," Viktor said carefully.

"I don't want to be here at all," Raoul said.

"Take a break from repairs," Viktor said. "Good for spirit."

"Think they'll have spirits?" Marc was still bubbling from the news.

"We're not out of alcohol yet," Julia said.

It was somehow Viktor-like to tell Marc the news just before entering the critical discussions with the Airbus crew. He had a theory, maybe typically Russian, that people worked best when they were responding to a quick challenge. Or maybe he just occasionally liked to jerk people's chains; nobody's perfect.

"Yeah, but after launch, we'll want to celebrate," Marc said. "We should save our own, drink theirs."

"After lunch, somebody's got to drive back," Raoul said.

"So who's the designated driver?" Marc grinned.

"No drinking for anyone," Viktor said. "Still work to be done in this day. And I want no loose tongues inside."

They all nodded, though Marc was still grinning maniacally. The Airbus lock was small and they showered down their suits using the one hose. She was first into the living quarters. Chen greeted them with plum wine again. She got hers before Viktor was in the room, and the others politely took their glasses but didn't sip any. She downed hers, though Viktor frowned. She gave him an impish smile. Marc saw it and took a sip himself. Discipline was breaking down all over the place.

"We have a little lunch laid out," Chen said, ushering them into the tiny dining area. No food was visible. "First, however—"

He led them into the staging bay. There Gerda and Claudine stood proudly beside—

"Trailblazer!" The 2009 rover/prospector craft stood there, showing the wear that almost a decade of service had inflicted upon it. Julia automatically bent down and touched it.

It had roved over a lot of Gusev Crater after its 2009 landing, helping make the case for human exploration there. When they arrived, it was still serviceable. She had steered it herself, from inside the hab, on further excursions, until it had broken down near the northern crater rim sixty kilometers away. They had left it there, since Raoul did not have adequate repair parts, and the dune buggy could do many of Trailblazer's tasks now.

"We ran across it," Gerda said, "and thought to take it home."

"To repair?" Raoul asked, puzzled.

"No, to have as keepsake," Claudine said.

Julia frowned. "To take it back to Earth?"

"A collector has paid for its return," Gerda said.

"You're going to haul it all that way . . ." Viktor shook his head in wonder. "They must be crazy back there."

Chen stroked Trailblazer's badly pitted solar panels. "We can also learn much about weathering conditions here."

"You'll have plenty of time to do that," Marc said sardonically.

Chen blinked, his lips thinning under pressure. "Not so much as you."

Julia had worked with Chen enough to read his

subtle moods. "You'll spend your time on biology? With only three of you—"

"No," Chen said, turning to her. "Though I wish to discuss that in detail with you. I have brought different laboratory apparatus, some specially designed in light of your findings here. Particularly I shall study the fossil cells, and try to find many more."

Julia carefully did not give anything away in her face. It was going to be unbearably exacting to talk shop with Chen when she had a greenhouse of *the real stuff*—and could not breathe a word of it. *Aaaargh!* "That will help fill in the history of life here."

"We spent our first days collecting samples, some short-range drilling," Gerda said. "Your reports were correct. The labor is difficult in the suits."

"Wait'll you get calluses where you never expected them," Marc said to Claudine. "Those suits are murder."

"I would appreciate instruction in avoiding that," Claudine said, her voice softening.

"We expect to circumnavigate Gusev Crater in perhaps a week," Chen said. "We shall be taking drill samples every ten kilometers from the walls."

"You've seen my topo maps, right?" Marc said. "Space your holes between mine, we'll get a better sample grid."

Viktor was still studying Trailblazer, frowning. "We can map out complementary methods, cooperation, yes."

"In our stay here we can expect, in sixty days, only to augment your pioneering—"

"Sixty?" Viktor demanded quickly.

"We shall launch at the very end of the return window."

"You have a different class of trajectory in mind?" Viktor asked.

She saw what was coming in Chen's deliberately blank expression, the eyes studying Viktor like a laboratory specimen. "An accelerated one, yes. Faster than your Hohmann orbit."

In the long silence that followed she remembered the embarrassed quiet of only a few days before, one of suppressed giggles. Now all seven eyed each other as the words sank in. Flinty anger in Viktor's eyes, Marc's openmouthed astonishment, Raoul's mouth scrunched into a tight arc. A studied, calm gaze from the other women.

"To beat us back," Raoul said loudly.

"You knew it was a race," Chen said.

"But the Mars Accords!" Julia blurted. "You can't possibly get the range, the depth of our studies here! We've got hundreds of kilos of—"

"All invaluable, of course," Chen said smoothly. "We shall depend enormously upon your reports, to be sure."

"What? What?" Marc sputtered. "You—"

"We shall visit the sites you found most productive," Gerda said slowly, formally. "Taking parallel samples from nearby will nicely verify your work and provide an interesting set of—"

"Verify?" Julia's mind spun. "The Mars Accords require a *lot* of representative samples and a cross section—"

"We believe we will be able to persuade the Accord Board that we have complied with their essential minimum," Gerda said mildly.

They've rehearsed this, Julia thought. She could sense

the barely suppressed energy in the room. "Look, damn it, this makes no sense. Trying to run around, snatch up a few things—"

"Ah," Gerda pounced. "But we have your thorough work as a guide. In two days we were able to complete a satisfying fraction of the geological—"

"You're following in our tracks!" Marc shot back.

"Well, of course," Gerda said in the slow, pedantic tone that was really starting to get on Julia's nerves. And this cramped room, the seething anger—Gerda raised a finger, as if in a lecture. "There is nothing wrong with science building upon the work of—"

"This isn't science!" Viktor exploded.

"It's a goddamned race!" Raoul finished for him.

Julia said, "And you're trying to sneak in, grab stuff from where we've found it, and scoot back Earthside. Nobody believed you'd try that, because we've done real exploring here, and, and—" She gasped for air, suddenly aware that she had been holding her breath.

"We shall satisfy the minimum requirements," Gerda said. "I am sure we all realize that the Mars Accords have been, ah, reinterpreted several times during your stay here, to increase the work you needed to do. That was perhaps a bit greedy of the Accords Board. We intend to hold them to their original statement of work, and contest their decision in court if need be."

She's not an engineer, she's a goddamned lawyer, Julia thought giddily.

"You could not have done this," Viktor said tightly, "if not for finding the ice under the pingos."

Chen had been quiet the last minute, letting Gerda

carry the argument forward, obviously by arrangement. Now he said, "That was the break we had for so long hoped. Originally we planned to go to the northern pole and use the snows there. Conditions would have been difficult in the cold. Making the proper scientific studies would have taken much more time. But your discovery of the pingo hills, measuring the depth of the ice—yes, that did it."

Marc slammed his fist abruptly into a bulkhead, startling them all. "I cleared the way for you."

Chen said, "I wish we could all look at this as scientists." He smiled benignly.

It flashed to Julia that Chen was especially enjoying baiting Marc. *He's gloating. He still resents Marc for coming back to the Consortium,* she realized.

"Some of us are engineers," Viktor said ominously. "Pilots."

Chen nodded thoughtfully. "We do not take from you the glory of being the first."

"Just the first to return," Julia said sharply.

"Well, yes," Chen allowed civilly. "We shall win the Mars Prize. Races usually do go to the swift. Surely this outcome must have occurred to you."

24

THEY DIDN'T STAY FOR LUNCH AFTER ALL.

The ride back was irksome, and not just because they had to eat their emergency rations.

After Chen's announcement, there was no choice. Viktor had led them proudly out into the Airbus lock, refusing to sit down to lunch with "our sneak competition." Julia's stomach was in a knot anyway. She never knew what to do in tricky situations—thank God Viktor was captain. He hadn't hesitated for a minute.

Rover Boy's emergency kit stocked cereal bars and sugary water, yucky stuff at the best of times, and these were not the best. The one container of real food had been removed to make room while Raoul was moving his machine shop to the ERV.

They traded dour looks and munched, each so self-involved that nobody except Marc, who was driving, looked out at the midday view. The white dot of Phobos hung on the eastern horizon. Julia rode alongside Marc while the other two sat in the fold-downs behind.

"Bastards," Raoul said. "Steal our results . . ."

"We broadcast them to the world," Julia said. "The Consortium made a fortune selling those ride-along virtual reality shows. I guess in a way it served them right."

"Only *we* pay," said Marc. "Twice."

"Yes. Was big pain to make them," Viktor said.

"So now Chen can visit each site, know just where to look," Marc said. "Just great."

"We have a hole card, though," Julia said. "The vent life."

"Thank God we kept it secret," Marc said.

Raoul brightened. "The Mars Accord panel—right. When we get back, even if we come in second—"

"*Then* we spring our surprise—real life-forms," Julia said eagerly. "We say that to come back with a bunch of rock cores and miss the Marsmat is unacceptable. That Airbus did a smash-and-grab operation, not a scientific exploration at all."

Marc said happily, "Yeah, that's in the formal wording of the Accords; 'Carry out a thorough scientific exploration of a landing site of relevance to important issues, especially the past or present existence of life there.' Airbus sure isn't gonna do that."

Julia smiled. "You memorized it."

"Thirty billion riding on that wording," Marc said. "You bet your ass I did."

Viktor nodded soberly. "Good argument. No lawyers here, however. We do not know how will play to the Accords Board."

"I'm betting they'll buy it," Marc said.

Viktor said, "I like to think so."

Raoul said, "We have to keep it secret, though. Not give Airbus a chance to find the vent and go down it."

Julia said, "Absolutely." At Viktor's surprised look she added, "And I wouldn't have said that until about an hour ago."

"That'll fix the bastards," said Raoul gleefully.

Viktor said bitterly, "They melt pingo ice while they collect samples at our already explored sites."

Raoul said, "The nuke gives them all the energy they need to drill the ice, heat it up, drive pumps."

"Nice touch, to deliver to us the repair kit," said Julia.

"Why not?" growled Marc. "We found their fuel for them. And I thought I was so damned smart, getting into the pingos."

"Or another idea . . ." Raoul stared into space.

"Where else is fuel?" Viktor asked.

"Suppose they bet we would fail. The ERV wouldn't fly. Then they could use the ERV's methane," Raoul said bitterly.

"Very neat," Julia said ruefully. "They had backup strategies, and one of them paid off."

"Only if they can get back first," Raoul said vehemently.

Silence. Then, "Can we beat them?" he asked Viktor.

"Possible. We think so much in terms of Hohmann orbits, I must check with Earthside to judge non-Hohmann."

"There are a lot of choices of liftoff dates, plus added delta vee needed?" Raoul asked. "I remember some 3-D plot."

"Infinity of choices," Viktor said. "Maybe double infinity, I am not mathematician."

"They have to load a lot of melted ice," Raoul said. "Can't get that done and do much sample collecting."

Marc said, "They had half a year to sit in their little can and think how to do it."

"Will be great opportunity for gamble," Viktor said. "Old technology of chemical rocket, race against new nuke."

"Chemical rockets are tried and true," Raoul said. "They're more reliable."

"But in long run," Viktor said mildly, "nukes are the way to explore and develop the solar system. Mine asteroids, move things."

Raoul frowned. "Yeah, I guess. But the old tech had better come out ahead, this one last time."

They all nodded and munched their bars.

As Zubrin Base came into sight, they struggled into their helmets and gloves and prepared to disembark. Marc dropped Viktor and Raoul by the dune buggy, and with Julia continued around to the hab's airlock.

Viktor and Raoul took off for the ERV in a cloud of dust, the rusty fines falling with a leisurely reluctance.

To Marc fell the prickly task of informing Axelrod about Airbus's plans. "Although he won't be surprised," Marc predicted.

As he packed up his geology cores for transfer to the ERV, he would be on open comm with Julia. This informal kind of backup was a system they had worked out over the long months when any two of them were working close by.

"Okay, I'm off for Frankenstein's greenhouse," she said as she prepared to leave the hab in skinsuited garb.

As she entered her inflatable castle, Julia was surprised to see the clarity of the greenhouse walls obscured by a light coating of condensation. Puzzled, she walked the length of the greenhouse to check the controls. The heaters were set on high. *Of course!* She popped her helmet and felt warm air. She'd been keeping the heaters on high so she could work without getting cold. *Guess I forgot to turn them down when I left yesterday. Good thing we're not paying any electric bills. Still, I'd better remember today.* She gratefully removed her parka and outer gloves and left them and her helmet on the greenhouse bench next to the controls. *That way, I'll have to come back to retrieve them and I'll remember to reset the controls.*

She drew in a warm, foggy breath. Life! The only human-friendly biosystem within a hundred million miles. Until they had ventured to dear, dry Mars, nobody had felt, month after month, how barren the rest of Creation was. In this little space, cupped against the soil, was a tiny human garden. Its moist promise reminded her of the vent descent.

She walked back over to the mist chamber. It was hard to see inside due to the condensation, but there seemed to be a mass of Marsmat against the greenhouse wall. *Interesting. It's growing toward the light, like a damn plant. Only even thinking of it as a plant is wrong; it's alien. Oh, well, I'll check it later. Gads. There's so much to do here all of a sudden.*

In her head a list of studies was assembling. Now that the vent life was reproducing, she'd need more microscopic work to determine how it divided. If it had some type of chromosomes or was truly prokaryotic. And a whole bunch of interesting stuff about what environmental clues it responded to . . .

Her mind was whirling happily. There was enough

work here for years, not weeks! She sighed. If they lifted off quickly in order to beat Airbus back, she'd have to figure out how to keep her precious specimens alive for over half a year. But that was for later.

Today she was going to find out whether the vent harbored a distant cousin, or an alien.

She looked over her library of genes. They represented a wide spectrum of organisms, the soup to nuts of Earth life.

It was reasonable to expect that Mars life would most closely resemble Earth's primitive anaerobes, the archaebacteria, for a couple of reasons. If Earth and Mars had exchanged life early on, there would have been something like these organisms on both planets. Both worlds had an early CO_2-rich atmosphere, after all.

On Earth, wildly successful photosynthetic bacteria—once called blue-green algae—sucked up the CO_2 and produced oxygen as a waste product. So abundantly, in fact, that they altered the planetary atmosphere. After about two billion years, Earth's atmosphere contained only a tiny amount of CO_2, and about 20 percent oxygen. Soon afterward, multicellular life arose to take advantage of the energetic oxygen. The anaerobes retreated underground, where they remained still.

That revolution probably never happened on Mars. The atmosphere had bled away before the great blooming of the photosynthesizers. As the air thinned and the temperature dropped, the surface water froze, then sublimed away.

And life? Well, it went underground—and here it was, growing not a meter away.

Many people thought they knew life had never had a chance on Mars. Dead wrong! So what had been the real history of Mars life? And could she figure it out in three weeks? Or less?

Might as well go for it.

She picked three arrays of genes from different kinds of archaebacteria, at random, and set them up for testing against the solution of prepared Marsmat DNA.

She worked methodically, compensating for the inherent clumsiness of the glove box by being slow and careful. She remembered a poster in the office of one of her more obnoxious faculty advisors. Under a large picture of a rhino were the words "I may be slow, but I'm always right."

No one would argue with a charging rhino, but they would with her. She had to be very careful.

At last she completed the protocols and inserted the first incubated gene array into the little electronic reader that was hooked up to her slate.

The image of the gene array appeared. As she watched, the biological bingo board started to light up with a few fluorescent hits. *Aha, gotcha.* One part of the board in particular was live. When the reader was finished, she saved the results, popped the sample out, and put in the second one. This bingo pattern was similar: a few hits here and there, and a concentration in one area. Finally, the third sample was being read. She concentrated on where the hits were. *Lessee, somewhere in this program is the list of what genes are where in this field . . .*

Forty percent of archaebacterial genes did not match

any other Earth life genes. Were they too primitive, or what?

No one really knew. They were included in the arrays, however.

Through her intense concentration she felt something odd. *What . . . ?*

It was a slight breeze rippling her hair. This had just registered when her ears popped.

Pressure drop? The lock seal failing?

"Oh no—I'm busy!"

Her training kicked in. She nudged her comm connection in the collar of her skinsuit. "Marc, I've got a pressure drop out here." Always report trouble, even if you don't understand it.

He responded immediately. "Keep talking."

She pulled her hands out of the thin inner glove linings, looking around. The heat and humidity had painted the walls thick with beaded moisture. "The lock looks okay, but . . ." *You couldn't tell if a seal was failing without—*

The breeze increased. Not toward the lock. Blowing down and to her right.

She knelt and peered around. The footing of the glove box was firmly attached to the low greenhouse bench and she could see nothing beyond. The damp was pleasantly warm but obscured her view. She edged around the hard plastic of the box. With her right hand she wiped moisture off the side, peering inside.

Was that a thin whistling? "Might have a micro-meteorite puncture. Trying to find—"

She froze. Something was standing straight up from

the soil in the chamber. Pale, like celery in its sinewy rippling. It curved partway up, toward the side of the box. She looked toward the seal between box and greenhouse wall. A thin fog hung in the air there.

"Looks like one of my samples has grown like crazy. The Mars life, it's wedged itself into the corner where the box—"

The whistling suddenly rose to a shriek.

Startled, she rocked back on her heels. The wind whirled by her head. Toward the wall. Her ears popped again.

"Damn! The leak's growing."

She could *see* it now. The stalk stuck out from the corner where the box met the wall. It moved visibly, forcing itself through.

Falling into the crack?

She refused to believe it was moving on its own.

Why grow toward the edge?

The Mars plant had stuck through the tough plastic and into the greenhouse. The end of it was pointed, leathery. It had poked out through the absolute worst place, breaking out to Martian pressures and the greenhouse at the same point.

Automatically she reached for it. Cold, wet, slick, tough. She pulled at it. Rubbery resistance.

"Trying to patch," she reported.

But with what? Her hand slipped around it, air rushing past. She couldn't stem that flow with her palm.

She drew in a deep breath. Or tried to.

Time slowed. Her heart thumped in her ears.

Quickly she glanced around. Across the greenhouse

all the plants were whipping in the wind. Her kit—

It was on the other side of the box. And the patches in there probably wouldn't handle this awkward split, anyway.

Screaming wind. She grabbed a sample bag and crammed it into the corner. It stuck, but only over part of the crack.

Get more.

She leaped up and moved around the box. Marc's voice squawked at her from her comm. The damned sample bags were blowing around. She snatched for one, missed. Her ears popped again.

She caught a bag and started back toward the breach. Something tripped her. She fell in slow motion. Reached out, grabbed. Hand on the box edge. Caught herself, jerked upright. Went on. Something tapped her on the head.

She looked up. The ceiling was falling. No more pressure to hold it up.

She dropped down, struggled toward the breach. It was like an angry mouth, screaming. She slapped the bag over it, but—

Not enough. Where are the rest? Losing air fast.

Only then did she think about her helmet.

Idiot! Where did you—

She stood up and the collapsing heavy plastic smacked her in the face. Crouching, she waddled around, trying to remember where she had put the helmet.

Usually by the lock, on the workbench.

She duck-walked toward it. She was breathing hard but nothing was coming in. It took forever to cover the ten meters. Before she got there the ceiling settled down over her. She pushed up but it was surprisingly heavy. She could raise it a foot or so but no more.

Where's that helmet?

She couldn't see in the foggy air. The density was dropping fast and water condensed out in thick clouds.

She blinked to clear her eyes. Her eyelids were slow. *Freezing? Drying out?*

Helmet!

The idea came to her and without hesitation she knew it was right. The helmet was somewhere around here but already her eyes were getting a gluey feeling. She was not going to find it in time. Too hard to see.

Got to get to the hab.

The lock is right here!

She rolled sideways. The lip of the lock was easy to see. She felt upward under the still settling plastic.

There. The release was simple, a lever. She pulled.

The hatch swung open under the fading greenhouse pressure. The shrieking was thinner now, running out of air. Just like her.

She crawled through into the short space. Fumbled up for the outer hatch release. Found it. Pulled.

Her shoulder shoved it open. Dimly she remembered what they had said a few thousand years ago about low pressures.

Don't try to hold your breath.

She got to her feet and shoved the hatch open the rest of the way. It seemed heavy.

No sound at all now. But her heart hammered in her throbbing ears.

Keep the main air passages open and the pressure will not build up, she remembered that much. Opening her throat let a gush of air out, expanding so much she felt the rush of it.

Brilliant light all around. She blinked again. Something like sand in her eyes.

The sun was a hard bright ball on the horizon. Lancing light struck her face. *Full UV. And cold.*

She made herself run. The prickly sensation in her face was swarming down over her whole body and some part of her mind struggled to understand it. *Never mind.*

The blazing sunshine helped, framed each detail. She had never realized how much of Mars she was missing, seen through the helmet.

Go. Her legs pumped and her throat boiled with suppressed air. The one lungful of air was foaming out of her, a stream of vapor condensing into tiny crystals that glinted in the blaring light. Above the collapsing greenhouse a mushroom of rising vapor was turning into snow.

Her lungs still felt full. The last dregs of air expanded under the hundredfold pressure drop outside.

She set her course. Around the hab, first.

Each step seemed to take forever.

The skin makes a pretty fair space suit, a lecturer had said once, somewhere, somewhen.

Pressure wasn't the problem. Her pounding head could not think very well but it reminded her to keep her mouth open. *Let the gas laws work for you.*

She had gone ten meters and her legs were like logs, thumping her feet down. Coming around the round hab walls, she studied the landscape with a floating curiosity.

All details were sharp, hard. She was still exhaling, a fog falling from her, ice crystals shimmering in it. Her face was starting to hurt. Lips freezing.

Time for another blink. Her eyelids slid down and wanted to stay there. Run blind?

Thump, thump, thump, went her feet, so very far away.

An idea there—? Keep eyes closed, stop the corneas from freezing.

Maybe the eyelids will freeze to the corneas. Hard to open them then.

Thump, thump.

Cranking up the eyelids was like lifting weights. Gravel in the gears somewhere.

She was farther along the curve of the hab now. Here came the lock, looming on the hab horizon like a tarnished promise.

Stiff, slow, her legs churned. No more helpful air boiled out of her. Nothing but a hollow feeling left. Something biting hard in her throat. She tried to force out a last packet of air, *first shout ever on Mars,* but there was nothing, nothing.

The lock. She saw it coming toward her, wobbly as it came, like a child bounding out, glad to see her.

The exterior buttons were sharp and clear and all she had to do was bring her arms up to punch the green CYCLE button. It took a long time, though, long enough to wonder why everything was taking so much effort.

Her arms were not working right. It was dark all of a sudden except for a narrow tunnel of filmy light, straight in front of her, a flashlight beam. In it she watched her right hand come up and punch for the CYCLE and miss it.

Try again. Can't be that hard . . . Missed again . . .

Her hand would not do what she told it to.

Try the other? No, it would not get here anytime soon.

Something else. Movement. Not her hand.

The lock.

Opening out.

So fast, too. She stepped back and tried to get her breath and felt something pop in her chest.

Marc. He looked so big in his green suit.

But he tilted back and fell away and the sky was there. Soaring.

A dark hole at the top of it. Black on pink. Beautiful.

25

JANUARY 25, 2018

SHE FELT FRAGILE, JUST LYING IN BED LIKE A RAG DOLL.

She lay still and listened to the hab warm up. It stretched and groaned as the metal expanded, a slow long clamor that marked both dawn and dusk. Not the sighing of soft breezes through drooping paper-bark trees, but it would have to do.

She'd slept restlessly, moaning and thrashing intermittently, according to Viktor. He'd looked at her with a solemn, searching expression, a furrow between his eyes. Later he'd insisted that she just rest up the whole day, and part of her wanted to do just that.

A quiet throbbing ran down her throat and into her chest. At times she felt that she carried the medals of a Soviet field marshal on her chest, pinned not to a uniform but to her skin. Her lips were swollen from their near freezing and the dehydrating effect of the tenuous atmosphere. Her eyes still felt sandy, an effect Earthside medicos found intriguing—which meant they didn't understand it. Nobody had ever survived a "vac event," as space station jargon called it. Sure, there had been suit ventings, quickly patched, but nobody had run for their life before. The external cameras had caught most of her frantic, slobby sprint—big, loping strides in the low gravity, a wreath of pearly fog trailing her head the whole way.

And with the video had come her terse descriptions of Martian life ripping through industrial-strength plastics. The audio had gone out to Earthside, too.

She tried not to think about it, and of course failed.

But after a good sleep and an hour of lounging around past breakfast, she got restless. In her robe she ventured forth, to find that Raoul and Viktor were long gone for the ERV. Viktor had checked on her earlier, and she had drifted off immediately. "Oh?"

"You were asleep, prob'ly didn't notice," Marc said, offering her some tea. She had thanked him profusely as soon as he got her into the lock, and the wonderful sensation of filling her lungs again had passed. He got embarrassed if she brought it up any more.

She eased into her acceleration couch, the best place to snuggle.

She had a deep facial sunburn, eyeballs showing red veins, dead skin on her earlobes, and overall felt as delicate as antique porcelain. "I must still be a little rocky. Mmm, it's warm in here."

"Yeah, Viktor turned up the hab temperature for you."

That meant heating the water jacket. They had ample power reserves in the nuclear thermal generator they carried down near the work level, so everything was pleasantly warm to the touch. The walls radiated it, the water shielding out the cosmic radiation, providing the vital fluid of their entire biosphere, and warming them. It was always a source of quiet reassurance to her that at night, sleeping together, she and Viktor were each blocking for the other some small fraction of the background radiation that lanced down from the skies here. Human shields against the unrelenting danger of the universe beyond Earth.

"You're the big media star, now," Marc said. "Axelrod sent you a congrats message. Here, I'll play—"

"Belay that. I'm not strong enough."

"Yeah, he's going over the top a lot now."

"The test?"

"Remember Viktor's crack about there being an 'i' in 'win'? Well, that 'i' is Axelrod, for sure."

She smiled wanly. "He's worried his billions might slip away."

"You shoulda seen him last night, after you'd nodded off. Going over all kinds of details with the folks simulating the test, asking Raoul questions about the pressure levels. Man!"

"Does he understand it all?"

"Doubt it. He obsesses over it, though—knows how to do that."

"They think they can do the test today?"

"If everything looks right to Raoul, yeah. He'd much rather be out there working than in here listening to Axy yammer on."

She might as well get it over with. "How'd the greenhouse footage go over?"

Marc's mouth twisted. "Couldn't cover it up. You were yelling about the Mars life and that got onto the audio. We didn't know it until the autofeeder had sent the whole segment Earthside."

"Oh."

"Axelrod loved it, action scene and all. Aired it right away."

"He didn't hold off?"

"He—hell, everybody—thought it was just an accident. But the audio gave it away, once you played it through carefully."

She grimaced. "And only a million or two people bothered with that."

"Right. At the Consortium, nobody realized the implications until too late."

He thumbed on a stored video: SPECIAL MARSCAST. Massaged by the Consortium staff, the probable number in the audience was inserted at the bottom:

1,856,000,000. She often wondered how reliable these new smart estimator programs were, but the import was clear—the bulk of humanity that could watch was tuned in.

There she ran, looking like an idiot, mouth yawning and legs churning, eyes bulged out. Voice-over by a solemn commentator: "The greenhouse was punctured by a form of Mars life the team *had not reported* to anyone but the Consortium bosses. That is the only possible deduction from conversation mistakenly leaked by the Consortium itself, in the hubbub after Julia Barth's heroic miracle run—"

"Off, off." She waved it away.

"Look, it had to get out," Marc said.

"Not now."

"No kidding. Look at this."

A jump cut to: "Already dozens of activist groups— led by the Protect Earth Party, PEPA, Mars First! and the newly formed, fast-growing Earth Only Movement, seen here in their Paris offices—have moved to legally compel the Consortium to not allow a liftoff of the Earth Return Vehicle. This would—"

"Lotsa luck," Marc said dryly.

She chuckled. "A lawyer in Paris trying to stop Viktor from hitting the firing button, from a hundred million miles away?"

"They write out a writ or whatever, those guys think they've got the world by the tail."

"That world, maybe. Not this one."

"Hey, don't look so sad, gal. This is just media fluff."

She hadn't realized that her expression was so easy to

read. "I don't like word getting out this way. MARS LIFE ATTACKS JULIA."

"We went back over there and had a good look from outside. That spike, it's still alive."

"Surviving on the surface?" She blinked, eyes rusty.

"Tough sonofabitch. I gave it a yank, couldn't pull it out."

She nodded. "It's attached to all the rest of the mat in there. That figures. It's adapted to move in on any warm, wet site and exploit it to the full. What organization! To grow that fast—"

"Don't put it that way to Earthside. They'll all gang up on us."

"Ummm . . . It's tough, all right—but an anaerobe. Oxygen would kill it right away."

"Why didn't the greenhouse air do it in, then? The stuff in the vent was awfully sensitive to our oxy."

She frowned. "Good question. Probably a concentration effect. Our tanks carry pure oxy, under pressure. Stuff we're breathing here isn't. And also, the piece that broke through looked awful rugged. Maybe it's a specialized structure, with a nonporous skin, for exploring. That would let it tunnel through anything to get towards water."

"That's where it was headed?"

She snapped her fingers. "Of course! It grew towards the light, then vectored in on the seam, where water collects best and runs down to pool. The thing must have a water sensor that's very selective."

"So by pure bad luck, that's the place where it could burrow through—tough little bugger!—and breach both the outside wall *and* the seal on the greenhouse."

"Absolutely the worst luck," she agreed. "On the other hand, we learned a lot from it."

"You damn near learned how to push up daisies."

"Ummmm, true. Look, that spike can defend against oxygen for at least a minute or so, or else it would've wilted. It only needed to hang on until all the air was gone from the greenhouse."

"Yeah, but it's going to scare a lot of people."

"Ummm, right. Not me, though. A few minutes on Earth and all that life would be finger food for every microbe around."

Marc shrugged good-naturedly. "So we're caught, I figure. Airbus wants to beat us home and plenty of other people don't want us back at all."

She curled her lip. "So we consent to a quarantine after we land."

"Maybe. Listen to this—"

He fast-forwarded and started the video again. "—some are saying the Airbus crew should prevent the launch of the ERV if it carries the slightest trace of this revolutionary discovery, a form of life unknown to Earth. Terming it 'a dire threat to all Earth,' PEPA spokeswoman—"

"Good grief!"

Marc grinned. "The price of fame."

"No, the price of the unknown."

"You ready to hear Axy-boy?"

"No. Viktor said he was leaning pretty heavily on the test."

"The Consortium investors' board has gotten into it

pretty thick," Marc said soberly. "Kinda funny, picturing a bunch of investment types poring over orbital mechanics tables."

With a sinking feeling, she said, "Let me see."

Axelrod looked both frazzled and energized. His tie was knotted too tight and his eyebrows kept jumping around like insects looking for some place to settle. He scowled with almost comic ferocity as he said, "Julia, this is just for you. You and me, we been through a lot, and I was never so proud as when I saw you making that run. What a woman!"

"Fast-forward," she said.

As the tape sped Marc asked, "Sure you want me to hear this?"

"Sure. We can't be keeping secrets from each other."

Axelrod finished his praise with a flourish, leading a toast on camera from the Ground Control team. Then he said, "I want you to know that I'm covering for you here, to the hilt. I'll take the blame for not releasing the news. We need a little statement from you, laying out how you were trying to get definitive word on just what this stuff is and so on. Maybe drop a little hint about your findings? Just an idea."

"More ammo for PEPA, sure," she said.

Axelrod frowned theatrically, a false note that put her on guard. "It's a firestorm down here. Just catch the news, see how they're playing it. Real live *life on Mars*— and dangerous, too—plus the race. I don't mind the extra income we're getting from coverage, of course. We're playing you as the heroine of it all. You were keeping the whole discovery under wraps until you could tell if it was any kind of threat, see. But there's this panel of biologists, U.S. National Academy of Science and all. They're saying you've been exposed now, touched that nasty thing that caused the accident."

Axelrod paused, eyeing the camera as if he could see her.

Julia said, "They're right."

"—and so maybe you shouldn't be sharing even the same air with the rest of the crew. So these Academy people say. In case you got something, and it"—he spread his hands helplessly—"well, it spreads."

"Too late for that," Marc said.

"As the National Academy knows," she said.

"A minority report even said—now, don't take this seriously, it's just a bunch of lab guys, after all—that you shouldn't come back."

"What!" Julia sat up straight.

"That's the kind of pressure flying around here, is what I'm saying." Axelrod looked apologetic.

"Those plants are *anaerobes*," Julia said hotly.

"Not that most people know what that means," Marc said.

"That's nonsense talk, of course," Axelrod hurried on. "I'm gonna make a speech today, label these people for what they are. But we sure could use a statement back here from you. It would give the PR boys something to work with, to spin."

"What the hell is going on down there? What are they afraid of?"

"*The Creeping Unknown*, 1955."

"Huh?"

"It's an old sci-fi movie. The only survivor of a rocket ship that crashes on reentry is infected with some alien organism. It kills the guy, then goes on to terrorize London."

"But it's just a stupid movie. Patently false."

"Maybe, but people are profoundly ignorant about space, and science in general."

"You think the movies are where people get their ideas about space? Good Lord, I had no idea. I thought everybody knew they were just silly stories."

Marc shrugged. "Unfortunately, most of the sci-fi movies are about all the *bad* things that could happen with alien encounters. Invading monsters make a better movie. Cute aliens are for kids."

"So you think people believe that the Marsmat is a threat from space? And they got that idea from sci-fi movies?"

"That's my thesis. Oh, the guy on the street wouldn't admit it, but the movies are most people's exposure to ideas about the future."

"I have a hard time believing that."

"Maybe, but remember that NASA quarantined the Apollo 11 astronauts returning from the *moon*."

There was a short silence.

"Okay, okay," Julia said. "Time to go on the air."

Marc looked relieved. "I'll go down below, do some packing."

Julia narrowed her eyes. "Axelrod asked you to get me in front of the cameras, didn't he?"

Marc looked sheepish. "Yeah, you are the biologist, after all."

"Here goes." She said in a hollow bass voice, "Creatures of Earth, I speak to you from Mars."

Marc's head jerked up, then he noticed the record button was still red. "Ha ha. The PR guys would've edited it out anyway."

"Yep, they cut all our best stuff."

She made a brief, clear statement detailing the vent descent. Their discoveries. A few shots of the deep vent life. A promise of further developments from her greenhouse experiments—"Which were unfortunately interrupted, as you all saw, by the unexpected, marvelous robustness of the vent life. This is hardy stuff, the product of tougher times than life has had on Earth. Now, that does not mean it's going to walk all over us. Oxygen poisons these forms immediately—I tried it on several of them, and they withered into brown husks within minutes. There is no danger to Earth here!"

After she signed off, she said, "It shouldn't be just me talking about the Marsmat, it's your discovery, too, you know."

"Yeah, only I haven't got the investment you do. I didn't nearly get killed out there, for my research."

"Our research."

"You're the Lady of Life, as that TV show called you."

"Hey, your name will be on the research papers, with mine."

"Oh no, I have to write papers, too?"

She grinned. "Price of fame."

26

SHE THOUGHT OF THE FOUR OF THEM AS BEING A KEYHOLE, through which billions of people were peering at an entire world beyond.

How to squeeze the immensity of Mars through that tiny knot? First and foremost they were pilots, engineers, scientists—not popularizers, but doers. They had made innumerable "squirts," as Viktor called them, sent videos, commentaries, interviews. It had never been enough to feed the media maw, and now the appetite at their backs was far worse.

Still, the hardest message she had to send was to her parents. She had to sheepishly own up to not telling them the biggest story in history. DEADLY LIFE ON MARS! had screamed at them from the Sydney newspaper.

Her father's calm, ironic rendition of the coverage carried not a hint of irritation or distress. "We understand you had to keep this out of all transmissions, sweetie," he had said. She'd carefully scrutinized the vid: Did he look more tired? "Security and all, quite so, quite justified."

But she had apologized anyway, and meant it. With all they were dealing with, they didn't need to be awakened at 3:00 A.M. by some arrogant media type wanting their "reaction to their daughter's near-death accident."

Such seemingly minor emotional issues took up her time as she rested. Minor compared to the real issues coming remorselessly to bear, anyway. She had to keep matters in perspective. Her body had myriad little aches and oddities, all duly chronicled for the medicos.

By the next morning she was feeling fairly chipper. In a quick message for the doctors she said, "I got off easy, I know that. But a minute in vacuum! I'll bet your research never implied that anybody could survive so long."

Viktor overheard her and said, "Miracle now, standard trick in future."

She was glad to have him say something; he and Raoul were obsessively readying for tomorrow's test. "How so?"

"Big hassle to get in and out of suits, true? Easier in future to make short dashes as you did—not even holding breath."

Somehow this shocked her. "But it was—scary."

"First time must be. Second time will make news maybe." He grinned. "Third, is habit."

She recalled how staff at the Mars Society arctic station would run from the rover to the hab without bothering with the heavy down jackets and boots. There was a small *zing* to thumbing your nose at the elements. "Y'know, you're probably right."

"Danger is fun," Viktor said. "Of course, best way is to watch from distance. From Earthside, say."

Like tomorrow, she thought.

Then she resolutely put such thoughts away.

When Viktor came in from the ERV work he was carrrying her slate. "I inflated the greenhouse again, patched the break."

"Fantastic. I've gotta get out there. Did you look at the mat samples?"

He frowned. "No. Found this."

"My slate. Double fantastic!" She reached for it eagerly.

He held it away from her. "You will rest one more day if I give it to you?"

"Are you serious?"

He nodded. "I have enough to worry about with ERV."

"Okay, it's a deal. I've got a lot of correspondence to catch up with, now that it's all out in the open."

She punched up the power and the slate filled with the stored readout from the DNA comparison tests. She fairly hummed as she dug into the results.

By the time Viktor came back from his shower, she was euphoric. "I've got it! These results are great! Woese was right after all."

"Woese? Who is that?"

"The microbiologist who coined the term *archaea*. His idea was that the bacteria in the group were a whole new kingdom of life. It included a lot of strange anaerobes, known as extremophiles, that lived in places like hot springs, underwater thermal vents, or coal mines. When he compared the genes of the archaea to those of other bacteria, he discovered that there was only a sixty percent match. A full forty percent of the archaea genome was unique. But I've found it! The Marsmat DNA matches those genes! Not only did we find life, but it's related to us—very, very distantly, but it's clearly related!" She stopped all of a sudden and beamed at him.

Viktor sat down, toweling his hair. "So we are Martians? Or is vent life from Earth?"

"I don't know. What I *can* say is that the life on both

planets was once together, swapping genes, and then it separated, a long time ago. That means life originated on one planet, then migrated to the second. I suppose it could have arisen in a third place altogether, but there's no evidence either way for that. So, to be parsimonious, life probably arose once, on either Mars or Earth."

"Mars to Earth is much easier energetically. Easier to blast rocks off Mars, and they fall towards sun."

"Yes, of course, you're right."

"Is wonderful news—to find cousins in the solar system. You are going to be real big-shot scientist when we get home. Make lots of money on talk shows. I never have to work again!"

She threw a pillow at him.

They knew by now to pace themselves as a team. She would spend another day resting, spraying e-mail to half a dozen colleagues. Fair enough; the weight had nearly lifted from her chest.

She had planned to help Marc with some light packing, but during the day about fifty e-mails poured in. The biological community was electrified with the news. They suggested dozens of additional analyses, and each person had a slightly different interpretation of her work. As she answered them, she wondered why she had not heard anything from the other biologist on Mars, Chen.

Viktor and Raoul had the ERV ready to test in late afternoon, but experience had taught them to not perform critical jobs when they were beginning to tire. So they came in a bit early and ate a large meal. The secret lay in putting the future out of mind until it had arrived.

That night they watched a John Wayne western, *The Searchers*. Her Aussie instincts preferred vistas anyway and this classic was full of them, vast gorgeous landscapes of Monument Valley. As medical officer she had to be crafty, selecting adventure films—her crewmates were men, after all, not exactly addicted to relationship dramas—that featured outdoors adventure instead of, say, exploding cars and cut-to-the-chase movies.

The six-month voyage out had been the hardest. Studies on submarines and in arctic bases had shown that subtle effects could lead to big liabilities. Sub crews suffered vision changes, unable to focus accurately on distant objects after months of seeing nothing farther away than five meters. The U.S. Navy cautioned its sub crews against driving until they'd been ashore at least three days. Submariners on land mistook far objects for near ones. She didn't want accidents after their landing, so she had imposed a go-easy rule the first few days.

There were more insidious effects, too. Even on Mars they spent most of their time inside metal boxes with limited views. The hab's flatscreen video showed them the outside, but there was an elusive lack in looking *at* a picture instead of *through* a window. They all preferred staring out Red Rover's "windshield" (though it was really a vacuum shield), even after it got scratched and pitted.

So they had watched *The Searchers* for probably the tenth time, chanting some of the dialogue in unison, loving it all. Marc had brought as part of his movie allotment some cheesy movies about Mars itself, titles like *Mars Attacks!*, *Angry Red Planet*, *Mars Needs Women*,

Robinson Crusoe on Mars, Mars Calling, A Martian in Paris, Mission to Mars—good for laughs—and the quite decent *The Martian Chronicles*. This time they skipped looking at these. Instead, Viktor brought out tiny shares of vodka. They played a few hands of poker before turning in, ignoring a priority message from Axelrod.

"Pep talk before the big game," Raoul snorted.

Nobody mentioned the next day.

She and Marc were to stay at a safe distance from the ERV during the full-throttle test.

Viktor explained to them all around the breakfast table, his eyes veiled. "Axelrod, he is pushing for max delta vee on the return trajectory. To cut the flight time. So I need to test system at highest pump speeds. Lift a little, set down, is all."

Nobody said very much as they suited up. A billion people would be watching and talk would seem like playing to a stage.

Astronauts were not self-doubters. But in the long run, self-doubt was a trait you learned. This mission, doubt had developed into a reflex. Raoul and Viktor went through an elaborate checkdown, calling results back and forth to each other. She and Marc stood near the hab and sent a few commentary squirts for Earthside.

Time ticked on. Waiting was not her strong suit.

She went over to the greenhouse and went in through the lock without cracking her air seal. At the corner of the mist box she bent down. Here was the pale, crusty stalk that had caused it all—dead now, yet still piercing the thick walls with its spiked tip. She marveled at the rugged vigor of the thing, a lance apparently evolved for breaking through to the surface. After how many millennia of hiding below?

Marc helped her search; things had blown around. All their crops were dead, of course, already quite dried out. To her amazement, some of her samples seemed still viable inside the partially crushed glove box.

But in the mist chamber? She ached to do some simple examinations. It was impossible to do anything definitive, but they did seem moist and showed no color change.

"Maybe they can survive on the surface," she exclaimed happily.

"Not quite raw surface," Marc said. "This heavy-duty plastic kept off the UV. And they're sitting in wet soil you made, free of peroxides."

"Good points, dead on. If the atmosphere were thicker, say. If water had melted out locally and destroyed the peroxides in the dust. Then this place could have been like our greenhouse."

"When?"

"During one of your wet spells."

"Those were millions of years ago, my cores show."

"So? These guys were waiting around down in their vent."

She could see Marc's frown through his helmet plate. "So over time, why didn't they just get rid of this ability, this talent for living on a warmer surface?"

"Two reasons. A very slow mutation rate underground on Mars, plus it's an ability pretty close to what they need to make a go of it in the vent," she said. "It also happens to be what they need to break out."

"Pretty clever," he said.

"Makes you wonder what they're doing at the other end."

"The other end of the vent?" He blinked. "You still want to do that? After what you've been through with this stuff? That's twice now it's almost gotten you."

She grinned. "Guess I'm just a biological fool, but yes. I've been thinking about what you said down there in the vent—that Mars is a cooler planet, so the temperate region below ground could extend a lot farther down. Ten klicks deep, all the way over the surface of the planet, right? That's a lot of space to evolve in."

"Yeah, you're right. I wonder how we can ever get a look at it?"

Viktor's voice came over the comm. "Time to end idle scientist talk, be crew members. Take your positions. Start the live vid coverage."

"Yes sir!" she sent with a chuckle.

Julia started the running commentary for the live-action vid they would squirt to Earth. She tried to keep matters light for Earthside, but the unspoken mood on the spot was grim. Their lives were riding on the plume of scalding exhaust about to come out. She fidgeted with the microcams—Earthside wanted four viewpoints, supposedly for engineering evaluation, but mostly to sell spectacular footage, she was sure.

Her thoughts drifted briefly. *Home!* The call of it was an ache in the heart. "The cool green hills of Earth," a song had said.

Leaving Mars . . .

Viktor sent, "Checks completed."

"Let's go," Raoul called in a husky whisper.

"Start up," Viktor said in a matter-of-fact voice she did not believe for a moment.

Sudden exhaust. The slender shape rose on a column of milky steam. The methane-oxygen burn looked smooth and powerful and her heart thudded as the ship rose into a ruddy sky.

"Max pump speed," Viktor called. "Throttled flow."

Fuel feed was choked down. They did not want to push it high into the sky, wasting fuel. It handled nicely, standing on its spewing spire as Viktor called out flow speeds and made it hover. Then drift sideways. Up. Then back.

"All nominal," Viktor said, clipped and tight.

"Control A-sixteen and B-fourteen integrated," Raoul answered. "Let's set her down."

"Coming off from max—"

"Got three seventy eight on—"

Down they came through the ruddy sky, settling—

And a loud *thump* smacked into Julia's helmet, before she saw anything. The entire nozzle assembly was askew, the ship lurching in air. Ratcheting bangs rolled toward her.

It set down at a tipsy angle, spewing fumes, blowing sand over the damp smear that marked the takeoff.

Again, as if in a dream, she was running across the rocky ground, feet crunching, her shouts echoing in her helmet along with all the others, tinny over the comm.

	JULIA'S MISSION TIMELINE
12/20/2013	ERV launched from Earth
6/21/2014	ERV lands on Mars
1/20/2015	ERV is fueled
3/15/2015	Blowup at Cape Canaveral
2/20/2016	We launch from Earth!!
3/21/2016	~~Backup ERV launches from Earth~~
4/17/2016	Raoul and Katherine's baby due
8/9/2016	We land on Mars!!
1/20/2017	Backup ERV ~~lands~~ on Mars
1-19-2018	*{Vent descent – LIFE!!* *{Airbus lands!*
3/14/2018	Launch date!!
10/12/2018	HOME!!

PART IV
MARS NEEDS WOMEN

27

Once again she was swimming in the Adelaide community pool. Her dad was there, slim, young, and fit, her mom limping slightly from the accident, as she would for the rest of her life. She and Bill were racing across the pool. She dove below the lane separator, as her instructor yelled, "Blow bubbles when you go under the rope."

But something was wrong. She had no air left, and the surface was so far away . . .

She awoke, clutching her chest, heart pounding. It took several long seconds to realize she was breathing after all.

Viktor stirred beside her. "Time to get up already?" His voice was curiously flat.

They dragged themselves vertical, pulled on their worn coveralls, and got themselves out to the social area. Cereal and pseudomilk. Raisins and sugar. No music, just the hab popping as it stretched itself for the day.

Raoul sat over his breakfast, silent, staring at the oatmeal Marc had cooked. Nobody spoke.

They had said little the night before, as well. The hours of cleaning up after the crash had completely robbed them of energy. Then they had all taken refuge in what was normally an onerous task—reporting in. For Julia this meant a soulful message to her parents and a stiff-upper-lip, we're-studying-our-options stall for the Consortium PR flaks to work with.

For Viktor and Raoul it was harder. She could see it in their faces that evening, after each had listened to Axelrod's incoming priorities and then responded. They had recorded their reports in private, each sitting in his acceleration couch. Neither she nor Marc wanted to watch.

They had all retreated to their precious privacy after supper, and Viktor had said little to her. Long experience had taught them when contact meant conflict.

Raoul suddenly attacked his oatmeal, dumping extra sugar on it and wolfing down spoonfuls. They all waited until he was through, nursing their coffees. Julia had deviated from her ritual tea today, somehow feeling that it would help solidarity, and maybe she needed the caffeine, too. Certainly she needed something.

She dreaded the end of breakfast. When it arrived, Raoul drained his coffee mug and rubbed it, a sure sign that he was steeling himself to speak. She wondered whether he was aware that the floral ceramic made by Katherine had come to stand in his mind for Katherine herself. Often he cradled it obsessively, kept it in its own holder he had made of elastics, insisted on cleaning it himself, and would stare into it for long moments—like now.

Raoul said abruptly, "Seals failed, pumps jammed tight. I can't fix it. Nobody can."

Viktor nodded. They all knew this, but the words hung in the air for a long time. Julia let the minutes stretch.

Viktor said at last, "They have to send a second ERV. Launch in mid-May, arrives about nine months from now, in November."

Marc asked quietly, "Can we live off our supplies until then?"

"Marginally," Julia said. "The ERV has seven months' food for six, NASA's mission plan. But we'll have to play farmer with a vengeance."

Viktor continued in his flat, reporting voice, "ERV arrives, we transfer methane and oxy from the ruined ERV. Cannot launch right away. Delta vee is too large, no hope. We must wait for next window, about four hundred fifty days more."

"Oh no," Marc said. "There's no other window?"

"None we can make. June 2020 is first time planets are in right place, we can go. It's a Hohmann orbit but not a good one." He paused, as if unsure whether they were ready for what came next. "Need extra delta vee even so."

"How much delta vee?" Raoul demanded.

"Almost twice what we would have needed," Viktor said very precisely, "for this time."

"My God!" Marc's eyes widened in alarm. "That's nearly four times as much fuel as we have."

"They know that on Earth," Viktor said coolly. "They must build—very fast—ERV that can carry that much more."

"Good God . . ." Marc paled.

"I believe we can make it. Axelrod must fly us more hydrogen . . . or else we mine water from the pingos."

"And that's if everything works right," Marc said. "The ERV has to make it okay, land near us . . ."

A silence. The mountain of labor and time and sheer endurance that confronted them was overpowering. Julia felt herself forced to note, "We're headed into the southern summer."

That was the subtle point behind their entire mission profile. Dust storms raged across the southern hemisphere through its warm season. Though the winds rose to hundreds of kilometers per hour, they carried less mass. Still, nobody wanted to be there for months of stinging dust.

"Will not be fun," Viktor conceded. "May have to go on diet, too."

"I don't know *what happened*," Raoul suddenly blurted.

"I do not know either," Viktor said calmly, holding one hand palm up toward Raoul. "We ran the pressure profile we thought was best. Earthside approved."

"But they sure as hell can't explain," Raoul said bitterly.

"They say they are running fresh simulations," Viktor said with a slight edge in his voice.

Julia frowned. It was not like Viktor to blame anyone but himself. Derision he handed out in sometimes ample portions, but not fault. She said quietly, "It doesn't matter."

"I agree, does not," Viktor said, looking not at her but at Raoul. "We did best we could."

"Nobody'll ever know what made the whole system crash like that," Raoul said. "I went over it all yesterday afternoon, couldn't see what blew first."

"Standing out there for years, it got worked pretty bad by the weather," Marc said. Julia could see Marc was trying to soothe Raoul and Viktor, but she knew that only time could do the job. *Well, at least we have plenty of that . . .*

They were facing months of hardship and a long voyage back—at best. They all knew it and there was nothing to say.

Into the gathering silence came the beep announcing a priority message. Viktor glanced at the monitor. "Axelrod."

The slim, athletic, elegantly tailored frame had gotten a bit gaunt and tired. "Got your reports, Raoul and Viktor. Been through the slow-mo of the crash with the experts. They figure—well, hell, what's it matter?"

He sagged against his desk and eyed them bleakly. Julia felt a spurt of alarm. John Axelrod had always been buoyant, even when troubled. This deflated balloon did not bode well.

"Don't matter worth a bushel of dog turds, as my daddy used to say. You're stuck there and there's no way back. You've got enough food to hold out until I can get you an ERV—the one I damned well shoulda sent way back then, right after your launch. I know that now, in spades."

"Yeah," Raoul said with an icy spike of a voice, "you bastard."

"So I got nothing to say to you until I hear from the tech boys. Tell thee true, I don't expect much from 'em. Ever'body knows how much food you got. Air, water, the rest—keep making 'em with the thermal nukes. Goddamn they're good!" He suddenly brightened. "Wasn't that a good break, though? Didn't crack a single fuel tank when you came down, Viktor. That's good piloting."

"Failed in last ten seconds," Viktor said sourly.

"Else things'd be much rougher, guys. This way, that ERV arrives, you pump your methane and oxy over to it. We'll send a good pump for sure . . ."

Axelrod's voice trailed away and he gazed off-camera. "And I . . . I'm doing what I can for you here. Talking to Airbus. Now, this is the main point, so listen up." He turned to face the camera, again in command. "I don't want you talking to the Airbus crew there. Not now. We're negotiating with their people here. I'm trying to find a good angle on this for you all. Gotta see if they can take one person back. Maybe. Beyond that, I can't say. So that's the word—no talking."

There was some more meandering monologue, but Julia got up and went into her study. She and Viktor had a code, to retire to the study when the world got to be too much. He sat and listened while she fled. She sat on the narrow seat in the small room and let the tears come that had been waiting there for her for days, since the greenhouse blowout. Even last night she had not been able to let them out, but now, all alone, they rushed forth.

Delayed shock. Her medical training reasserted itself. *Physician, heal thyself.*

They went on for a long time. She knew it would be harder on the other three. They couldn't even cry.

When she came out another face was on the screen. Not Axelrod, not some member of the Earthside tech team, but . . . Chen.

"We expect to be there within two hours," he was saying. The view was from a handheld camera, showing the background of the Airbus control room. "To be of what help we can."

Marc said, "Sure didn't take them long."

"Or us," Viktor said. "To break Axelrod's rule."

"You're going to talk to them?" Raoul asked. "Those bastards?"

Viktor's smile was more like a thin gash across his face. "We have negotiations of our own to make, that I am sure."

28

SHE HAD KNOWN HIM AS MENTOR, AS COLLEAGUE, AND now as he came from the lock, as rival. Victorious rival, as his thin smile announced.

"I am sorry to come on such an occasion," Chen said with a formality that seemed fitting, despite the smile.

"We welcome any assistance," Viktor said, ushering in Chen and Gerda and Claudine. "Thank you."

They had made cocoa. Mars always chilled you, and coming in to a hot cup of milky reception had become a ritual often observed among the four of them, to mark a distant journey come to an end. Marc, not Julia, had thought of offering it.

Julia had noticed that usually the first thing their crew did after returning to the hab, especially after getting some food, was to turn and look out, "through" the large flatscreen. When not in receiving mode for messages from Earth, it reverted to one of the three external cameras. Safety protocols called for cycling among these three, but Marc had reprogrammed them so that the view outward toward the ERV had the most screen time.

All seven now stood before this view. The ERV was slumped slightly to the side as a result of the last landing. Panels were off, exposing a tangle of plumbing. Even in midday glare, the vista seemed somehow forlorn.

Nobody said anything at first. Then Chen broke the silence with, "Unfortunate. The fuel is intact?"

"Yes," Viktor said. The two captains stood together. "I got it back down when the pressure on line two dropped. Did not damage the main tanks."

Chen nodded and turned away. "You have a very pleasant place."

The Airbus Three, as the media had dubbed them, spent a few moments reconnoitering the hab, with Raoul as guide. They noted with skill the design features and compromises the four crew had imposed on the basic design that had lifted off from Canaveral a thousand years ago. They admired most the space. The hab was the size of a New York condo at best, but still more than half again larger than the Airbus living quarters.

Which quickly developed to be the point of the visit. They sat around the social table, the guests getting the seats with Viktor.

"We are sorry for the accidental failure of your test," Gerda said.

"At least no one was hurt," Claudine added.

Viktor said, "Starvation will be at least slower."

A tense pause, then, "Surely not that," Claudine said.

"We can take one more crew member," Chen said gravely.

"That is all?" Viktor blinked in surprise.

"It is not a matter of payload, you understand."

"We have a good food reserve—"

"We do not have the room." Chen nodded toward Marc. "As he can confirm."

"Yeah, there's sure not much," Marc grudgingly agreed. "We all saw that. Big limitation is in the systems.

The one I trained with, it was rated for a crew of four. The air and water filtration systems, everything."

"We have higher shielding needs," Chen said, "for the reactor."

"It limits the payload mass," Gerda said.

Viktor nodded. "I appreciate your limitations. We are all here living close to knife edge."

"There are severe constraints upon our mission," Gerda said, apparently trying to be helpful.

"Management?" Viktor said.

Chen smiled again. "It is amusing to find ourselves, the entire human presence on another world, carrying out the dictates of people who are on the other side of the solar system."

"We are in command here," Viktor said, "you and me."

"There will be an accounting when we are home," Chen said.

Viktor grimaced. "For those who get home."

"I am offering one berth upon our return flight," Chen persisted. Julia could see he was getting irked with Viktor, though the only sign was a slight lift at the corners of his mouth.

"And who will fill this berth?" Viktor asked edgily.

"I believe that is up to us," Chen said.

"I am captain of ship and I say who will go back," Viktor said stiffly.

"Our ship, we say who goes," Gerda said.

Both men turned to look at her. Chen said nothing. Gerda realized she had violated the levels of command and visibly swallowed. Nobody said anything for a long moment. Julia had no idea where this was going and was fairly sure that Viktor did not, either.

"I trust what we say here will not become an issue for Earth to know of, on either side," Chen said.

Marc grinned. "Too late for that. I'm getting all this on interior camera. With audio."

Chen was genuinely shocked, eyebrows shooting up. "I had assumed—"

"We made no promises," Viktor said. "Axelrod wants to know what goes on here."

Chen bristled. "When I came aboard—"

"At own invitation. We did not invite."

Julia could see that in Chen's mind the frontier between irritation and outright anger had grown thinly guarded, and as his irked mouth twisted she saw that he had crossed the border without slowing down. "We came offering *help*—"

"At price, I think," Viktor shot back. "Only not announced yet."

Chen stood up, loudly scraping the chair back. "I believe we could all use a time to think upon these matters."

"Leaving?" Julia asked. "No, don't. We can't let things get out of control—"

"Then let us take time to slacken the trouble here," Chen said. "Julia, I would like to have a word with you, a technical word."

"No one negotiates but you and me," Viktor said. "Captains."

"No negotiations," Chen agreed readily. "Scientific talk only."

Claudine said in a blithely conversational manner, as though nothing at all had happened, "I would appreciate very much seeing more of this ship."

Marc snapped this up. "Sure, lemme show you."

The two of them moved away, buzzing. Their animation contrasted sharply with the stiffness of the others. Julia was suddenly aware of being on camera, though she had been there so much for years she felt foolish even noticing the camera near the ceiling, whose snout tracked whoever was speaking, following its software.

She said, "All right, Dr. Chen, perhaps if you would step into my office . . ."

Her cabin they had outfitted with two tiny workspaces with pop-out seats. They sat on either edge of the drop-desk. Chen smiled at her, two feet away, and said, "I hope we did not all get off to a bad start today."

"On Mars, just about everything is a staged event."

"Just so," Chen said. "I wanted to discuss the implications of your accident."

"Better ask Raoul. He—"

"No, the greenhouse incident. You were studying living specimens. That much was clear from your own description, as heard over the suit comm."

"Uh, yes."

"You have found subterranean life."

"Yes."

"Down a thermal vent?"

"Yes, we finally located one." How much to give away?

"I would very much like to see those samples."

"They're in the greenhouse."

"I saw you had reinflated it. The samples are now dead?"

"Not all."

"Really!" His face lit with eagerness.

"They're tough to kill, all right."

"Tell me all about them."

"Well, for starters, they're carbon-based—no surprise there. And simple vital staining on frozen sections confirmed that their metabolism is similar to Earth organisms." She reached for her slate, called up her results. "It appears to be an advanced biofilm, well organized, with several distinct cell types."

"But prokaryotic?"

"So far it seems so. I did some quick SEMs, didn't see anything resembling a nucleus or chromosomes. But they cooperate in a manner more typical of advanced life-forms on Earth. Say, on the level of a sophisticated jelly-fish. And the structures get quite large . . ."

"Like stromatolites?"

"Bigger, with more complex shapes."

He leaned back. "I have often thought that stromatolites were limited by their environment. The ocean-air interface imposes strict physical limitations. What if they'd been set free?"

She nodded. "I think that's what happened here. Unlimited time, a source of energy, and nutrients from the thermal vent. Anaerobic life went wild."

"I must see them. My ideas about hydrogen sulfide ecology, do you think they apply?"

"I can't tell yet, but yes, some of what we talked about at NASA, in the training seminars—that might be the right way to think about it."

He shifted in his seat, hunched over to press his case. "I must see them."

"I can't do that yet."

"Why not?"

"We're trying to contain exposure to them."

"But I would be inside the greenhouse pressure envelope."

"Look, there are a lot of very squirrely people on Earth who are totally paranoid about this whole subject. You get uplinks, you know all this. Some of them don't want us to go home, fearing some kind of contamination." The hell of it was, she had no good reason to deny him access except the real one. She didn't believe that crap.

"What other tests have you done? Maybe we can find some way to reassure them."

She looked at him carefully. He seemed entirely guileless, and she was relieved to be able to finally talk about the biology. The constant edginess and fencing wore her down.

"You have been carrying out DNA comparisons?"

"Oh, yes, let me show you. That's the best of all. First I tried Venter's essential three hundred genes—not much luck. In fact, I can't really interpret what I got."

"I would like to help. Theory's my game, you know."

"Well, you're going to love this." On her slate she punched up the results of the archaea bacterial gene comparisons. "There. The vent life's genes have an eighty-six percent concordance with the so-called unique part of the genome of the archaea."

Chen seemed dazed. "Which means—"

"Common origin. Those unique genes are Martian genes."

"This is incredible. It's the biggest story in biology since Darwin. I must see it. We need to reconfirm your results."

She hesitated, then stepped off the cliff. "When things have settled down a bit, maybe we can do a joint descent in the vent, and you can see for yourself."

Chen smiled broadly. "That would indeed be interesting. But why wait? You have samples in the greenhouse."

"I'm sorry, I can't . . ."

He recovered himself, his face hardening. "You will not let me see because of your company," he said sternly.

"They say so, yes."

"You and I, we are the only biologists. We must work on this together."

"You're going back in a few months. If I show you all my work, what's—"

"To stop me from claiming it?" he smiled warmly. "Only that billions of people already know the truth. You found it. Not I."

"I don't want to let out results until I've had time to check—"

"I will help you check. There is much to be done."

"It's Consortium property. We can't just—"

"As you assert, I will be gone soon. This is your only chance at collaboration."

"Look, I really would like to work with you, but—"

"Then I can make that possible. Come back with us."

"What?" She had not seen this coming.

"We will have six months to work together. To think, to compare—"

"No, I can't leave—"

"You will bring the samples of course."

"No, I meant I can't leave Viktor."

"Most important, you cannot leave your great discovery."

"If you listen to the Earthside media, plenty of people want us to leave it all right here."

He waved this aside. "Fools. Western journalists."

"Even if we ship them back with you, they'll be quarantined."

"So that for a long time no one will be able to work on them."

She caught his drift. "So our work will be all there is."

"That is quite possible."

Something in his rapt gaze, blazing with excitement, put her off. *Let's see just what the offer is.* "I don't think the Consortium will let the samples go with you."

"Why?" He seemed affronted.

"Because Airbus will scoop up all the Mars Prize. That hadn't crossed your mind?"

"I do not think of the race, compared with the science."

"I bet." *Really?*

"Neither should it concern you so much."

"Look, what if I come back, we have time to discuss all the biology, you look at all my data—there's a lot— and we maybe write a paper on it in transit. But no samples." *What's he gonna say to that?*

His eyes narrowed. "We must have the samples. No one will be satisfied with merely your—"

"Nope, that's a condition. The Consortium won't let the samples out of their hands."

"Your hands. We make the decisions here, as Viktor your captain said, and they are your hands."

"So no berth without the samples?"

"You wish to force my hand this way?"

"Let's call it a legitimate question."

"A negotiation, you mean."

"You don't really want me, you want the vent life."

"Your captain said only he and I, we carry out negotiations."

"So it is the samples or else no berth for me?" *As if I would go alone under any conditions.*

Chen ground his teeth suddenly, as if no longer caring how he appeared. "The biological specimens, yes, they are essential."

"Nuts."

"What?"

"Nuts."

29

AS THE AIRBUS ROVER FELL BELOW THE HORIZON, THROWING dust, Viktor said, "We talk."

"You bet," Marc said, beating the rest of them to the communal table.

"First, what did Chen say in there?" Viktor asked Julia.

"Biology, mostly. I showed him my slate data. We discussed genetics, that the vent life is related to the early Earth life. We're distant cousins."

Viktor nodded. "He wants samples?"

"Yes—asked for them several times. Or to at least see them."

"Show him a video," Marc said.

"Not of the vent descent, no," Viktor said. "Maybe of the samples in their little dishes. That would be okay, I suppose."

"He wanted to go to the greenhouse," Julia said.

Raoul said, "Did you notice him stop and look at it when they were headed back to their rover?"

Marc said, "Yeah, he wanted to walk over there so bad you could feel it."

Viktor sniffed. "Knew we would come out if he did."

"Yeah," Marc said, "but it takes five minutes minimum to suit up."

Julia grinned wryly. "Me, I'd just make the run without the suit again. He's not getting *my* samples."

"Offer to work on them with you?" Viktor persisted.

"Sure. And to go down the vent with me."

The men all looked stern. "Sure, help him win the prize money," Raoul said. "I bet he'd like plenty of help, maybe toss us a free dinner or something."

Viktor said, "No descent with him, no."

Julia said nothing. Somehow they all knew there was more. Nobody spoke. At last she said, "He offered me the berth home if I would."

Predictably, each exploded in a different way. Raoul smacked his palm on the table, Marc shot to his feet, Viktor gave a loud, derisive grunt.

"Bastard!" Raoul shouted. "He's going to bargain us down for it, I *knew* it."

"Not all of us," Marc said, pacing back and forth. "What've the rest of us got to offer?"

"True for now," Viktor said gravely. "Have pilot. Doubt would want Marc's rocks, but his core samples might help them. I am thinking that Raoul may be useful to them."

Raoul blinked. "How come?"

"Getting ice from pingos, nobody ever done. Need good engineer. Engineers. Gerda is able but there is lot of labor to do."

Raoul could not disguise his interest, not from people who had lived with him for years. "Think so?"

"If cannot get enough water, they cannot lift in the best launch window. More they wait, more they need. Orbital mechanics very clear. Could be they will need smart worker."

Marc said, "Sheesh!"

"I doubt that," Raoul said, measured and not very convincingly, to Julia's ear.

"I do not like this," Viktor said. "Captains should decide who goes. Not bargain."

"What'd you say?" Raoul asked her.

"I told him no, of course."

Raoul kept his face carefully under control but his voice was strained. "Really? You'd sit on those samples and not go home?"

"You bet."

Nobody said anything, but Julia could feel the furious calculation going on in the room. She could not tell whether they believed her. The signal bell rang and she was glad to hear it. It was Axelrod, of course. Marc started the priority message and sat down.

"I heard it all, guys. That Chen sonofabitch! One slot, he says."

Axelrod was pacing before his desk and the view through the broad window behind it was of city lights winking in the night. They had long since ceased keeping track of the mismatch of times between the planets; their clocks gained half an Earth hour every day. Yet somehow Julia was surprised to see the moon hanging in a luminous evening sky. Comfy Earth was indeed a long way from raw Mars.

Axelrod looked frazzled, gray. "Well, don't think you guys have to deal with him up there. I'm talking to his bosses right now. They're playing cagey. Not saying how many berths they could squeeze out. One, Chen says. My engineers say that's a pretty plausible number, given the uncertainties we have about their detailed designs."

"Fits with what I know from the training," Marc said.

Axelrod waved away his own reservations. "They're hinting like crazy about those samples of yours, Julia. I figure we got 'em there, I really do. You're not to tell him *anything* that might help him find that vent. Nothing. He might be able to just follow your tracks back. In fact, don't talk to him at all about this stuff."

"A little late, Axy," Raoul said sardonically. "The old time delay strikes again."

"We discussed theory, genetics," Julia said defensively.

Axelrod looked at the camera cannily. "One thing I learned in tight negotiations like this. Make damn sure you know your opponent's true position. What's valuable to him. So he doesn't get that for a cheap price, while you're imagining he wants something else."

"Gotta admire him," Marc said. "He's holding no cards but he's still playing the game."

"He knows this sort of business," Viktor said. "We do not."

Axelrod spread his hands. "Say, suppose, they need a part or something. Have to come to you, Raoul. Or maybe they really do need fuel, after all this talk about mining those pingo hills. Nobody's ever done that, right? They couldn't have trained for it—Marc hadn't even drilled through to the ice until after they'd boosted on their way. Could be they don't have all the equipment they need. Or can't do it at all, and that engineer, that Gerda, has already found that out."

"He's got a point," Marc said.

Axelrod waxed on, thinking out loud. This was not

prepared material, carefully scripted to keep their spirits up. "Hell, maybe they'll come begging for that methane of yours. They get more lift than we do out of a pound of liquid, right? Two, three times as much, the engineers tell me. They might not need nearly as much as you guys do to get back here. So they'd bargain for some."

"He's just winging it," Raoul said. "All his people, they haven't found out a thing."

"Not yet," Julia said. "But they could."

"So what I'm saying here is, tell them zip, nada, zero. Wait for word from us, from me particularly." Axelrod blinked. "I know you guys are hanging on by your fingernails there. Stay with me on this. We can wangle somethin' out, I'm sure of it."

"Sure about a lot, isn't he?" Marc mocked.

Axelrod straightened and stared into the camera. "Julia, you're the crucial one here. Your message about the vent life, that went over real well in the media. Real well. We're playing you as scientist hero, see. Protecting Earth by studying this thing, before we ever even *think* of bringing it back. The vent—hey, let's come up with a better word for it, huh? 'Vent life'—that doesn't have a ring to it, seems to me."

There were some more sign-off phrases, his energy running down, and then he was gone.

Nobody said anything. Julia mused, "Do you think the spin doctors would like my 'Marsmat'?"

Viktor said, "Still like 'Marshroom' better."

The others laughed dutifully at that, then became quiet again.

"He's so damn sure he can cut some deal," Raoul said sourly.

"He means for a share of the Mars Prize," Marc said.

"Means for all of us," Viktor said loyally.

"Maybe he can get two berths back," Julia said.

Raoul scowled. "Cold equations time here, folks. There is only so much room in that cramped little ship. Want to spend half a year crawling all over those three?"

"And vice versa," Marc said.

"Not that you'd mind," Raoul said.

"Huh? What's that mean?"

"You and that Claudine have taken every chance you could get to go off and rub up against each other," Raoul said tightly.

"What the hell?" Marc demanded.

"It's pretty damn obvious."

"We knew each other in training. Went out a couple times, is all."

"You'd love to fly back with them," Raoul said hotly.

"Well, who wouldn't?" Marc shot back.

Raoul said sharply, "And you do know where the vent is, right?"

Marc leaped up. "You think I'd—"

Raoul glowered. "You've got motivation, is all I'm saying."

Marc's hands twitched. "Geeze! I'd never—"

"Of course he would not," Viktor said mildly. "Sit down, Marc."

"He accused me of—"

"He spoke too quickly," Viktor said rapidly. A cool, steady look at Raoul. "I am sure he is sorry he did."

"Look, I didn't mean you'd really do that." Raoul looked down at his mug. "Axy said we should think through possibilities, right? Well, that's one that will occur to Chen, too."

This seemed a weak comeback to Julia, but Viktor nodded. "He could try to pull us apart."

Raoul muttered darkly into his mug, "Thing is, I've had to watch my son grow up on the goddamned *vid*. When he walked for the first time, I saw a tape a day later, 'cause we were out on a rove. His second birthday is coming up!"

Julia said awkwardly, "We know, it has been hard."

Raoul looked her square in the eye. "And what do I have to offer Chen? Nothing but helping get water from the pingos. If they need help at all."

"He does not decide," Viktor said patiently.

Julia's throat felt tight, as though she were holding something in. She had never been able to talk to Raoul about his separation from Katherine, even though she was the unofficial Empathy Officer here. Apparently he had not been able to talk about it to anyone else, either. "We'll all decide together, really."

Viktor said, "No, I will. For us."

"Can't say as I like that," Raoul said. He slurped from his mug, as if to underline his point.

"I decide for best of mission," Viktor said.

Raoul studied Viktor and from his expression Julia judged that he had evidently decided not to challenge Viktor directly, at least not now. Raoul said carefully, "It seems to me that my chances are best if we just draw straws."

"Judgment is always better than gambling," Viktor said.

"Especially with lives," Julia said loyally. She felt warm, as if she were getting angry herself. Or maybe, she thought ruefully, it was just thwarted self-righteousness. *She*, after all, had already turned down the slot Raoul was whining about. Viktor sat up straighter, a visible sign that he wanted to move the discussion forward. "We should discuss methane."

Marc tilted his head. "You mean Axy's idea?"

"No, the methane we need to get back on next orbital opportunity, two years from now."

"It's a lot," Raoul said, shaking his head. His guttural tone told Julia that he was not satisfied at having his drawing-straws proposal brushed aside.

He was so obviously in pain. It was an impossible situation for each of them, but Raoul was taking it much harder than the others. *Machismo is exacting another toll.*

"Delta vee is nearly twice our max rating, in present ERV." Viktor pressed a command into his slate and it sent his display to the flatscreen. They all studied the details for a long moment: the required rendezvous speeds, expenditures, trajectory times—all for a family of return trajectories in the flight window. "So is nearly four times original fuel requirement."

Raoul said in a flat, factual voice, free of emotion, "They'll have to send us an ERV with lots bigger tanks. Plus plenty of hydrogen."

"Unless we do different scheme," Viktor said. "Use water for hydrogen, keep oxygen separated. Be ready with fuel when ERV lands."

"How?" Marc asked, then snapped his fingers. "Sure! We use the pingos, melt 'em for water."

"Before," Viktor said, "was impossible. Did not have hoses, circulation chambers, storage. Now Airbus comes. Must have such things."

Marc said, "Claudine was saying she had worked for days setting it up. They've got plenty of heat with that nuke, so they run a simple heat cycle through the reactor."

Raoul said, "Their reactor's big, but we have one hundred forty kilowatts available here. Three nuke heaters that give mostly electricity, but I could modify them. Build up a chamber out of spare parts, if we have to—"

"So we could have fuel ready when the ERV arrives?" Julia asked. "Could we use it right away, not have to wait for the ERV to make methane out of Martian CO_2?"

"Might make some difference in our choice of trajectories," Viktor said.

"Let's propose it to Earthside!" Marc said happily.

"Requires some thought," Raoul said carefully. "But I don't think it can help much."

"Why not?" Marc was surprised.

"Because there's no good window, right after the ERV touches down. Sure, there's a window a few months from now, to lift from Earth. But there's no easy, low-cost way back, once it gets here."

Viktor nodded. "So as I have calculated. But Earthside may be able—"

"That's a pipe dream," Raoul said with sudden anger. "You're feeding us false hope here."

Viktor's face stiffened. "I explore all possibilities."

"You want to talk methane," Raoul said hotly, "I'd

say we take care of what we got. That ERV over there has plenty enough methane to fly the Airbus nuke back to Earth. They'd be fools not to try for it."

Julia's heart sank. *Not this again.*

Marc blinked. "Try—*steal* it?"

"Axy was right. If they can't bargain for it, why not just take it?" Raoul demanded. "Let the lawyers fight over it afterward, when they're already on their way Earthside."

Marc said thoughtfully, "Yeah, it's really NASA's, isn't it? Axy, he cut a deal, but it's got so many extra clauses and stuff in it—"

"We would not let them," Viktor said sternly.

"Suppose they just fly their nuke over here and take it?" Raoul shot back.

"They're not going to try," Julia said in what she hoped was a reasonable voice, though her face felt hot.

"I wonder," Raoul said suggestively. "I mean, they could show up, force us to cut a deal."

"For what?" Julia asked.

"For the extra berth, say?" Raoul said archly.

"What a mind! A conspiracy theory nightmare," Julia said.

Viktor said slowly, coolly, "I have thought about it, since boss suggested this problem. We do not need to protect methane."

"How about Axy's idea?" Raoul said hotly. "That maybe they need some parts or something? They could come over at night, take it."

"I do not think threat is there," Viktor insisted stolidly.

"You don't see a problem anywhere, do you?" Raoul said loudly, waving his right hand in a half-clenched fist. "You just wanna be in charge, like, like some goddamn *emperor*—"

He emphasized the word with a sweeping gesture— and knocked his mug off the table. It hit the deck and shattered.

Everyone gasped. Raoul turned, dumbfounded. He gazed down at the shards that clinked to a stop against the walls. His horrified look, mouth half open in wrenched despair, froze the moment in Julia's mind as the depth of their own disintegration swept over her.

30

JANUARY 29, 2018

THIS TIME HER DREAMS WEREN'T ABOUT SWIMMING. THEY were short, disconnected fragments. She couldn't seem to really get to sleep. She finally gave up and sat up in bed. Her throat was raw, her shoulders ached. She felt goosebumps on her legs. Realization dawned slowly. *I'm sick. I must have a fever. Feels like the flu.*

But how? An infection? But Mars was sterile. *We've been isolated together for over two years. We can't get sick anymore.*

This phenomenon was first noted on submarines. Any incubating viruses made the rounds once. Then the crew were all immune and nobody got sick anymore. *It must be Airbus. Just my luck. I caught something from that weasel Chen.*

A thought prickled the back of her mind. *The vent life.* She had been exposed without her helmet. *That's absurd. This is real life, not some tabloid fantasy.* She tried to push the thought back, failed.

Viktor stirred, reached for her in his sleep. She gently removed his arms. But he was persistent. Finally, after a couple more skirmishes, he awoke. "Something wrong? What time is it?"

"It's not quite midnight. I think I've got a fever, and I don't want you to get it."

He was instantly concerned. "You are sick? With what?"

"It's probably a virus from Airbus." She hesitated. "At least I hope it is."

"What else could it be?"

"Viktor, what if it's a reaction to the Mars life?"

"I thought it was not likely to react with us."

"No, it isn't. That's really a far-fetched idea, but I can't absolutely rule it out."

"Is fever speaking, not biologist. You have Chinese variety of flu, probably."

"Oh, God, when they find out about this on Earth, I'll never be allowed back home."

"We say nothing. You be careful in front of camera, is all."

"Well, they have nothing to worry about, since I'm not going back."

"Maybe you should. Chen offered you the berth."

"How could I live without you for two years?"

"Have busy time with ticker-tape parades, TriVid shows, lectures."

"That's not what I want to do."

"Work on vent life in fancy lab on Earth, then."

"Hah. I'll probably never be able to touch my samples again. Every A-list microbiologist on the planet will want to work on them. I have no special credentials. I'm just the discoverer. Besides, Axelrod will sell 'em to the highest bidder anyway."

"Will be tough here. I would feel better if you were safe."

"Viktor, I'm not going to go without you. And that's final."

"Three guys here could—"

She put a hand over his mouth. "Wait a minute. What's that noise?"

He sighed. "Marc and Raoul, drunk and singing."

"They're drunk?"

"After you went to bed, Raoul brought out bottle of tequila. That one he was talking about opening after launch, remember?"

"Sounds like bad news. Depression plus alcohol."

"I had one shot only, then came in here."

"Well, it sounds like they've patched things up."

"Both pretty tense today."

"What's the captainly thing to do here?"

"Sleep."

She wasn't going to sleep, not with a red-raw throat. And something in the tone of the words, though she could not make them out, sounded faint warning bells. Viktor believed in a rather formal standard of leadership, however, with strict compartments between professional and private behavior. How to get around that? "Um . . . I could use some entertainment."

"I get your slate and headphones."

Was he being deliberately dense? "I am going to breach protocol and eavesdrop."

In the faint light she could see him grin. "Captain cannot do this."

"But he can lie here and let sounds blow by him?"

"Captain can do that. Not his fault."

She grunted as she slipped out of bed and moved quietly to the door. Carefully she turned the latch and cracked the door open. As she got back under the covers Marc's voice came through clearly, though slurred.

"—knew he was a prick with a ramrod up his ass alla time 'bout somethin'."

"Bastard sure hasn't changed," Raoul agreed.

"Trainin' in China, he'd make us run drills till we dropped, but no feedback about what was wrong. We were supposed to 'discover it ourselves,' he'd say."

Julia whispered, "Well, at least it's not about you." Viktor grinned again, lazing back. Even the captain could bend the rules and enjoy it.

"Ask me, he's got somethin' goin' here," Marc muttered.

"Cards he hasn't played, like Axy says?"

"Can't read the guy. That always makes me suspicious."

"He got all the breaks, right." Raoul poured more coffee into a plastic mug.

"Glad he can't get the bio stuff, at least."

"Hell, he sure wants it. And more."

"An' ever'body talks about the bio, sure. Thing is, he was trying to work it so he gets to fly home with three women, ever' damn one of 'em."

"That's true. Leave us here with nothin'."

"One sly guy, three women, two of 'em single." Marc's voice got fainter. Was he looking down into his glass in self pity? "Six, seven months to Earth."

"Crowded, maybe they have to double up on bunk space."

Marc laughed sourly. "Li'l adjustment, right. Captain's orders an' all."

"Li'l threesomes, maybe even?" Raoul's voice was low, muggy.

"Why not, he's the cap'n."

"Goddamn Captain Chen—he's the one we should yank outta there."

"Hey?"

"Pull him off, take that damn nuke for ourselves."

"Huh? How?"

"Four of us, three of them. We got three guys, they got one tightass we could use for a punching bag, we wanted."

"Uh, wow." Marc sounded dazed.

"Take them when there's two outside, one inside."

"Using what?"

"I can rig something that looks dangerous, never mind that."

"What if Chen has a gun?"

"Who'd take a gun to *Mars?*"

"Chinese, I wonder."

Raoul said rapidly, "You and me, *we* take the two slots. Leave the two biologists here to work over the Marshroom or whatever the hell it is. We fly home, got a woman apiece."

"My God."

"Y'know, I just thought it through," Raoul said carefully, his diction more precise. "It makes some kind of sense, right?"

"Well . . ."

"We get what we want. Axy does, too. Sure we're using the Airbus nuke, but we're running things. We fly back your rocks, Julia's samples—dead, sure, but the real stuff. With thirty billion bucks in his pocket, Axy can do the legal for us."

"Good Lord, I dunno."

"You just think about it. That's all I am saying."

"They'd maybe throw us in prison."

"You know who runs Earthside? Not laws—no, just lawyers. And those Axy can provide."

"For the boys who bring home the bacon."

"Right. With Marshroom sauce." Raoul chuckled.

"I . . . I really dunno . . ."

"Look, we're tired—"

"And drunk on cheap tequila."

"Best tequila there is."

"*That's* the best? Whoosh."

"Look, point is, you sleep on it. We talk some more tomorrow."

"I . . . okay."

Scraping chairs. Closing doors.

Julia looked at Viktor. He got up and silently closed the door, securing it with the lever that would make a good vacuum seal if necessary.

"My God," she said. "What . . . ?"

"Drunk talk. It may go no farther than this."

"But if it does—"

"I will stop it."

"How?"

"I do not know, but there are tricks."

"What tricks?"

"Captain tricks."

"Like?"

"Raoul did not think anyone would take a gun to Mars."

31

JULIA BRACED HERSELF BEFORE ENTERING THE COMMON area for breakfast.

She felt as if she were walking on eggs. Not only unsure of what Marc and Raoul would be like, but suddenly aware of the camera. She and Viktor had agreed that, as a fallback, she would claim "lingering effects" from the near-vacuum run for her hoarse voice. Best thing would be to talk as little as possible. That she was prepared to do.

Viktor and Raoul were already at the table, reading their electronic newspapers and trading items of interest. She was momentarily startled to see Raoul drinking his coffee from one of the generic plastic mugs before remembering that his special ceramic one was gone. He appeared tense and withdrawn, as he had since the engine test failure.

The psychological support team had insisted that the crew receive daily news summaries from Earth to reduce their feelings of alienation. This was in addition to the mission-relevant news summaries prepared for them by Axelrod's communications people.

So each had picked a newspaper, and the features they wanted to see. Raoul got the *Los Angeles Times*, with augmented coverage of South American soccer. Viktor read the London *Times*, and was deeply into European geopolitics and soccer. He and Raoul had spent most of the time they were fixing the ERV happily comparing and arguing soccer minutiae.

Marc stuck with the Dallas *Times*, the paper of his birthplace. He followed most traditional American sports, especially volleyball, of which he had an encyclopedic knowledge. Only a minor knee injury at a critical time in college had turned him away from a pro career in the game. Julia had found it was possible to be utterly bored in conversation with Marc if he got going on stats, spiking versus blocking, and arcane rule changes. But he was a bright and well-read scientist, so she tried to keep their conversations on a professional level. Still, she genuinely liked Marc. He seemed to be a more cautious version of her much-missed brother Bill.

Julia had opted for the Sydney *Morning Herald*. It was partly a lark, to see the world again through Aussie eyes, and it helped her keep in touch with Harry and Robbie in Adelaide. It carried a diffuse piece about her—pride of Aussies, on Mars!—the life discovery, and endless speculations. This one had not made it into her "filtered" personal news summary. There were probably thousands like it, long on imagination, short on information.

She cleared her throat and tried a tentative "Morning." It came out as a croak. Raoul looked up with a frown and stared at her.

She tried a smile and a half shrug, and went over to make herself some tea. Glancing furtively at the camera, she was relieved to see that its little ruby light was dark. *Makes sense.* At some point last night, Raoul and Marc must've turned it off. She wondered briefly how much of their conversation had been beamed Earthside before they remembered about that ever-roving eye. The psych team would be busy this morning if anything had gotten through. In any case, it was a lucky break for her.

Julia made her tea and gratefully slurped the hot liquid down her aching throat. She sat at the table and scanned the comics.

Recently Viktor had been following closely two minor brush wars being put down by the German army. Despite the traditional Russo-German enmity, he approved heartily of its role as the policeman of the New Europe. "Let 'em pay the price of being big shots," was how he put it.

Julia managed a few grunts at appropriate moments in their one-sided conversation, and picked away at her crossword puzzle. The painkillers and tea began to kick in. She started to feel human.

When Marc finally appeared, unshaven and bleary-eyed, Raoul and Viktor were well into their second coffees. This was normally a very pleasant time for the crew. For all of these highly motivated people, the morning was an optimistic time. With plans for the day, and energy levels high, they would trade funny bits from their respective newspapers. Julia hoped desperately today would be the same.

"G'day, Marc," she said with feigned cheeriness.

He grunted something and shuffled over for coffee.

Raoul drained his mug and joined him at the food prep center. They talked, their words drowned out by the noise of the microwave. Julia shot a quick look at Viktor, but he was absorbed in his electronic news. She felt a gathering storm in the air. To give herself something to do, she grabbed a deck of cards—the fourth they had worn out on this mission—and started laying them out for solitaire.

For a while after Marc and Raoul returned to the table, the loudest sound was the gentle slapping of the cards. Viktor resolutely stared at his slate. *He's not going to give them any openings.*

The silence stretched between them.

Finally, Raoul looked at Viktor and said, "We want to talk about who goes back with Airbus."

Viktor looked up. "Who is 'we'?"

"Marc and I."

Viktor shrugged. "What is there to discuss? Axelrod is making deal with Airbus for space, but I have final decision about who goes."

"We don't agree with that." Raoul frowned. "We want a more equal shot at that berth."

"Look, Viktor," Marc cut in hurriedly. "You've been very fair so far on workloads, assignments, and all that. You haven't favored Julia, everyone knows that. But this is different. There's no way you could make this decision without personal considerations coming into it."

"Yeah," said Raoul. "This could mean life or death. But we're not in the military, and we're not gonna stand for a battlefield command decision. Each of us has an equal right to that slot."

"I remind you that Airbus captain thinks *he* will pick," said Viktor mildly.

"I'm not worried about Chen," growled Raoul. "And I don't want to have a fight about it here. Let's just draw straws. That way I have a one in four chance to get home and see my son."

"I agree," said Marc. "It's the fairest way."

"I agree with Viktor. We should use other criteria than the luck of the draw to pick," said Julia.

"Figures," said Marc.

Julia steamed. "May I remind you that I was offered that berth, and I turned it down."

"So you say," said Raoul.

"Yeah, why did you?"

"What?" Julia was furious. "Are you implying that I didn't?"

"I just find it hard to believe, the way you described it," said Raoul. "You sure there wasn't more to it?"

"Like what?" she demanded.

"Like some kinda agreement to say no publicly, and then have Viktor pick you." Raoul shrugged.

"Or Axelrod," said Marc. "You're his favorite. He kicked me off when you asked him to."

"Either way, you go home, but you look noble," said Raoul grimly.

"I can't believe I'm hearing this!" said Julia. "I said no to Chen without thinking a lot about it. It just seemed wrong, that's all. Anyway, what he wants is the Marsmat, not me. I suspect he'll ask each of you in turn the same thing. And from what I hear, neither of you would hesitate to sell the rest of us out."

She glared at them.

"Okay. Let us draw straws," said Viktor's calm voice.

"What?" Julia looked at him in astonishment. "Viktor, what are you doing?"

"Uncertainty is tearing us apart. Is better to know."

"That's more like it." Raoul smiled and visibly relaxed.

"Anyone have any spare broom straws?" asked Julia bitterly.

"Yeah, what do we use?" asked Marc. He looked around. "We don't actually have any straws."

"We play Russian Roulette with cards," said Viktor. "Is old Russian military tradition for settling disputes."

"Huh?"

Viktor reached for the deck of cards, still laid out on the table for solitaire. He hunted around, pulled out the ace of spades, held it up. "This is short straw. I bury it in the deck," he said, demonstrating. "Shuffle it, person to pick cuts deck, takes card. Wrong cards are not replaced. Shuffle after each pick. Finally, someone finds ace."

"Sounds okay to me," said Raoul.

"Me too," agreed Marc.

"Julia?" Viktor looked at her. "All must agree."

"This is crazy. It's like a bad old movie."

"Julia doesn't have to play if she's already refused the berth," said Raoul. "That betters my chances."

"All must pick, or no deal. If all are equal, all have same chance," said Viktor.

"Well, Julia?" asked Marc.

Damn. What does Viktor want me to do? Am I supposed to refuse, or go along? I just can't read him on this one. It's like when we play poker—I can never tell when he's bluffing. Still, he suggested it. "All right," she said reluctantly.

Viktor ceremoniously showed each of them the ace,

put it in the deck, shuffled it, and placed it in front of Raoul. "Cut, then pick."

Despite herself, Julia was fascinated.

"Seven of diamonds," said Raoul. "Shit card."

"All same, but one." Viktor reshuffled, passed the deck to Marc. "You next. Cut, then pick."

"Jack of clubs. No good."

It was Julia's turn. *Ohmigod, they're serious. We're really doing this crazy thing.* With a sense of unreality, she cut the deck, hesitated, turned over the card. It was a black ace. Her heart leaped. *No.* "Ace of clubs," she heard herself say. She placed it in the reject pile and sagged back in her chair.

Viktor drew the four of spades.

They played as if nothing else in the world mattered.

Two rounds in, the comm chime sounded.

Julia made a move to get up.

"Forget it," growled Raoul. "It's probably the eavesdroppers wanting to know why we turned off the vid."

She shrugged and sat down again. It was her turn anyway. Earth could wait.

The reject pile grew steadily.

Three rounds. Nothing. Raoul cursed more violently at each failed pick.

Four.

Five.

"Fuckin' thing isn't in here," Marc muttered under his breath.

Julia couldn't see how this would all end. She felt exhausted by the tension. She tore her eyes away from the cards and looked at her fellow crewmates. Who were these two frenzied, ragged men?

They seemed like strangers, suddenly.

Viktor seemed very tense. He cut the deck, flipped over the card. Stared at it for a long moment, then closed his eyes and sighed with relief. "Ace. Of. Spades," he said slowly, turning it so all could see.

32

JANUARY 29, 2018

AFTERWARD, THEY SAT FOR A FEW MINUTES, TRYING TO understand the implications. Raoul frowned into his plastic mug, rubbing it absentmindedly. Julia wondered how he was going to last for more than two years without seeing his family.

"So, Viktor, you won," said Marc in a flat voice. "You'll get to see how a nuke flies before I do. That's a turnabout." He laughed, a short bark.

"I will not leave Julia here. But the seat is mine to decide."

Raoul sighed. "Yep, so it is." He looked at Marc. "Time for us to get moving. You about ready?"

"I want to pack a bag, is all." He shuffled slowly off.

Julia raised her eyebrows. "Where are you going?"

"Moving to the ERV," said Raoul.

"What for?" Julia was dumbfounded. This she had not anticipated.

"Safeguard the fuel, Axelrod's orders," said Raoul.

Julia's brief hopes for normalcy shattered.

"I don't think is necessary," said Viktor. "Boss has funny ideas of what can happen here. Is not bad sci-fi movie."

"Well, we're not gonna sit here on our asses wondering when Chen makes his move."

"You really think he's going to try for the fuel?" Julia was dazed.

"What I said is I don't wanna worry about it. We stay in the ERV, there's no question of him trying anything funny."

"And Marc is going too?" asked Julia hoarsely. "But his samples, his work, everything's here."

"We're not exactly moving out of the neighborhood, although God knows we tried."

Julia struggled to clear her throat. *They're serious.*

Raoul looked at her coldly. "And there's another reason to go. This place is so small we'll catch whatever she has. And I don't want it. Especially if it turns out to be a Mars bug."

"It's from the Airbus crew."

"No one else caught it. You were the only one exposed to the Marshroom."

"Marsmat," she corrected him automatically. "Yeah, my immune system was down after the accident, so that's why I got it first."

"Whatever," Raoul said, getting up. "I don't fancy spending the rest of my life in quarantine."

Viktor looked thoughtful. "Is time to plan maintenance for hab. These last few weeks we have not been on correct schedule."

"No kidding," said Raoul. "We were trying to get the hell outta here."

"Is not criticism, just observation."

Over his shoulder he called, "You make up the schedule, get back to us, we'll come over." She heard the door to his cabin bang.

"Damn," Julia said. "I thought it was all over."

"Just beginning, is more likely."

"They were looking for any excuse to move out of the hab."

"My guess also."

The red light on the comm was blinking steadily. "Damn again. We forgot about that vid that came in earlier."

Axelrod was indeed anxious. He delivered his rambling soliloquy while pacing back and forth. "Hey, what's wrong? You've been off the air for damn near twelve hours now. What's happening? You know, I worry about you guys alla the time. And—well, I've already apologized for not sending a backup ERV. I'm doin' all I can here to get you guys home, but it's sorta limited at this point." A grimace.

"Airbus is still holding tight. They won't come right out and demand Julia's samples, we'd blow them outta the water in the international press if they did. Might jeopardize their getting the prize also. Blackmail isn't cricket, y'see."

He stopped pacing and looked straight at them. "I was worried that you didn't agree with my Airbus negotiations. When you turned off the camera, I thought you might have taken matters into your own hands or somethin'." He laughed nervously.

Why did he think that? Maybe all men are alike. Or somebody talked to his supposedly personal advisor.

"So just hang in there, guys. I can imagine how tough it is, and I feel really bad about it.

"Well, turning to something else, my PR boys are okay with calling Julia's alien the 'Marsmat.' Everybody on *this* planet has gone crazy about it. This is some hot property we've got! The U.N. is going to debate whether Mars life should come to Earth. I mean, how could they stop us? Give me a break. There's talk about permanent quarantine—in orbit—or worse. Meantime, every guy in a lab coat wants to get his hands on those samples. So, what d'ya think we get the scientists to fight the PEPA crazies? Julia, you got any ideas?"

Julia said sourly, "Sure, lots."

"So, guys, lemme hear from you. Soon. Okay?" He signed off.

"What are you going to tell him?" asked Julia. "About this morning?"

"I tell only truth," said Viktor stolidly. "But I volunteer nothing. I am going to do it live, to show we have nothing to hide."

She sat behind him while he did the broadcast. She even waved cheerfully, but said nothing.

"Hey, Boss, relax," said Viktor. "Camera was accidentally left off all night. We have just turned it back on."

That is true—as far as it goes.

They had regretfully turned it back on. Besides the privacy, leaving the camera off also made them feel farther from Earth, which felt surprisingly good.

Viktor continued blandly, "There is nothing wrong here, as you can see. Apart from ERV, that is. We think you are on right track with Airbus. I am content to let you handle it."

"I" not "we," but maybe he won't notice.

Viktor continued, "You are professional at sit-downs, not us. As you wanted, Marc and Raoul are moving to the ERV to guard the methane. That way we keep all options open. We give nothing away here."

If only he knew how true that is!

"You arrange for space on nuke, get as many slots as possible. As captain, I will make final choice of personnel. We all agree on this."

Very neatly done, that. She had to admire his ballsy attitude. He really was good at command.

"Have not heard from Airbus crew since visit yesterday. We have sensor near their ship, though, shows they are getting ready to melt pingo water. Laying hoses, setting up connections to their reactor."

A beaming smile.

"As for us, we have to do schedule of maintenance around here. We let it slip working on ERV so much. Could use help from tech staff to make sure we have forgotten nothing."

She was amazed how Viktor could carry on as if it

had been just a normal day. *But maybe that's how he copes. A familiar routine is calming.*

For her part, Julia was exhausted. Flu and worry combined to make her very sleepy. After Marc and Raoul left, taking the dune buggy, she decided to hide out in her cabin, reading backed-up e-mail and catching up on long-neglected correspondence. That way she would have a plausible excuse not to be on camera.

The hab felt strange, with just the two of them. They'd been alone before, when Marc and Raoul had taken days-long trips in Red Rover, but this felt different. They didn't talk about it in the public rooms—out of long habit they saved such talk for their cabins, out of range of ears and cameras.

Julia went to bed early. She brought her usual evening mug of hot cocoa in with her, and stretched out under the covers blissfully.

Viktor joined her a short time later, saying, "Is too quiet out there."

"A li'l spooky. Why do you think they really left?"

"Easier to hatch plans alone."

"You think they still want to attack the nuke?"

"Raoul is very unhappy man, but not crazy."

"Yeah. I'm more afraid they'll try to cut a deal with Airbus."

"With what?"

"With whom, you mean."

"Ah, the women." He propped up on one elbow. "Tell me what you think."

"For starters, we've all noticed Marc and Claudine.

Maybe Raoul wants Marc where he can watch him."

"Yes. Good thinking. But what about Gerda with Raoul?"

She shook her head. "I don't sense any interest there, and I remember seeing her once or twice with typical Germanic types. But we never talked about anything personal, so I really have no idea what she likes."

"Eight months in a rocket can change tastes."

"For sure, but we don't know anything about those kind of arrangements on the nuke."

"Is something we must watch from now on, for sure."

"Yeah, I think so too. Even though you won this morning, fair and square. I was so relieved. What great luck!"

"Good commander never relies on luck."

"What?"

"Marc was right. Was never in deck."

"Viktor! Don't tell me you cheated! A gentleman doesn't cheat at cards."

"Am captain, not gentleman."

She put her hand to her chest theatrically. "I'm shocked, shocked, to discover that you would do something underhanded!" She frowned. "But you looked so relieved when you turned over the ace. I'd have sworn it was genuine."

"It was. I wasn't sure trick would work. Had only done it once before."

33

JULIA AWOKE FEELING MUCH BETTER. AFTER THE INITIAL shock, she'd recognized her virus as an absolutely standard Earth-type bug. Viktor still showed no signs of catching it, but that was no surprise—they rarely shared colds. In fact, they joked about whether that was good or bad news for their future children. Either they'd catch none, or get twice as many colds as anyone else.

They rattled around at breakfast, just the two of them. She thought of calling over to the ERV just to say hi, but Viktor discouraged her with a shake of the head. As they all had been early in the mission, she was aware of the intrusion of the camera. By unspoken agreement, she and Viktor did not allude to the problems the crew was having while on camera. Having to hide things put her on guard.

Viktor was obviously enjoying the privacy. She realized that with the others he was forced to be always on duty: Viktor the captain, not the man. This being together felt more like it had been in their apartment on Earth, so long ago.

They both took advantage of it to be physically affectionate, something she had missed over the long months of enforced togetherness. She even indulged him with a neck rub as he read his London *Times*.

He grunted with pleasure. "Could get used to this, easy."

"Say, look—" She stopped and pointed. "They're taking the dune buggy."

Marc and Raoul were already churning away in the open light rover. "Going north," Viktor said.

"Toward Airbus."

"There are other things north."

"Sure."

Viktor shrugged. She let it go. Instead of fretting over the situation, very little of which they could do anything about, she settled into her acceleration couch and called up her e-mail. *Ah good, one from the folks.* It was a vid. When her dad appeared on the screen she studied him carefully. He seemed animated and happy.

"Hi, honey. Hope you're doing okay. We think we understand your situation and understand it's pretty difficult. Axelrod's folks keep us informed, but I'm sure they put their own spin on things. Thanks for cc'ing me on your bio e-mails, they're fascinating. But we'd love to hear how you're feeling, when you can spare the time."

Oops. How long since I last e-mailed? She checked her "sent" file. *Almost a week. The prodigal daughter screws up again.* She'd been assuaging her conscience by sending copies of her scientific transmissions. *Guess that only works so long.*

She went back to the message. "On the other front, I have some better news. I've found a group of doctors with an experimental treatment for liver cancer. Not drugs or radiation, but ultrasound." She listened carefully. "It's from the same folks who invented the ultrasound arterial cleaning technique. They had both ideas at the same time, but it's taken a lot longer to get the bugs ironed out of this one. Lotsa tech stuff, but basically, they can zap the cancer without harming the healthy liver tissue. And that's the main threat of this type of cancer—it's all mixed up with healthy tissue. They've done all the animal tests and some small-scale human trials, and the results are good."

Wow, she thought.

He stopped and took a deep breath.

"So, we're flying to Los Angeles in a couple days. Your mother and I feel pretty optimistic about this treatment. It won't do any harm, and at the very least it'll buy me more time. So don't worry about me, sweetie. You have some tough decisions to make and I don't want to make them any harder."

A bit of unrelated family news, and he signed off. She got up and stretched. Long ago she had learned to kick back from problems when somebody else was doing the right thing. No fretting, no burning of useless anxiety. Time for some fun.

She donned her pressure suit for a trip to the greenhouse. After days in the hab, she was longing for some different scenery.

"No taking helmet off," Viktor reminded her sternly. "I will be watching."

The greenhouse welcomed her, as always. *An oasis of green in a red desert . . .*

Except that the plants had frozen during the night after the blowout. Dead, brown vines hung from their support lines. Upright plants had simply collapsed in place.

"Viktor," she called over the comm, "while you're making up the maintenance schedule, don't forget that the greenhouse needs replanting ASAP."

"I make note. Everything dead?"

"Just about. I haven't done an inventory but I don't see any green."

After checking the readout on the internal atmosphere, she opened the faceplate of her helmet, sniffed tentatively. It was just hab air with a faint tinge of vegetation. She sighed. It wouldn't smell fresh again until plants grew.

She went straight for the repaired mist chamber. Viktor had strengthened the joints, and they seemed secure. She peered through the transparent walls—

And was astounded by what she saw.

A riot of diminutive shapes. And even—yes—colors! Faint, but definite.

Over in the far corner was the original celery-like spike. Underneath the nozzle that sprayed the nutrients was a small pool covered by a pinkish scum. *Bet it's teeming with Marc's "shrimp."* At the center of the chamber was a tangle of pale blue filaments. The remaining mat surface was smooth or sported bumps of varying size. It was larger than before the blowout.

Her thoughts were racing. How could those pale blobs of mat have spawned this diversity?

She saw two possibilities. The mat could be a community of different organisms, finally large enough to express its true complexity. Microbes on Earth had chemical systems that allowed them to count their neighbors. If enough were present, the microbes turned on new genes and assumed different characteristics.

Or . . . it was one organism of extreme plasticity. And minute differences in the environment were causing radical changes in the organism.

Like slime molds. They spend most of their life as single wandering cells. As such, they cruise their landscape of wet, rotting wood like the familiar amoeba. But a drop in moisture causes a radical change in behavior and morphology. Using chemical attractants, great numbers of individual cells aggregate and differentiate into an elaborate reproductive structure of great beauty and brilliant color.

Hmmm. On second thought, that's a cooperative effort also.

She went back to the microscope slides she'd made. Those cell types really did look different. But the slime mold model was also attractive. She didn't have enough data to be able to decide.

Two heads would be way better than one.

Damn Chen anyway. Why couldn't we have cooperated on this discovery, rather than be at swords' points?

What had really surprised her during the vent descent was how large and complex the structures were. It was a throwback to the grand old days of the Precambrian on Earth, three billion years ago, when anaerobes had ruled the Earth. With the exception of the stromatolites near Perth, living anaerobes on Earth were minute, and most lived solitary lives. Even biofilms, communities of bacteria, were microscopic.

On Earth, evolution's crown went to the oxy users, the animals. They had grazed away the bacterial mats with their superior energy. But here the anaerobes ruled, and they'd evolved new forms.

Hmmm. Maybe the best analogy was the marsupials of Australia—furry vertebrates, not true mammals. They breed more slowly than true placental animals, like rodents, and thus were eliminated all over the Earth except for the huge, isolated island of Australia. Free of superior competitors, they populated an entire continent, evolving completely unique forms such as kangaroos, wombats, and the duck-billed platypus.

Was that what had happened on Mars? A planet that never evolved plants because it cooled off too quickly, so it never got an oxygen atmosphere to poison the original life-forms? Without the superior energetics of the oxy users to compete with, the anaerobes had slowly colonized, evolved, *blossomed.*

She did some quick calculations and saw that the available volume of warm, cavern-laced rock below Mars was comparable to the inhabitable surface area of Earth. Plenty of room to try out fresh patterns.

But would evolution have produced the same answer to the riddle of survival on Mars as on Earth? Something tickled the edge of her mind, but she couldn't quite get it.

Out of the corner of her eye she saw movement outside. The dune buggy with two suited figures was returning to the ERV. She sighed inwardly.

They weren't any different here on Mars than they'd been on Earth. Competitive, unruly, passionate oxy users all. Driven. They were only a microcosm of the larger strifes and divisions on the home planet.

34

"Well, well, this is very interesting," said Marc.

He was doing a routine download from sensors they'd left at various sites, mostly for weather monitoring. Despite the chilly relations between the two men living in the ERV and Viktor and Julia in the hab, they all understood that routine maintenance had to continue. For almost two years, their lives had depended on well-functioning equipment. Raoul and Marc had come over earlier in the dune buggy, and Raoul quickly got to work checking the life-support system.

"Um?" Julia looked up from her slate.

"The Airbus rover is parked at the vent. So that's where they went."

"What? I don't follow."

"Raoul and I called on Airbus yesterday, only they weren't home. At least no one but Claudine. And she was real close-mouthed about where the other two were. Well, now we know."

"What are they doing there? Can you see the crew?"

"Nope, just the rover, and a climbing rig. My guess is, they're inside."

She leaped to her feet. "That sonofabitch! I can't believe it! Last I talked to Chen, it was going to be a joint descent."

"How so?"

"I was going to go with them, or rather, him. I figured a two-biologist trip was optimum."

"Boss know about this?"

"Not yet. He knows I talked biology with Chen, showed him my results. And that I refused to trade the samples for a ride home. I'm sorry now I told Chen anything. If I'd known what he was gonna do . . ."

"Well, he'd have found the vent with or without you."

"I didn't tell him where it was, or much about what the interior was like. I didn't do a travelogue. We talked biology."

"How'd he find it, then?"

"Probably followed our tracks backwards. He knew we were coming from there when they landed. We can always ask."

"So he doesn't know what to expect?"

"Not in any detail. I said it was slippery and dangerous, that Viktor'd been hurt there. I was still pissed off with the bastard, wanted to pick his brain on theory, not help him win the prize."

"Well, we're screwed now," Marc said wanly. "There goes our last card."

In her Sydney newspaper there was a lurid spread on the "Mars flu."

"What?!" she cried. "Listen: 'Julia Barth lies near death from an affliction caught from the Martian life she found—' Where did they get this?"

Viktor said, "No leaks, Axelrod said."

Raoul was doing his systems maintenance in the hab, so they had a meeting. "I told only my personal counselor," he insisted.

"So means there is leak from counselor," Viktor said.

"As we suspected before," Marc said.

"Damn!" Julia fumed. "We can't trust anybody now."

"Maybe is best, keep us on guard."

"It'll be a media firestorm Earthside," Marc said.

It was, and she soon sickened of reading even her "filtered" news summary. Axelrod came on soon, rueful at the leak. "A goddamned media tabloid paid Raoul's counselor a million for the story," he said angrily. "Said he didn't want to stick around anyway, listening to Raoul die. The bastard!"

"I wonder if Axelrod didn't know before?" Marc asked.

Viktor asked, "You mean, is Axelrod getting copies of all our counselor sessions?"

"Could be. Would explain some leaks," Marc said.

"We cannot know if he is," Raoul said. "We just don't know what or who to trust anymore."

Axelrod's news did not make any difference to her. For each of them the whole nightmare of quarantine and panic suddenly became solidly real.

They were all having a rather glum midafternoon tea when the comm console lit up with a flashing red light. The unexpected chimes startled Julia from her seat.

Emergency message! But from who?

Claudine's voice came across thin and tense in the sudden hush. "'Ello hab, are you there? Something's wrong. Gerda and Chen are away from base in ze rover and zhey 'ave missed their second check-in. Can you do anything?"

Marc was closest to the console. "Where are they?"

he asked blandly, knowing full well that the rover hadn't moved from the vent.

"Zhey're at a big fissure about twenty kilometers north of here. It's the vent where Julia found the lifeform. They went underground again this morning, and I 'aven't 'eard anything since."

"Again today? How long have they been out there?"

"Since yesterday. They did a short descent in ze afternoon, then prepared to go deeper today."

"And check-in time was . . . ?"

"Well, roughly *midi*, ah, middle of the day. They took extra air tanks down, but they are on their last ones by now. Maybe they're trapped in there." Her voice rose before it pinched off.

A brief silence. Conflicting emotions boiled up in Julia's mind in rapid succession: worry, fear, sympathy, rage, envy, satisfaction, then shame. Through the fog she heard Marc's soft drawl.

"Ah, Claude, we're going to talk about this for a bit and get back to you."

"Oh, *merde*. Please, do not take too long. Zhey could die out there. It is not our fault, we did not make the rules for this trip . . ."

"Yeah, well, we didn't either. And we're a long way from the vent."

Marc switched off. He swiveled in his couch and looked at the others quizzically. "Well?"

"Serves them right!" exploded Julia. "I warned that little cocksure bastard that it was dangerous!"

"How do you like that? They expect us to help them!" said Raoul grimly.

"I wouldn't give them a sample, so they went to get their own," said Julia. "They've paid the price of competitiveness."

"They got what they deserved," agreed Marc.

Viktor held up his hands. "First thing to do is find out if they need rescue," he said mildly.

Julia took a deep breath, let her anger drain off. *Slow . . . easy . . .* She shot a grateful smile at Viktor. "Right," she said. "Any ideas?"

"Try them again on radio, check sensors again."

"*Oui, mon capitaine,*" said Marc. He turned back to the console. "We don't even know what radio frequency they use, they were so determined to keep their plans so goddamn secret," he said. "I'll use a broad-band sweep."

They all sat and waited, Julia's mind whirling.

"Situation unchanged," he reported after a long three minutes.

"Maybe they're having cable problems," said Julia. "It's easy enough to get tangled, in those clumsy suits."

"Maybe it's a phony distress call, to get us away from base while they steal our fuel," said Raoul.

"Why do they need it?" asked Marc.

"True, race is over," said Viktor.

"Not quite," growled Raoul. "What about Julia's samples in the greenhouse?"

"But they're in the vent," protested Marc. "They can get their own."

"How do we know where they are?" Raoul shot back. "I wouldn't put anything past that arrogant squint."

Julia thought rapidly. After her accidents, Viktor would automatically object to her going back to the vent.

But maybe this gave her the crack she needed. "Look, if the two of you stay here, Airbus can't pull a surprise visit if they're *not* at the vent. Then Marc and I can go see what the matter is." She glanced at Raoul, added quickly, "Or *if* there is anything the matter."

Viktor frowned, but said nothing.

"We owe them nothing," said Raoul bitterly. "Still, the law of the desert says you don't leave someone stranded on the side of the road."

"They were eager enough to abandon us," said Marc.

"That's the difference between them and us," said Raoul. "Where I was brought up, you didn't."

Marc considered for a moment, then nodded. "Yeah, you're right. I don't see a lot of choices here. Okay, I'll go."

Julia was aware that Viktor was hanging back while the rest of the team came back together. *Careful now . . . you're still on pretty thin ice.* "Well, we can't just leave them out there."

Viktor looked unhappy. "I agree. I think we must go see. But you two are not to make another descent, understand? It will be dusk when you get there. Too late to set up safely."

"We won't take any chances," Julia said.

"We will monitor you on radio." Viktor scowled at them both, one at a time. "Stay in touch. That is captain's order."

35

AS THEY REACHED THE VENT, PHOBOS ROSE IN THE RUBY west.

It was a lump of white, about a third the size of the moon's disk, and if she had taken the time to watch she could have seen it crawl across the sprinkling of stars now poking through the gathering dark. She wondered whether she would ever have time to watch that happen again.

The Airbus climbing rig looked first class. Chen and Gerda had worked from a single heavy-duty winch, which meant they'd alternated their descents and ascents.

"I prefer one man, one winch," said Julia.

Marc shrugged. "I've heard of these, never seen one. Look over here. The differential transfers power from one cable to the other depending on which one is sending a signal. Same idea as the rear axle in a car, actually. Hmm. Saves mass, I guess. Now where is the test switch?"

"You look while I check their internal radio."

From inside the Airbus rover, which took some trouble getting into, Julia tried to raise them on radio. Nothing. She came back out quickly, since she had taken her helmet off to go inside. After the greenhouse, she wasn't going to let it out of her sight again.

"This motor is jammed, or burned out," he reported over the comm. "I can't get a rise out of it."

They looked at each other grimly through their face-plates.

"They could have just gotten tangled up," she said hopefully.

"Uh-uh," Marc grunted. "More like they got trapped, tried to power out, and overloaded the motor."

"Well, there's nothing for it but to go down."

"Yep. Better tell base. Viktor'll scream bloody murder, but he can't stop us."

His prediction was exactly right. Viktor even shouted over comm, something she had never heard him do.

"They knew what they were doing! We are not responsible to get them out. I sprain my leg there. If something happens to you—"

"I'll be *very* careful."

"So was I!"

"Look, Chen was a scientist—" She stopped, realizing she had used the past tense. "What if they found something really important down there? And are cut off?"

"I do not like—"

"We'll just go—"

"It is *night*. Soon so cold you are not able to move joints in that suit, maybe."

"The vent gets warmer pretty fast."

"That is not enough to—"

"This is an on-the-spot decision, Viktor. We're going in."

"I, I *order* you not to—"

She switched off. Immediately she felt terrible about doing it, but she left it off.

Marc had heard. They said nothing, just checked their harnesses, securing the yokes.

"How about carrying oxy tanks this time?" Marc asked.

"Theirs?" She nodded at the rack of bottles on the rear of the Airbus rover.

"Ummm. I was thinking ours."

"Both, why not? Look at their rack—four gone. They took two extras, but by now they'll be low."

"That'll up the mass on our lines a lot. They're Mars-rated for one ton metric, so . . ." He calculated. "Okay, there's plenty margin. But they'll be pretty damn awkward."

They put two tanks apiece on their lines, double-clamping them five meters above the yokes. She did not like the idea of that much mass ready to fall on her, and checked the clamps three times.

Backing down the slope, playing out their cables, Julia looked up into a bowl of sharp stars. Already her suit felt chilly. Her heater was ticking away, fighting the frigid plunge as the skimpy warmth bled out of the thin Martian atmosphere.

The crew never operated outside at night, an absolutely solid rule. Mechanical parts stuck, valves jammed, suit power ran out fast. They had a power connection in the line to Red Rover's inboard nuclear power source, but they would have to stop to tap into it. She gritted her teeth and wondered if Viktor had been right.

Sure he was. This is foolish.

But another part of her knew that if she walked away

from here without trying to find them she would answer for it the rest of her life. Not to others—to herself.

She glanced over at Marc as they played out line. Something in his face told her that he was having the same thoughts. Had reached the same conclusion. And neither of them had needed to talk about it.

They got the oxy tanks past the Y-frame that routed the lines. It was awkward getting the bottles set right. Then the two of them backed over the lip and negotiated the bottles into place above them.

In their suit lamps she could see him concentrating on where his feet were, how his weight was displaced—the riveting attention trained into them by the years. After all the gut-churning tension of the last few days, it actually felt good to be *doing* something—clean, direct, muscles and mind.

They went down gingerly, parallel to the Airbus monofilament cables. Marc said, "I wonder if that differential was built after seeing our plans?"

She grimaced, puffing as the winch lowered them both into an inky well. "Why not? All's fair in a race."

"Look there," he called.

From below seeped a soft ivory glow. The darkness above them made the seeing different this time. A thin mist boiled up and cloaked the radiance in streamers of gossamer finery.

"Careful not to touch the mat," she said.

"Marshroom, you mean."

"I certainly do not."

They moved down fast and the glow ripened. The Airbus cable plunged straight into inky nothing.

They passed by the increasingly lush mat. Some phosphoresced in pale blue and ivory. Others seemed to have earlike fans to catch moisture. She had memorized parts of this, the pieces she had caught on video.

"It all seems different," Marc said. On comm she could hear him breathing steadily and deeply. Heavy work at the end of the day, not recommended . . .

"No sunlight. The mats do seem brighter."

"Maybe something's stirred them up."

"It's misting pretty heavily."

"I was thinking maybe Chen and Gerda."

Down, as fast as the winches could go.

In the torch beam they found the ledge where they had gone to the left.

"That way led into the large horizontal cavern," Marc said.

The Airbus cables went to the right. "It looks steeper their way," she said. The Airbus lines sagged into the turn, not taut, not bearing any weight. "Wonder what that means?"

"The mist is getting heavier," Marc said.

"There's a wind." She watched coils of speckled moisture rise past them.

"Hope this vent isn't getting set to do something big."

"Unless the mat is giving off some vapor."

"Why would it?"

"Transport of water from the interior. The top is always drying out, getting cold."

"You mean the system has circulation?"

"Outflow, yes. I wonder if the mat somehow regulates it."

"Could it?"

"Earth's whole atmosphere and climate is regulated by plants and animals."

"Sure . . ." He looked at the luminous mat gliding past as the winches carried them down. They were far enough out to keep the oxy tanks from smacking into the sides, but she knew some damage was inevitable.

No chance for pristine intrusion. I'll catch hell for this with the Earthside biologists.

At the edge of her vision she sensed something and stopped her winch. "Look, some mat is dead."

"Yeah. I don't remember doing anything like that when we came through here."

"Me either. Turn off your lamps."

They plunged into blackness.

The glow gradually built up in their eyes. "Right, there's a lesion on the closest mat," said Marc.

She swung gently over, peered at it. The oxy tanks above were handy for this, providing a local pivot. "Probably they stopped here and their exhales did this."

"Pretty big patch."

"If I'd told him about my descent he could have avoided doing this."

"Hey, don't blame yourself. He was calling the shots, remember, making deals."

"Well, at least we'll get a look at some new territory."

They turned their lamps back on and let the winch take them down. She pulled out her microcam and began shooting the mat as they went. The mats were growing ever larger and thicker as they went lower. They covered most of the tube walls now, stacking thickly on every available out-jut, then working up the verticals.

"How far along are we?"

Marc looked at his digital readout from the winch control above. "Three hundred point four meters."

"Let's pick up the pace. If—what's that?"

"Another lesion." Marc swung over to look. "They must've—"

"Look! It's the same shape as the damage above."

The mat around the wound glowed brightly with pale phosphorescence.

"They made the same pattern each place?" Marc asked. "Some kind of experiment Chen was trying?"

"Beats me." It seemed to be changing as she watched. "Look at it out of the corner of your eye," she said. "See?"

"It's spreading downward."

She leaned over and peered around. "The glow increases below." They looked down the vent.

Marc said, "It's definitely brighter down there."

"Let's go." They descended carefully, playing out line. Their lamps washed the mats in glare that seemed harsh now. Twenty meters down she said, "Lamps off again," as they rested on a shelf.

When her dark vision came back her eyes were drawn to a splotch of light. "Damn! How—?"

"It's the same shape again."

"Right."

Marc asked, "What the hell?"

"A mimicking image."

"Naw, can't be . . ."

"Parrots imitate sounds, this mat imitates patterns imposed on it, even destructive ones. But why?"

He drawled, "I'd say the question is, how the hell?"

"The mat here learned about the wound above."

In the blackness Marc's voice was baffled. "Learned?"

"Echoed, at least. Maybe automatically."

"Okay, they're connected. But why the same shape?"

She wondered herself, and guessed, "It's a biological pictograph. I have no idea why. But I am sure that any capability has to have some adaptive function."

"You mean it has to help these mats survive."

"Right."

On with the lamps and they dropped again. This tube was very nearly vertical, which made their descent quick. Still, time was narrowing. Julia felt incredulous, wondered if she was imagining the similarity in the damage patterns. But no: the image repeated on successively lower mats twice more, five meters apart.

Off with the lamps again. She gazed back up. The blurred gleaming above had faded. So it was not just a simple copying, for some pointless end. "The pattern, it's following us down."

Alarm filled Marc's voice. "Tracking us?"

"See for yourself, up there—the image is nearly gone, and the one next to us is brightening."

"Are you implying it knows we're here?"

"It seems to sense what level we're on, at least."

"The one here is stronger than the others."

"I think so too. Brighter the deeper we go. The glow is purely chemical, some signaling response I would guess. Maybe the denser vapor here deep in the vent helps it develop."

"Signaling?" Marc sounded worried.

"Maybe just mimicking. Light would be the only way to communicate downward here. It couldn't use chemical means to signal downward, the updrafts of vapor would blow them away. Sound could go either up or down, but it doesn't carry well in this thin an atmosphere."

His voice was strained in the blackness. "There's got to be a simple explanation."

"There is, but it doesn't imply a simple organism."

"Maybe it's . . . signaling something else . . ."

"And if it's brighter the deeper we get, maybe that means . . . something below?"

"The Airbus cable, it's still slack." He kicked it and waves propagated both up and down. At the next ledge down the lesion image began to swell into a strong, clearer version.

Something beyond comprehension was happening here and she could only struggle with clumsy speculations as she worked. Somehow the mat could send signals within itself. There were many diaphanous flags and rock-hugging forms, getting thicker, most of them pasty-colored. Somehow they all fit together, a community. They used the warmth and watery wealth here and could send signals over great distances, tens of meters, far larger than any single mat.

Why? To sense the coming pulse of vapor and make ready? A clear survival value in that, she supposed. Could organisms evolve such detailed response in this harsh place? Could a biofilm do it? On Earth they were considered to be early, primitive forms with severe limitations. Or had biofilms just been outrun by other forms in the rich, warm, wet oceans?

With their lamps off she took video shots of the ghostly lesion images with her microcam, though she was pretty sure the level of illumination was too low to turn out. She would memorize all this and write it down in the rover. Careful notes . . .

"Their lines just keep going," Marc said, looking down as they descended.

"I'm nearly halfway through my oxygen."

"So would they have been, when they got this far."

"This goes nearly straight down. Not like the way we went."

"There's been no plate tectonics for a long time, remember. Nothing to shear a volcanic passage like this, twist it around. So lava just came pretty much straight out. This tube, it's probably a couple billion years old." Marc seemed a bit spooked by the mat, but more confident with geology.

"Getting narrower though."

"This mat is getting thicker, too."

Her lamp was on high, poking down, so she saw it first. "What's that?"

Far below was an oatmeal-colored floor. They stopped just above where the two Airbus cables forked straight through the middle.

"Where'd they go?"

"They got through this thing," she said.

It looked like two massive, cupped palms pressed together at the center. The whole structure was perhaps three meters across. *Maybe not an accident that it's here, where the vent narrows down.*

"Some kind of valve?" she speculated.

"Looks pretty solid."

"Reminds me of stomates," she said. "Plant cells that guard openings in leaves. The plant opens or closes the holes by pumping fluid into the stomate cells, changing their shape."

"The mat is a plant?"

"No, it's something we have no category for. A film, a biofilm—but one incredibly more advanced than the simple ones that grew in the early oceans of Earth. These have had billions of years to follow a different path."

"Well, it's sure good at blocking our path."

"But it didn't stop Chen and Gerda."

"Maybe it was open when they came through?"

"That's it. This structure seals the tube, maybe to protect the lower vent—"

"From what?"

"Peroxide dust? Maybe *they* irritated it, so it closed up."

"So if we poke at it . . ."

"Good idea."

She lowered directly onto the thing, boots sinking in. "It can hold my weight. Wow, that's strong."

"For a plant, yeah."

She walked around on it. "Some give to it, but— wait, I have an idea." She winched down so she could sit down. "Ugh, not easy in these suits."

"What's up?"

"Maybe my air exhaust will tickle it."

Abruptly it flexed. She automatically reached for her winch control, but the membrane gave way faster. It retracted and she lost her footing. A hole opened at the middle and she skidded through. The surface was slick now and she stopped halfway through the opening.

"Hey!" Marc called.

She stabbed at her winch control and played out the line, slipping fully through. As she looked up the opening widened. She was dangling just below the roof of—

"My God, it's huge," she said.

Below and around her was a murky vault that stretched beyond view. As her lamp swept around the fog reflected back its glare. But to the side she could make out a sweep of radiance that dwindled into the distance—the ceiling of a vast cavern.

"You okay?" Marc peered down at her through the opening.

"Fine. Come on through."

"What if it closes up on us?"

"We'll kick our way back out."

"What if we can't?"

"Look, the Airbus cables just keep going straight down, so they didn't get trapped by this . . . this *valve*. Let's find them."

"Valve?" Marc asked as he lowered himself through.

"Maybe that's what it does. I dunno. Theory later. *Look*."

With lamps quenched, the gloomy grotto came alive with shimmering luminescence: burst golds, dapplings of orange, vermilion splashes that laced through turquoise filigree.

"My God, how big is this?" Marc whispered.

"Can't see the walls."

"Or the floor, through this vapor."

"So bright, the walls— Turn off your beam."

Without the back-scatter from the fog she could make out dim glows tapering away on all sides. *Like the signature of a distant city . . .*

"It's moving. See, on the ceiling." He gestured up.

She played out line to watch the shifting pale patterns above them. Hanging in the blackness, she could see, achingly slowly, the complex seethe of radiance.

She was too stunned to think. *Okay, so act.* "Well, nowhere to go but down."

"Yeah . . . What's *doing this?*"

Damned if I know. On Earth, mats of bacteria luminesce when the bacteria get thick enough. Quorum sensing, it's called. Here, who knows what could have evolved—colors? shapes? patterns?

"Come on." She winched down, leaning back in the yoke to watch how her line fed through the hole in the membrane. The cable did not rub against the edges of the thing. It had opened further, maybe two meters.

Marc followed her. "Could all this be directed by intelligence?"

"Doesn't have to be. Sentience is not the same as intelligence. There'd be a huge selective pressure in favor of controlling the loss of gases. Maybe that's what the valve does."

"This is some kind of instinct, then?"

"Can't tell from what we've seen so far." She turned and gazed down. The flush of light from below was getting well defined. More of the curious swirls and blotchy colors, as above. How close to the floor were they? She let herself down a few more meters and called, "I'm going to turn on a beam. Close your eyes, so one of us keeps night vision."

"Roger."

When the beam stabbed down she took her hand off the winch command instantly. About five meters below them were two space suits, one orange, one blue. Facedown. They did not move.

36

FEBRUARY 1, 2018

THEY DANGLED OVER THE TWO FACEDOWN SUITS AND Marc carefully lowered himself to within a foot of the orange one.

"Gerda," he called on comm. Nothing. "Chen?"

They looked at each other, only a few feet apart. "Turn her over. Be careful—it looks like the mat has partly grown over them."

"This *fast?*"

"Don't think of it like a plant."

"I wonder if I can turn her over from here."

"Try. Don't put your weight on the mat."

Marc pivoted in his yoke and took hold of Gerda's suit with both gloves. "Man, this stuff pulls hard." His angle was bad, and finally he had to lift Gerda. The pale mat growths resisted, stretching until they popped free. In normal Earth gravity lifting that much would have been impossible, but with some grunting he managed to get her turned over. Her eyes were closed. No expression.

"I can make out her internals," Marc said, shining his beam through her faceplate. "Air's to zero."

"See those tanks lying to the left?" She craned her neck. "Reading full."

"So they're . . . dead."

"No way to be sure unless we crack their helmets."

"They're way beyond the time limits on their tanks."

"Explains why they didn't answer. Their audio connection shorted out along with the winch, I'll bet."

Marc turned over Chen with the same difficulty and same result. Chen looked peaceful, somehow. "This damned mat, it's all over them."

"Maybe they got snagged in it somehow. Looks like ropes of blue linguine."

"For some reason they couldn't hook onto their oxy."

Marc gestured at the small distance between the bodies and the tanks. "They were close enough. I can't see how the mat could stop them."

"I have no idea what it can do." She suddenly remembered the pale blue filaments in the mist chamber. "Marc, I saw some of these same shapes and colors in the mat growing in the greenhouse. Only much smaller."

"It's just a *plant*," he insisted.

"It may be a lot stronger than it looks. That valve thing up there, it was pretty—"

"I'm not touching it, tell you that."

"But they did . . . They must've detached their tanks from their line. Dropped them onto the mat. It would be hard to put them on, dangling here."

"So they landed and tried to get their oxy—wait, what's that?"

Their beams found scattered instruments—cutters, sample bags, a big box. She said, "Chen was taking samples. Look at those filaments to the right—they're sliced. He was partway through with the job, looks like."

"Did it before they changed tanks. Not smart."

"They're new, not much real experience."

"See that?" Marc swung toward the spot. "Looks like an oxygen burn, right by Chen."

"He was testing it, maybe. Look, there are other burns over there. Deliberately spraying it with his exhale exhaust?"

"I still don't see what killed them. This film thing, how could it—"

They both looked up. A tremor had come down their lines.

"Oh damn," Marc said. He started winching up at max speed, training his beam upward.

Julia thought she knew what was coming but turned back to Chen and Gerda. For a moment she was alone with them. *Why try to do it all? If you had just asked we would have warned you, shown our videos—*

No point in going there, not now.

"That goddamn valve thing," Marc called. "It's closed around the lines."

"We've got to get out."

"Right." She could hear his breathing quicken. "Only we're down to around ten percent left on our tanks. I don't wanna get into the jam they did."

"I agree," she said, looking away from the bodies and trying to think. "Let's do the switch right now."

"Agree." He came winching down.

The change of tanks proved to be even harder than she had feared. On their last descent they had done the switch standing on a ledge. In air, even with lower gravity, it was a struggle to detach their nearly finished tanks and get the new ones in the sockets. They kept the old tanks secured to their lines. Each helped the other but it took over ten minutes.

"Whoosh, glad to get a full one," Marc said.

"We had better think through what we do. It looks to me that Gerda and Chen didn't."

"Okay, what'll we try? Me, I say we hammer at that valve up there. Leave these bodies."

"I hate to leave them in the mat. Not just humanitarian reasons—don't want to contaminate this community."

"Community?"

"This mat is a complex structure. Rootlike filaments, thick petals, moss, lichen . . . those are just analogies. Maybe it's like a higher plant in level of complexity and organization, even though it's a mixed community of microbes."

"Ummm. I wonder if there's another way out of this place?"

"Another vent? Could be—but do we have time to look?"

"No," he said decisively, "not with just a few hours left."

They hung just above the mat and watched the slow, strange ebb and flow of phosphorescence. A chill came into her, not from temperature, but a shiver that ran along her spine with icy fingers as she felt the hair at the nape of her neck stand up. *Something more here . . . something different . . .* She looked to both sides, at the churn of somber luminosity that stretched away into the foggy darkness beyond their lamps' ability to penetrate. There was a sense of *presence*, a weight in the slow, ponderous seethe of vapor and light, like a language beyond knowing. As a field biologist she had learned to trust her feel for a place, and this hollow of light far beneath a dry world had an essence she tried to grasp, not with human ideas, but with a blunt, root perception . . .

She was looking behind him and so saw the movement first. "It's rising."

"What?"

By the time Marc had spun around the bulge in the mat was a foot high. A spaghetti swarm of pale blue strands was lacing through the dark mat, stretching and expanding like tendons in some strange muscle that rose just fast enough to see the change. It was a few meters away and tilted toward them as it sluggishly rose. Tubular stalks slid among cakes of brown crust. Fibers forked into layers of dark yellow mass and seemed to force up slabs of porous mat. An outline shaped itself and the whole structure seemed to bud up, as if a wholly new plant were emerging from the moist conglomerate surface.

Julia's heart thumped wildly. She held herself absolutely still in her harness and watched, timing the movement of the thing with her own breaths. In utter silence the mass forced itself up and toward them. She felt a palpable sense of something struggling, putting vast concentration into this one focal point.

"My God," Marc said. "It's . . ."

A chunky rectangular form, the top turned toward them. Two branches sprouting at the top, shaped by the blue strands. She blinked. At its base, two more protrusions, slabs of dark mat forming with aching effort into thicker tubes . . . And from the upper sides, above the two thickening tubes that now jutted from each side . . . a third blob, of ebony as thick as tree bark, pulling itself out from the main trunk.

A part of her did not want to say it. *This is impossible. It can't be* . . . "A . . . human shape."

No mistake. The mat was creating a pseudopod, pseudohuman. *Responding?*

"What . . . ?"

"It's the mat's idea of us."

"Another kind of echo?"

Marc could not take his eyes off the changing shape, which had now stopped thrusting out. It stood there, fully two feet above the surrounding mass, a blunt but recognizable outline of the human body. She tried to ask herself questions, to make her mind work. How could a mat enlarge itself into a particular mold, so quickly . . . ? How could it know . . . ?

She said through a dry throat, "It can see us, somehow. At least enough to work out our outlines."

"It has eyes?"

"Maybe that's what all this glowing is about. It communicates across the cavern with light."

"Sentience?"

"Must be. Of some kind. It has developed enough to control its environment. Life does."

"But why'd it kill Gerda and Chen?" Marc asked as he twisted in his harness. His microcam flashed on and he took a long pan of the thing in available light. Was it glowing more now? He might capture its image, though the moist darkness seemed to absorb light. They had kept their beams away from the mat, relying on back-reflection from the mist to light up the area. The mat glow seemed stronger around the form. She aimed her own microcam at it and carefully swept the area to take it all in.

"It didn't," she said softly, "except maybe by accident. Holding them, feeling all over them . . . to find out what they were?"

"They were out of their harnesses, couldn't winch out anyway. Then the mat got them."

Can it hear us? What senses does it have . . . and are they remotely like ours?

She spoke rapidly, to quell a rising wave of unease. "Maybe in response to them, the Marsmat protected itself. That valve membrane above, it closed automatically. Its major threats come from above—peroxides and cold and vacuum. The mat could build up vapor pressure in here by sealing that exit. Chen and Gerda were trapped below it and got stuck in the mat itself."

Marc spun carefully around the axis of his line, peering uneasily at the vast darkness that now seemed to close in, clasping them in gossamer veils of haze. "How do we convince it to let us go?"

"I expect it's sentient but probably not intelligent."

"So?"

She was unsure of everything, and every breath narrowed their options. Was this extruded shape an attempt at communication? Or a threat? How to get it to release the valve above? Noises? Thin atmosphere, unlikely it would respond to sound. The flashlights? What signal to send? They had been sweeping their beams all over this cavern.

Her heart thudded harder. To fight the rising panic she knew she had to keep her thinking crisp, direct. *React later.*

"Look, it must be responsive to chemical stimuli. If the gases coming up from deep in the interior are wrong for it, there's got to be a way to filter them, expel others."

"So we make it want to let us go by poisoning it?"

"Maybe Chen figured that, too. That's why the burns in the mat."

"Which failed."

"Maybe to irk the whole system we have to pour it on."

"With what?"

"Their oxygen tanks."

"They're our reserve!" Marc was getting impatient.

"Notice their connectors? They're screw type, not

the pressure clamps we have. So we can't tap them anyway."

"Damn, no, I didn't."

"So we might as well try with them."

"Me, I'd rather bang on the door up there."

"No reason we can't do both."

"Not like I can think of anything else, either."

She sent a call to Viktor, for the Rover to relay. At least they would know what had happened down here . . .

The winches labored hard—*don't burn them out!*—to lift them away from the glowing, phosphorescent mat with its strange humanoid shape, its elephant ears and festoons of every blobby shape, its mass of essential strangeness.

In the haunting darkness her muscles now ached and her breath came in ragged gasps. *Tired? Or scared? . . . Both.*

A part of her thought of what message they would be sending to this strange place, how they would appear to this being, a truly advanced Martian life-form. No way to tell. But what choice did they have?

She looked down at the crude humanoid shape, still plain against the mat. A part of her wanted to stay and study it, but her nerves screamed *get away!*

React later, she reminded herself. *Think ahead.*

During the ride up she opened the screws on her Airbus tank. It spewed out, a moist plume condensing immediately into crisp snow. Water in the compressed tanks froze on expanding. The air around them was still very cold.

This vapor is from the mat itself, not coming up in warm gas from below. The mat is releasing it . . . why?

The unseen oxygen made gusts in the foggy banks around their beams. She glided upward through a universe unlike anything she had ever imagined—a shadowy, clouded world of diffuse light that throbbed with a slow, softly radiant energy.

No easy explanations here. No immediate explanation for the deaths. This was life unlike any analogy with Earthly biology, still evolving from forms older than the continents, still hanging on, indestructible, still dealing in its own strange way with the hard conditions dealt it, still coming.

She directed the Airbus tank spout at a nearby outhanging. Frosty gas vented onto it. The mat jerked visibly.

"Good," Marc called, and did the same.

They approached the valve membrane, drawing up through a somber fog that thickened toward the ceiling. Their lines slid easily through the narrow puckered center of the membrane.

"I'll give it a squirt," Marc said.

Playing the Airbus reserves over nearby thick mat surfaces produced a curious rippling revulsion. The glow heightened here, ebbed there, in no apparent pattern. In her beam she saw tubers seem to swell with liquids, like fat roots. Without a sound she caught the sense of growing agitation.

"Now to knock on the door." Marc brought himself up to the membrane and slammed his gloved hand into it. Nothing. He took a screwdriver out and punched a hole in the leathery pale skin, but it was thicker than the tool. He could tear away some fragments but the strength of the valve was obvious.

"Marc, stop!"

"Why? What's wrong?"

"I don't think we want to send the wrong signal. We want to *tickle* it open, induce it to cooperate."

"What's wrong with a little force?"

"It's not a threat, and I don't want it to become one."

"No, huh? It just killed two of us."

"Accidentally. Their inexperience was probably as much to blame."

"Chen was sawing some big chunks off just before. Maybe it reacted to that."

"I really don't know. But I don't want to find out what a full protective reaction is. Okay? Let's try it my way for now."

He grumbled something inaudible, but put the screwdriver back in his belt pack.

Julia took her turn. They were both bleeding Airbus oxy and she could think of nothing more to do.

Yet she felt around them the same gathering sense of urgency.

Glowing patterns flowed in the mat nearby.

"Hey, pressure's building," Marc said. "Fast."

The atmosphere around them was thicker. Their beams now penetrated only a few meters into it. A wind brushed the banks of murky haze. *Wind?*

"It's giving off gas," Marc said, reading his instruments. "Must be, to build this fast. And—what's blowing?"

"A breeze from below," she said. "Look down, you can see currents coming up."

The cavern now brimmed with light. Vapor, glows—

all somehow coupled in the complex system this place had evolved to . . . what? Survive. Irritate an organism and it will—

A crack formed. The membrane valve abruptly began to open.

Immediately the wind tore at them, rushing past.

She could hear the rising roar of a hurricane gale.

"What?" Marc looked down in alarm. "Hold on—"

"No, spread your arms. Catch the wind."

"Catch—?"

The valve snapped open with an audible *pop*.

The blast of pressure from below swept them up, through the hole. She got tangled in her own winch cable and tumbled through the opening feetfirst. She slammed into the side, whirled, scrambled for a grip on anything. A piece of mat came away in her glove. She got a grip on a rock and pivoted, out of the direct wind.

A fountain of vapor sprayed up into the dark vent. Moisture turned to snow, a white gusher that drove upward in eddies.

"Marc!"

"Here."

She saw him clinging to the other side of the vent, five meters away. "It's . . . *sneezing* us out."

The storm died quickly. The irritant oxygen was expelled into the vent, to find its way to the surface.

They followed, shaking from the aftereffects. It was a long ride up out of the swallowing dark, into a glittering sky rich in cold and stars.

PART V
MARS CITY

37

THE NEXT DAY CRAWLED. MARC AND JULIA SLEPT LATE IN Red Rover, exhausted and depressed. Breakfast was a silent meditation over acidic coffee and warmed-up instant oatmeal with hard knots of raisins.

Neither felt like waxing long over comm on the events in the vent. Julia made a brief report and they didn't answer the comm as they drove back south through the pingo hills.

When they reached the classy Airbus rocket, proud tower in the ruddy midday, there was nobody home. Or so it seemed.

Claudine saw them from the pingo two hundred meters away, where she had been hooking the hoses into the autodriller.

She came running. "I thought work was best, to keep from thinking," she gasped over comm.

"It was . . ." Julia did not know what to say. "Strange.

They died in some way we do not fully understand."

"Viktor called, told me, last night. I wanted to be out in the open today." She looked drawn through her face-plate, eyes hollow.

"At least Earthside can't reach you while you're in your suit," Marc said. "Come on inside."

Claudine walked around the rover with an awkwardness that Julia knew would go away within another week in 0.38 g. The blue-suited figure pointed toward the rocket. "Maybe I should go into the ship first. I want to shower, change—"

"Nah," Marc said. "We'll take you to the hab. Shower there."

When Claudine came inside she marveled at some of the rover's "customized" features—a scent catcher, cool water spigot, self-warming meal dispenser; all Raoul's retrofitting.

Only then did Julia call Viktor. "Let's have conference," he agreed.

On the ride they spoke little, and mostly of Mars, of landscape, of the many small ways to adapt to a world that is always trying to kill you.

When they came into the hab Axelrod was on the screen.

"—hold steady there, guys. We've got a good horse to ride now, Airbus can't think they've got much in their hand. You should see how stiff their lawyers' faces are now! And my engineers, they figure no way can she fly that package back alone—"

Viktor cut it off and turned to them. "Welcome." Some ritual condolences, all in tones soft and hushed.

Viktor embraced Julia. They moved to where Raoul had already prepared a high tea, appropriate for late afternoon. On the wall the big screen reverted to the exterior scene, shadows stretching across the cluttered landscape that was the human signature upon the rusty plains beyond.

"He is right," Claudine said. "I cannot fly the ship by myself."

"Chen, he must have talked about how severely the life-support apparatus is limited," Viktor said.

"He did," Claudine said. "We can take only four."

"Not five, not at all," Viktor said. It was a question.

"Not possibly."

"Then he was telling the truth," Marc said. "We weren't sure. I mean, where did he think you'd get the fuel?"

She blinked. "Why, the ice."

Raoul pressed, "You didn't want the methane?"

"It is yours. And we would have to move the ship to land nearby . . . too dangerous, such a close landing."

"So I believed," Viktor said mildly, quite obviously not looking at Marc and Raoul.

"So one person must stay," Claudine said dejectedly. "Unless we all do."

"What?!" Raoul said loudly.

"To load the ship with water will take drilling, steam cycling, pumping . . . and we do not have Gerda."

"I can handle that," Raoul said quickly.

"Sure, we'll all pitch in," Marc added.

"Of course," Viktor said. "That is a given. I wish to discuss one principle, before we go to details."

Claudine frowned. "I do not understand how we can plan the return flight."

"Principle is," Viktor said soberly, "we decide here all such matters. Not Axelrod, not Airbus. We."

They all nodded.

They went back in force to recover the bodies.

Julia had made the case for it, expecting opposition, but there was none. "We can't let the mat get into the suits," she said anyway. "It may find a way to breach them. Intermingling cells, who knows what damage that could do?"

Plus it could mess up doing clean science down there!

Only then did she think of the more humanitarian reason—the way Earthside would play it, of course: a decent burial.

Five Earthlings, two rovers, and three winches strong—the team of four prepared with aching detail. Viktor remained in Red Rover, to keep Earthside informed and to brood. His ankle was still not up to a major job.

They brought every spare air tank on the planet. Triple-checking every step, they planned meticulously and in the first leg of the descent made no mistakes. Raoul and Claudine unjammed the Airbus winch so they had enough lifting power to make the recovery possible. In the end it wasn't that difficult.

As she lowered into the vast main chasm Julia felt a prickly sensation returning, a feeling she had not had the time to register before. Not fear, not curiosity . . . something with wonder in it: awe.

The mat was dim, hardly glowing at all. Their beams did not excite it. "Maybe it's exhausted from the last time," she said to Marc as the two lowered themselves gingerly. "Plants have a recovery time."

"You said it's not a plant."

"Right. But basic metabolic laws should apply. Anaerobes are not as efficient as oxy users."

The big valve they had found open, and so left Raoul and Claudine above it. Insurance, and to handle what was to come.

"I sure don't want to wake it up," Marc replied, dimming his hand beam.

The bodies did not seem to have changed at all. To all sides the mat lay like a dim, dormant rug. It did not seem to have swarmed further over the suits. The blue filaments were flaccid. The mist was less dense, and she got a clearer look at them. They looked more like giant tube worms than linguine. *So much to learn.*

But today was not for science.

Julia was cautious as they attached clasps and ties and stays to the Airbus lines, hovering over the bodies, but no awaking radiance rose from the surrounding mat.

They gave the signal. The Airbus winch labored to break free of the mat that encased the suits. They both came out with some hard pulling and the mat slithered away, collapsing below. Still no luminosity from it.

They rose together up into the misty atmosphere of the enormous vault. She longed to study it, watch its reaction to their breathing exhaust. As they neared the valve membrane some shifting colors came through the fog, as if from distant features. She still had no idea how far away the walls of this huge place were. It could go on for kilometers, part of an underground web of intricate implications . . .

They got the bodies through the narrow passage of the valve—and she was sure that term did indeed describe its function. Somehow the mat kept this region thick with vapor, and by ordinary gas dynamics that could not be sustained for long. The valve must cut off the losses to the surface, manage this eerie environment. A pressure lock.

But how did it know to close? How to respond to pressures and moisture densities? She was convinced that the glows and gas densities somehow carried messages, organizing this whole shadowy realm.

Raoul and Claudine were of great help in maneuvering the bodies around the edges and angles of the ascent. They were all careful of the bodies, working almost without speaking up through hundreds of meters of the vent. Sunlight beckoned above like a promise and she felt a surge of an odd, joyous energy. Still, when they got back to Red Rover, they were all exhausted.

"It's the spookiness does it," Raoul remarked. "I never figured on that."

"Who could?" Marc said tersely.

They rested and ate in the hab. Inevitably, reaction from Earthside had to be at least considered, though no one felt in the mood. Billions were jostling to peer through the media knothole at five people many millions of miles away . . . who didn't much want to talk, thank you.

On her personal slate she saw that Airbus had accused her and a Consortium conspiracy of "driving the two to their deaths" because she wouldn't share her Marsmat samples.

Axelrod's PR people had been massaging the events, issuing a list of reasons to retrieve the bodies: salvage the suits; not contaminate the mat; most featured: "It's just not right to leave them there."

She glanced at the immense backup of files and shuddered. "ALIENS KILL TWO ON MARS!" screamed the tabloids.

In all, it was like reading a barely understandable foreign tongue.

38

FEBRUARY 5, 2018

THEY MADE A LITTLE PROCESSION, A SHORT CORTEGE, SHE thought, following the dune buggy and its burden to the site.

With unspoken agreement they walked slowly up a low rise. A crimson sunset spread across the sky. Raoul brought the backhoe down the slope below the stone cairn they had erected early in the mission, at the christening of the base.

Julia glanced up at Claudine walking ahead, her suit still a deep blue, barely dusted with the pink stain of Mars. She walked tentatively, bouncing, uncertain.

They came upon the little perimeter circle of rocks. In the ensuing months, small pink sand dunes had invaded, piling up skirts on the lee side of the cairn. Raoul dug a pit with the backhoe on the buggy's rear. Viktor and Marc picked up some nearby rocks and started building two more cairns. As they worked, Julia recorded the scene on vid. No one spoke.

She thought about all the little outposts on Earth, each with its tiny cemetery. Cemeteries behind ghost towns, underground catacombs dug out of rock, mummies in desert caves, single graves lost forever in the wilderness.

The act of remembering their dead connected them to all the rest of humanity, down through uncountable myriad millennia and across a vast black star-studded void. How long had people been doing this? she wondered. From before we were fully human. Neanderthals, unnamed, lost hominids . . .

This mission, cloaked in technology and driven by both greed and desire and something as old as the species—it, too, was part of an unstoppable exploring impulse that had conquered an entire planet, and now was starting on a second one. "Wagon Train in Space," some wag had described an old sci-fi TV series. An apt description for them as well.

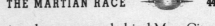

They were starting the cemetery behind Mars City. Boot Hill.

The cairns were nearly complete. Raoul finished and they laid the bodies to rest, wrapped in white parachute fabric. They stood and watched the backhoe push the ruddy dirt over the first humans to lie beneath the soil of another world.

When he was done Raoul handed two flat rocks to Claudine, who placed one at the top of each little tower. Through her helmet plate she looked dazed. She was probably cold, too. Cold, and in shock. As she stood up the sun slid below the sharp horizon. A dust devil churned across the dunes to the north. Mars went on in its endless cycles.

They all stepped back and tidied up the rock circle. Marc put a hand on Claudine's shoulder. "Come on, let's get something hot to drink."

"I have something hard, too," Viktor said. "Right time for it."

They returned to the hab, showered down, dressed warmly in cotton sweats, and headed for the round metal table in the common room. Raoul and Marc were the first there, preparing five mugs of steaming cocoa. They all knew what was coming.

Julia relished the comforting sweetness of cocoa. They had sat here hundreds of times, eating, working, talking, arguing—even making love when Raoul and Marc were away in the rover, she recalled somewhat guiltily. Now suddenly she was aware that it was all coming to an end, that this was one of the last times they would be here. Already the feeling had changed, with the addition of Claudine. Soon this whole immense experience would all be reduced to memories.

Viktor stared at the steam lazing up from his mug. "Well, what next, eh?" He gave a short sharp laugh. "Mars is full of surprises once again."

Marc looked solemn. "Right, what happens now?"

Claudine shook her head. "I'll have to return with you. Forfeit the prize, of course. Airbus has lost." She spoke slowly, struggling to control her accent.

They exchanged glances as a pause extended itself.

Raoul was tracing imaginary circles on the table with his fist—somber, even grim. Julia saw that he took the ERV failure as a deep personal rebuke and was too embarrassed to speak.

Claudine sat woodenly.

Julia tried to assess the extent of her shock. She didn't seem to be grasping the situation very well. Had she forgotten that the ERV couldn't fly?

"Bottom line is, we can't lift off, you can't crew nuclear rocket alone," Viktor said carefully. "No mission is going home."

"Yeah," Marc said wryly. "A real Martian standoff."

There was another pause. They looked at each other around the table: dusty, worn, ragged, all.

It came to her in a flash, then. "No, not a standoff, a Martian *solution*. We have to combine forces."

Viktor looked skeptical but supported her with, "Is obvious, yes, but how?"

"Well, for starters, at least one of us has to stay here," said Julia.

"What!"

"No."

With a waving hand she cut off the beginning protests. "There's no other way and we all know it. We're still too many for the available transportation."

Claudine looked alarmed. "But what about food?"

"There are more than enough supplies—the ERV is fully stocked for six people for a return trip of seven months. And there are two extra people's supplies on the nu— on the Airbus ship."

Claudine cut in, "Gerda's and Chen's."

"Right, in your larder. We even have all their extra gear. So no problem there."

Claudine said slowly, "Sums to . . . forty-two person months of supplies on your ERV, plus twenty-four person months on my ship. Which we use if three people return."

"But you said *one* person has to stay," said Marc.

"One person is too vulnerable." Julia looked around the table.

"I agree," said Claudine. "One, he would die out here." She said slowly, "But how long do they have to stay?"

"Until a . . . a rescue mission reaches them." Viktor was not liking the idea any better this time.

Julia took a deep breath. "Earth can launch another ERV in three months. It can be here six months later with fresh supplies—if needed."

"Will need," Viktor said. "Stuff wears out."

"Right. But we can't lift off for Earth for another twenty-six months from now, at the next minimum fuel window."

Raoul said sourly, "Hell of a note. The rescue ship is too small to carry the survivors." He laughed mirthlessly, a sharp, dry chuckle.

Claudine looked up sharply. "You know all that was not our idea. We were never a rescue mission, never wished you to have trouble. Maybe some at Airbus, but not us. No one asked the crew before . . . before *somebody* started that idea. It was Airbus managers talking, and maybe not even them. They claim not to know who started it."

"Well, they were right after all," said Julia. She looked deep into her empty mug, as if the solution could be found there.

Finally, Marc said slowly, "I accept your argument. Three go back, two stay." He looked around the table. "How does anyone else feel about this?"

She could see a growing acceptance in their faces.

"It's not all bad, this solution," she said. "For one thing, it forces Earth to launch another mission. That's what we all want, isn't it? Not to abandon another planet, like we did the moon, after a brief fling. But to move toward colonization."

Marc nodded. "I'm not sure we thought of ourselves as the colonists." He paused. "I sure didn't."

"Neither me," Viktor said.

Marc continued, as if provisionally trying out the idea, "So how do we pick? Short straws again? Volunteers?"

"Should be captain's orders." Viktor spread his hands.

"True," Julia said, letting him feel his way through this.

Viktor shook his head slowly, staring straight ahead. "Decision is too hard."

Claudine nodded without speaking.

As if from a great distance, Julia heard herself saying, "I'll stay."

Viktor was stunned. "Why would you . . . ?"

It was suddenly so clear. "Random picks won't cut it. We have to have the best team possible to both go *and* stay. Claudine *has* to go back, she has the only experience on the nuke. Learning all those systems will be hard enough for us." She paused. "I suspect Raoul is too valuable *not* to have on the ship."

Raoul started, "Thanks, but I screwed this up and—"

"No, you're essential, is true," Viktor said.

Julia rushed ahead. "And besides, he has a new family waiting for him. After that . . ." She shrugged. "But look, I can't make any decision except for myself."

"Why would you want to stay?" asked Marc. "Your Marsmat?"

She frowned. "I guess so. I don't think I'm ready to never see it again. And I got a funny feeling up at the . . . the cemetery this afternoon. I suddenly felt like a resident in a frontier settlement, not an astronaut on a space junket." She looked at Viktor. "Sorry, I should've said something to you first."

"Maybe we should all think about this some more before we make any final decisions," said Marc.

"We don't have time anymore," said Raoul.

"We should inform Earth, at any rate. Maybe they'll have an idea," said Marc.

"Earth can suggest, but we decide. New law of space," said Viktor.

Heads nodded. There was a little pause. Julia felt curiously light, but she could almost see the stresses coursing through the others.

"I'm curious about one thing. Why did you say you had a Martian solution?" asked Marc.

She was relieved at the chance to talk about science for a bit. "I'm just feeling my way through this, but I think the Marsmat is not a single organism at all. It's a cooperative community of different kinds of single-celled organisms. Like a stromatolite, maybe, or a primitive jellyfish."

"Remind me about stromatolites," said Raoul.

She was surprised at such a question from Raoul, who was never much interested in biology. She guessed he needed a break from the intense conversation they were having.

"Stromatolites are huge living mounds, basically layers of blue-green algae and silt. As a life-form they're very old, maybe three billion years. At least there are wavy layers in rocks of that age that may be their fossils."

"Earth's past is Mars' present?" asked Claudine.

"Oh, they're not just fossils. I've seen living ones on the west coast near Perth, just off the beach in the shallows of the Indian Ocean."

"They've been around for three billion years? *Mon Dieu.* I had no idea."

"Well, my point is not their age, but how they survive. Anaerobes with different metabolic requirements can work in tandem, one thriving on the output of the one before it. It's a community survival strategy."

Raoul asked, "Adopted because Mars was under stress from its beginning?"

"Makes sense. In a way, it's the old Earth solution too. Before the oxygen-using multicellular forms raised the competitive stakes, the anaerobes used a different system. Well, in fact they still do. Bacteria faced with a poison in their environment don't have to wait around for a random mutation that would help them out. They just pick up a useful gene from another bacterium. And not just other strains of the same kind, but even species not closely related. That's why antibiotic resistance spreads so rapidly."

The others looked a bit blank, so she finished up hurriedly, "I'm just saying that the anaerobes work together instead of at cross-purposes. Instead of competing with different organisms in a race to get ahead, they all move forward together. I think that's what the Marsmat has done. That's what we're doing too."

"An incredibly positive spin, that," said Marc, smiling. "You've learned a lot from your trivid career so far."

"That's not what I was trying to do, sugarcoat it." Julia looked at him sharply. She glanced over at Viktor. His face was unreadable.

"Not to put too fine a point on it, but we're up against the wall here. What other choice do we have?" asked Marc.

Raoul looked up. "Yeah, but who's number two?" He gestured with his head at the Earth-Mars chronometer mounted on the wall. A long, tense silence. "Anybody volunteer?"

Around the table Julia saw compressed lips, worried eyes.

Raoul pressed. "This is bigger than us, y'know. Anybody wanna call Earth?"

Marc nodded. "Can't put it off forever." He started to get up.

"Before we call we should have the solution," said Viktor. "I have decided. Captain should stay with his ship. Claudine leaves with hers, I stay here with mine."

"You sure?" Raoul gaped. "We could find some other way to decide."

Viktor shrugged. "Besides, someone needs to keep Julia out of trouble."

Julia's heart soared. Quick tears stung her eyes, spilled over and started down her cheeks. She bent her head and furtively brushed them away with her napkin. She desperately wanted to rush over and hug him, but made herself sit still.

She really was going to stay. Another two years! Until this moment the idea had seemed remote, unreal.

"Okay. Are we agreed?" Marc looked around the table. Heads nodded in assent. "Then let's call Earth."

The others walked to the comm center. Julia and Viktor stayed. She took his hand, pressed it to her cheek. It felt so good to touch him.

"Are you sure you want to do this? I didn't mean to maneuver you—"

"You wouldn't come here without me, back on Earth. How do you say it? Is payback time."

"Is that your only reason? You don't want to stay even a little bit for Mars?"

He shrugged, then smiled. "Is only a little worse than Siberia in winter. We belong together, in Siberia or Arctic or Mars."

She looked at him. "I didn't want to stay without you." She realized her cheeks were wet again.

The moment stretched between them.

"Is truly settled then. We stay."

She nodded. "Mars City."

"Now comes hard part. We have to convince Earth."

"You thought this was easy?" She blew her nose.

"No. Was not easy. But Earth will be harder. You'll see."

Viktor was right. Axelrod demanded that "his" crew commandeer the nuke so the Consortium could win. His battery of lawyers would argue that it was like marine salvage, he said.

When the crew resisted he became infuriated. Claudine relayed this to Airbus, who called it the first instance of Martian piracy. They argued that it was the reverse, and the Consortium had lost.

Legions of lawyers began arming for their paper wars.

All five were stunned, debating over a long dinner how to handle it. Julia argued forcefully that they reject all "Earth way" solutions with only one winner, and propose the "Mars way": cooperation. But they couldn't just ignore Earth's wishes. Someone had to send a rescue mission.

They told Axelrod to find some angle in the rescue trip to profit by.

"More drama," Marc said dryly. "Gotta sell."

Finally, they got Axelrod and Airbus to understand

that the Consortium crew couldn't fly the nuke alone, but neither could Claudine. Both teams would lose without some middle ground. Axelrod and Airbus had to work things out amicably.

Then, in a daring trivid message, all five announced their solution to Earth, and declared that the true Mars Prize was the cooperation. Through this they hoped to appeal directly to the public.

They broadcast a little ceremony of them rechristening the nuke *The Spirit of Ares* with melted water from the pingos, in Viktor's used vodka bottle. It seemed to work.

But they needed an end run. Through her father, the one route Axelrod could not "creatively edit," Julia got to the Mars Accords board. She explained the compromise in detail: It was truly a joint mission coming home.

Two days on tenterhooks followed.

Then a U.N. emergency panel agreed to help sponsor the rescue mission.

Once more, Viktor turned out to be right: What seemed so logical and neat on Mars, amidst the stark desert isolation, turned out to be horribly complicated in the festering media-driven swamp of Earth.

Mars had become a Rorschach test. Every faction with the most tenuous axe to grind instantly jumped into the fray. Religious leaders decried three unmarried people alone in the return ship. The Mars Protection Society, a Mars faction of the animal rights lobby, demanded they sterilize their landing site and leave immediately. The Terraform Today Society wanted the Marsmat destroyed. Two cult groups—one in India, the other holed up in

Montana—tried to commit mass suicide to avoid the incoming Mars plague.

"Let 'em," Marc said.

Media bloomed with florid discussions between completely uninformed people about every detail imaginable. Their entire lives were dissected, their predicament analyzed, philosophized over, chewed at.

Julia came to believe in the ensuing weeks that she and Viktor had, in fact, chosen the easy way out. They would just hang out quietly on Mars while Claudine, Marc, and Raoul took the brunt of the hysteria on their return.

39

IT HAD BECOME SO SIMPLE, MUSED JULIA, ONCE THEY HAD understood the Mars way.

They were now a crew of five. Claudine was incorporated smoothly and as a whole they prepared for the departure. Cooperation ruled. They'd swapped expertise for space, and everybody won.

Just like the Marsmat. Just like bacteria on Earth.

You want antibiotic resistance? Swap with another bacterium and get the gene you need.

The vexing part was that this kind of solution had been available to them all along. Nobody had to die.

But Earthside was aboil with negotiations between the Consortium and Airbus. Lawyers angrily slapped writs on each other, over fuel and ships a hundred million miles away. Airbus argued that the Consortium team failed if it could not get home without Airbus help: they should at least split the $30 billion prize money.

This provoked a brief flurry within the governments who had to pay the bill. The Mars Board announced that the terms of the contest specified only that the first team returning successfully from Mars would be the winner. Anything else was between Airbus and the Consortium. Politicians carefully tiptoed away from the problem.

Intense public interest greased the negotiations. Airbus couldn't refuse the team their only chance to get home with the whole world watching. And none of the negotiators could have stopped the crew from taking the ship anyway.

Finally they agreed. Overnight, four billion dollars changed hands. They even made a little meaningless ceremony of it; she saw it on her news squirt. Deep in the bowels of a Swiss bank, a dolly heavily loaded with gold bars was wheeled from one vault to another.

She did some bargaining herself.

"I want a done deal," she told Axelrod. "Here's how. I send samples back. Not live, preserved. Dead. No threat to Earth, so you have no problems with the crazies. After you get the prize, you don't own the samples, either. They belong to science. This is too big for proprietary secrecy."

She took a steadying breath. Part of her training did not like talking back to The Boss. *Well, get used to it. Get used to years of it, probably.*

"In return for sending the samples, I get the DNA analyses. Also a ton of biological lab gear, sent on the next ERV you're launching. Literally a ton—a thousand metric kilograms. I'll pick the equipment."

She paused for the big leap. "And a biologist. I need somebody to work with here. Find a list of candidate astronaut biologists. I pick one. You send him—or her— on the next ERV."

She smiled to take the edge from all this. It really disabled you, pitching to a camera with no feedback. "I get this—or you get nothing. No more information on what I find here. No videos of future vent descents. Zip, nada, zero."

She allowed herself a raised eyebrow. "I expect my colleagues to send me the research papers based on my samples for review. First. Before leaking them to trivid or journals. That's the way it's done in science. Real science."

She smiled to herself. The joke was on the pure-Earth fanatics. The samples were technically dead, but the way she was preserving them, the DNA wouldn't be harmed. Fat chance those samples wouldn't be sliced and diced every which way before a week was out. Every hot-shot DNA lab on Earth was working up its protocols already, in anticipation. Eager hands would identify and slice out the specifically Martian genes, splice them into Earthly anaerobes, and have working pseudo-Martians within a month.

The march of science. Competition. She could count on it.

She couldn't prove any of her speculations, of course. Not without knowing more about Martian DNA.

One evening in the hab, after they were all tired out with the sheer grunt labor of farming water from the pingos, she had seen it. What to look for, once her samples reached the labs of Earth.

The DNA code might just hold the answer. Earth's code was mercifully redundant: a mistake in the coding was like a change in spelling that doesn't always alter the meaning. There were alternate spellings for the same amino acid. And of course proteins themselves have regions where a substitution of a different amino acid doesn't really matter. Room for error, with no consequences.

She had always thought that was a response to a rapidly evolving planet with lots of mutating agents: a Darwinian hotbox world. A rich world struck a balance between conservatism and experimentation, achieved over billions of years on a planet where evolution's lathe was always spinning.

Earth's climatic fluctuations changed the rules of survival, flipping from warm to cold and back again. It led some to postulate the Red Queen hypothesis: you have to keep running to stay in the same place, the entire biota evolving in fast lockstep to avoid being left behind. The pace was grueling, and a species lasted on average only a million years or so before running out of steam.

What would happen on Mars, where there may have been only one golden age of evolution, and a long twilight of one-way selective pressure? The young soil got ever colder, ever drier, the atmosphere ever thinner. Tough times . . . forever.

On Mars, would the DNA code be more conservative, simpler, and more precise?

Without sudden climatic shifts, the need for redundancy disappeared. Every error would be significant.

The price? Evolution would be slower. Even on Earth, most mutations were unfortunate, spelled gibberish, and killed the organism. Only a very few were useful.

On Mars, the chance of a successful mutation would be much smaller in the steadily worsening, harsh conditions.

But there had also been brief eras of warmth, when water flowed on the surface. Then what would happen? Evolution couldn't work fast enough to take advantage of the new conditions.

So . . . what else? Could *cooperation* have become the winning rule, and not competition?

She looked around the tiny hab commons room at her teammates. Five tough-minded types with different skills, fitting together into an efficient whole. Four had survived near disasters and a grueling eighteen months in this freezing, near-vacuum rustbowl because of their efficiency. That's what her subconscious had been trying to tell her.

Could it work on a planetwide scale?

Find a partner with the desired characteristic, instead of trying to evolve it yourself. A short period of wet and warm brought the mats out of the vents and into the lake beds. Light-sensitive organisms loosed from the mat—those "shrimp"?—could colonize the seas, making hay in the brief summer while the atmosphere lasted. Maybe they could even photosynthesize!

Life that found partners to help it maximize the wet-era opportunities would be successful. Glowing mats and photosynthetic microbes. Free-swimming forms and protective films. Peroxide eaters and watery membranes, all somehow trading their resources.

An entire ecology, now driven far underground, nonetheless finding a path through the great Dar-winnowing . . .

But always meshed into the spreading network of organisms, great and small . . . evolution in concert. Organisms still died their pitiful deaths, genes got erased . . .

And the system could grow even more interlaced, she saw . . . deep in the guts of a slumbering world.

She worked in the slowly reviving greenhouse to soothe her soul and spark her imagination. Although Viktor insisted she keep her helmet on, she opened the faceplate to the soft air. And in time . . .

The Marsmat in the mist chamber had reached some kind of limit, and was not growing much anymore. When she had more time, she would start changing its environment and see what happened.

After the liftoff, she thought. Vast stretches of time beckoned from beyond that horizon.

Meanwhile, she planted another crop of vegetables. Marc was busy at the nuke every day, and she would have to tend the greenhouse alone after he left, anyway.

Marc had never really moved back into the hab. He

and Raoul spent most of their time working at the Airbus site, driving back in late afternoon only to eat and sleep.

One day Raoul had come back alone. His only comment to Julia and Viktor was that he felt like the odd man out wherever he went on Mars these days.

Today she had promised herself a special treat. Over in the corner was a large plastic pot, holding her green soul mate, a western white pine. The seeds she'd gathered herself on a last break before their Earthside launch, a short hiking vacation in California's High Sierra. Buffeted by winds, sheared by ice storms, the pines clung to the stony soil in small groups. Just below timberline they were no taller than shrubs. Finding a partially gnawed cone in a snow bank, she'd tucked it into her pack.

Adapted to cold and dry, living at high altitudes under reduced oxygen, the pines were already partially adapted to living on Mars. And her tree had thrived in the greenhouse, growing to be an astonishing two feet high, with many side branches. The only wild Earth organism on Mars.

She brought her chair and sat beside it, looking carefully at the tips of the branches. She wasn't an expert on pines, and had never grown one before. The needles on this one were dark green, consistent with the reduced sunlight. The cold nights following the blowout had nipped some of the younger needles, but—*what's this?*

Pale green needles at the branch ends! Yes, the tips were growing. *Well, look at that, you're going to make it after all.*

She smiled broadly. The first tree on Mars.

40

THEY STOOD ON THE HILLSIDE AND WATCHED THE spreading rusty sunset, stamping their feet against the cold.

What was going to be a midafternoon departure had succumbed to the inevitable last-minute delays. Julia and Viktor had thought they'd watch the launch from outside. It would make better vid footage, to be sure, but it somehow just felt right, too.

Over her suit comm came the last-minute chatter between Claudine and Marc.

"Pressurizing all okay."

"Flow regular."

"Max two four seven."

"On profile."

"Got the temp envelope steady."

She let it wash over her, remembering their own departure, and how she'd felt.

There came another delay, something about the nuclear pile running a little too hot because the plates of high-grade uranium were squeezing a bit close together, not kept apart by the gas flow between them. Raoul said that would correct once they were full throttle, pouring water by from the high-pressure pumps. The water flashed into steam in an instant, heated by the plates. But it all had to synchronize.

This Airbus design used the workhorses of chemical rockets, valves and pumps and nozzles, but at vastly higher power levels. Just as the once-newfangled steamships still used hulls and decks and rudders, inherited from the Age of Sail. Perhaps they were witnessing the end of the Age of Liquid Oxygen, outmoded because no one would open up the solar system that antiquated way anymore, burning chemical energy into hot gas.

An era ending, an era beginning.

She shivered and her suit clicked with supporting warmth. Viktor said, "Earth rising."

So it was. She close-upped the white dot on the horizon and again saw the two points of light, one a gray-white and the other a definite ocean blue. *Home.*

The desert night fell quickly, applauded by the brilliant jewel starscape.

"Three, two, one. Ramping," came Claudine's voice.

Below the slender ship the first bright steam blossomed. Cottony clouds billowed up, licking up past the square port, almost swallowing the rocket.

"Flow standard. Zero eleven seven."

"Profiling steady."

Viktor had started the vid and narration. "The *Spirit of Ares* launches for Earth on water from Mars. This is the first return from another planet since Apollo astronauts walked on the moon."

It climbed up a growing spire, the alabaster banks of it lit from within with a hot orange glow.

The nuclear rocket climbed gracefully into the darkening butterscotch sky, leaving a huge plume behind. The gases fizzed away into nothingness.

Quick tears stung Julia's eyes. She imagined being on the ship, on her way home. *They're going home, and I'm not.*

Telling her parents had been difficult, but they'd been very good about it. Her father was looking better, the results of the ultrasound cancer treatments optimistic. He would see her when she finally returned, he had said. However long that took.

The ship rose quickly, almost soundlessly, into the deepening blackness of Martian night.

She and Viktor shouted good-byes.

Marc called out altitudes, speeds, voice calm and flat.

She felt a sadness as they angled over at several kilometers up. The rocket plume blazed across the hard blackness.

Reluctantly she looked away from the hard spot of light above to a suddenly empty world, her world.

Then she saw it. A smudge of light toward the horizon. It was a pale white cloud, linear, fuzzier at one end. It seemed to point downward. She realized that she was looking north, and that the cloud glowed. A pale ivory finger of illumination spiked up from the surface, broadening.

It came from the vent, she knew instantly—an impossibly brilliant outpouring.

"Viktor, look. Swing the vid to the north. The vent is outgassing."

To poke such a glistening probe of light into the sky must have cost the matting enormous energies, she thought. To make it, the vent would first have to be expelling a gusher of vapor. Then the mats would all have to pour their energy into the pale glow, coherently.

What coordination . . . and what control, over the

venting of vapor itself? Could life have attained such levels?

And why did life *allow* vapor to escape? Was there some chemical clue she was missing?

The pearly lance, jutting up: a signal? Celebration? Mating dance? Her mind whirled giddily. With so much energy expended, there must be some purpose.

It was natural to see this as a pointed message, but there are many behaviors in biology that defy easy logic. She knew what she would like to believe, but . . .

Science was a systematic way to avoid fooling yourself, after all.

She closed her eyes to fix the image in memory. An ivory plume, towering kilometers into the sky, mingling with the gleaming stars.

So much to learn . . . She could stay here a lifetime and not know it all.

Hello, Mars. From a member of the Martian race.

Acknowledgments

THIS NOVEL ATTEMPTS A PORTRAYAL OF HOW HUMANITY might explore Mars in the near future, at low cost and with foreseeable technology.

Undoubtedly reality shall prove the details wrong. Still, I hope to sound a note of realism in the sub-genre of exploration novels, to depict just how demanding true planetary adventuring will be.

Going to Mars could be a defining moment in the twenty-first century, precisely because it will be hard, tough and exciting. Our most basic and meaningful questions about life there simply cannot be answered by robots.

Thanks are due to many who have contributed technical knowledge and advice: The Mars Society (http://www.marssociety.org); the Planetary Society (http://planetary.org); Bob Zubrin and Richard Wagner, whose Mars Direct scenario (*The Case for Mars*) I employed; and the Mars Underground.

At NASA Ames I gained much from conversations with Nathalie Cabrol and Edmund Grin, who supplied lore about the Gusev landing site, and the Viking photo used herein. Roger Arno, Geoff Briggs, Chris McKay and Carol Stoker (*Strategies for Mars*) provided many insights. Yoji Kondo of NASA Headquarters offered constant advice.

Michael Carr of the U.S. Geological Survey patiently explained puzzling Martian features to a neophyte. His *Water On Mars* illuminated further.

Penny Boston related spelunking stories with a Martian angle. The SETI Institute (http://www.SETI.org) offered encouragement and arguments. Mark Adler of the Jet Propulsion Laboratory discussed rovers and their problems. Bruce Murray of Caltech offered realism, though I sometimes ignored it. John Connolly of Johnson Space Center provided the orbital "pork chop" plots and expertise. Douglas Cooke of the JSC Exploration Office filled in many details. Jon Lomberg gave sage advice. Joe Miller read the manuscript and augmented some of the biological ideas. Michael Cassutt worked on the script outline for a miniseries, contributing valuably to the novel that followed.

Betsy Mitchell gave unstinting editorial support. Marilyn Olsen kept track of innumerable details.

The novel was based on the novella "A Cold, Dry Cradle," co-authored by Elisabeth Malartre, who continued to provide many ideas, creations and criticisms.

Thanks to all. They have labored to make Mars not just a dot of light in the sky, but a destination.

Gregory Benford
June 1999

Orbit titles available by post:

❑ Foundation's Fear	Gregory Benford	£6.99
❑ Cosm	Gregory Benford	£6.99
❑ Against the Fall of Night/	Arthur C. Clarke	
Beyond the Fall of Night	and Gregory Benford	£5.99
❑ Rendezvous with Rama	Arthur C. Clarke	£5.99
❑ Rainbow Mars	Larry Niven	£5.99

The prices shown above are correct at time of going to press. However the publishers reserve the right to increase prices on covers from these previously advertised, without further notice.

ORBIT BOOKS

Cash Sales Department, P.O. Box 11, Falmouth, Cornwall, TR10 9EN
Tel: +44 (0) 1326 569777, Fax: +44 (0) 1326 569555
Email: books@barni.avel.co.uk.

POST AND PACKING:

Payments can be made as follows: cheque, postal order (payable to Orbit Books) or by credit cards. Do not send cash or currency.

U.K. Orders under £10	£1.50
U.K. Orders over £10	**FREE OF CHARGE**
E.E.C. & Overseas	25% of order value

Name (Block Letters) _____

Address _____

_____

Post/zip code:_____

❑ Please keep me in touch with future Orbit publications

❑ I enclose my remittance £_____

❑ I wish to pay Visa/Access/Mastercard/Eurocard

Card Expiry Date

_____